THE LAST GUARD

SOUTHERN STAR TRILOGY BOOK ONE

By K.J. Taylor

Published by Shooting Star Press

http://www.shootingstar.pub

First published in 2017

2nd Editions 2023

Copyright © K.J. Taylor 2016

The right of K.J. Taylor to be identified as the author of this work has been asserted by her under the *Copyright Amendment (Moral Rights) Act 2000*.

This work is copyright. Apart from any use as permitted under the *Copyright Act 1968*, no part may be reproduced, copied, scanned, stored in a retrieval system, recorded, or transmitted, in any form or by any means, without the prior written permission of the publisher.

National Library of Australia Cataloguing-in-Publication entry:

Taylor, K.J. (Katie Jill) 1986–

Fantasy—Fiction
The Last Guard/K.J. Taylor
Speculative fiction--Young adult fiction.
A823.4

Cover design by Sabrina RG Raven
Map by Allison Jones

ISBN-13: 978-1-925821-91-8

Shooting Star

*Dedicated to everyone who has stuck by the series
for all these years. I couldn't have done it without your support.*

Contents

FIRST MOUNTAINS
MALVERN
TARA
NORTHGATE
MOUNTAINS
ISLAND OF THE SUN
WITHYPOOL
CANRAN
LIRANWEE
former Canran borders
WYLAM
THE SOUTH
FORMER SITE OF EAGLEHOLM
SUNTON
former Withypool borders
NEW EAGLEHOLM
former Wylam/Eagleholm borders
THE COPPERTOPS
WILD COUNTRY
MONAG

CYMRIA

Chapter One

The Guardsman

The body appeared on the streets of Liranwee early one morning. Nobody knew how it had come to be there, or why.

Red, on dawn patrol, was the one to find it. As the morning advanced and people gathered to see what was going on, he kept his place beneath the hanging corpse and prevented anyone from coming too close. Other guards appearing on the scene quickly formed a ring, pushing people back if need be and stolidly ignoring the questions that came their way.

Red stayed where he was, nervously running a finger over his moustache, and waited until his commander finally arrived. The ring of guards parted to let him through, and Red straightened up and saluted smartly. 'Sir!'

Commander Talmon, a middle-aged man with short grey hair, nodded back. 'At ease, Sergeant. Tell me everything.'

Red relaxed slightly. 'There's not much I can tell, sir. Me an' Ranulf were comin' along the street from the south end around dawn, and found it just like this.'

Talmon glanced at Red's partner, who was standing nearby. 'Nothing's been touched?'

'No, sir,' said Ranulf. 'Me an' Red here took one look at it, and sounded the alarm. We've stayed here ever since.'

'Good job.' Talmon took a few steps back, and looked up at the body. Somebody had tied a noose around its neck, and hung it up from a post holding a sign with a picture of a white snake on it. It was impossible to tell if the victim was a man or a woman – the clothes were baggy, and the head was covered by a sack.

'Could be a suicide, sir,' Ranulf put in helpfully.

'Don't be daft,' said Red. 'What kind of suicide ties their own hands an' feet together?'

'Right,' Ranulf muttered.

Talmon took his helmet off, and scratched his head. 'Were there any witnesses?'

'No, sir,' said Red. 'We've talked to the tavern owners; none of them heard a thing. Mind you, it was Springday yesterday. Bit of a noisy night, sir.'

'Unbelievable,' said Talmon. 'Someone hangs some poor bastard, probably alive, from the sign of the White Serpent on Springday Eve, and *nobody hears anything*? Nobody comes outside and sees something?'

'It must've been put here later, sir,' said Red. 'After closing. I touched it when we found it, t'see if it was still alive, like. I'd swear it was still a bit warm, sir.'

'Hmph.' Talmon put his helmet back on. 'I know these places. They don't close until nobody wants another drink. On Springday Eve, that means never. Still, you did well here. We'll get this taken down an' have another chat to the innkeeper. See if we can't find someone who can help.'

'Yes, sir,' said Red.

'I'll go find us a ladder, then,' said Ranulf.

Red smirked at him. 'Don't worry about it; I got this.' He made a small jump, and caught hold of the signpost. Holding on with one hand, he drew his dagger with his other hand and sawed through the rope. The body thudded onto the street, making several people jump back.

Red dropped onto the ground beside it. 'Probably should take a look at the face…'

He loosened the noose and pulled it off. The bag over the head hadn't been tied on, so he removed it. He grimaced when he saw the face underneath.

The victim was a man, and it was immediately obvious that the hanging had indeed been what killed him. His face had turned an ugly shade of purple, the eyes bulging, red with burst blood vessels. The mouth was jammed open in a final gasp for air, and the rope had left a vicious looking bruise just under the jaw.

'Ye gods,' Red mumbled.

Talmon shook his head in disgust. 'Take the poor bastard to the Temple, and ask the priests to let us know if any of his relatives show up.'

'Yes, sir.' Someone had already brought a stretcher, so Red rolled the body onto it. He jerked his head toward Ranulf. 'C'mon, get over here an' give me a hand.'

Reluctantly, Ranulf came over and lifted one end of the stretcher. 'Ugh. Let's get this over with.'

'Right.' Red shifted his grip on his own end, and waited until the other guards had cleared the way. Fortunately, Liranwee's Sun Temple wasn't far.

Ranulf huffed along at his end of the stretcher, hampered by his impressive gut. 'I'm gettin' too old for this,' he muttered.

Red said nothing. He had spent his entire adult life as a guard, ever since he had joined up at the age of sixteen. Years spent patrolling the streets, chasing thieves and murderers and, once or twice, helping to put down a riot. But he had never seen anything like this. Murder was one thing, but the sight of someone left hanged like this, there for everyone to see, had shaken him more than he was going to admit.

Not wanting to look at the corpse again, Red kept his attention on the people moving in around him to get a good look. It was the usual assortment of people you'd find in the streets at this time of day, mostly traders who had been on their way to work, and kids who were too young to have a job they cared about.

Further back, though, someone caught his eye. A man slightly taller than those around him, and very thin. He was bald, and had a strip of cloth covering his eyes, but his head was turned toward Red.

For a moment Red looked straight toward the stranger, and even though there were no eyes to see he had the uncomfortable feeling that the man was looking straight at him.

He shook himself, and went on toward the Temple. Fear and foreboding didn't matter, not when he had a job to do.

He and Ranulf reached the Temple, with several other guards following to keep people away. Somebody must have already alerted the priests, because a group of them came out to meet them.

'Where did this one come from?' one of them asked.

'He was found this morning,' said Red. 'Hanged outside the White Serpent Inn.'

The priest's face twisted with disgust. 'Who would do something like that?'

'Someone I'd like t'get my hands on before he does it to someone else,' Red said grimly. 'Can you take care of this poor sod, and let us know if his family turns up?'

'Of course.' The priest gestured at two of his fellows. 'Take him to the vaults.'

Red gladly handed over the stretcher, and stood by respectfully with Ranulf while it was carried inside.

'Right,' said Ranulf, once the priests had gone. 'Back to business as usual, I s'pose.'

'Yeah.' Red rubbed his eyes; he had been up since before dawn, and his shift wasn't even close to finished yet. 'Let's get back to the tavern.'

'Maybe we can grab somethin' to eat while we're at it,' Ranulf said as they set out.

'Good idea.'

Red and Ranulf settled into their usual pace on the way back, walking side by side, always on the lookout for trouble, as they had done on every patrol they had shared over the years. Since Ranulf was older, Red had been paired with him to learn just as younger guards always were. At least, that was the idea, but the reality was that Red looked much more interested than Ranulf did. Fat and balding, Ranulf had been a guard for nearly thirty years, and nothing seemed to interest him much about the job these days.

Red kept pace with him, frowning. While his partner tended toward the paunchy, Red tended toward the muscular. Wide shouldered and stocky, with big hands, he wore his carrot-coloured hair short like most guards did, to keep himself from overheating under his helmet. His moustache, on the other hand, was more than bushy enough to make up for it.

Back at the tavern, most of the other guards had dispersed and gone back to their proper duties. Commander Talmon, though, had waited behind.

Red saluted smartly. 'Job's taken care of, sir.'

Talmon offered him a rare smile. 'Well done. You handled all this very well, Sergeant.'

Red was careful not to let his satisfaction show. 'D'you want me an' Ranulf to talk to the innkeeper again?'

'No, I took care of that while you were gone. You two can go start making enquiries elsewhere.'

'Yes, sir,' said Red. He was glad; interrogating witnesses was never much fun, especially the second time around.

'Got it, sir,' said Ranulf. He grinned at Red. 'C'mon, let's get going, mate. You've run the show enough for one day.'

Red flushed. 'Right, right. See y'later, sir.'

Once they were out of sight, Ranulf slowed to his usual pace. 'Now then, no need t'go running off ahead,' he said. 'We ain't in a hurry.'

Reluctantly, Red fell back to join him. 'You didn't have t'go telling me off in front of the Commander like that,' he complained.

Ranulf chuckled. 'Red, I like you an' all, but you gotta learn to calm down a bit. The job is just a job, an' you'll do better if you treat it that way.'

'Will I?' said Red. 'We're supposed to be protectin' people, Ranulf. That's something I'm always gonna treat seriously.'

'But it ain't something you do better by rushin' about, right?' said Ranulf. He stumped along reflectively. 'Y'know, I heard after you ran off with that Winged Man or whatever he was, you came back different. He tell you you had a mission or somethin? Somethin' from Gryphus or whatever?'

Red started. 'What? No. Kullervo and those griffiners just needed someone t'help them on the journey. Y'know, making food an' tidying up an' whatnot. There wasn't anything like that.'

'But he was the Winged Man, wasn't he?' said Ranulf. 'Holy an' that. Didn't he have anything important t'tell you?'

'Not really,' said Red. He squared his shoulders. 'My Dad was the one who taught me it was important t'be loyal. Loyalty's my family code an' has been for centuries, that's what he said.'

'Yeah, but wasn't your dad a traitor?' Ranulf sounded suspicious. 'Lady Isleen had him killed for—,'

'Shut up.' Red said it firmly, but not angrily. 'I was fourteen. Nobody told me nothin'. All I know is my dad never would've done something like that. You know how griffiners are. They do things like that an' say whatever they think us commoners will believe.'

'Yeah.' Ranulf sighed. 'It's just…you oughta be careful about that stuff. I heard some things from people…other guards an' whatnot, sayin' someone from your family can't be trusted. After Eagleholm an' all.'

Red scowled. 'Look, my dad wasn't from that side of the family. That was my mum, an' she died when I was tiny. I got nothing to do with any of that.'

'Yeah, but you still call yourself Re—,'

'Oh, stop it,' Red snapped. 'Wasn't your dad a stableboy? Shovellin' ox shit doesn't sound like a noble heritage t'me.'

Ranulf winced. 'Low blow, mate. Low blow.'

'Look,' said Red. 'Nobody's gonna judge me by where I came from. They're gonna judge me by what I do. And I'm gonna make it something t'be proud of. That's a promise.'

'Like what?' asked Ranulf.

'Like…' Red scratched his ear. 'Like I'm gonna catch the son of a bitch who hanged that man.'

'Are you now?' said Ranulf.

'Yeah. I'm gonna get him,' Red vowed. 'An' when I do, he's gonna wish I'd never been born.'

Chapter Two

The Wild Griffin

Somewhere far away from Liranwee, high in the sky, the clouds seemed to darken.

A chilly breeze stirred in the treetops, and a flock of parrots flew up, shrieking in alarm as a shadow fell over them.

Kraego was on the move.

He soared over the land, riding the wind, wings barely moving. Occasionally his tail would twist, the feathery fan adjusting for every slight change in altitude.

The massive griffin kept his eyes on the ground, watching for any sign of movement. He hadn't eaten in several days, and any food would be welcome.

It had been a long time since he had left the North, where he had been conceived, and returned to the South where he had hatched. In all that time he had never returned to human cities, and had rarely encountered humans up close. He had chosen the life of a wild griffin instead – a dangerous life, with humans about, but his sheer size had kept him safe from hunters. That and the fact that his feathers were black. Nobody anywhere in Cymria, human or griffin, lived without fear of the dark griffin. And with his father Skandar dead, Kraego was the dark griffin now.

Of course, fear alone wasn't enough. Rather than find a territory and defend it, he had chosen to live as a nomad; flying anywhere he chose, and eating whatever prey came his way. Wild animals or livestock were equally welcome. He wouldn't eat humans, of course. Eating them was a good way to be slaughtered by the city griffins. And besides, humans were…different.

Kraego might have spent his whole adult life living wild, but he had hatched among humans and had spent his early life living with them, talking to them, being fed by them. Humans were pathetic creatures, not worthy of a true griffin's attention, but they were not food.

Wings spread wide as he rode the wind, Kraego idly wondered where he would go next. Cities were, of course, out of the question. An unpartnered griffin couldn't go near one without being attacked on sight. Mostly he had kept to the open country, farmland and mountains that had plenty of places to roost and to hunt. At one time he had even gone to live in the Coppertops, where his father had been born, but they weren't much good as a territory any more. Humans were building a new city near their edge, and even without that the hunting was poor. Still, Kraego had spent some time there and had found some wild griffins still clinging on. He had fought some of them, mostly for the sheer challenge of it, and had won every time.

So…would the Northgate Mountains be a good place to try next? They were the border between North and South, and wild griffins probably still lived there. Kraego had spent the last few years living in what had once been Eagleholm lands, and hadn't gone that close to the North in a very long time. But surely the Northgates would be safe.

Humans didn't climb them; they used the pass with the fort called Guard's Post. And any wild griffins he found could hardly be a challenge. Kraego hadn't even reached his full size yet, but he was already larger than any other griffin he had met. Aside from his father, of course, but his father was dead.

The thought of his father, and of the North, reminded Kraego of something he had never quite forgotten. He remembered the reason why he had left the North to begin with.

Shar.

When Kraego was barely more than a chick, the red griffin called Shar had challenged the Mighty Skandar and won. She had helped her human, Caedmon, to take over the North. It was because of her that Kraego had chosen exile. But he had left swearing to return one day and challenge Shar. Kraego was not an ordinary griffin; he was a dark griffin, and that meant he was the one meant to rule, not her. It should have been *his* right to challenge Skandar, not hers. She had stolen his victory from him, and he would make her pay for it. And he would do it without choosing a human partner.

And maybe now it was time. Kraego leant on one wing and made a leisurely turn until he was facing north. He would go to the Northgates and find a territory there. And then… he would wait.

Wait and watch, and think. From the Northgates he would be able to see straight into Shar's territory. And, when he felt ready, he could enter it once again.

He had bided his time for nearly ten years. A little longer couldn't hurt.

*

Prince Caradoc Taranisäii of Malvern was afraid. But he didn't let any of it show on his face. It wasn't right for a Taranisäii to show fear, and certainly not here, or now, or in front of his father.

King Caedmon Taranisäii was looking at him expectantly. 'Are you ready?'

Caradoc swallowed. 'I… think so.'

'Either you are or you aren't.' His father's face was as stern as always, and there was no humour in his voice.

'I am,' Caradoc said hastily. 'I'm ready to go in now.'

'Good.' Caedmon reached out and put a hand on one of the grand double-doors in front of them both. He glanced at his partner, Shar, and she obligingly lifted a forepaw and placed it on the other door. Once they were both ready, man and griffin pushed.

The doors opened in front of Caradoc, and all at once a rush of sound hit his ears. His eyes went wide.

'Go in,' said Caedmon. 'Don't hesitate!'

Caradoc stepped forward. Beyond the doorway a vast space opened up in front of him. It was shaped like a massive beehive, and like a beehive it was full of holes in the walls and ceiling. But these holes were enormous. Above his head, hundreds of huge rafters criss-crossed the room, seemingly at random. Wherever two or more of them crossed, huge platforms had been built and were covered in messy heaps of straw and dried reeds. In several places, Caradoc saw bones draped over the rafters, held together by dried flesh. More bones littered the floor – great thick ox bones, most of them broken apart.

Only one creature could do something like that.

Everywhere in the room, in the rafters, on the floor, and in the air, there were griffins. Big griffins, smaller griffins, young and old, perching above or flitting about in search of somewhere to land. Some were barely more than chicks. Most were adults, big enough to carry a man in the air, and those were almost all on the floor.

They might have been disorganised and unruly before, but the moment the door had opened all of them took notice.

Every huge, beaked head was turned toward the entrance. On the floor, the large adults were already coming forward in a group. Above, others were trying frantically to land. Youngsters and the old were retreating, knowing they were too weak to take part.

Caradoc stood in the doorway, looking up into dozens of sharp, curved beaks, hundreds of staring, animal eyes. Terror rooted him to the spot, and for one instant he nearly turned and ran away. But he didn't move. *Don't move!* he told himself frantically. *Be strong!*

Caedmon came to his side. He stood there protectively, and allowed Shar to go forward.

Lean and scarred with rich red-brown feathers, Shar made a threatening lunge toward the griffins who were too close.

'Move back!' she screeched at them. '*Do not touch my human!*' She was speaking griffish, of course, because that was the only language griffins could speak. Caradoc could understand it easily — he couldn't remember a time when he hadn't known griffish.

Sure enough, the griffins — the Unpartnered, they were called — backed off. Some bowed their heads toward Shar. Others merely stepped away and soon returned their attention to the two humans.

Shar soon cleared a circle, and glanced at her human. Caedmon came to stand beside her, motioning at Caradoc to join him.

Caedmon stood there a moment, frowning and stern. Like his predecessor, the great King Arenadd, he wore a black robe. A silver circlet gleamed on his black hair.

'Griffins!' he said at last. 'Griffins of Malvern! I am King Caedmon Taranisäii, partner to Shar.' They knew, of course. 'Today,' Caedmon continued, 'I have brought my son to you.' He nodded to Caradoc, who quickly came to stand in front of him. 'This is my son, Prince Caradoc Taranisäii,' said Caedmon. 'Heir to the throne of Tara, and heir to the great Taranisäii line. He is ready to become a griffiner, and so Shar and I have brought him to you. Choose him, and make a partnership that will last the rest of your lives. He is worthy.'

All of them knew what he had been going to say, of course. They had known that Caradoc would be shown to them today for years, ever since Caedmon and Shar had decided to bring him on his eighth birthday.

The instant Caedmon stopped speaking, every single griffin there rushed forward.

Shar threw herself in the way. '*Stop!*'

They backed off once again.

Shar paced up and down in front of them, tail swishing. 'You will be calm!' she warned. 'You will not charge at the youngster as if he were prey; you will kill him, and his death will mean yours.'

Silence followed.

Shar glared at the Unpartnered. 'Come forward now, whichever of you is bold enough.'

It didn't work. More than twenty griffins immediately advanced. Seeing the competition, they began to snap at each other. Shar charged them, breaking up the group, but after that chaos broke loose. Some of the Unpartnered tried to get at Caradoc, some went after Shar, and others merely began attacking each other.

Caedmon took Caradoc by the shoulder. 'We may have to leave,' he said over the racket. 'Let them work it out amongst themselves.'

The two humans started to move back toward the door, but at that moment a screech rose above the rabble.

'*Enough!*'

But it was not Shar who called. The voice came from among the Unpartnered, and Caradoc saw a ripple of angry griffins as something fought its way through.

The flock parted, and a griffin emerged who was bigger than the rest. Female, pale sandy-yellow, with streaks of white in her wings.

She raised those wings proudly and called. 'I claim the human, and if any of you think you should have him, then come and fight me!'

The others there took up the challenge. Two griffins immediately charged at her. She smashed one into the ground with a brutal talon-blow, and turned to grapple with the other.

Caedmon took his opportunity, and hustled Caradoc out of the chamber. Shar followed, stopping anyone from following, and helped her partner to close the doors.

'Right, then,' said Caedmon. 'I should have expected something like that.' He looked a little shaken.

Caradoc could feel himself trembling. 'Won't I be chosen now, Father?'

Caedmon crouched to look him in the face. 'Don't worry,' he

said. 'You'll be chosen. Didn't you see? Every griffin in there wanted you to be their human.'

'I don't like them.' Caradoc could feel his voice rising as his throat tightened up. 'They're horrible and scary.'

'It's all right,' said Caedmon. 'Griffins are dangerous creatures.'

'To you, perhaps,' Shar said in her dry voice.

'And to each other,' said Caedmon. 'This isn't anything to worry about, Caradoc. With an ordinary person, the Unpartnered would have come forward one at a time to inspect you and decide if they wanted to choose you. But you're not ordinary. You're a Prince. The only Prince in Malvern. One day you'll be King. They already know they want you, and they want you enough to fight for it. You should be honoured.'

'But they'll kill each other!' said Caradoc.

'No. Griffins hardly ever kill each other in a fight like this,' said Caedmon. 'They'll fight until one gives in.'

'Killing is not necessary here,' Shar agreed. 'This is not war – it is only a contest of strength. We will wait until a victor has emerged, and return then.'

Caedmon straightened up. 'I'm sorry I took you in there, Caradoc,' he said. 'If I'd known that would happen I wouldn't have. But you're going to be a griffiner, and that means you'll have to learn not to be afraid of something like that.'

'In war, you will see fighting like that many times,' said Shar. 'But do not be afraid. You will not be expected to fight a griffin yourself – your partner will not allow it.'

'This is good, really,' said Caedmon. 'For them to decide it like this. My son will have the strongest partner possible.'

'Not stronger than me, surely,' Shar said lazily.

'Of course not.'

Caradoc listened to them talking, deciding his future for him. There didn't seem to be anything he could say. And what could he say that would make a difference? He was going to be a griffiner; he had been going to be one since he was born, just as he had always been going to be King. And then he would wear the crown, and probably a robe like his father's. And he would have a griffin beside him just like his father did, maybe one even bigger and meaner than Shar.

That thought, at least, gave him comfort. *His* griffin would be his protector, as Shar had said, and maybe his friend as well. And he would be able to fly, too. He'd flown on Shar's back before, with his father, and it wasn't so scary. Maybe being a griffiner could be fun as well as big and important like his father said.

They waited a while, the two humans and the griffin, and listened to the sounds of chaos coming from inside the Hatchery. Fortunately, the doors were enormously thick and reinforced with steel. Otherwise they might have broken down by now, and more than once Caradoc thought they would be anyway, as massive blows from the other side made them shudder.

But they stayed intact, and eventually the noise of battle began to die down.

'I should check,' said Caedmon. He went to the doors, but rather than open them he slid a little hatch open and peeked through. 'I think it's just about over now,' he said.

Shar came and looked through, before wordlessly putting her shoulder against the door and giving it a shove.

It swung open, and Caradoc looked through at a sight that made him feel sick with nerves.

The huge crowd of griffins was gone. Some of them were up in the rafters, but many must have flown away through the openings. Only a few were left on the floor, and of those most looked as if they had fought – and lost. Some were even lying down, either hurt or showing submission. Others hunched in corners and licked their wounds. The floor was littered with stray feathers and clumps of fur, and even a few broken talons.

Nearest to the door, one final struggle was still taking place.

Three griffins made a knot, beaks, talons and claws hooked into flesh, wings flailing. It was impossible to tell who was winning, or even who had hold of who. But, as Caradoc watched, the knot broke. A griffin jerked sideways, twisted, and fell. It was a large dark brown male, and he must have been one of the main fighters, because everywhere on his body patches of blood showed up starkly against his feathers.

He landed on his side, and did not get up again.

That left only two griffins to the struggle. They let go of each other and moved back, both breathing heavily. One was the yellow female Caradoc had seen before. The other was another male, this one with a very attractive silvery-grey coat and violet eyes. Caradoc thought he looked striking and special, and hoped he would win.

The two griffins leapt at each other one last time. Or, rather, the male leapt. The female appeared to leap, rearing up as he did, but midway through her leap she suddenly twisted sideways and rammed into his belly, beak-first.

The male's fur seemed to slide away from his flesh, showing red muscle for an instant before blood welled up and turned his silvery coat dark.

The yellow female didn't wait to let him recover. Now she reared up, onto her hind legs, and ruthlessly brought her talons down on his head.

There was an ugly crunch, and a thud, and the male griffin thumped onto the floor, twitching horribly in his death throes.

The female griffin contemptuously shoved his body aside, and advanced on the two humans. Her yellow feathers were bloodied, and she had talon-cuts down the sides of her face, but she was big and powerful, and victorious.

She ignored Caedmon and Shar completely. All her attention was on Caradoc. Her eyes were a rich brown, fixed on his face, and as she came closer they seemed to fill his whole world.

Caradoc looked around frantically for his father, but suddenly Caedmon wasn't there. Nor was Shar. Without even seeming to move, they had left him standing alone.

It was just him, and this yellow griffin who had killed for the right to be here.

Sides heaving, she sat on her haunches. He could smell her sweat, mingling with the musky odour of feathers and the dry scent of fur. She was so close he could see the tiny black veins in her eyes, and the soft place where her skin merged into her beak.

The griffin looked down, putting her head on one side to see him better.

'Little human,' she rumbled. 'I am Ereska. I am the mightiest of the Unpartnered, and I have fought away all others who would choose you. You are now mine by rights.'

Every griffish word Caradoc knew seemed to have fallen out of his head. He looked up at the bloody conquerer, and felt as if he were falling.

'I choose you, Caradoc Taranisäii,' said Ereska, unmoved. 'You are my human now. You may touch me, if you wish.'

Caradoc had been raised among griffins, and he knew what this meant. Very slowly, he reached up toward her.

Ereska lowered her head to meet his hand. Her feathers were warm and soft.

Emboldened, Caradoc rubbed her face the way he had seen his father do with Shar. She liked that and pushed against his hand to encourage him. A purr began in her throat.

'We are partners now,' she crooned. 'My strength for your cunning. Your power for my magic. My wings for your status. Together, we will fight and lead. Together, we will dominate. Together, we will become great.'

Caradoc finally found his voice. 'Yes,' he managed. 'Together.'

*

That day there was a feast in the Eyrie, to celebrate the choosing. The weather was good, so they held the feast on the roof of the Council Tower, which was flat and had plenty of room for the griffins.

Every griffiner Caradoc knew was there. Lady Isolde, Master of Law, was one of the first to talk to him. 'How does it feel to be a griffiner?' she asked.

This was a question that hadn't occurred to Caradoc yet. 'I dunno,' he mumbled.

'Don't you feel honoured?' Isolde prompted.

Most of the griffins were off at the carcasses provided, but Ereska had stayed proudly by her new human. 'You should be honoured,' said the yellow griffin. 'There is no greater honour for a human to be chosen.'

'I'm honoured,' Caradoc said hastily.

'That's good!' said Isolde. She gave him a bright, encouraging smile. 'Now you'll have to be properly trained, of course. And don't worry; it's not as hard as it looks. Once you know griffish, the rest is easy.'

'You must learn to fly,' said Ereska. 'But you will be easy to carry!'

Caradoc did his best to look excited. 'Maybe we can go see the other cities.'

'Yes,' said Ereska. 'Now that I am partnered, I can leave Malvern whenever I wish.'

Meanwhile, Lady Isolde had already lost interest in him. 'I think

I'll go and have something to eat. Ceinwen is here – you should go and find her.'

Caradoc nodded, and wandered off through the crowd.

Ereska kept close behind him. 'Who is Ceinwen?' she asked.

'A girl,' said Caradoc.

'Young female?' Ereska translated. 'Tell me about her. You must tell me about other humans who are important; I must learn.'

Caradoc felt unexpectedly pleased to be asked for something. 'Ceinwen's Lady Isolde's daughter,' he said. 'I'm going to marry her one day.'

'A mating?' said Ereska. She looked slightly confused. 'But you are too young.'

'I know, so we're going to wait until I'm older,' said Caradoc.

'Surely it is too early to think of that,' said Ereska. 'Why have you chosen a mate already?'

'I didn't,' said Caradoc. 'My father decided, and my mother before she died.'

'But it is not for them to choose your mate,' said Ereska, now thoroughly lost. 'You must wait until you are an adult, and then you must wait until your human females are in heat and fight other males for the finest of them.'

Caradoc stared at her in complete bewilderment for a moment, and then he burst into a fit of giggles. 'We don't do *that!*'

Ereska snorted. 'Do not laugh at me! The way to find the strongest mate is to fight for her! Why would you allow the choice to be made for you?'

Caradoc stopped giggling immediately. 'Because my dad and I are the last Taranisäiis, and I have to marry and have children as soon as I can, or we might die out. They picked Ceinwen because she's high born.'

'What does that mean?' asked Ereska.

'Her parents are important, so she is too,' Caradoc said lamely. 'I don't know. I just do what they say.'

'Not any more,' said Ereska. 'You are a griffiner now, and so even if you are only a pup you must make your own choices. When you are an adult, I will help you to find a mate.'

'All right.' Despite all his confusion and lingering fright, Caradoc felt encouraged by her words and massive presence. She was big and scary but, he reminded himself, she was on *his* side. He stood a little taller, and went in search of Ceinwen.

She was over at one of the food tables with her father. When she saw Caradoc she hid.

Her father, Lord Druson, smiled at Caradoc. 'Hello! Congratulations on being chosen. Ceinwen, why don't you come out and talk to your betrothed?'

Ceinwen peered out shyly from behind her father's leg. Druson gently guided her out into the open, and she stood and looked silently at Caradoc.

Caradoc managed a smile. 'Hello. This is Ereska.'

Ceinwen smiled back hesitantly. 'Hello.' She was only six, and her eyes looked big and nervous like a rabbit's.

'This is your mate, then?' said Ereska. She came forward and snuffled at Ceinwen. The girl knew griffins well enough not to run away, but she tensed as Ereska's breath ruffled her hair.

'She looks small and weak,' Ereska said brusquely. 'Surely you would need a more powerful mate than this to bear your eggs. Where is her partner? Is she a griffiner?'

'She's too young,' said Caradoc, aware of Druson's smirk as he tried not to laugh. 'I couldn't be chosen until my birthday, but she's only six.'

'Not old enough to be partnered,' Ereska concluded.

'Not yet,' said Druson. 'But in a year or two she'll be brought to the Hatchery too.'

'Then perhaps she will be worthy of my human,' said Ereska. 'Until then…' she turned her back on Ceinwen, and returned to Caradoc's side.

Instantly, Ceinwen went straight back to hide behind her father. This time she refused to come out again.

'You scared her!' Caradoc told Ereska.

'Then she must learn not to fear,' said the yellow griffin.

Even though it hadn't been his fault, Caradoc felt guilty. He walked away along the food table, and ate some grapes from a dish. At the far end he found a plate of little honey cakes, and picked one up.

He went back and offered it to Ceinwen.

She took it with a barely audible 'Thank you'.

'I'm sorry you got scared,' said Caradoc. 'Ereska doesn't understand about humans.'

'Then it's your job to teach her,' said Druson, from above. 'She needs training just as much as you do, little Prince.'

Caradoc looked up at him. 'How do I teach her?'

'Just tell her things,' said Druson. 'She's smart enough to know she has to learn. She'll listen.'

'All right,' said Caradoc. 'I know lots about people.'

Ereska was keeping her distance this time, and Ceinwen had started to look more cheerful. 'You can tell her that we don't have eggs!' she said.

'Yes, I'll tell her that,' said Caradoc.

Druson smiled indulgently. 'What else will you tell her?'

'I'll tell her that… um…' Caradoc thought quickly. 'I'll tell her…'

A screech cut across him.

He turned hastily. 'That's Shar!'

Sure enough, Shar was standing tall in the middle of the celebration. The musicians had already stopped playing, and everywhere people and griffins turned to look at her.

Caedmon was at her side. 'Prince Caradoc, come to me,' he called.

'Ereska, to me,' said Shar.

Caradoc hurried over, with Ereska close beside him. The pair of them went to stand beside Shar and Caedmon, and waited while the King spoke.

Caedmon had changed into his finest robe, and his look was proud. But he sounded as businesslike as usual. 'Lords and Ladies of Malvern, I present Prince Caradoc Taranisäii. From today, he is one of you. A griffiner of Malvern – and of Tara.'

'And I present Ereska,' said Shar. 'Hatched in Malvern. She has chosen a human, and now is one of us. Welcome her!'

There was a respectful muttering from the humans there, and huffs and chirps of acknowledgement from the griffins.

'Now,' said Caedmon. 'Every new griffiner must be apprenticed for training. Normally he or she would be brought before the council and offered up to be chosen, but in this case the choice is already made. My son will be apprenticed to me. I will teach him how to be a griffiner, and I will teach him all he needs to know to rule after me, just as every apprentice must become a Master.'

Caradoc had been expecting this, of course. He wondered why the others there wouldn't know already too.

'And so,' Caedmon continued, 'since Caradoc is my apprentice now, he must stay with me. The Emperor of Amoran has agreed to our offer, and we will soon be ready to leave Malvern. My son will be going with me.'

Several people there looked openly surprised.

Caradoc's heart skipped a beat. 'But I—,' he began.

Caedmon held up a hand. 'I know that some of you will say it's too dangerous. But Caradoc is more than a griffiner; he is a Taranisäii, and every member of our great family must know danger. Our founder, King Arenadd, once told me that every great man is forged in fire. To be a true Taranisäii, and to learn how to be a true King, Caradoc must come with me.'

As the shock faded, excitement began to pulse through Caradoc's body. *I can go with him!* he wanted to say. *I can go and learn how to be a warrior.*

Nothing, he decided afterwards, could have been better than that. Knowing that he wouldn't have to stay in Malvern and have his lessons every day, but instead would be allowed to go with his father and see real fighting. He would be able to see what evil men looked like. And he would get to see them die.

Chapter Three

The Hangman

The White Serpent was as busy as it usually was, even now, weeks after the murders had begun. In fact, Red thought it looked busier. Murder worked wonders for bringing in the customers.

He wasn't surprised. Public death always seemed to bring out either the bravado or the ghoul in everyone. Oh, they'd put on a show of being shocked or horrified, but once they'd made sure everyone saw them being normal and decent the showing off would start, or the morbid questions, or the bloodthirsty gossip. It was just how people were. At least seven more bodies had shown up, all hanged in the same way, and it was all people wanted to talk about these days.

He thought on that while he and Ranulf bought a beer each and found a place to sit at the end of a long table full of chattering drinkers.

'Did that hit the spot?' Ranulf asked cheerfully.

'Yeah.' Red put his mug down. 'Y'know, I was thinking…'

'Yeah?'

Red looked around at the other customers. He could catch snippets of conversation easily enough, and predictably, most of it was concerned with the Hangman. 'I wonder why people are so fascinated with death,' he said. 'I mean, can y'hear them?'

Ranulf took a healthy gulp of beer. 'Of course they're fascinated,' he said. 'Death's the one thing what happens to *everyone*, along with birth. Everyone's got it in common, even us and Northerners.'

'Even us and animals,' said Red.

'Yeah, exactly,' said Ranulf.

Red stopped at that. 'Oh, c'mon. Northerners are just people, y'know.'

Ranulf paused with his mug halfway to his mouth. 'That ain't what I'd call them,' he said. 'You know what they did. Inviting Lady

Isleen North t'make a peace treaty, then tryin' to kill her instead!'

'So she says,' said Red. He scowled. 'For myself I don't believe a thing that woman puts about.'

'Oh, right,' said Ranulf. 'Sorry, forgot.'

Red wasn't in a forgiving mood. 'Anyone who calls my dad a traitor is a liar, an' that's all there is to it.'

'Never trust anything a griffiner says,' Ranulf agreed.

'Right,' said Red. He drank for a while in silence.

'Actually,' said Ranulf, 'I've always wondered about that.'

'About what?' said Red.

'Well, Isleen had your dad killed, right?' said Ranulf. 'Or so you reckon.'

'She did,' Red said sharply.

'But if that's true, then why are y'still here?' asked Ranulf. 'Why stay an' be ruled by her? If it was me…'

'Liranwee's my home,' said Red. 'I grew up here. I helped *build* it, come to that. My sweat went into these stones. Yeah I hate Isleen, but this city's a part of me, an' no power on earth is gonna make me leave.'

Ranulf finished off his beer. 'Ah. So that's why you don't have a woman. You're in love with the city.'

'You might say that,' said Red. 'But that doesn't mean I'll look the other way when I meet the woman what's right for me.'

Ranulf grinned at him. 'But you'd break the city's heart!'

'It's a big city; it can cope. I'm the last of my family as far as I know. I'm not gonna let us die out.'

Ranulf finally became serious. 'Honestly, though, you care way more than you oughta. It's been what – a month since the murders started, and you've refused to go off-duty once. You look like you're gonna keel over – is it really true Talmon forced you to take the night off?'

Red stifled a yawn. 'Yeah… I guess he was right. A tired guard can't think straight and shouldn't be on duty. I just…' He sighed. 'I couldn't just do nothin', y'know? All those people the bastard's hanged by now, and no-one's come close to stopping him. I've tried everything and gotten nowhere—' He broke off mid-sentence, and his head turned sharply as a shout rose above the crowd. 'There's trouble!'

'Leave it, Red,' said Ranulf. 'You're off-duty, right?'

But Red had already left his seat and gone to investigate.

Over near the doorway that led to the street, a pair of drunks was harassing a man with a cloth tied over his eyes.

'C'mon!' one of them said. 'Give us a look!' He made a grab for the cloth.

The man backed off, clumsily trying to shield his bandaged face. 'I said no, didn't I?'

The drunks, however, were in the sort of mood that didn't need any encouragement.

'Why not?' one asked. 'Just a peek!'

The victim fumbled for the door handle. 'The light hurts, right? Please just leave me alone.'

One of the drunks gave him a not-really-playful shove. The blind man fell backward with a pathetic cry, and before he could get up the second drunk had lunged for the bandage.

'Oi!'

Red's shout made both of them look up. 'Whaddya want?' one growled. 'Mind yer own business.'

Red knew exactly what to do in these situations. Careful not to look overly threatening lest he start a fight, he glowered at them. 'I'm a member of the city guard,' he said. 'An' you're about to break the law. Now move it.'

The drunks abandoned their victim and confronted Red instead. 'What law?' one demanded. 'We weren't doing nothing wrong — what law were we breakin'?'

'The law that says only rat-arsed lowlifes like you go botherin' old blind men,' said Ranulf, appearing at Red's side. 'Now beat it, or get beaten.'

They took the hint, and sloped off back to the bar.

'Thanks, mate,' said Red.

He went to help the blind man, who groped for his offered hand and let himself be pulled upright.

'You all right?' Red asked.

'Fine,' said the blind man. 'Thanks.'

'No problem.' Red eyed the man for a moment, wondering why he looked familiar. Then he remembered — it was the same man who had "stared" at him on the day he and Ranulf had carried off the Hangman's first victim.

The blind man shook his head slowly. 'Old No-Eyes knows that voice. You're the guard with the red hair.'

'I am,' said Red. 'How d'you know that?'

No-Eyes grinned – it was a slightly uncomfortable sight on a face with no eyes. 'A blind man uses his ears for eyes.'

'Hear colours, can ya?' said Ranulf.

No-Eyes turned his blind face toward him. 'No. But your friend's a guard an' he calls himself Red. An' you're a fat man if I'm any judge.'

'How'd you know *that?*' asked Ranulf.

'It's in your footsteps,' said No-Eyes.

Red laughed. 'He's got you there. You need any more help, No-Eyes?'

'No. But…' No-Eyes came closer. 'You helped old No-Eyes, so he'll help you.'

'That's fine,' said Red. 'I was just doin' my duty.'

'When you were s'posed to be off-duty,' No-Eyes observed. 'Listen…' he took another step forward, until he was so close he could speak directly into Red's ear. 'A blind man hears many things. I hear how you're killing yourself trying to catch the Hangman. But I hear things about the Hangman, too.'

Red's pulse quickened. 'Like what?'

No-Eyes' voice dropped to a whisper. 'There's a place at the city's edge where a new building is being made. No-Eyes heard that on some nights a man goes there to steal rope. Good thick rope they use for lifting wood an' bricks. The day after he takes the rope, someone turns up dead.'

'*No,*' said Red. 'Are you sure?'

'Sure I'm sure,' said No-Eyes. 'It's always the same rope he uses, always the same kind. Didn't you wonder where he got it from? Go there on the right night, I reckon you'll find him.'

'On the edge of the city?' said Red.

'Where they're buildin' a tower,' said No-Eyes. 'Go there, an' see if you can't stop the bastard. Thanks again.'

He turned and shuffled out of the tavern.

Red stayed where he was for a while with a thoughtful expression.

'What was that all about?' Ranulf interrupted. 'What'd he tell yer?'

As if the sound of his voice had galvanised him into action, Red straightened the hang of his tunic, checked his sword, and strode for the door. 'Come on,' he said. 'We're goin'.'

Ranulf followed. 'Goin' where?'

Red kicked the door open, and ran off into the streets. 'To catch the Hangman.'

'What?' Ranulf jogged to keep up. 'Where?'

'At the city wall,' Red said grimly. 'Where they're building the new guard tower!'

*

Darkness had fallen over Liranwee, but it wasn't late. Plenty of people were still out and about in some of the better-lit areas. But there was an air of nervousness about most of them, and none of them looked very happy to see the two guards.

'Useless bastards!' one woman yelled at them.

'We'll see about that,' Red said through gritted teeth.

'Oh, c'mon,' said Ranulf. 'You really think this is gonna work? What'd some blind man know about any of this?'

'It's a lead an' I'm following it,' said Red. 'It's the only damn one we've had since this thing started.'

Ranulf was already puffing. 'I'm just saying there's no point in chasin' after rumours! Next we'll be goin' after the monster what lives in Eagle Lake down south!'

'It's not a rumour,' said Red.

'Yeah it is,' said Ranulf. 'Just 'cause you only heard it from one man doesn't make it not a rumour.'

'It's – not – a – rumour,' Red insisted.

'How d'you know?' Ranulf was beginning to look genuinely annoyed now.

'Because unlike you I pay attention to stuff,' said Red. 'An' *I* remembered that we had a report last week about a theft at that building site.'

'Theft of what?'

'They didn't say,' said Red. 'But I'm willin' to bet it was rope.'

'Oh, fine,' said Ranulf. 'Let's go have a look, then. But we'd better be damn careful. We're not on duty an' if anyone catches us snoopin' around we'll be up before the Commander in a heartbeat.'

'I know,' said Red. 'I just wish I had my armour. Got my sword, at least.'

'It'll do,' said Ranulf. 'We're not goin' in for heroics tonight, right?'

'Right,' said Red. 'We're just lookin'.'

Both of them knew the edge of the city quite well, since after all it was where the city's walls were and any defensive structure needed guards to keep it going. Earlier in the year they'd been assigned to the wall, and had spent several tedious months patrolling along its top or helping to run the guard towers built just inside it. Liranwee had never been attacked, but with the Northgate Mountains just beyond it – and Northerner territory beyond that – there was always a danger, or at least a healthy dose of paranoia. Plenty of times in the past, impatient young guards had been reminded that if war ever broke out, the city would be very well served by those towers.

The tower that Red and Ranulf made for, however, was only half built, since there had been some problems with clearing a space for it back when the city was still under construction. The building site had been left open, since there was supposedly nothing worth stealing on it and anyone stupid enough to wander around in a tower with half its flooring missing clearly deserved to die.

The ground around the tower's base was a mess. Stacked crates were interspersed with piles of wooden beams too heavy for anyone to steal, and heaps of bricks.

'Time was when we woulda had a gang of blackrobes t'deal with this stuff,' Ranulf observed.

'Yeah, I bet the griffiners would've loved that,' said Red. 'No wages to pay. But I'd rather give jobs like this to good honest Southerners. Men need jobs, y'know.'

The pair of them shook their heads ruefully. Nobody in the South kept slaves nowadays; not since the Northerners had rebelled. They'd taken back their homeland and now ruled themselves there, and no Southerner would set foot in their territory unless he wanted to die.

'Now, let's look around,' said Red. 'Find out where they keep the rope.'

'Should be in one of these crates,' said Ranulf. He approached the nearest one and peered inside. 'Argh, why didn't we bring a bloody lantern?'

'Just feel around,' said Red. 'Rope's hard to miss.'

'Right.' Ranulf groped around inside the crate, shook his head, and moved on to another.

Red went to inspect another nearby. It was empty, so he tried the next. This one was full of what felt like nails.

He glanced over his shoulder. 'Hey, we should stick together…'

Ranulf was nowhere in sight.

'Oh, great,' Red muttered.

He went in the direction he thought Ranulf had gone, closer to the tower. No sign of him, but he spotted more crates inside the building and went to investigate those.

Most of them turned out to be empty, or had things in them he couldn't identify. Maybe they kept the ropes hanging up somewhere instead?

As he went to grope his way around the walls, he heard something moving off to his left.

'Ranulf, is that you?'

There was no reply.

Instantly, Red tensed. Moving slowly and carefully, he edged his way toward the door. Realising that he had already given himself away, he kept his voice loud and confident as if he had no idea what was going on. 'Ranulf? C'mon, stop foolin' around.'

Still there was no reply. There were no other sounds of movement either.

Red reached the doorway, and quickly glanced through it. The cluttered ground beyond the tower was utterly still. Ranulf was nowhere in sight.

The back of his neck prickled. He couldn't see anything, or hear anything, but some other sense, some deep, animal sense, spoke up. *There was someone behind him.*

Keeping as still as possible, Red slowly drew his sword.

The faintest breeze moved over his head. He heard a soft intake of breath.

In one swift movement, he turned around and thrust his sword in an upward stab.

The blade hit something, and a muffled cry split the air.

Red moved back hastily, out into the dull moonlight, and something followed.

For an instant, he had a vision of something huge and horrible. A man, a giant man, bigger than himself, and even more powerful looking. Blood had darkened a patch on the front of his tunic, but he didn't look even slightly bothered by it.

There was a coil of rope in his hand.

He held a club in the other.

Pure shock stopped Red from acting. Stupidly, he raised his sword – not to attack, but to try and protect himself. 'No—!'

The giant brought the club down. Red's wrist slammed into his head, and the hilt of his own sword hit him with an audible *crack*.

The night exploded.

He woke up an instant later, on the ground. Pain burst behind his eyes, making the world spin. He couldn't move, but he was moving. Hands turned him over, and tied his wrists behind his back.

'No…' Red's voice came out thick and mumbled, and he kicked out feebly.

Hands caught his feet, and tied them together too, so fast and easily. *He's done it before, so often,* Red thought.

Even the agony in his skull could not numb the terror. He thrashed about like a landed fish, fighting back with all his might as the hands turned him over again and lifted him up by the shoulders.

The face of the giant appeared once again, hard and square and brutal, carved from wood.

Red finally came to his senses, and opened his mouth to yell. '*Ranulf—!*'

The giant smacked him in the face, hard enough to make his head spin horribly again. Then the sack went over his head, and the noose around his neck to hold it in place, and he was being dragged backward, effortlessly.

Red fought. Like every victim before him, he fought. But like every other man or woman the Hangman had claimed, his struggles could not save him.

The dragging stopped, and he felt the rope being thrown upward. Then it began to pull.

The noose went tight around his neck as it lifted him up, and up, until his feet were off the ground.

No, he tried to say, and *Gryphus save me.* But the noose had taken away his voice, along with his breath.

Like those before him, Red thrashed on the rope. But every kick of his bound legs only made the noose tighter. Agony pounded in his head, in his throat. It spread to his lungs soon enough, and his faltering heart.

Redness filled his vision, and as it blinked away he thought he saw a face. A lean, hungry face, there for an instant. Hands reaching out. *Come to me. Join us now. Die.*

From somewhere far, far away he thought he heard a voice call his name.

Then true darkness came.

Chapter Four

Heroes

Darkness, he was in darkness. Darkness, and freezing cold, and terror ripped his mind apart. He could not move or breathe or make a sound, and the void opened up before him – empty, unforgiving, and terrible. Red tried to scream, but nothing happened. He tried to turn away and flee back to the light, but he couldn't. Something had hold of him – freezing hands, pulling him forward, taking him away from life to claim him for their own. They felt like claws, ripping into his skin, and a face flashed up before his eyes – evil, twisted, barely human, the eyes whitened and full of hunger and unspeakable despair.

Red struggled weakly against the thing, eyes wide with terror, but as the void swallowed them both he felt himself begin to fall away. His memories faded out of his head, one by one. He forgot the Hangman, and Ranulf, and No-Eyes. He forgot about Kullervo, and their journey together. He forgot the sound of his father's voice.

Only one thing remained, clinging on in his mind. *Red… Red… my name is Red…*

But the monster would not let him go, and nor would the void, and he knew, then, that he was dead.

Thud.

The noise sounded muffled and distant, and it would have been unimportant, but it brought pain with it. It thumped through his body, and a moment later it had hold of his throat. Pain began there, and spread downward and then upward as well, and he felt himself jerk and gape, unable to cry out. Blackness turned to redness around him, and light came, horribly bright.

Confused and suffering, he tried to turn away from it, suddenly aching for the comfort of oblivion and forgetfulness. In the void, he would not have to feel.

For a moment, he thought he could still feel the icy hands that had hold of his soul.

Then they let go.

A voice spoke, so faint it was barely there. *He got away, master.*

I got away, Red thought. And then—

'Red! *Red!*'

Sound slammed back into his ears like a blow to the head.

Hands again, hands pressing on his chest, hands lifting his head, and a voice growing louder.

'Breathe! Red, *breathe!*'

Red's mouth jerked open, and he started to cough.

'Breathe!' said the voice.

And Red breathed. It spread more pain through his body, but that didn't matter. Pain was life, and it pulled him back to the real world just as the hands had pulled him into the void.

'Yer all right,' said the voice. Ranulf's voice! 'Just rest an' breathe. I got you.'

Red shuddered. He wanted to open his eyes and try to get up, but the impulse only produced the slightest, feeblest jerk of his limbs. Ranulf gently pushed him back and propped his head up on something soft.

The Hangman, Red thought, as pain pulsated in his crushed throat.

'It's all right,' Ranulf said from somewhere above him. 'We got him. You did it, Red.'

Did not, Red thought. *He killed me.*

He fell asleep.

He woke up again once or twice after that, but only briefly – just long enough to know he was being carried. He heard a babble of voices around him, but they were friendly voices, friendly and concerned. No danger there.

His head ached, and his throat hurt, and he felt weak all over, but not afraid any more. Everything was all right now, he thought, and he allowed himself to slip away again. The next time he woke up, he didn't open his eyes. He felt himself being laid down, and someone removed his boots. Then a blanket covered him.

Red stirred.

'Rest,' someone told him. 'Just rest now.'

The blanket warmed him, and he dozed off again. He was vaguely aware that when he woke up properly it would be time to pay the full price for the beating he had taken, but for now he could put it off.

*

He woke up in pain again. This time, it wasn't dulled or distant.

His eyes opened, and he tried to breathe in. Pain flared in his throat. He gagged on it, and began to cough.

Instantly, voices rose up around him.

'He's awake!'

Red blinked and peered upward. His vision was blurry, but it cleared soon enough, and he saw faces looking down at him. All familiar faces, all worried.

'Ranulf,' he tried to say. But the name caught in his swollen throat, came out strangled and hoarse.

Ranulf seemed to understand. 'It's all right, mate.'

Red tried again. 'Ranulf,' he whispered. This time he got the word out properly.

'Yeah, it's me,' said Ranulf. 'You feelin' okay?'

'Throat… hurts,' Red managed.

'Not surprised about that,' said Ranulf. His tone was casual, but he looked pale.

Red blinked some more, and looked at one of the other faces. 'Sir,' he whispered.

Commander Talmon nodded formally. 'You've done an excellent job, Sergeant. You went above and beyond the call of duty, and you succeeded.'

Red closed his eyes, as dark memories came back. 'The Hangman…'

'We've got him,' said Talmon. 'He's in custody. Thanks to you.'

Red opened his eyes again. 'How…?'

Talmon offered him a rare smile. 'Before he knocked you down, you managed to stab him. The effort of lifting you up made his bleeding worse, and by the time Ranulf arrived he had collapsed. He might not even live long enough to be executed. And you're going to be fine.'

Red nodded jerkily. 'Like to… ask for… another day off, sir,' he whispered.

Even Talmon laughed. 'Request granted, Sergeant. You'll be on paid leave until the healer says you're strong enough. But try and get some strength back soon – you don't want to miss your ceremony!'

Red peered at him. 'Miss what?'

'You and Ranulf are both going to be honoured,' said Talmon. 'The Eyrie Mistress herself will present you with an award for bravery. The whole city will know you're heroes – especially you, Red.'

It was all too much just then, but Red smiled by way of reply.

'Anyway,' said Talmon, 'you need rest, and I've got work to do. Well done, Sergeant, and I'll see you later.'

He nodded formally and left. The other guards there left with him, with grins and congratulations.

'Well done, Red. Y'sure showed us!'

'So much for needin' the rest of us!'

Red grinned. 'Let you do it next time, Bear.'

Ranulf stayed behind. 'How about that, then, eh?' he said, sitting down on the edge of the bed. 'Heroes!'

'Yeah,' said Red. Even whispering hurt, so he fell silent and let Ranulf do the talking. The truth was that his partner looked shaken.

'Red, I'm so sorry,' Ranulf's eyes looked a little bloodshot. 'If I hadn't wandered off like that, then this wouldn't've happened.'

Red shook his head.

'I found a lantern, see,' said Ranulf. 'I was tryin' to light it when I heard you yell. I got it lit an' came looking, but I couldn't tell where you were. Then I saw him. That bastard, staggerin' out of the tower with blood on him. I went to get him, but he just fell down an' I heard… heard you in there. So I went in, an' saw…' Ranulf cringed visibly. 'I tell you I'm never gonna forget it. Seeing you hanging there was the worst thing I ever saw in my life.'

Red shuddered too.

'Yeah…' Ranulf shook his head. 'If you'd died, I never would've forgiven myself. But I cut you down in time. Used the hanging rope to tie up the bastard, just in case.'

Red nodded, telling him to go on.

'I tellya,' said Ranulf, 'we owe that No-Eyes a beer. An' not just because he told us where t'go. Seems he heard us say we were goin' there, so he went an' fetched some of the lads just in case. Then he came back t'help me. Even helped us carry you back to the barracks. He was here just now before you woke up.'

Red smiled again. Who would have thought an old blind man could be so much help?

'But I'm sorry,' said Ranulf. 'Gryphus' talons, I must be the most useless partner any guard ever had.'

Red shook his head. 'Good partner,' he whispered. 'Good friend. Saved… my life.'

Ranulf smiled. 'That's what friends are for. Now I'd better go – got stuff t'do. But there'll be lads in an' out of here just as always, so you tell 'em if there's anything y'want.'

Ranulf left, and Red was alone. He lay peacefully in his comfortable old bunk – the same bunk that had been his ever since he had joined the guard. After all that time, and so many troubled nights, he had done it. The Hangman was captured, the city was safe, and he, Red, had done what he had always wanted: served his city above all others, and done something great for its people.

He thought of his family too. His proud old family, which had been disgraced and nearly wiped out. He was the last of the line, but by Gryphus he had done everything in his power to honour his heritage and bring back some of the greatness they had lost. He hoped that his ancestors would be proud of him now – and especially his father, wherever he was now.

It had been a while since Red had thought of his father. Dan, his friends had called him. But most other people had called him Lord Danthirk. Once he had been a guard, but he had ended his life as a griffiner. A new griffiner, chosen after the destruction of Eagleholm, when the unpartnered griffins had decided to leave the ruins with whatever humans they could find. Once upon a time, Red had been raised to believe that one day he too would be a griffiner. After all, the children of griffiners nearly always followed in their parents' footsteps.

But Lord Danthirk had died, and that hope had gone with him.

Red had never seen him dead. Danthirk had simply gone to the Eyrie for a meeting one day, and never returned. But Red still remembered that day vividly. He remembered how worried his father had looked, and he remembered the last words he had said to his son.

Our family's code is duty, Red. Not just duty t'family, but duty to our people. Live by duty an' you'll live a life without regrets.

I did my duty, Dad, Red thought. *I nearly died doing it, but I've got no regrets. I hope you're proud of me.*

There could be no reply, of course, but there didn't have to be. Red knew what it would be.

*

Red slept on and off for most of that day. Food was brought to him, but his throat was too swollen to eat. He didn't feel that hungry anyway. Nearly dying, he thought, really took it out of you.

The next day, however, he woke up feeling much better. Ranulf brought him breakfast, and he managed to get it down. He could speak above a whisper now, and when the healer came to look at him after breakfast she was encouraging.

'You're doing well,' she said. 'Looks like you'll make a full recovery.'

'Can I get up?' Red asked.

'Yes, but take it easy. You might be a bit unsteady.'

Red got out of bed with some help from her and Ranulf. His legs were fine, but for some reason the left one felt a little weak.

'Neck wounds can give people trouble with walking,' the healer explained. 'We're not sure why.'

She gave him a crutch, and showed him how to use it. Once he had it wedged under his arm, he could limp around easily enough. 'I'm not gonna be a cripple, am I?' he whispered.

'Probably not,' said the healer. 'Walking around should give you your strength back. Don't worry – you're young and strong, and that'll help you heal faster.'

Red nodded gratefully. For a guard, being crippled could mean early retirement.

Now that he was up and about again, he took the opportunity to go for a walk. He didn't go far, but he visited the mess hall and followed it up with a lap around the training yard. Ranulf, who'd apparently been given the day off as well, went with him.

'It's good yer doin' this well,' he said. 'You'll want to be in good shape by tomorrow.'

'Sure I will be,' Red rasped. 'Why?'

'They've decided they'll hang the Hangman at noon,' said Ranulf, grinning at his own play on words. 'Afterwards, if yer up to it, they'll do the ceremony.'

Excitement quickened Red's heartbeat. 'I'll be there!'

'You sure?' asked Ranulf.

'I'm fine, honest,' said Red. 'Bit beat up, but it's mostly just my throat.' To emphasise the point, he handed the crutch to Ranulf and strode off across the yard. His leg felt stronger already.

Ranulf came after him with the crutch under his arm. 'All right, calm down, mate. No need t'prove to me how tough you are; everybody knows it. Here.'

Red took the crutch back. 'Right. I'd better go polish my armour, then.'

He returned to his bunk, feeling much more alert thanks to the exercise, and occupied himself with sorting out his armour. He'd kept it pretty clean and been sure to oil it regularly, but he gave it a thorough going-over this time. Once it was clean he brought out a pot of beeswax and rubbed it over the outside, polishing the stiff leather with a rag until it had a good sheen.

Someone had been kind enough to clean his sword and put it away for him, so he unpacked it now and gave it a sharpening and some oil. Nobody would see the blade at the ceremony, but that didn't matter. This sword had helped to save his life. He buffed up the scabbard and, just for the sake of it, polished the belt it hung on as well.

The preparations made him start to anticipate tomorrow's ceremony with great pride and excitement. As for the execution… well. That was just another part of the duty, and he would go through it because he had to. But he wouldn't take any pleasure from it. A guard did his duty to the city, and personal revenge should not come into it.

By the time he finished cleaning up his arms and armour it was about time for dinner, and he felt strong enough to have it in the mess hall with everyone else.

When he went into the hall and chose a seat, several other guards immediately came over to join him.

'Hey, Red!'

'Good t'see ya up an' about!'

'How are yer, Red?'

Red looked at his admirers with some surprise, but he quickly hid it. 'I'm doin' good.'

'Here, lemme help,' said a guard to his left, pouring out some water for him.

Red took it gratefully. 'Thanks, Elthan. I'm feelin' much better now.'

'Tell us about it, sir!' said one of the younger guards. 'Tell us how y'caught the Hangman!'

Red shook his head, and winced when the motion made his neck twinge. '*He* caught *me*, really.'

'Tell us!' someone else encouraged. 'Go on, we've all been dyin' t'hear the whole story.'

'All right, then.' Red coughed, and groaned at the pain that caused. But he massaged his throat and drank some water before he began.

They listened excitedly, asking questions every so often, and what he'd meant to be a short, simple version of the story ended up as a complicated one. Other guards, noticing what was going on, came over to listen as well, and he wound up having to go back and fill them in on what they'd missed.

By the time he finished his throat felt like it was full of gravel, but his audience was enthralled.

'You're crazy,' said Elthan. 'No wonder y'nearly got killed if that's what you was up to every night!'

'I know,' said Red. He was back to whispering by now.

'What was it like?' another guard asked. 'What's it like to nearly die?'

It was the deepest question anyone had asked yet, and it caught Red by surprise. He started to reply automatically, but stopped. A frown settled over his face.

The others there went quiet, apparently hoping for something special.

'What's it like?' the one who'd asked persisted. 'I mean, didya see something? They say the gods talk to people who nearly die.'

'Don't be daft,' said someone else. 'It's all just stories.'

'I saw something,' Red whispered.

Silence fell.

'What?' asked the first guard.

Red hesitated. He half wished he hadn't said anything. But it was too late now. 'Thought I saw something,' he whispered. 'Everything went dark, an' I felt like everything was going away. Couldn't feel my body any more. Then I saw...' Memory came back to him, and he shivered.

'Saw what?' several people asked at once. 'What was it? Was it Gryphus?'

'Saw a face,' Red whispered. 'Reaching out to take me away into the dark. But I got away,' he added, half to himself.

His listeners looked disturbed.

'Is that really true?' asked Elthan.

Red's throat was agony by now. He clutched at it with one hand, feeling the deep bruise under his jaw. 'Maybe imagination,' he whispered. 'Or maybe I saw death.'

'I *hope* it was just yer imagination,' said Bear, who was among the listeners. 'I don't wanna see anything like that when *I* die.'

'Well,' said Elthan, 'We'll tell the Hangman t'say hello to him tomorrow morning, eh?'

Mutterings of approval went through the group of guards. Red said nothing, but scowled his agreement. He imagined that hideous face he had seen reaching out to drag the Hangman into the void, and thought it would be the punishment he deserved.

There didn't seem to be any more questions for him, so he picked up his spoon and ate his bowl of stew. It had gone cold by now, and swallowing hurt, but eating it made him feel better.

While he ate, he thought about the Hangman. He wondered if the murderer even knew that his last victim was still alive. If not, it would be a nasty shock for him when he went onto the gallows tomorrow and saw Red waiting there for him.

Red scowled again at the thought of the man who had nearly been his murderer.

His admirers, apparently sensing that he had talked enough for one day, dispersed. Maybe some of them felt bad for bothering him, but Red wasn't annoyed. The truth was that he felt flattered, and honestly touched by their concern for him.

All the talking *had* taken its toll on him, though, so when he had finished eating he went back to his bunk for an early night's sleep. Tomorrow could be the most important day of his life, and he wanted to be ready for it.

Chapter Five

The Dark Griffin

Red woke up the next morning feeling much better. The swelling in his throat had gone down considerably overnight, and the weakness in his left leg had eased as well.

He went for breakfast in the mess hall, where his fellow guards were all talk about the hanging that would soon take place. And afterwards, the ceremony for Red and Ranulf.

Red ate quickly, and returned to his bunk to put on his armour and swordbelt. Once he had finished neatening himself up, he unhooked something from a nail at the head of the bed. It was a thin leather loop, long enough to wear as a necklace. But instead of a medallion or a pendant, there was a feather on it.

The feather was about the size of his hand, coloured a mottled grey. Other than its size it would have looked like any old feather, except for one thing. At one end, where the soft vane gave way to the central quill, something other than downy fluff grew. At the point where the vane broke up, fine black strands of hair were scattered in among the down. More hairs appeared further along, poking out incongruously from the quill.

Human hairs.

Everyone knew he had a lucky griffin feather, and that was how he was happy to keep it. But if they'd known just which griffin it came from, it would have been stolen by now.

Red hung the feather around his neck, and tucked it away under his breastplate. Then, feeling a little light-headed with nerves, he left the barracks and went to face his destiny.

Ranulf joined him along the way. 'There y'are. Scared?'

'A bit,' said Red. He started involuntarily when he realised how normal his voice sounded now. It was still rather husky, but it was much better. No more need to whisper.

'You sound better,' said Ranulf, as if he could read his partner's mind.

'Yeah,' said Red. He rubbed his throat. 'Great!'

'Yeah,' Ranulf echoed. 'Don't you need the crutch any more?'

'Don't think so,' said Red. He had a feeling he'd be taciturn for a while longer, if only out of recent habit.

Both of them knew where to go. The city's prison had been built right next to the guard barracks, and that was where executions always took place. A crowd was already gathering around the hanging platform, but as guards Red and Ranulf were allowed to go in through the back of the building and approach it from behind.

A line of guards had been posted along the front of the platform to keep back the crowd, and there were more behind it in case of an escape.

Talmon, who always personally oversaw executions, was among them. 'There you are,' he said. 'They're about to bring out the prisoner. You can go up on the platform, or wait back here 'till you're called; it's your choice.'

Red glanced at Ranulf.

'We'll go up,' said Ranulf. 'May as well.'

Red shrugged by way of a reply. He'd decided to save his voice in case he was asked to say anything during the ceremony.

Together, he and Ranulf went up a set of steps and onto the platform, where they stationed themselves off to one side and out of the way.

The noose was already hanging from the scaffold. Red looked up at it, and felt a cold shiver move over his skin. On his throat the rope mark pulsed, as if in sympathy.

Below, the crowd was full of chatter. It was the usual half-festive mood you saw at any execution, but this time there was an ugly edge to it. This wasn't just an ordinary criminal today. Red doubted that any previous execution had been of a man as hated as the Hangman. He suspected that plenty of the people below him had come to see their loved ones avenged by the noose.

Ranulf, a veteran of a dozen other executions, seemed completely unaffected. 'Y'know they say the Dark Lord Arenadd survived a hanging,' he said. 'Over in Malvern before it was lost.'

Red nodded. 'He used his powers to come back to life, or somethin'.'

'Some people reckon the rope just broke,' said Ranulf. 'But there's always some who just don't wanna believe it.'

'Huh,' Red wheezed a laugh. '*I* survived a hanging. I must have dark powers too.'

'Must have,' Ranulf said gravely. He looked up, and started. 'Watch out! Here come the griffiners.'

Both guards turned their heads skyward, and shuffled aside cautiously. Overhead, two griffins were coming. Their huge shadows fell over the crowd, which reacted with fear and excitement.

Fortunately, the two massive creatures didn't try and land on the platform. Instead they touched down neatly on either side of it, and their human partners stepped off their backs and straight onto the platform. It was a nicely planned little manoeuvre, and it certainly impressed the crowd.

Red and Ranulf kept their distance, as the two griffiners went to take centre stage. One was a man that most of the more senior guards knew – Lord Eadion, Master of Law. Talmon, up on the platform now, saluted him and went to stand beside him.

The other griffiner was a woman. She was middle-aged and somewhat chunky, with a face as bland as the feathers of her grey-coated partner.

Red's eyes narrowed when he looked at her. He knew who she was, but so did everyone there. Lady Isleen, Eyrie Mistress and ruler of Liranwee.

Isleen glanced briefly at Red and Ranulf, and went to join Talmon and Eadion. Beside the platform, the two griffins sat bolt upright on their haunches, and looked impassively at the crowd.

Neither griffiner spoke, but once everyone was in position Eadion turned and gave Talmon the slightest of nods.

Talmon stood to attention. 'Bring the prisoner!' he bellowed.

Immediately, two guards came up onto the platform from behind it. They walked slowly, and no wonder. They had the Hangman between them.

Red's breath caught in his throat.

In daylight, without the added menace that shadows gave, the Hangman should have looked less impressive. But if anything he looked even more so. So big he towered over the two burly guards, he would have looked even taller if he hadn't been hunched over. His arms were huge and muscular, his hands the size of dinner plates. Seeing him now, it was not at all surprising that he had managed to haul Red around like a doll on a string.

But it was very clear that he wouldn't be able to do that now. Even without his manacles he looked ill and weak. The square face was pale, the eyes bloodshot, and it was obvious from the way he moved that the wound Red had given him was causing him pain.

As the Hangman appeared on the platform, the crowd let out a collective hiss and growl. He acted as if he hadn't heard it, and kept his eyes down. But as he was taken toward the waiting noose, his head turned sharply. His eyes were dull, bleak grey. They were fixed on Red.

Fear stung him for one sickening instant.

The Hangman's expression did not change. Once again, his face was wood.

The glance only lasted an instant before the two guards pushed him on, and he turned to stare at the noose. Behind him, unseen, Red shivered.

Once the Hangman was in place, one of his guards took the noose and pulled it tight around his neck. But afterwards the two of them stayed where they were, holding onto the murderer's elbows.

Now the Master of Law came forward, and his griffin screeched for silence. It came, and Lord Eadion spoke.

'Grafton Carpenter, you have been found guilty of eight counts of murder and one count of attempted murder. For these crimes you have been sentenced to death by hanging. Do you have anything to say before the sentence is carried out?'

Absolute silence fell. Even the crowd went quiet.

The Hangman finally raised his head. 'You are evil.' His voice was flat and deep, as emotionless as his face. 'Liranwee is a city of corruption and soon you will all die. Gryphus sends his punishment!'

The crowd bayed its fury.

'*Murderer!*' voices shouted.

'*Kill him! Kill him now!*'

One of the two guards holding the Hangman let go of him, and silently pulled the lever by the scaffold.

A trapdoor opened under the Hangman's feet, and he fell. The rope pulled him up short, and everyone on the platform heard the muffled snap as his neck broke.

It was all over in a heartbeat, as the crowd roared, and the Hangman's body swung gently to and fro.

Red could not look away, but he wanted to vomit. His head span, and for a moment he thought he was going to black out.

The executioners waited for the allotted length of time to pass before they released the rope. The Hangman's corpse fell onto the ground under the platform, and a group of waiting guards discreetly carried it away, back into the prison, to be disposed of.

With the trapdoor closed again, the executioners left and Lady Isleen took her turn to speak.

'We are gathered here today for more than a mere execution,' she said. 'Today we are also here to honour two members of the city guard, who were responsible for bringing this murderer to justice. Come forward!'

Red and Ranulf took their cue, and came to stand beside the Eyrie Mistress.

Talmon came too.

'Sergeant Ranulf Ranulfson,' Lady Isleen intoned. 'For bravery, and for going beyond the call of duty to do a great service for the city, I present you with this. May it be a token of our thanks.'

Talmon handed her a gold medallion, and she put it around the grinning Ranulf's neck.

'Next,' she said, turning to Red. For a moment, as she looked at him, a slightly puzzled expression crossed her face.

Red looked back stonily at her.

Isleen shook herself, and resumed. 'Sergeant Kearney Redguard,' she said. 'For bravery, and for going beyond the call of duty to do a great service for the city, I present you with this. May it be a token of our thanks.'

Red accepted the medallion as graciously as he could, and he and Ranulf turned to face the crowd. And now the people who moments before had cheered for the death of the Hangman cheered their appreciation for the two men who had helped bring it about. Red resisted the urge to wave to them, and instead squared his shoulders and did his best to look… well, brave.

'Ahem.' Talmon spoke up as the cheering died down. 'There is one final thing to announce here today. Sergeant Kearney Redguard, come forward.'

Red obeyed, frowning his puzzlement.

'Sergeant,' said Talmon. 'Of the two of you here before us today, you were the bravest. You were willing to do whatever it took to protect this city and its people. You nearly died in the process, but you stopped the murderer. We owe you a great debt. You've proven your worth to us all, and to me. Therefore, I and the Master of Law have together decided that you will now be promoted to Captain.'

Red gaped. *'Captain?'*

Talmon smiled at his expression. 'Yes. From today, you can call yourself Captain Redguard. Congratulations.'

Red stood there in stunned silence. Captaincy was one of the highest ranks in the guard, second only to the Commander himself. From now on he would have command of one of the guard towers, and would be in charge of a squad of fifty men. Normally only the most senior and experienced of guards were ever promoted that high, but here he was…

'Captain Rattrapper is retiring,' Talmon said aside to him, as the crowd resumed its chattering. Some of those at the back were leaving. The spectacle was over for today.

Or so they thought.

As Talmon began to leave with Red and Ranulf, and the two griffiners moved back toward their partners, a woman down in the dispersing crowd screamed.

Red turned immediately, his hand going to the hilt of his sword. Below, others had begun to cry out as well. Heads turned upward, and the crowd surged away from the platform in a confused mess of shouting and shoving.

A massive shadow moved over them, and Red drew his sword and looked up at something that put ice into his heart.

A griffin was coming, and it was huge. As it descended on them its talons opened wide, and its wings beat slowly to steady it in the air. Enormous wings, with feathers as black as coal.

Panic shot through Red's mind. *'It's the dark griffin!'* he shouted.

The two griffins there had already started up angrily – and with fear. Both of them were much smaller than the intruder, and that must have been why they didn't immediately move to attack him. Lady Isleen's partner put his front paws up on the platform, and stretched out his beak toward his human. She, very sensibly, ran straight to him and let him lift her down and hide her under the platform.

The giant griffin landed. He landed in front of the platform, where the last of the spectators were still trying to make their escape. He didn't seem to care that they were there at all, and Red saw at least two people fall under him.

The dark griffin stood there for a moment, surrounded by fleeing humans. One of those he had knocked over was thrashing pathetically under his front talons. He shoved her aside with an irritable huff.

The Eyrie Mistress' grey partner was first to act. Having put his human out of harm's way, he moved aggressively toward the intruder. On the other side of the platform, the Master of Law's russet partner took her cue and came forward too.

The dark griffin regarded them both without any sign of fear. He was definitely male – the feathery tufts over his ears gave that away – and he was not actually black all over. The feathers on his front half were, but the ear-tufts were white, and the furred hindquarters were the palest brown, tipped with silver. His eyes, slanted behind a dark grey beak, were a striking sky blue.

Lady Isleen's partner hissed a challenge. But the dark griffin didn't look about to attack. He sat on his haunches in what Red knew was an unthreatening gesture, and spoke. To most people his speech would have sounded like nothing more than a string of hisses, rasps, clicks and chirps – and that was exactly what it was. But it was a language all the same. Griffish.

Red, standing frozen on the platform, listened as closely as he could. He was slightly surprised to find that, after so long, he still understood it.

'I have come to find the ruler of this city,' said the dark griffin. 'Where is he?'

'That is me,' said Lady Isleen's partner. 'I am Arak, and this city is my territory. Where is your human?'

'I have no human,' said the dark griffin.

Arak's neck feathers fluffed out aggressively. 'Wild griffin! Leave my territory now or die.'

The dark griffin showed no fear. 'I have come to bring you a warning, Arak. You are not prepared for—,'

Instantly, Arak reared up. 'Humanless scum! Fly away now, or I will kill you!'

The dark griffin hissed. 'If you will not listen, then you are a fool.'

Arak charged. On the other side, the Master of Law's partner attacked as well.

The dark griffin managed to jump back out of the way, but the two griffins were on him in an instant. Arak's talons raked down the side of his head, and the other, the red griffin, leapt forward and hit him between the wings with her beak.

The blow might have crippled another griffin, but it did nothing here. The dark griffin shook off his two attackers like a pair of fleas, and struck back. In an instant he had knocked Arak down, and the red female as well. Hidden under the platform, Lady Isleen screamed for her partner.

But the dark griffin did not close in for the kill. His attackers disabled, he backed away from the platform. 'You will not hear my warning, and so you will die,' he rasped. 'But you have a traitor here. Believe that.'

He opened his black wings wide, and effortlessly jumped into the air. Arak and the red griffin, recovering themselves, took off too and went in pursuit. The moment the ground was clear of them, people came running back to watch.

The dark griffin circled up and away from the city, but if he had intended to fly away easily he didn't get to. Everywhere in the city other griffins, alerted to the presence of an intruder, flew up from among the buildings and rushed to the attack.

Outnumbered by dozens to one, the dark griffin turned tail and flew away northward with surprising speed. The other griffins chased him in a big, murderous flock, and drove him on until he was out of sight.

Meanwhile, down in the prison yard, chaos reigned. Lady Isleen emerged from her hiding place and ran to Arak's side. Neither he nor the red female seemed to be injured, but several people from the crowd who had been caught up in the fight were.

Red jumped down from the platform, and went to help. Others of the guards there were doing the same, and Red, gathering his wits, shouted to one. 'You! Go find a healer, right now!'

'Right, S— Captain.' The guard hurried off.

Red allowed himself a moment of smug pride. Captain!

Ranulf had joined him, and together the two of them attended to the wounded as well as they could. Most of them were lucky enough to have gotten away with bruises, but one or two had been clipped by talons or claws and the woman who had been crushed under the dark griffin's paw was unconscious.

Luckily the prison employed several healers, and one had already been standing by to verify the Hangman's death, as was customary. He arrived soon enough, and his colleagues were quick to emerge as well. Red's throat was hurting again, but he stayed to help carry people indoors.

Once the wounded had been taken care of, he found Talmon. 'Sir! What should I do now, sir?'

'Now you should go back to the barracks and take it easy,' Talmon said sternly. 'No need to overexert yourself this soon.'

'Yes, sir.' Red looked skyward. 'What *was* that, sir?'

'No idea,' said Talmon. 'Griffin's business, and we don't want any part of that. I just wish those things didn't make so much mess. Honestly, every time one of them gets into a fight we get property damage, injuries… the things are more trouble than they're worth.'

Most commoners would never have talked about griffins that way, but Red knew his commander well enough. Anyone in the guards who was as senior as him didn't hold much in reverence anymore. Even Gryphus himself would probably be just another bit of work if he showed up.

'Right, sir,' he said. 'If everything's under control here, I'll get going. But sir…'

'Yes, Captain?'

Red tried not to let his pride show. 'What should I do tomorrow?'

'Nothing, Captain. You're still off-duty until you're completely recovered.'

'All right, sir, but I meant… now I'm a Captain, what should I do?' Red started to feel stupid, but he ploughed on regardless. 'Where do I take command an' so on?'

'You can worry about that later,' said Talmon. 'You'll be assigned to a tower once you're better, and your predecessor will tell you everything you need to know.'

'Yes, sir.' Red coughed and winced, and saluted before he left.

Ranulf joined him as he was leaving. 'Damn me,' he said. 'You, a Captain.'

'Yeah,' Red mumbled. 'I just hope I don't have to deal with griffins.'

'Don't be daft,' said Ranulf. 'That's griffiner stuff, thank gods. Wouldn't've wanted anything t'do with griffins even before today.'

'I just wish I knew what that griffin was on about,' Red said thoughtlessly. 'But Arak didn't let him get anywhere.'

Ranulf gave him an odd look. 'Who knows? Who cares? I don't know griffish. Didn't sound like talking t'me anyway.'

'Right,' Red said hastily. 'But he must've come here for a reason. He wasn't looking for a fight or he would've attacked from the sky instead of landing. They're vulnerable on the ground.'

Ranulf gave him an even odder look. 'Oh yeah? An' you know all that stuff do ya?'

Red felt confident enough just then to say, 'Yeah, I do. He wanted t'say somethin' – that's why he came. I just dunno what.'

'Huh,' said Ranulf. 'My mate Red's a Captain *and* a griffiner now.'

'Griffiner?' Red grinned to cheer him up. 'Yeah, right, sure thing. They always go for the likes of me, griffins do.' He certainly wasn't going to admit that he could speak griffish; for a commoner, knowing that sort of thing was a good way to get into trouble. The griffiners were very protective of their secrets.

The medallion around his neck turned on its cord, and the sunlight shone off its surface and hit him in the eyes. As he flinched away from the sudden flash of light, he realised that he hadn't looked at the medal yet, and caught it in his hand to inspect it.

The medal wasn't actually round, but oval shaped, and it looked like it was made from real gold. One side was smooth except for an engraving. Red ran his fingers over the two lines of neat runes. *Kearney Redguard, From the City of Liranwee*, they said.

The other side of the medal was embossed with a wattle sprig – Liranwee's symbol – flanked by two griffins on their hind legs. Above that were a crossed spear and sword – the symbol for guards used all over Cymria.

Underneath were three words. *COURAGE AND DUTY.*

'Nice, ain't they?' said Ranulf.

'Yeah, an' they put our names on 'em!' said Red. 'So no-one else can take 'em an' pretend they got given them, I s'pose.'

Ranulf squinted at the engraving on his own medal. 'Is that my name there?'

Red glanced over. 'Yeah, Ranulf Ranulfson from the City of Liranwee, it says.'

'Oh, right,' Ranulf said grumpily. 'I forgot you can read. Bet that's why they promoted you an' kept me a Sergeant for twenty years.'

'All right, but how many Sergeants have got a medal like that one?' asked Red. 'Eh? None, except you, an' I bet a man with a medal probably gets lots of free drinks.'

Ranulf looked much more cheerful. 'Yeah, I'll take that bet. *You're* gonna be too busy captaining for drinks, even if they're free.'

'Maybe, but I'm not captaining yet,' said Red. 'Not tonight, definitely.'

'Yeah?' said Ranulf, as they entered the barracks. 'You're on, then. I'd say a couple of heroes like us deserve a good session at the Serpent.'

'Why the Serpent?' Red asked idly.

'It's our lucky tavern,' said Ranulf. 'Ain't it?'

Red grinned. 'True. Let's just get out of uniform an' get some lunch first, an' then we'll go.'

'Gotcha.'

They entered the dormitory, and Red went straight to his bunk. Ranulf, however, was apparently too hungry to bother about his armour because he headed straight for the mess hall.

Alone in the dormitory, Red gratefully took off his breastplate and laid it down. His lucky feather was still underneath his tunic, so he fished it out and took it off.

An idea occurred to him, and he sat down on the bunk and removed the medal as well. After some trial and error, he took the feather off its leather strip and attached it to the loop at the top of the medal, so the two talismans hung together. He put the medal back around his neck, feather and all, and decided that he liked the effect; the medal lay on top of the feather, which stuck out around it, giving it a kind of tasselled appearance. Luck and courage, hanging together.

… hanging.

Red grimaced at that word, and opened up his clothes chest. Inside he found his lucky red tunic, which someone had washed for him. He shed his uniform tunic and put the red one on, and reached down into the chest to shuffle things around and make room for his breastplate.

As he dug downward to move a spare pair of boots, his fingertips hit wood.

He frowned. Something wasn't quite right, but he wasn't sure what. He'd touched the bottom of the chest – so what? Nothing odd about that. But some part of his mind insisted that it was.

Red prodded the wooden surface experimentally. It felt different. Too rough, too splintery.

He lifted out some of his belongings, and had a look at the bottom of the chest. Sure enough, it was different. It looked paler than the rest of the wood the chest was made from, and it was indeed rough and splintery. It looked too *clean,* as if it hadn't been there for very long. It looked like new wood, that was it – newer than the rest of the chest.

Red's frown deepened. Someone had put a new bottom in his chest? Unlikely.

He took out the rest of his possessions, and had a proper look at the unfamiliar wood. Now he could see all of it, he became absolutely certain that it hadn't been there before. For one thing, the chest was shallower now. Was the new bottom thicker, or was there something underneath it?

There was a knothole near one edge. Red put his finger through, and pulled. The piece of wood lifted out easily, and he put it aside.

Underneath it was a cavity, with raised edges that must have held up the cover he had just removed. Several folded sheets of paper were hidden in there, along with a small leather bag and a dagger.

Red blinked. 'What the——?'

He took out the bag and opened it. It was full of money – gold oblong that looked shiny and new. But a moment's inspection told him that these weren't proper oblong; they were embossed with spiral designs, and the writing was in some language he didn't recognise.

Underneath the bag, he found a tiny stone bottle with a cork sealed in wax. A skull had been carved into the side of it, and he didn't try and take the cork out.

He unfolded one of the pieces of paper, and his eyes widened. It was covered in writing – writing in his language, this time.

Sire, it read, *The walls around the city are approximately three metres thick, and are manned at all times by as many as ten men per mile——*

The handwriting was rough and uneven on the page – and it was absolutely identical to his own.

'*What?*' Red exclaimed.

Dumbfounded, he looked at another paper. This one was grubby and torn, and featured a detailed diagram of a guard tower, showing every level and featuring notes on how many men worked inside them and what their duties and routines were. And all of it looked as if it were written in his own hand.

His head spinning, Red stood up. This was insane. Who could have put all this here, and why? And how had they managed to copy his handwriting so well?

Red's stomach dropped straight into his boots. If anyone saw this, he was done for.

'Red, what—?' said a voice from behind him.

At the sound of Ranulf's voice, Red panicked. He snatched up the treasonous papers and made a frantic attempt to stuff them back in his chest, but one of them floated away onto the floor, out of his reach.

Ranulf picked it up. 'Red, what in the hell are you doing?'

'Nothing,' Red said hastily. 'It's nothing—,'

Ranulf looked at the paper. 'Wait – did you draw this? This is one of our guard towers, isn't it?'

Red tried to snatch it back. 'I told you, it's nothing. Give that here, would you?'

Ranulf looked past him, and took in the bag of money, the dagger and the bottle of poison. 'Red, what have you done?'

'I didn't do anything!' Red blurted. 'I dunno how any of this got in there, I swear—,'

Ranulf looked down at the papers strewn through the chest, and picked one up before Red could stop him. On it was a simple note – and once again, the handwriting looked like Red's.

Ranulf waved it at him. 'What does this say, then? I know your handwriting when I see it.'

Red stared at it, and his eyes widened as he read what was on it. *They trust me but they're idiots. Isleen will pay for my father's murder.*

Ranulf looked down at the bag of money. 'Those are Northern oblong,' he said slowly. His face slackened with disbelief. 'Oh dear gods – what've you done? Who gave you all that money?'

'They're not mine!' Red exclaimed. 'I never saw them before!'

Ranulf looked at the sketch of the guard tower again. 'Oh my gods,' he said. 'You're sellin' us out to the Northerners, aren't you? You're a traitor!'

'I'm not!' Red snatched the piece of paper off him and crumpled it up. 'I'm tellin' you—,'

Ranulf shook his head. 'I'm such an idiot. Trusting a traitor's son… I always thought it was weird how y'just didn't seem to care that Isleen had yer dad killed. This is about gettin' back at her, isn't it?'

Red backed away from him. 'I'm telling you, I didn't. I didn't do anything. It's all fake…'

'It's your handwriting, Red!' Ranulf shouted. 'How are you gonna explain *that*?'

'Someone must've faked it,' said Red – there was sweat all over his face now, and his heart pounded.

Ranulf took a deep breath. 'I'm gonna give you some time before I tell anyone about this,' he said. 'Get out of here, Red. Run.'

Red gaped at him. 'But I—,'

The paper crumpled in Ranulf's hand. 'Run!' he said. 'I'm givin' you a chance 'cause you're my mate. Run, Red. Run now.'

Panic seized hold of Red. He turned and ran out of the barracks as fast as he could.

Chapter Six

Traitor

Red made it out of the barracks before his comrades raised the alarm. As he ran out into the city, he heard the bell ringing in the tower that rose over the barracks – the bell that was only used when every guard in the city had to be put on full alert. Any in the barracks themselves had to report to the barracks Captain immediately. Then they would be sent out to hunt down the criminal. To hunt *him*.

Red didn't know where to go, or what to do. His only thought was to run.

And so he ran.

He kept away from the main streets, and used alleys and other shortcuts wherever he could. All he knew was that he had to get as far away from the barracks as possible, and as far away from other guards as he could. For now those who were out in the city would be heading back to the barracks. They weren't supposed to, but they would anyway. They would want to know what the alert was about. Others would do as they were supposed to and stay at their posts, ready for when word came.

Until then, he had this brief time of confusion before anyone knew exactly what was going on, and whether he used it well or not could make the difference to whether he would be caught, or escape.

Running made his neck hurt, and it wasn't long before his left leg started to weaken again. He slowed, gasping for air, and the panicked struggle to keep going made his thoughts go faster.

He had to find a place to hide. Getting out of the city now would only be possible for a short time, and trying would probably only get him captured. A better option would be to hide somewhere until things calmed down.

The west side, then? That was where criminals usually hid…

Criminals, he thought, and the word plunged sickeningly into his stomach. *Am I a criminal now?*

Of course not. He had been framed, that was obvious. But by who? And how could he possibly prove his innocence if he didn't know?

He shook those worries off; they didn't matter now. All that mattered right now was escaping. If he was caught, he was done for – they'd hang him in a heartbeat, innocence be damned.

He skidded to a halt, as a pair of guards came around a corner in front of him. It was too late to run back the way he'd come without being seen, so he flattened himself against a wall.

'Hey!' a voice hissed off to his left. 'This way!'

Red turned his head, and his heart leapt when he saw a familiar face peering out from a doorway. But it couldn't peer, not really. Not with the bandage over the eyes.

No-Eyes reached out blindly and caught him by the arm. 'Hurry!'

Red glanced at the oncoming guards. They hadn't spotted him yet. He ducked in through the doorway, and hid under a table in the room beyond.

No-Eyes hid behind the door, and the two of them waited in tense silence.

'They've gone,' No-Eyes said eventually. 'Let's go.'

Cautiously, Red came out from under the table. 'You sure?'

'I've got good hearing,' said No-Eyes. 'Come on, hurry up. There's not much time.'

Red left the building with him, through a back door. The coast was clear. 'Where are we goin'?'

'To my place. Stay close behind me, and hiss if you see anyone!'

'Right.' Red fell in behind his friend, and followed him on a winding route through the city toward the west end. No-Eyes travelled quickly, and with surprising certainty – so much so that it was a wonder he was blind at all. Twice they encountered guards, but managed to evade them the first time. The second time they were seen, but the guards who saw them mustn't have known that Red was a wanted man, because they only glanced at him and went on their way.

Finally, No-Eyes led him to a door in a small house on the edge of the west end. He opened it with a key, and ushered him inside.

The house was dark, and no wonder – No-Eyes had covered the windows with various rags and bits of wood, and there were no lamps in sight. Not that a blind man would need any.

No-Eyes closed the door behind them, and wedged a chair under the handle. 'There,' he said. 'Safe. Sit down if you want.'

Red sat down at the small table which was one of only two pieces of furniture in the house. 'Thanks so much, No-Eyes. You saved my neck.'

'No trouble.' No-Eyes gave him an unsettling eyeless grin. 'Why were they after you, anyway?'

Red took a deep breath. 'They think I'm a spy. For the Northerners.'

No-Eyes' grin disappeared. 'They never! You, a spy? The hero what caught the Hangman? A *spy?*'

'Yeah.' Red put his head in his hands, and groaned. 'Oh Gryphus, what'm I going to do? If they catch me, I'm a goner. I know what they do t'people they think are spies. Forget a fair trial; the griffiners would take charge of me. They don't give proper trials to traitors. I'd be tortured until I confessed, an' then cut to pieces. *Shit!*'

'It's a bad situation,' No-Eyes said gravely.

Red sat there for a while without looking up. 'An' you know what?' he added. 'You know what they're gonna say? They're gonna say "why didn't we see this coming? His whole family's made up of traitors. His uncle was Bran the Betrayer, for gods' sakes. His dad was Lord Danthirk, who got killed for tryin' to make himself Eyrie Master an' reach out to the Northerners." Godsdammit!'

'Bran the Betrayer?' No-Eyes repeated in a gently puzzled kind of way.

'Yeah,' Red muttered. 'I don't put that about. My name's Kearney Redguard an' my uncle was Captain Branton Redguard, who they say betrayed Eagleholm. I spent my whole life thinkin' how I'd fix that. Win back our family's honour. Now it looks like I'm gonna die a traitor as well. An' that'll be it. The last Redguard, executed as a spy. The end.'

'But you're not a spy?' said No-Eyes.

'Of course I ain't!' Red snapped. 'I never betrayed nobody. This city was my life. Someone set me up. Hid things in my clothes chest. Northern money, information on paper, an' a bottle of poison. They're probably gonna think I was about to murder the Eyrie Mistress or somethin'.'

'Spies and assassins aren't so different,' No-Eyes admitted. 'So I reckon. What are you going to do now?'

'I dunno,' said Red. 'I gotta get out of the city. Wait until things cool down, an' then escape. I can't be caught, or I'm dead.'

'Where will you go?' asked No-Eyes.

'Somewhere,' said Red. 'Anywhere that's not here. I got no family or friends in other territories. I s'pose I could hide out in Canran lands. Out in the countryside. Become a farmer or somethin'. Guarding's what I know, but it'd be too dangerous, even in another city. They'd hand me over in a heartbeat.' He sighed. 'I was gonna be a *Captain*. I could've been Commander one day... So much for honour.'

'If only you knew who framed you,' said No-Eyes.

'If I knew who it was, forget turning them in,' Red growled. 'I'd snap his neck with my bare hands.'

'But if you're gonna run' said No-Eyes, 'Old No-Eyes knows a place to go. Knows a way out of the city, too.'

Red looked up. 'You do?'

No-Eyes nodded. 'You say guarding's in your family. Cunning's in mine. I can help you escape. Get you out of the city and show you where to hide.'

'Why?' asked Red. 'Why're you sticking your neck out for me like this?'

'You're a good man,' said No-Eyes. 'You stand up for what's important. You care about the big things, like catching the Hangman, an' you care about the little things, like looking out for an old, blind man like me.'

'Thank you,' said Red.

'It's nothin',' said No-Eyes. 'Now, we can get out of the city tonight once it's good an' dark, but you're in a bad way. Get some sleep before then, while I get some things ready.'

'*Tonight*?' Red repeated. 'No, we should wait. Tonight the city'll be crawling with guards. It'll be that way for days.'

'Tonight,' No-Eyes said steadily. 'It can be done, even with extra guards. It's been done before.'

'By who?' said Red.

'Men who got away free,' said No-Eyes. 'Trust me, the longer you stay in the city the more chances of being caught. An' if you're caught here, I'll be dead too. So we're escaping tonight or you're on your own, right?'

'Understood,' Red said gloomily. 'But you'd better tell me all about how this is gonna work.'

'Later,' said No-Eyes. 'You rest now an' I'll get some food together. I don't have to tell you not to go outside, do I?'

'No, you don't,' said Red.

'Good. You can have the bed.'

Grumbling, but seeing sense, Red lay down on it. The mattress was stuffed with straw and the blankets smelled nasty, but the truth was that he was tired enough not to care. Despite that, he was convinced he wouldn't be able to sleep with so much fear burning at his insides. But he was wrong. He had barely lain down before exhaustion smothered him, and he slid away into troubled dreams.

*

The moment Red was asleep, No-Eyes went to work.

There was still plenty of time left before nightfall, so he didn't need to hurry. He didn't have that much to prepare besides; things had been close to ready for some time now anyway. Still, it was always good to take extra time with these things. There was always something you forgot until the last moment, so the more last moments there were, the better.

Careful not to make too much noise and wake up his guest, No-Eyes picked up a leather rucksack and started to fill it. First went a spare tunic, carefully laid out to cover the bottom of the bag. After that went a few personal belongings and a water bottle. Finally, he used the rest of the space to hold all the food he had left in the house – leaving some bread and a couple of apples on the table for a snack. He'd share it with Red before they left; dangerous activities were always best done on a full stomach. At least that was what his brother had always said.

No-Eyes smiled to himself at the memory, and went to the window.

There, he took down one of the hanging rags, and opened the window. It was small, but he was narrow enough in the shoulders to fit through. Balanced awkwardly on a chair, he hoisted himself through the window and reached up onto the roof.

A small metal spike poked out of the thatch. No-Eyes found it by touch, and delicately hooked the rag onto it. He twisted to inspect the results, and sure enough the rag stayed where it was, fluttering in the breeze like a little flag.

It should do the job.

No-Eyes pulled himself back in through the window, and closed it carefully behind him. Hopefully his partner would see the rag before it got too dark, and would remember what it signalled. No-Eyes was fairly certain that he would; he was more than bright enough. And thank gods for that; his help would be just about vital for this mission.

With everything ready, No-Eyes sat down at the table and breathed deeply. Everything hinged on tonight. It was a huge risk, he knew, and one that could easily cost him his life in several different ways. But he had long ago decided that any risks would be worth it if he succeeded.

Red snored softly on the bed. No-Eyes sat and listened to him. The red-haired guard was a good man, and a strong one as well, that was obvious.

His words repeated themselves in No-Eyes' mind. *I'd snap his neck with my bare hands.*

No-Eyes shivered involuntarily. He wondered if Red really would do something like that if he got the chance.

Well, why wouldn't he? This morning he had been a hero, loved by the city and about to be given a medal and a promotion. And now he had lost all of that, and his home as well. He'd gone from hero to fugitive in one instant. Why in the gods' names wouldn't he want to murder the one who had done that to him? Anyone would.

Either way, No-Eyes hoped Red was as strong as he seemed. He would need to be.

No-Eyes rubbed a thin hand over his bandaged eyes and waited, patient as a rock, for night to come.

*

Red couldn't breathe.

He lay on his back, paralysed, and icy panic made his heart thud against his ribs. His throat was closed, squeezed shut by some unseen force, like a massive hand wrapping around his neck. Why couldn't he wake up? Why was he just lying there and doing nothing when he was being suffocated?

No, he thought. *No, no, no!*

It was the rope, that was what it was. The rope hadn't been taken off his neck. It was still there, pulling tighter and tighter, crushing his throat, lifting him up. Up, to where death was.

'Argh!'

Red's eyes snapped open, and he lashed out. *The Hangman—!*

His fist shot into empty air, hard enough to throw him off-balance. He yelped in surprise and rolled off the bed and onto the floor.

He scrambled up at once and stood against the wall, gasping like a landed fish. 'What…?'

His throat was fine. He could breathe. No rope, no Hangman.

That was when he finally realised he had been dreaming.

'You all right?' asked No-Eyes from the table. He sounded absurdly calm.

Red slumped down on the bed. 'Just a dream,' he mumbled. Embarrassment had already replaced fear. 'Sorry.'

'No need for sayin' sorry,' No-Eyes said placidly. 'Nobody goes through a thing like that and doesn't have a few nightmares. Take it from me.'

Red wiped the sweat off his forehead as the dream left him, and the recollection of what had happened came to torment him instead. 'Take it from you, huh?' he said, to distract himself.

'If you want,' said No-Eyes.

Red glanced around the room. It was hard to tell with the covers on the windows, but it looked like night had come. 'Do you get nightmares too is what I meant.'

No-Eyes stood up. 'I got some food ready. Eat up before we go. It's just about time.'

Red went to join him at the table, and helped himself to some bread. 'Thanks. I'm starved.'

'Trouble does that,' said No-Eyes. 'And yes, old No-Eyes has nightmares sometimes. We all got things we can't forget.'

'Like what?' asked Red.

'If a blind man's born with eyes, he's not likely to forget it,' No-Eyes said solemnly.

Red chewed slowly as he tried to straighten that sentence out in his head. 'You were blinded?'

'By Northerners,' said No-Eyes. 'It was in the war.'

Red shuddered. 'How'd it happen?'

No-Eyes took an apple. 'I lived near the mountains. Little village there, you know. Northerners came, looking for any of our people left in what they said was their land now. Most of us had to leave. But they killed some too, just because they could. Some of them were out for revenge, see, for whatever reasons they had. One of them said he didn't like my eyes. Green eyes, they were. So…' No-Eyes made a slashing motion across the place where his eyes had been.

Red grimaced. 'Ugh, you poor bastard.'

No-Eyes shrugged. 'No-Eyes was lucky. The unlucky ones never got away at all.'

'What *is* your name, then?' asked Red. 'Because it can't be "No-Eyes".'

Another shrug. 'Red's happy with Red, so No-Eyes is happy with No-Eyes.'

'Fair enough,' said Red. Privately, he wondered if it was such a good idea to entrust himself to an oddball like this. But No-Eyes had saved his life once already, and really, who else was he going to trust? Not Ranulf any more, that was for sure.

Red tried not to think about the confrontation at the barracks, but he couldn't help it. So many things he should have said or done. But no, he'd acted like an idiot. A guilty one. Feeling miserable, he fell silent while he finished his food.

'Now,' said No-Eyes. 'Time to go.'

Red swallowed a last bite of apple. 'You'd better tell me the plan now.'

No-Eyes nodded. 'Sneakin' makes people suspicious, so we'll be calm about things. You'll be an ordinary man just helpin' his blind friend along, so keep lookin' down in case I trip. Oh, an' before I forget…' he picked up a bundle of cloth and held it out. 'I reckon you better keep that red hair hid away.'

Red took the cloth and unfolded it. It wasn't really a hood; more a rather sad looking scrap that happened to have a couple of frayed bits hanging off it that could serve as fastenings. He tried it on anyway, and found it was big enough to cover his head.

No-Eyes had already stood up and retrieved his walking cane from its spot in a corner. He picked up a bag as well, and offered it to Red. 'Some food an' things. You're bigger an' stronger, so they'll expect you to carry it.'

Red slung it on his back. 'All right, but how are we gonna get out of the city? What's this way out you're taking me to?'

'There's a tunnel,' No-Eyes said briefly. 'On the west side's edge. Someone dug it right under the wall, an' now criminals use it to get away when things get real bad. Get out of the city 'till the guards lose interest.'

Red frowned under his moustache. 'Really? You've seen it?'

No-Eyes cackled. 'Been there an' touched the edges. Heard about it from men who've used it. But not *seen* it. It's hid inside a house.'

'An' there won't be anyone there who wouldn't want us usin' it?' Red asked.

'No. House is abandoned. Nearly fallen apart. No-one owns the tunnel, but the secret's worth some oblong. See?'

Red took a deep breath. 'All right, I'm willin' to give it a try. Let's go.'

No-Eyes gave another of his eerie smiles, and opened the door. He stood there in the entrance for a while, then nodded and stepped out.

Red followed, feeling slightly sick.

Outside the coast was clear, and the two of them set out.

No-Eyes didn't seem to have an exact route in mind, because he muttered to Red to find a quiet way to the city wall. Red did his best, leading the blind man on a slow and winding pathway through alleys and quiet streets.

There were plenty of people around, though the sun had just about gone down. None of them paid much attention to the blind man and his helper.

The lack of any obvious danger only made Red's nervousness grow. Any moment, he thought, any moment something would happen. And then what?

If guards found them, he decided, he wouldn't try and fight them off. But he wouldn't surrender either. He would have to make a run for it. But he couldn't leave No-Eyes behind.

Red eyed his blind guide critically. He was certainly thin. Slight, in fact. If it came to it, Red decided that he could easily throw the old man over his shoulder and carry him that way. That shouldn't make running too much harder.

Having a plan made him feel better, but it didn't do much for his nerves. To distract himself, he concentrated on choosing the best route to the wall. That was easy enough when he thought about it the right way. He had patrolled on the west side plenty of times in the past, so now he made sure to choose streets and ways he would have avoided if he'd been on duty. That was nice and simple. If it looked unwelcoming to a guard, it was right for him now.

Slowly, painfully slowly, the city wall grew closer. Red found himself wishing he could just carry No-Eyes – the old man moved at a snail's pace and might not have minded being carried. But he knew that it would only attract attention if he did.

They were close to the wall, when No-Eyes suddenly tensed. 'Someone's comin',' he said.

Red had already tensed too. 'So?'

'I hear armour,' said No-Eyes. 'Hide!'

Red didn't waste any time. He had already noted a tiny alleyway to his left, so he hustled No-Eyes over to it and helped him in. No-Eyes squeezed through the gap and ducked behind some garbage.

The space was too small for Red to follow. Panicking, he turned and dashed over to the other side of the street, where there was another alleyway. This one was bigger, so he dived into it.

There was no garbage or anything else to hide behind. Heart fluttering, Red pressed himself against a wall and waited for the oncoming guard to pass by.

'Red?' said a voice.

It was so loud, and so close, that Red panicked. He leapt away and nearly fell over. 'Argh! Oh no—,'

There was someone standing in the alley's entrance, blocking his escape. A guard, armed and armoured. 'Red, is that you?'

Red backed away slowly. 'Bear?'

Bear took a step toward him. 'It *is* you. What're you *doin'* here?'

'Hiding, what's it look like?' Red snapped. 'Go away.'

Bear breathed out slowly. 'Holy Gryphus. The whole city's lookin' for you, Red.'

Red glanced back over his shoulder. The alley was a dead end. Wonderful. 'Yeah, well, you found me,' he said. 'Now what? You don't believe all that bull about me bein' a spy, do you?'

'I don't wanna believe it, mate,' said Bear. 'I really don't.' He looked grim. 'You know what they'll do with me if I let you go.'

'I know,' Red said quietly. 'Your life or mine. And you've got kids…'

'Yeah,' said Bear. 'Look, tell yer what – just get over here an' we can—'

He broke off midsentence, and gave a surprised, gasping groan. Then, without another sound, he crumpled to the ground.

Red stood over him, dumbfounded. 'What the—?'

In the alley entrance, beyond Bear's still form, No-Eyes stood. There was a bloody dagger in his hand. 'Come on!' he rasped.

'No...' Red knelt by Bear's head, and tried to turn him over. But the other guard was heavy and limp. He was still breathing, but the red slit on the back of his neck told a fatal tale.

Red stood up. 'What did you *do?*' he roared. 'You've killed him!'

No-Eyes snarled under the bandage. 'Shut up and come with me. That one's partner is coming.'

Even in this midst of his horror, Red saw sense. He clambered over Bear's body, toward No-Eyes. Sure enough, as he looked up the street, he saw a second guard hurrying toward him.

Red had made his plan, and he stuck to it now. He grabbed No-Eyes, slung the old man over his shoulder, and ran for it.

The only hole in his plan was that he didn't know exactly where he should run *to.*

Fortunately Bear's partner was slow to come after him, probably because he was trying to help his fallen friend. Knowing how important the first dash was, Red sprinted away toward the city wall, took the first left turn he saw, and hid behind a stack of rotting crates.

He waited there – not bothering to put down the startled No-Eyes – until he heard the pursuing footsteps go past and fade into the distance.

Then he left the crates and went on through to the next street along, and ran on.

At last, at long last, he reached the city wall. With the great structure looming overhead, he went to ground beside a garbage heap and finally put No-Eyes down.

The blind man looked shaken and bedraggled from his ride. He adjusted the bandage over his eyes, and said, 'Where are we?'

'By the wall,' said Red. 'Where's this house of yours?'

'Between the tower with the old seige weapon next to it an' the one with the broken window,' said No-Eyes.

That wasn't far away. 'Good,' said Red. 'Let's go then. Walking, this time.'

'I've lost my cane,' said No-Eyes. 'I'll hafta hold onto you.'

'Fine,' Red growled. 'But if we get into trouble, don't expect me t'help you.'

'That's nice considerin' I just saved your life,' said No-Eyes.

Red finally lost it. 'Saved my *life*?' he shouted. 'You just killed me! D'you know what happens t'people who kill guards? Forget arrestin' us; if the lads find us now they'll kill the pair of us on the spot!'

'Better'n bein' executed,' No-Eyes said calmly. 'Or tortured.'

'Bear was my friend,' said Red. 'An' now thanks to you, I'm a murderer as well as a spy.'

It was hard to read an expression on an eyeless face, but nevertheless No-Eyes looked unmoved. 'Let's argue about it later, when we ain't dead.'

Red sighed and rubbed his face as he accepted that No-Eyes was right. 'Fine, just lemme check for anyone comin'.'

He peered out from behind the garbage heap. Thankfully, there didn't seem to be anyone about.

He helped No-Eyes up, and offered him an arm to lean on.

Then, moving slowly once again, they started to follow the wall.

Fear and guilt made Red feel close to vomiting. He couldn't stop seeing Bear's dying body in his mind, or remembering his last words. If only he'd acted sooner – but how could he have known what No-Eyes would do? What sort of blind man knew how to stab a man in the neck like that, in just the right place to paralyse him instantly? Sheer luck?

However it was, Red decided that the moment he was safely away from the city he was going to leave No-Eyes behind. Whatever this man was, he was dangerous, and it would be best to leave him as soon as he, Red, didn't need him any more.

Thankfully, though they saw a few more guards along the way, they made it past the tower with the seige weapon without being chased again.

From there, Red helped No-Eyes to feel his way along the wall, sometimes clambering over bits of junk or squeezing past houses that had been built too close. It was against building regulations to have anything made right up by the wall like this, but regulating everything had turned out to be too impractical, especially on the west side. Knock something down today, and tomorrow three more things would have replaced it.

Sure enough, about halfway between the tower with the seige weapon and the next one along, No-Eyes stopped. He didn't have much choice: a tumbledown shack had been built right up against the wall, so close that there was no room to go around it on that side.

Wordlessly, No-Eyes climbed in through a hole that had once been a window.

Red glanced around cautiously, and followed.

Inside, the shack was in such bad shape that it was impossible to stand upright except in one corner. Everywhere else the roof had caved in, and bits of rotting wood hung down from the ceiling like reaching fingers. The floor was invisible under a layer of rubbish and bits of fallen wall and roof. The wall furthest away from the city's own wall had fallen down completely, which was probably why the roof had caved in.

The wall closest to the city wall… *was* the city wall. Whoever had built the shack had apparently decided to save time and wood by building close enough to use a small section of stonework as a wall for his home. Time and damp had given it a nasty layer of green slime.

'Is this it?' Red asked.

'Help me clear the floor,' No-Eyes said by way of an answer.

Red obligingly knelt and helped him to push away the layer of detritus on the patch of floor nearest to the stone wall. Underneath was a board made from some planks crudely nailed together, and the whole thing was rotted badly enough that Red could see why no-one had stolen it for firewood.

'Lift it away,' said No-Eyes.

Red hooked his fingers underneath it, and lifted. It was heavy, and for a moment he thought it was going to fall apart, but he heaved it out of the way and leant it against the wall.

And, sure enough, there was a hole. It was lined with nothing but dirt, but it was big enough for Red to fit through.

'See?' said No-Eyes. 'I'll go first. Pull the cover back on after you when y'follow. An' take the bag off an' drag it or you'll get stuck.'

'Got it,' said Red.

'It's dark in there,' No-Eyes added, 'But just feel your way along an' don't panic. It goes a good long way.'

'Right,' said Red.

No-Eyes grinned. 'See you on the other side, then.'

He climbed into the hole, and in a moment he was gone.

Red wasted no time in following him. The moment he had taken the bag off his back and pulled his tunic over the hilt of his sword so it wouldn't catch on anything, he went in feet-first and pulled the cover after him.

The hole opened up a bit inside, enough for him to turn around. He tied the bag to his ankle, crouched down, and crawled on into darkness and the smell of cold earth.

Chapter Seven

Lies

The journey through the tunnel was a long one – painfully long.

Most of the time the space was just barely big enough to crawl through. In other places it got so narrow that even crawling was impossible and he had to wriggle along on his stomach.

It was utterly dark, and the weight of earth above felt suffocating. Fear, too, pressed down on him – steady, pervading fear. If the tunnel collapsed, or if he came across a blockage, he was doomed. Turning around would be impossible, and moving backwards would be just about impossible as well. He would die here, deep underground, in this tunnel which already felt like a tomb.

Sometimes he thought he could hear scratching or scuffling up ahead. Hopefully it came from No-Eyes, but as time dragged on his imagination conjured up pictures of giant snakes and other monsters that might live underground. And here and now, when he was lying with his shoulders twisted at a weird angle so they would fit, and his arms were pinned to his sides, he would never be able to fight back.

He shut those images out, and struggled on laboriously with his eyes and mouth closed to keep the dirt out.

Once or twice he even fell asleep, when he stopped to rest. Waking up in utter blackness was horrible, and jolted him awake every time.

For the first time, he came to understand what life must be like for someone like No-Eyes, or blind Lord Derrick, who was one of Isleen's councillors.

But if this was how the world looked to No-Eyes, how had he managed to stab Bear in the neck?

With nothing else to do while he journeyed through that tunnel, Red began to obsess over that question. How could it be possible?

It shouldn't be, he decided. Couldn't be. And whatever the real answer here was, one thing was clear. No-Eyes couldn't be trusted.

Red wasn't afraid of him. The old man might have supernatural skill with a dagger, but he'd be no match for a powerfully muscled and fully trained guard like himself.

Once he was out of the tunnel, Red decided he would ask some important questions. And if he didn't like the answers he got… well, every guard was taught how to be persuasive when they had to be.

The tunnel widened again, and Red managed to free his arms. He stretched them gladly and took a moment to rest before he began to crawl again.

Light touched his eyes, and he cautiously opened them.

Light, there was light! Real sunlight, coming from up ahead!

Greatly relieved, Red sped up. Deep down he had begun to doubt that he would ever see daylight again.

The tunnel finally ended in a small cave, like the one that had begun it. Red pulled himself out into it, and stood up, groaning as his legs twinged in protest. He untied the bag from his ankle, and slung it back onto his shoulder.

His clothes were covered in dirt. He dusted himself down and checked that his sword was still there. It was, and he straightened his lucky tunic with relief.

'Hey, what the——?'

Suddenly alarmed, he groped around inside the tunic, and then inspected the ground. His medal had come off, and he couldn't see it anywhere around him.

Swearing, he crouched down and checked the ground around him. It wasn't there either. It must have come off while he was underground. By now it could be anywhere in the tunnel.

Red shook his head sadly, and climbed out of the cave and into the open air.

He emerged into a forest. Dawn had come, and the trees all about were silvery with it. A cold breeze rustled among the leaves, and made him shiver.

Red looked back. The tunnel had come out in the side of a small embankment, and a heap of old cloth that must have covered the entrance lay nearby.

As he stood there, rubbing his eyes and wondering where No-Eyes had got to, he saw the blind man coming toward him. He was just as grubby looking as Red must be, but he looked lively enough.

'There y'are,' he said. 'I thought you must've died down there.'

'Thought I was going to a few times,' Red said ruefully. 'What next?'

'Here.' No-Eyes groped his way over to the heap of cloth. 'Help me cover it up.'

Forgetting his suspicions for the moment, Red picked up one end of the cloth and helped No-Eyes drape it over the tunnel. It was brown cloth, and coarse, and it blended in with the soil quite well.

'Put leaves over it,' No-Eyes advised. 'We don't want nobody findin' it.'

Red scooped up some fallen leaves and bark, and threw them over the cloth. Once they were on, the entrance was just about invisible to the casual eye. 'How'd we ever find it again?' he wondered aloud.

'There,' said No-Eyes, pointing vaguely toward the embankment. 'There's a mark on a tree, see it?'

Red squinted. Sure enough, someone had cut a row of grooves into a spice-tree that grew directly behind the entrance. 'Oh, right.'

'Now,' said No-Eyes. 'Let's get going.'

Red folded his arms. 'No.'

No-Eyes stopped in surprise. 'No what?'

'I ain't going with you,' said Red. 'Not until you answer some questions.'

'There's no time for that!' said No-Eyes. 'You wanna get caught?'

'We're far enough away by now,' said Red. 'They're not gonna come all the way out here. An' I'm not goin' with you until you tell me what's really goin' on here.'

'What d'you mean?' said No-Eyes. 'I'm helpin' you escape!'

'Yeah, an' I'm grateful, believe me,' said Red. 'But I don't trust you. Who are you, really?'

'Just an old man with no eyes who felt he owed a debt,' said No-Eyes.

'You stabbed Bear in the neck,' Red said flatly. 'In the spine. You did it like an expert would. Nobody from off the street knows how t'do that. How'd you manage it?'

No-Eyes shrugged. 'I just made a stab at him. Didn't know where I'd hit him. Got lucky, I guess.'

But Red wasn't fooled any more. 'You know too much,' he said. 'You *see* too much.'

There was an awkward silence.

'You're not really blind, are you?' Red said at last.

'What're you going to do, then?' No-Eyes asked unexpectedly.

'Whatever I have to,' said Red. 'But not until after you've told me the truth.'

No-Eyes straightened up. In some subtle way, he seemed to grow taller. 'The truth is that you're comin' with us,' he said. 'Now.'

'Us?' said Red, immediately reaching for his sword. 'Who's us?'

No-Eyes seemed to hesitate. Then he shrugged again, reached up, and took the bandage off his face.

Red tensed instinctively, but underneath the bandage there was nothing but—

'*Eyes*!' he roared. 'I knew it!'

No-Eyes grinned, and his eyes crinkled with the expression. 'Yeah,' he said. 'But not eyes I'd show to anyone. Not here.'

The voice had changed too. Red took a step closer, hunching in readiness for a fight. 'Who are you?' he asked again.

No-Eyes glanced past him, and grinned. 'Look into my eyes, and see for yourself.'

Stupidly, impulsively, Red looked. The eyes were ordinary enough, shining in the dull light, but they were unlike any eyes he had ever seen before. But that was because he had never gone North, and had never looked into the black eyes of a Northerner.

He backed off, and drew his sword. 'Holy Gryphus! You're a bloody blackrobe!'

No-Eyes' black eyes narrowed. 'Watch it, Southerner. There's no 'robes in my family; I'm a free-born darkman.'

But Red was too shocked to listen — and an instant later, too angry. 'It was *you*,' he snarled. '*You're* the spy. *You* put that stuff in my chest!'

'Aye, I did,' No-Eyes said coolly. 'They were on to me. I had to get myself off the hook somehow.'

'But you helped me get away,' said Red.

'It was time to report back,' said No-Eyes. 'I thought I'd take you with me. The King will have plenty of use for you.'

Red had heard enough. He thrust the sword straight at the Northerner's smirking face.

No-Eyes dodged the blow and darted away.

'Get back here, you son of a bitch!' Red shouted.

No-Eyes looked completely unafraid. He ducked behind a tree, and made an odd screeching sound.

The undergrowth to Red's left exploded. He yelped and lurched away from it, but too late. Something huge bounded toward him, and before he could even think the word *griffin*, it leapt.

He hit the ground face-first, and a massive grip closed around his body like a hand. His sword had disappeared somewhere. He struggled against his captor, but the griffin's hold was iron. It squeezed tighter in response, and he felt the talons pierce his skin.

'Aaargh!'

No-Eyes' voice spoke somewhere above him – in griffish! 'Don't hurt him! We need him alive.'

The grip loosened.

'Why alive?' the griffin's harsh, rasping voice demanded. 'Why is he here?'

'A prisoner,' said No-Eyes. 'For the King. He has information.'

'We will take him, then,' said the griffin. 'Tie him up, and I will carry him.'

There was nothing Red could do. The griffin pinned him down effortlessly while No-Eyes tied his wrists and ankles together. After that he climbed onto the griffin's back. Red lay there helplessly, until the griffin took him in its grasp again and lifted him off the ground. He heard its wings beat, and felt the wind from it on his back.

The griffin took off and flew up over the trees. Hanging from its talons, Red saw the ground fall away below. He could even see his sword, gleaming among the leaf litter.

As the griffin flew higher, he turned his head and saw the walls of Liranwee. His home and all he loved, beyond his reach.

Deep down, Red knew that he would never be able to return. Even if he survived whatever happened to him next, Liranwee would never welcome him back. But all the same he knew that his heart would always be behind its walls. For better or for worse.

*

No-Eyes and his partner flew northward, away from Liranwee, for the next four days, stopping only to rest. Naturally, Red had intended to escape at the first opportunity he got, but neither of them gave him that chance. They kept him tied up at all times, tethering him to a tree at night, and took turns watching him. He knew that if he tried to attack either of them he would be subdued and possibly killed by the griffin, and that if he did ever escape the beast would track him. Griffins had excellent eyesight, and a good sense of smell as well. They were, after all, the most powerful predators in the world.

All he could do was wait, and watch, and listen. Neither No-Eyes nor his partner ever spoke to him, but they didn't know he understood griffish, and carelessly used it in front of him. Red took in every word, hoping they would give him something useful.

'I have gathered plenty of good information,' the griffin boasted one day. 'And I remember it all. Have you done as well?'

No-Eyes smiled at him. 'Brag away, Echo, but I've done well myself. I've got everything about the walls, and I stole plans for the guard towers. And I smuggled out this guard. I know for a fact that he worked on the walls and in the towers as well; he's not just a member of the ranks. He's a Sergeant – they were about to make him Captain, come to that. He'll have plenty of good intelligence for us.'

'Shar will be most pleased with us,' said Echo. 'Her human will give you many rewards, and she will reward me!'

'With what?' No-Eyes asked.

'With a mating,' said Echo. 'She is a fine female. And I want many shiny rings to wear on my forelegs.'

'You'll have them, never fear,' said No-Eyes with a grin. 'As for me…'

'Yes?' said Echo. 'What will you ask for?'

'A marriage,' said No-Eyes. 'I'm hoping I'll be big enough after this that one of those Eyrie ladies will want me. Jumped-up commoner my arse! I was made for finer things than this!'

'You will not attract many mates now,' said Echo. 'You are ugly and furless.'

'Oh, my hair will grow back,' said No-Eyes. 'I couldn't very well keep it while I was surrounded by Southerners. Then again, that lot are stupid enough that maybe they wouldn't've noticed. Thank the Night God I don't have to keep pretending to be blind. It worked well, I'll grant you, but it was such a pain.'

'I did much pretending in the Eyrie,' said Echo. 'I changed my coat so many times I was exhausted and they thought I was a weakling!' he huffed.

Red listened to all this with a kind of fascination, but with rage as well. *Stupid Southerners?* he thought. *I'll show you who's stupid the moment I get my hands free. I'll beat you around the head so bad you'll wind up a dribbling idiot.*

Bravado like that helped to sustain him during the journey, but he had to face up to the truth as they went further North and the air grew colder; bravado was just a shield. A way of stopping himself from facing up to the danger he was in. And when the Northgate Mountains came in sight at last, he finally began to understand just how great that danger was. And not just for him, but for everyone in Liranwee.

No, he thought numbly, as the sight of it sank in. *Not just Liranwee. Everyone in the South. All of us.*

Below him, spread out over the plain that backed onto the Northgates, was an army. An army so big it beggared belief. Thousands upon thousands of human figures, swarming over the ground below him like ants. And among them there were griffins. Everywhere tents studded the ground, and smoke rose from campfires. He saw oxcarts loaded with boxes and barrels, and even a herd of goats in a pen.

As Echo flew lower, Red could see the banners that had been hung up here and there. Every one of them was white, with a black symbol of a triple spiral on it. He had never seen a banner like it before, but it didn't matter. He already knew who these people were, and why they had come.

The nightmare of Liranwee had come true, and the Northerners had come through the mountains at last.

As Echo came in to land in the middle of the camp, the other griffins there noticed him. Several of them flew up to intercept him. He showed no fear of them, but they weren't overtly hostile. The moment they were close enough to have a good look at him, they circled round to fly beside him, guiding him downward.

Before Echo landed on an open patch of grass, he unceremoniously dropped Red. He hit the ground with a painful thud, and managed to roll onto his back in time to see the griffin land right beside him.

No-Eyes dismounted and came over to Red's side, roughly hauling him up by his tunic and forcing him to kneel.

Already people and griffins were hurrying over to see what was going on. No-Eyes gestured imperiously at them. 'You and you, come here and guard this bastard. You – go and fetch the King.'

'Yes, sir!'

One man ran off, while the other two came over and stationed themselves on either side of Red, weapons drawn.

Red had too much common sense to try anything. He sat as still as he could and didn't even make eye contact with his captors. If there was a time to escape, it wasn't now. He looked up at the growing crowd of onlookers instead. All Northerners, with a few griffins sprinkled in among them. Dozens of pale faces, and black eyes all fixed on him.

He heard them talking among themselves. Most of them spoke some language he didn't recognise, which he guessed must be their own native tongue. But some of them were using Cymrian, albeit with a lilting accent.

'That's a Southerner?' one of the younger men said.

'Aye, that's one of them,' said the older man next to him.

'Do ye think they all look like that?' the young man asked. He sounded fascinated.

'More or less,' said his friend. 'Ugly, ain't he?'

'Look at his big stupid face!' someone else jeered. 'His eyes are all watery like a cow!'

'Yeah, an' his skin's all tanned,' said another. 'He's all big an' lumpy like a sack o' potatoes. An' look at them hands! They're huge! How'd he even hold a spoon with those?'

Red sat there in silence, and felt the insults rain down on him like rocks. He had never thought of himself as big or clumsy, but next to them, with their narrow shoulders and long-fingered hands, he suddenly felt that way. And he felt ashamed, as well – ashamed in a way he had never felt before in his life. Ashamed that he was so different from them.

But beside the shame, there was also resignation. This was all the proof he needed to know that he couldn't expect any mercy here. They hated him. He was a Southerner, and therefore their enemy, and that was all there was to it.

As he steeled himself to accept that, a sudden silence cut off the jeers from the crowd. Red looked up, and saw the Northerners moving aside hastily to make a path, bowing low to the one they were letting through. Red's heart sank before he even saw who it was.

The leader of the Northerners was a griffiner, of course – his partner, a scarred female with reddish-brown feathers, walked just behind him. And Red's heart froze at the sight of him.

The man was clad all in black – a long black robe, black leggings, and black leather boots. His long hair too was black, like his eyes, and he wore a pointed chin-beard. His face was pale and suspicious, with a naturally bitter expression, one cheek marked by delicate, spiralling blue tattoos. He carried himself very upright, and there was an aura of cold, haughty authority about him.

A silver circlet rested on his forehead, set with a large blue stone.

When Red saw him, his throat closed itself up as if the noose were around his neck again. Sweating with terror, he sagged between his guards, who pressed their swords into his throat to stop him from making a move.

The robed man came to stand over him, tall and terrible. A creature of the night, a patch of darkness in the sunlight.

'Southerner,' he said. 'Look at me.' His voice was flat and cold.

Obediently, Red looked up. The man's black eyes were on his face, and they looked like a pair of holes into the void.

'Southerner,' said the man. 'Do you know who I am?'

Red's voice didn't want to come. He nearly choked when he tried to speak.

The man gestured impatiently at the guards, and they withdrew their weapons. The man leant down to look Red in the face. 'I said, do you know who I am?'

Red finally managed to speak, but his voice came out thin and high with terror. 'The… the Dark Lord Arenadd.'

The robed man straightened up, and laughed. His laugh was cruel and mocking. Around him the other Northerners joined in, many of them taking the opportunity to throw more insults.

Their leader silenced them with a wave, and turned his attention back on Red. 'So! The Dark Lord has finally come South again. And what about you, Southerner? What's *your* name?'

'R… er… Red. I mean…' Red coughed. 'Sergeant Kearney Redguard. From Liranwee.' There was no point in lying about any of that; No-Eyes would catch him out if he did.

The man – the Dark Lord – looked at No-Eyes. 'Morgan, is that you?'

No-Eyes came forward, and bowed. 'Yes, Sire. Finally reporting back after all this time, Sire!'

His King laughed, and gave him an affectionate clap on the shoulder. 'Well done! I knew I could depend on you.'

'You haven't seen my information yet,' No-Eyes pointed out.

'That doesn't matter now; you did well just getting in and out of there,' said the King. 'Was there any trouble?'

'Not much, Sire,' No-Eyes said lightly. 'I thought they were getting close at one point, but I managed to pin the blame on this great clod of a guardsman. He ran off before they could arrest him, so I got him to come with me and brought him here for you. Thought he could be useful, Sire.'

The King's smile at him was a genuine one, Red noticed, one with true warmth in it. 'You're my best, Morgan, you really are. And you're just as devious as your brother was.'

In the midst of his horror and panic, Red nearly laughed. "Morgan" was such an obvious name for a Northerner. Any time you wanted to tell a story and there was a Northerner in it who wasn't important, you called him Morgan. Come to that, "Morgan" was the name of the faithful slave in the *Adventures of Alaric* books the griffiners liked to read.

But there was nothing comical about this Morgan, even if he looked every bit as faithful to his master as his imaginary namesake. 'Well, you know Henwas taught me all his tricks,' he said. 'Now if you'd like, we can go somewhere more private and I'll show you what I gathered.'

'Yes, of course,' said the King. 'And you too, Echo?'

The griffin stirred. 'I have brought information for your human, Shar.'

The red griffin with the King clicked her beak. 'That is good. Come with us, and we will talk.'

The King nodded. 'I think that's everything. We'll deal with the Southerner later. You two—,' he looked at the men guarding Red. 'Take him away and lock him up. I want at least two men watching him at all times, is that understood?'

'Yes, Sire.' One of the guards gave Red a spiteful kick in the ribs. 'Get up, ye sun-worshippin' bastard.'

Red struggled up, but his feet were still tied and he immediately fell onto his face. The crowd laughed viciously at him while he lay there, waiting until one of the guards had taken the rope off his ankles.

After that he was able to stand up, somewhat stiffly, and allowed himself to be marched away. The mocking crowd, and his aching legs, felt completely unimportant now. His head was spinning.

The Dark Lord Arenadd! It should be impossible – the dreaded King of the North was supposed to have died nearly ten years ago. But who else could he have seen? The man who was his captor fit every description of the Dark Lord he had ever heard. The robe, the beard, the crown – everything. And who else could have led this massive army through the Northgates?

It was an old fear, one Red knew well. Like everyone born in Liranwee, he had grown up knowing what every adult around him dreaded, and it had become one of his earliest memories. One day, they had all said, any day, the Dark Lord Arenadd could come through those mountains. Riding on his giant black griffin and leading his army of Northerners. He'll come South to kill us all, and Liranwee is the first place he'll strike. He won't spare anyone. He hates Southerners, and his master the Night God gave him dark powers to kill us. He'll destroy everything, and we won't stand a chance.

Those old words ran through Red's mind now, and despair ate at his heart. How could his home city ever hold off an army this big? On the journey to wherever it was they were going to lock him up, he passed hundreds of Northerners, all armed and armoured. And griffins. Dozens and dozens of griffins, many of them unnaturally big.

There was no hope for Liranwee, none at all. The Dark Lord had brought enough soldiers to populate two cities the same size, and he probably had more griffins with him than Liranwee did too. The place would be overrun within a day.

And it would happen with his help, he thought. They would torture all the information he had out of him, make him tell them all about the defenses and the inner workings of the guards. He wasn't a traitor, but they would force him to become one.

With that thought, all of Red's terror froze and hardened inside him. He squeezed it in his mind, and let it become rage.

No, he thought. *NO. I won't. I won't help them. I won't tell them a damn thing. No matter what they do. I'll tear my own tongue out first. I'll escape and force them to kill me. But I'll never talk.*

His guards finally took him to a clearing near the edge of the camp, where an iron cage sat on the ground. They opened it and untied his hands before they thrust him inside and locked the door behind him.

Red sat down on the floor of his prison. It was barely big enough for him to stand up, and only just long enough to lie down, and there wouldn't be much comfort there – the bars were underneath him as well, making it impossible to escape by digging or by just lifting the cage off himself.

He rubbed his swollen wrists, and tried to pull himself together. It was only a matter of time before they started interrogating him, and he had until then to try and think up a plan. Escape – or death.

Chapter Eight

The Prince and the Bear

Red's captors left him alone for the rest of that day. His two guards kept watch over him, and the two others who relieved them brought food for him.

It wasn't much; just some bread and a piece of cheese, but he ate it gladly – he hadn't had anything since that morning.

After that, he lay down on the cage floor, using his arm as a pillow, and tried to get some rest. May as well be properly awake when the time came – it would keep his head clear and make it easier to think.

Commander Talmon's words came back to him as he lay there. *A guard who's tired can't think straight, and he shouldn't be on duty.*

'Right, sir,' Red muttered to himself. 'I got it.'

What with his troubles and the uncomfortable floor, sleep should have been next to impossible. And it was, just about, but he drifted off eventually. Days of captivity and constant travelling had taken the last of his strength.

Once again he dreamt of the noose, cutting off his breath just as his fear had done that day.

He woke up when it was still dark, but the sting of fear brought him out of sleep too well for him to go back. After trying to drift off again for some time, he eventually gave up and went to sit with his back against the side of the cage. His guards had a couple of lanterns burning, and the light let him see them standing just where they had been, straight-backed and alert. Clearly, these guards knew their job. There'd be none of that conveniently falling asleep at their posts and allowing the prisoner to escape stuff that storytellers loved so much.

Never liked them stories, Red thought irrelevantly. *A real guard does his job how it should be done.*

Eventually, when the sky began to lighten, two more guards came to relieve them. Red watched them swap over, and felt a weird kind of connection to them. It was so much like how it was back home. But that was how it was, he thought. No matter what race they belonged to, a guard was a guard.

Bit by bit the sun rose, and the last of the night finally faded away. The new guards snuffed out the lamps and stood patiently in position, keeping watch over the cage and its occupant. A boring job, Red knew, but it had to be done. A guard's duty was often a thankless one.

Tiredness finally got to him, and he dozed on and off while he waited for something to happen. He vaguely wished that he could have explored the cage properly, and maybe found some weakness somewhere he could use, but with the guards watching him he knew he couldn't. They tensed the moment he moved at all.

Everything in and around the cage was so still, then, that when he did finally see movement it was a shock.

Not long after dawn a man appeared out of the early morning mist. The guards immediately turned to look, and stood to attention when they saw his face. In his cage, Red, too, straightened up.

It was Morgan.

The spy nodded to the guards, and addressed them in their own language. A brief conversation ensued, and a nervous Red, unable to understand any of it, watched. Morgan had stopped shaving his head after the flight from Liranwee, and a thin stubble of black hair had now covered his scalp. With it, and without the cloth on his face, it was astonishing to realise just how effective his disguise had really been. Not only was he not blind, but he wasn't old either. In fact he looked younger than Red himself.

Looking at him now, Red could hardly believe that he had ever thought he was old. True, there hadn't been any visible wrinkles or liver-spots on him, but they hadn't been necessary. It had all been in the slow, hunched way he walked, and the rough edge to his voice. Everything about the way he acted had said "old", and it had been done so well that Red hadn't seen through it for a moment.

Beneath his hatred, Red found room for some grudging respect. The Northerner was a genius master of disguise. No wonder he'd become a spy.

Now Morgan turned his attention on Red. He came closer to the cage, and inspected him. 'Good morning, Red,' he said. 'Did you sleep well?'

'Shut it,' Red growled.

Morgan only smiled and shrugged. 'All right. You're the one who's supposed to be doing the talking today anyway.'

'Not a chance,' said Red.

Another shrug.

The two guards came closer. Both of them had spears, and now they thrust them between the bars and rested the tips against Red's throat.

'Put yer hands behind yer back, through the bars,' one ordered.

But Red had had enough of doing what they said. He reached up, grabbed one of the spears behind the point, and wrenched it away. Immediately the other spear stabbed into the side of his neck, but he managed to lurch away from it before it broke the skin. Acting fast, before they could react properly, he stood up and gave the spear in his hand a hard shove. The butt hit the guard holding it in the stomach, making him stumble. Immediately Red pulled, hoping to get the weapon away from its owner.

The guard, however, managed to keep hold of it. He pulled back, and a brief tug of war ensued.

Red kept hold of the spear, and put all of his strength into the struggle. His confidence was rising already; these guards weren't as good as he'd thought. And he was stronger than this one.

The other guard had pulled his spear back out of the cage. Now he turned it around and, holding onto it by the point, he thrust the other end through the bars and smacked Red hard in the head with the butt.

With a yell of surprise, Red let go of the spear and fell hard against the cage wall. The guard who had hit him reached through and grabbed him by the arm, pulling it through the bars. 'Help me!' he yelled to his friend.

The other guard was there in a moment, catching Red's other arm, and a pair of manacles snapped into place around his wrists.

With a groan, Red fell down into a sitting position. There were a couple of bars between his wrists, and he couldn't pull his arms back into the cage. His head was still spinning from the spear-blow.

Morgan had stood by and watched all this in silence. 'Idiots,' he said at last. 'You're lucky he didn't hurt either of you. Trust me, that one's strong. Now give me the damn keys. And then one of you can go and bring us a couple of men to replace you.'

'Yes, my Lord.'

Resignedly, one of the guards handed over a ring with a key on it and hurried off.

Sitting in his cage, Red sneered at Morgan. 'You lot ain't got a clue how to train good guards.'

To his surprise, Morgan nodded. 'It's true,' he said. 'Southerners make the best guards. I saw enough of you and your friends on duty to know it. It's probably because mindless obedience is so easy for your sort.'

'You're scum,' said Red. 'I wish I'd snapped your lyin' neck when I had the chance.'

Morgan didn't bother to reply to that. He waited patiently until the replacement guards arrived, and gave them a few curt orders in Northern.

One of them took up station behind Red, spear in hand.

The other waited while Morgan unlocked the cage door, and then went inside. Morgan locked the door behind him. Then he came closer – close enough that he and Red could look each other in the face.

'Now,' he said. 'You're going to tell us about the guards in Liranwee. Were you trained in what to do if the city's invaded?'

Red looked at him for a moment, considering what to say. In the end, he closed his mouth and looked stubbornly away.

Immediately, the guard standing over him punched him in the face. His head jerked sideways with the blow, and he gasped.

'Again,' said Morgan.

Another blow, to the other side of his head.

'Now I'll ask you again,' said Morgan. 'How are you trained? Can any of you handle bows?'

Once again, Red kept his mouth shut.

Once again Morgan signalled to the guard, and more blows rained down on his face.

That was how it went, for however long it was. Morgan asked questions, and for every silence, a hit to the face came. After a while, frustrated, the guard took a wooden cudgel from his belt and used that instead.

The first time that hit him, Red felt as if his whole face had caved in. His head slammed back against the bars, and he heard an ugly crunch as his nose broke.

The guard raised the cudgel again, but Morgan held up a hand to stop him.

Twisted sideways where he sat, but held up by the manacles, Red groaned. 'I…' he mumbled.

Morgan came closer. 'Yes, Red? What is it? Speak up.'

Red could feel the blood soaking into his moustache. His mouth hurt, but he wanted to talk now. 'I swear,' he said thickly. 'To protect the weak. I swear to serve my Eyrie, my territory and its people. I swear to find lawbreakers an' bring them to justice. In Gryphus' name…'

'What's he saying?' the guard behind him murmured.

Morgan shook his head in disgust. 'He's reciting the guard's oath. Shut him up.'

The cudgel hit him in the face once again. This time, when it struck his already broken nose, the pain was unbelievable. Red cried out pathetically, but once he had slumped down again he continued to mumble the oath.

'Duty… honour… loyalty… that is the creed of the guard. I swear t'follow it every day of my…'

Smack.

This time, the cudgel hit him in the mouth.

'That's enough,' Morgan's voice said from behind the clanging in his ears. 'We're done for now.'

The guard with the cudgel left, and Red heard the cage door close. Finally, the manacles were removed. With them gone there was nothing to hold him up, and he silently toppled onto his side.

Morgan's voice spoke again, from somewhere above him. 'He's got a strong will, but don't worry. That was just some softening up. We'll start the real torture tomorrow. I think the hot iron should do the trick.'

Red knew the words were being said for his benefit. Dizzy, and trembling in shock and pain, he wrapped his fingers around a bar and slowly pulled himself back into a sitting position. The beating had left him confused, but he still refused to cower at the spy's feet.

His vision was a little blurred, and closed off on one side by a swollen eye, but he could make out Morgan, standing close by.

The spy spoke, this time to him, and his voice sounded almost gentle. 'You think I'm a monster. But did you know I had a brother once? His name was Henwas. One of your lot tortured him just like this, and it killed him in the end. He was a true Northerner. Are you that loyal to your own people? They betrayed you. All your friends turned on you the moment they thought you'd done something wrong. No doubt, nothing. They were that ready to believe you'd betray them.'

Red spat out a mouthful of blood. 'Duty. Loyalty. My family's code.' His tongue felt too big for his mouth.

The wavering shape of Morgan shrugged his signature shrug. 'Very inspiring, Southerner, but we'll see how long that lasts. Sleep well.'

He started to leave, but Red managed to find his voice again. 'Morgan…'

Morgan stopped and turned around. 'Yes?'

Red looked him in the eye. 'One day I'm gonna kill you. Promise.'

Morgan stared at him for a moment, and then walked away without saying anything.

Left alone, Red let himself lie down again. He felt close to fainting.

But he hadn't talked. He forced himself to focus on that, and pride made him feel better. They had beaten him to a pulp, but he hadn't cracked, not once. Hadn't said a damn thing.

But tomorrow… what would happen then? When the so-called "real torture" began? Would he be able to hold out under that?

Duty, he reminded himself fiercely. *Loyalty. You're a Redguard, dammit, not a traitor!*

The pain made it hard to think. He kept trying to concentrate on his family motto, using it to give himself more courage, but in the end the pain in his head won out and he drifted into a kind of trance. Lying on his side with his mouth and nose bleeding, he let the pain consume him, and thought of nothing. It was too much just now.

In the end, when the shock wore off, exhaustion consumed him. He closed his swollen eyes, and went to sleep.

*

'Is he dead?'

Red heard the question as he woke up. He tried to open his eyes, but cringed and closed them again immediately. His head hurt so badly he thought it was about to burst. Afraid to move, he lay completely still and listened. Had someone spoken?

'I said, is he dead?' the voice repeated. It wasn't one of the guards. The voice was high and a little nervous. With a dull shock, Red realised that it was a child. What in the gods' names was a child doing here?

Curiosity was enough to make him try opening his eyes again. Instantly the pain flared up behind them, but he forced them to stay open. His fingers twitched, and he groaned.

The child cried out in surprise. 'He's not dead, he's waking up!'

Very slowly, Red pushed himself into a sitting position. The motion made his headache rise to agony pitch, but he fought the urge to lie down again.

Cautiously, he touched his face. While he was asleep the swelling had gone up horrendously; his eyes were puffy and his broken nose was so bunged up he could scarcely breathe through it. His lip was split, too, and when he probed around in his mouth with his tongue he found two broken teeth.

I must look like a horse's arse, he thought.

To take his mind off things, he looked around blearily for the child who had spoken. Sure enough, a small boy was standing outside by the cage door. He was about eight years old, and Red immediately noticed how expensive his clothes looked. He was wearing a neat little red tunic with silver trimmings, and his pants were a rich shade of blue. He even had a fine leather belt with a miniature sickle tucked into it – the signature weapon of Northerners.

Seeing Red looking at him, the boy took a cautious step back. 'Hello,' he said. 'Are you the Southerner?'

Red rubbed his face. Dried blood flaked away under his fingers. His moustache had stuck together into a row of stiff bristles.

The boy scowled at him. 'You've got to answer me when I ask questions.'

'Mnph?' Red managed.

'Do you even talk?' the boy persisted. 'Everyone says Southerners are stupid, but they didn't say you couldn't talk.'

Red finally managed to focus on him. 'I talk,' he said, hoping that would be enough. While the boy digested this, Red glanced over at the guards. They'd moved away to a respectable distance, but they were still keeping a close eye on the pair of them. Clearly, this boy had some authority.

'I came to see you,' said the boy. 'I've never seen a Southerner before. Do they all look like you?'

Red's eyes narrowed. 'Not really,' he said. '*I don't look like this usually.*'

'You don't?' said the boy.

'No, 'cause usually I ain't been beaten about the head with a lump of wood,' Red growled.

'They just did that to make you talk,' said the boy. Suddenly, he giggled. 'It would've been stupid if they were doing that and you couldn't talk anyway!'

'Far as they're concerned, I can't talk,' said Red. 'An' I didn't.'

The boy came closer. 'Why not?' he asked, sounding intrigued.

'I ain't gonna betray my home to this lot,' said Red. Even talking hurt. 'They'd better just kill me because they won't get nothin' out of me.'

'Even if they hurt you?' asked the boy.

'Even then.' Red rubbed his moustache between his fingers to try and get some of the blood out. 'Who are you, anyway?'

The boy lifted his chin. 'I'm Prince Caradoc Arenadd Taranisäii. My dad's the King.'

Red squinted. 'Prince, are you? Am I meant to bow or somethin'?'

'Yes,' Caradoc said sternly. 'Everyone has to.'

'Tough,' said Red. 'My head hurts too much for that nonsense, an' you're not my prince. We don't have Kings in the South.'

'No, you're led by griffiners,' said Caradoc. 'They're all nasty and greedy and they lie.'

Red opened his mouth to disagree, but he changed his mind. 'Yeah, you got that right,' he admitted. 'I don't trust griffiners. Bunch of backstabbin' scumbags. They don't have honour. It's up to us guards to be honest an' upright.'

Caradoc giggled behind his hand. 'Are you a guard, then? What's your name?'

'Red,' said Red. He wondered if he should risk standing up.

'That's not a real name!' Caradoc objected. 'That's a *colour.*'

'True.' Despite himself, Red started to like the boy. 'My friends call me Red, so you can call me Captain Redguard.'

'Your name's Redguard, then?' said Caradoc.

'No, it's Kearney. Redguard's my last name.'

'Then you should've just said you were Kearney!' said Caradoc. 'You really are stupid.'

The pain in Red's head was starting to die down a bit by now. He settled down with the bars to his back, and decided he may as well keep talking to the prince. After all, there was a good chance that this was the last pleasant conversation he'd have before he died. 'You're right,' he said. 'I ain't the cleverest man around. That mate of yours, Morgan, he had me fooled.'

Caradoc nodded. 'He's very clever. Sometimes I'm scared of him, but he's funny sometimes too. My dad likes him a lot.'

'Yeah, I saw that,' said Red. 'Like old mates, they were.'

'They're not mates,' said Caradoc. 'Morgan's my brother.'

Red started. 'What?'

'Well, he's like my brother, but not really,' Caradoc admitted. 'He used to live down in the city, but my dad went and found him before I was born and took him into the family.'

'Why?' asked Red.

''Cause my dad had no children and he was the last Taranisäii. He didn't want us to all be gone, so he made Morgan a Taranisäii too. His brother was my dad's best friend, but he died.'

'Oh,' said Red. That explained the "jumped-up commoner" remark, then.

'But I'm the only child here and there's nobody to talk to,' Caradoc went on. 'Except Ereska but she's too scary. She didn't want me to come here.'

'Who didn't?' said Red.

'Ereska, my griffin,' said Caradoc. 'I wanted to come look at you. She didn't want to and said I shouldn't, so I snuck away. I'm good at sneaking,' he added proudly. 'I'm like my grandma. She was the Shadow That Walks, you know, but she died before I was born.'

The boy's chatter was making Red's headache come back. But there were more important things to worry about now. Slowly, he grasped hold of the bars and pulled himself upright.

Caradoc watched him unfold to his full height with a fascinated stare. 'You're big,' he said. 'You've got such big hands an' shoulders! You're like a bear.'

Red frowned. 'I had a friend called Bear once,' he said. 'We called him that because he was so hairy. Your friend Morgan killed him. I saw it happen.'

Caradoc's eyes widened. 'You saw your friend die?'

'Yeah.' Red shuffled closer to the front of the cage, where the boy stood. 'Your friend stabbed him from behind, like a coward. Now everyone in my city thinks I did it. But I still want to go back there.'

'Why?' asked Caradoc. Nearby, the guards were already alerted.

'Because it's my home,' said Red.

He lurched forward, and thrust an arm through the bars. Too late Caradoc realised the danger, and before he could reel away a big, callused hand had caught him by the front of his best tunic.

Savagely, Red hauled the screaming prince toward him. Holding him against the bars, he took him by the throat and yelled at the two horrified guards.

'All right, one of you come here an' open this door right now! Run off or leave it shut an' I'll snap the kid's neck.'

'Help!' Caradoc shrieked.

The guards stood there, frozen.

'*Now!*' Red bellowed. 'Open the door right now! You got until the count of three!' To emphasise the point, he squeezed Caradoc's throat more tightly and began to count.

One of the guards ran over. 'All right, stop it! I'll unlock the door!'

Red loosened his grip slightly, and glared at the man. The petrified Northerner fumbled with the key, but as promised he fitted it into the lock and opened the door.

'Now back off,' said Red. 'Go back an' join your mate.'

The guard hurried back to his friend.

Once he was at a safe distance, Red let go of Caradoc with one hand and slowly reached around through the open door. Working his way around the bars, he left the cage without letting go of his hostage.

'Right,' he said once he was out in the open. 'Both of you, get in there. I mean it!'

Reluctant, but knowing they couldn't risk the prince's life, the two guards obeyed. Red snatched the key from one of them, and locked the cage door.

'Have fun losin' your jobs,' he said, and with that he threw Caradoc over his shoulder and ran.

Chapter Nine

Reunion

Caradoc had never been so frightened in his life. Even the day of his choosing by Ereska hadn't been this terrifying.

He bounced roughly on the Southerner's back as the man ran, unable to break free. Once he tried to reach for his sickle, but his captor's arm was in the way and he couldn't twist around enough to get to it.

He watched as the camp disappeared behind them both, and before long, as the forest closed in, he had lost track of where he was. Even if he got free now, he'd never find his way back.

'Help me!' he yelled. 'I'm here! The Southerner's got me!'

Red jostled him roughly. 'Shut up or I'll stuff yer mouth with leaves!'

The man's deep, growly voice was scary enough to make Caradoc stop. There was no telling what he might do; Southerners were barbarians who hated Northerners and had done all sorts of horrible things to them in the past. His father had even told him what they had done to his grandmother. She'd fought back against them, so they tortured her and then cut out her heart.

Maybe this Southerner would do the same to him. He was a Taranisäii, after all, and Taranisäiis were the biggest enemies the sun-worshippers had.

Caradoc whimpered, and tried not to cry. Princes weren't supposed to cry. *We have no tears, only ice,* he reminded himself frantically.

Red charged on through the trees, through some undergrowth and down into a gully. He kept on going up the other side, and his sheer strength and endurance terrified Caradoc. It was as if he couldn't get tired or scared, or feel pain. Even in the cage he hadn't seemed like he was in pain; he'd just looked angry.

Red stumbled up the other side of the gully and onto a hilltop. There he stopped, and risked a look back.

'Is anyone following us?' he asked harshly. 'Well?' He gave Caradoc a jab in the ribs with his shoulder when he didn't answer.

Caradoc still kept quiet. Not out of courage, though; fear had left him mute.

'Come on, you were lookin' back the whole time,' said Red. 'Did you see anyone?'

To Caradoc, the big Southerner's impatience sounded like murderous rage. 'There's no-one,' he gabbled. 'I didn't see anyone! Please can I go back? I'm scared and I want my dad, and...'

Red put him down. 'Shut it, kid,' he said. 'You'll give us away.'

Caradoc shut his mouth obediently, but his lip was trembling.

Red frowned and lifted the boy's chin with his finger. 'Stop that now, lad, I'm not gonna hurt you. Us guards got a reputation for thuggery, but I never hit a child yet an' I'm not starting now. Now listen. I'm off an' I'm not taking you with me. You can stay here.'

'No!' Caradoc burst out. 'Take me back; I don't know where this is!'

Red actually laughed. 'Go back? Yeah right. Listen, lad – you just climb up a tree an' stay there. Give out a call like griffiners do. Your partner'll find you soon enough; griffins are good at that. Now I gotta go. I'm sorry for scarin' you like this, but it was the only way to get out of there. I wasn't gonna hang about until they got around to sticking hot irons up my arse.' He gave Caradoc a gentle push toward the nearest tree, and turned to leave. 'Good luck, an' tell your dad the sun'll go cold before a Redguard lets his people down.'

He ran off through a wattle thicket like a charging boar, leaving Caradoc to fend for himself.

Alone, the prince fought down another sob and began to climb the tree. But he felt oddly comforted by the Southerner's words. He was just about safe now, and Ereska would find him easily enough as long as he got somewhere high.

Luckily the tree was a good wide one with lots of branches, and a Northerner's long fingers were perfect for climbing. Caradoc went up as far as he could, and perched on a spot near the trunk. Just to make certain, he reached up and snapped away as many twigs as he could so he had a clear view of the sky.

Then he turned his head up, and called out his own name as loudly as he could.

*

Red, running for all he was worth, heard the cry. Even in the midst of his panic-stricken flight, the sound made him smile for a moment. The poor kid would be all right. From now on it was just a question of whether Red would be all right.

So far he hadn't bothered to take much notice of direction; "away" was enough to be going on with. Now that he had put a decent amount of space between himself and his enemies, however, he slowed down a little and began to take stock. The sun was moving toward the horizon, so that had to be west. Then that meant…

Red staggered along for a few moments while he worked it out. Once he had figured out which way was South, he corrected his path and sped up again.

Even at the time, he was amazed by how far and how fast he went. But in moments of the greatest need, anyone could become faster or stronger than they had thought they could be.

The trees began to thin out, and hope soared inside him. He was going to make it!

Then he heard the sounds from overhead, and his hope turned into despair.

Even a commoner knew the sound of griffin wing-beats when he heard it. Any city dweller would.

Of course, he thought in despair. *Of course they bloody well sent bloody griffins after you, you godsdamned twit! What'd you expect?*

He started looking for hiding places, but it was already too late. Griffins had very good eyesight, and the ones chasing him had seen him. Now it was only a matter of time before they hunted him down.

Red slowed his run into a jog. No point in going as fast as he could now; they were faster than him, and he may as well keep some energy for… for whatever happened when they got to him. A fight to the death, hopefully. He had no intention of being taken alive.

Above, the wingbeats grew louder. He looked up, and saw them coming. One, two, three griffins flying in a loose flock. In a moment one of them would swoop down on him, and that would be the end of it.

A shadow fell over him, and he darted away to the shelter of the nearest tree. Maybe the branches could protect him, maybe…

He made it there, and pressed himself against the trunk. From there he looked up, expecting to see a griffin dropping out of the sky toward him.

But they weren't coming. All three of them had stayed in the sky – wait, no, there were four, he realised, but one of them was flying toward the others, and it was… enormous. The three smaller griffins must have been startled by its approach, because they were falling back, circling higher and leaving their prey forgotten.

Red took advantage of the confusion to crouch and search the ground for a weapon. He found a heavy branch and quickly broke the end off to make a crude club. It would have to do.

Above, the giant griffin had flown upward just as the others did. Before he could reach them, all three suddenly swooped at him. Red saw the outstretched talons, and realisation flashed across his mind. They were attacking!

The giant griffin kept on coming, apparently unconcerned. But when the first of the three other griffins was close enough, he struck the air hard with both wings and rushed forward and upward. The two collided, and in a moment both were falling. Red saw feathers falling away from the grappling griffins as they dropped straight toward him, and common sense finally broke past his amazement.

He turned tail, and ran.

The two smaller griffins saw him and went in pursuit, but their massive attacker wasn't finished yet. He came after them, and as the exhausted Red looked back over his shoulder he saw one of them come crashing down into the branches of a tree. It struggled there for a few moments, but he could see the blood on it and knew it wouldn't be coming after him again.

The giant griffin was already attacking the one remaining hunter, but this one had seen sense. It broke free of his talons and flew back the way it had come. The giant griffin chased it a short way, but Red soon saw it come back to circle over him.

'What in the gods' names?' he finally muttered. From the way the giant was circling directly above him it looked as if it were claiming him in some way, like a prize it had won.

Red's heart sank. That must be it. The beast had fought off the other three and so won the right to catch him and get all the credit. Griffins didn't understand loyalty – not to each other, anyway. They were more than happy to kill each other if there was some prize at stake.

When the giant griffin started to descend, he immediately decided that his fears must have been right. There was no time to run for cover now, so he planted his feet firmly and raised the stick ready to strike. It had to be the most pathetic weapon ever used to fight a griffin, but that didn't matter. He would never win, but he'd give the monster a good whack across the head before he died.

But the griffin didn't try to snatch him off the ground. Instead it braked with its wings, and landed neatly in front of him.

Red took a step back and braced himself to attack, but in that moment, face-to-face with the giant griffin, he finally recognised it.

'*You*!' he exclaimed.

The griffin regarded him through a pair of ice blue eyes. 'I do not know you, human,' it said.

But Red knew it. 'You're the one who came to talk to Arak,' he babbled. 'The dark griffin!'

The giant beast sat on his haunches. 'I am,' he said. He flicked a black-feathered wing. 'The fool would not listen.' Suddenly, he stood up again and gave an impatient rasp. 'Why am I talking to you? You are a commoner and cannot understand me.'

Red had had enough of being called stupid for one day. He lowered the stick and scowled. 'I understand you just fine, thanks.'

The dark griffin jerked slightly. 'You know griffish?'

'Yeah, I do,' said Red. He coughed nervously. Then, slowly and clumsily, he broke into griffish. 'I know griffish. I learned it from my father, who was a griffiner.'

The dark griffin shook his head slowly. 'You are not what you seem, human.'

Red relaxed slightly. The dark griffin was wild, and therefore not with the Northerners, and if he was going to attack he would have done it already. But there was something nagging at him as he looked at the giant animal. Something…

He shook himself. 'What are you doin' here? Why did you attack that lot?'

'They were Shar's griffins,' said the dark griffin. 'I am her enemy, and the enemy to all those who follow her.'

'But I ain't,' Red said hastily. 'One of hers, I mean.'

'Of course not,' said the dark griffin. 'You are a Southerner.'

'Yeah, but…' Red trailed off. 'Wait. Don't I…?' he shook his head slowly. 'No. No way. That can't really be you.'

'What are you talking about?' the dark griffin asked irritably.

But the truth had finally dawned on Red. 'Holy Gryphus,' he said.

'It's you! You're Kraego, aren't you?'

The dark griffin put his head on one side. 'How did you know my name?'

Red grinned in disbelief. 'It's me, Red! Don't you remember me?'

'Red!' said Kraego. 'But… but Red was only a youngster.'

'So were you,' said Red. 'We used to play together, remember? You put scratches all down my arms. I still got a few little scars left. Dammit, I was there when you hatched!'

Kraego brought his huge head closer, and sniffed. 'Yes,' he said slowly. 'I remember you now. Your scent has not changed.'

'Dear gods, you got big,' said Red. 'I never saw a griffin bigger.'

Kraego drew himself up proudly. 'I am as big as my father, the Mighty Skandar. Now that he is dead, I am the largest griffin in Cymria. I am the one true dark griffin, the heir to the Mighty Skandar.'

'Oh yeah?' said Red. 'I thought your sort didn't believe in that stuff. Wait, did you say your father's dead?'

'He died when I was only a chick,' said Kraego. 'Why are you here, Red? Why are you not with your people?'

'Ah, they threw me out,' said Red. 'It's a long story.' He glanced back over his shoulder. 'Actually, I gotta get goin'. That lot back there will be sendin' someone else after me pretty soon.'

'Then I will come with you,' said Kraego. 'You must tell me what has happened as we travel.'

'All right,' said Red.

The two set out walking together, and along the way Red told the giant griffin everything that had happened since the execution of the Hangman.

Kraego listened in silence. He moved quite fast for his size, and Red was more than happy to have him there. If more griffins came hunting for him, he would be the best protection possible. And, he realised, it was just good not to be alone any more. Ever since Morgan had framed him, he had been completely friendless. But now Kraego was back with him, and if a griffin could be called a friend then Kraego was one of the oldest friends he had.

'I gotta say,' he said once his story was finished, 'I never thought I'd see you again. What happened to you? How'd you end up livin' wild?'

'I chose the wild life,' Kraego said proudly. 'No human is good enough for me, and to live in their territories is stifling. I chose a life that meant I could fly wherever I wanted and do what I pleased.'

'Then why'd you come into Liranwee?' asked Red. 'You nearly got killed!'

Kraego hissed at him. 'They could not have killed me! I am too powerful to be defeated by lesser griffins. I came to your home to warn you of Shar's coming. She and her humans plan to find your nest unprepared so that they can capture it easily. I wanted to warn you and so make her attack more difficult. She is my enemy.'

'Mine, too,' said Red. He groaned. 'Argh, this is awful. It's a godsdamned disaster is what it is. Even if our lot *were* prepared, they'd still slaughter the lot of us.'

'Arak's followers deserve to be slaughtered for their stupidity,' said Kraego. 'They would not listen, and now it is too late.'

'But we gotta do something!' said Red. 'If we flew back there together, they'd listen.'

'No!' Kraego huffed. 'They do not listen to wild griffins and spies.'

'I ain't no spy,' said Red. 'But listen…' he paused, timidly. 'If… if you chose me, I'd be a griffiner an' you'd be partnered. They'd listen to us then.'

Kraego made an ugly *chark* sound. 'I, choose a human? And for the sake of some puny human nest? Never! And besides, Arak's human should be an enemy to me as much as Shar.'

'Lady Isleen?' said Red. 'Why? What'd she ever do to you?'

Kraego huffed again. 'Shar killed my father, but not in a fair fight. The Mighty Skandar was weakened by poison. Poison given to him by Arak's human. She is a liar who tried to take over the North through trickery and betrayal. That is how Shar was able to become master of that territory, not through her own strength, but through deceit!' The giant griffin screeched as his voice rose with anger.

'But what about everyone else in Liranwee?' Red persisted. 'All my friends are there, an' lots of just ordinary people who never hurt anyone. They've got to be protected.'

Kraego gave him a gentle shove with his beak. 'You are my friend, Red, and the closest thing to a brother I have had. But I am a griffin. Human lives mean nothing to me, and I would not care if every one of those living in Liranwee were slaughtered. Only Shar's defeat matters to me, and I will bring it about myself. No human can help me with this; I see that now.'

Red stared at him in disbelief. 'You can't mean that.'

Kraego chirped. 'You do not know the mind of a griffin, red-furred one. We do not care for each other – why should we care for such weak creatures as you?'

'Because…' Red trailed off. 'Because we… I mean, you're really not gonna help?'

'I will be there for the battle,' said Kraego. 'And if the time seems right I may challenge Shar. But your territory is not mine, and I will not fight for it.'

'Then do it for me,' said Red.

'Why?' said Kraego. 'You are not my human.'

Red glared at him. 'Fine. Be useless. But I'm going back. I'm gonna warn them myself, even if you won't.'

'They will not believe you,' Kraego said flatly. 'You will be killed.'

Fear chewed away inside Red, but he squared his shoulders and said, 'I don't care. Liranwee's my home an' I'd rather die than let it down.'

'Go, then,' said Kraego. 'Be a fool and die that way. But do not expect me to join you. Now I must go and hunt.'

'Wait,' Red called after him.

Kraego turned his head.

'Will you at least help me back to Liranwee?'

Kraego paused a moment. 'I will try and find you again,' he said eventually. 'But do not wait for me.'

He took off. Red stood and watched him fly away for a little while, but he soon reminded himself that he had to get going. Time was short, and he had to get to Liranwee before the Dark Lord did.

Chapter Ten

Apprehension

By the time Caradoc flew back to camp on Ereska's back, he wasn't scared any more. His partner had found him, just as Red had promised she would, and now he was with her, he was safe.

Ereska reached the camp in no time, and immediately flew to its centre where the royal tent had been pitched. The King was standing in front of it, with Shar beside him.

Ereska landed, and crouched to let Caradoc off her back. He ran to his father.

King Caedmon's face had turned pale. 'Caradoc!' he shouted. 'Are you hurt?'

Caradoc had been going to hug him, but the rage in his father's voice made him hesitate. 'No, Dad, I'm fine. I got scared but I didn't cry, and Ereska came and found me.'

Caedmon took him by the shoulder. 'What about the prisoner?'

'He ran away,' said Caradoc. 'He said he wouldn't hurt me.'

'Did Ereska save you from him?'

'No.' Caradoc stared at the ground, realising that he was in trouble, though he wasn't sure exactly why. 'He let me go and then ran away. He said to go up a tree and call Ereska, so I did.'

'He escaped because of you,' his father said stonily. 'Look at me, Caradoc Taranisäii.'

Caradoc obeyed, and his stomach went all fluttery when he saw the angry look on the King's face.

'Why did you disobey me?'

All of Caradoc's fear had come back now. 'I'm sorry, I just wanted to see what he looked like!' he babbled. 'I just wanted to *look*, because I never saw a Southerner and I wanted…'

'You went without Ereska, and put yourself in danger,' said his father. 'What did I tell you when we came here, Caradoc?'

'Dad, I—,'

'*What did I tell you?*'

'You said never go anywhere without Ereska 'cause it's dangerous,' Caradoc mumbled. He didn't dare look his father in the eye.

'But you ignored me,' said the King. 'You decided that you could go off without her, so you could go visit a dangerous prisoner. You could have died, do you understand that? He didn't have to let you go. He could have taken you with him as a hostage, and he could have done anything to you. You could have *died*. Do you understand that?'

Caradoc wanted to cry again. 'I'm sorry! I didn't mean it! I won't do it ever again, I promise!'

'But it's worse than that,' said his father. 'Because you disobeyed me the prisoner escaped, and if he makes it back home then our invasion will be in danger. Lives will be lost. Lives that could have been saved if we had been able to make our attack a surprise. Do you understand that as well? We have to do this on our own until the Empire's troops arrive – the Southerners outnumber us a hundred to one. Do you know what could happen if we're defeated?'

His voice was relentless and fierce, and every word hit Caradoc like a blow. He felt like the most worthless, stupid person in the world. Tears started to prick at his eyes. 'I'm sorry!' he wailed.

The King shook his head. 'When I told you I was going to bring you with me, I told you that this was serious. This isn't a game, Caradoc. It's war, and nothing is more serious than that. People live or die depending on what we do here. *Our* people. But we've barely even started and you've already managed to get in the way.'

Now Caradoc really did start to cry. 'I didn't mean to!'

'I shouldn't have brought you with me,' his father muttered. 'It was a mistake. I should send you back to Malvern.'

'Please!' Caradoc sobbed. 'Please don't send me back, I want to stay, please! I won't do anything wrong again, I promise!'

He felt movement behind him, and Ereska was there. 'Shar,' she said. 'I apologise. I should not have allowed my human to stray. If you allow us to stay, I will watch over him more carefully. I will not let him leave my sight again, and if I do, you may strike me for my stupidity and I will not strike back.'

Shar looked regally at her. 'That is a large promise to make. Can you be certain that your human will not make another mistake like he has today?'

'He is young,' said Ereska, moving closer and enveloping Caradoc in her protective warmth. 'And has much to learn. This conquest will be a perfect way for him to grow and become as wise as your own human.'

'And perhaps it will be a good place for you to learn and grow as well, Ereska,' Shar said meaningfully. She clicked her beak. 'I will allow you to stay, but my human must agree.'

Caedmon had listened to all this. Now he nodded, and turned to Caradoc.

'Your partner knows how to argue your case for you, that's for sure. You can stay. But only if you stay with her all the time, and listen to what she tells you.'

Caradoc, tears forgotten, nodded hastily. 'I will!'

'That's my boy.' His father's expression softened. 'Please try and understand, Caradoc. I was very frightened today. If I lost you, I don't know what I'd do. You and I are the only true Taranisäiis left. The Southerners nearly wiped us out. We can't let them succeed.'

'We won't,' said Caradoc. 'They're all bad and cruel, aren't they?'

'They're power-hungry,' said his father. 'They always have been. And they've always been our enemies. Since ancient times they've tried to make us their slaves and take everything from us. This invasion might seem cruel, but it's the only way for us. It was only a matter of time before they did the same to us.'

'Like they did before,' said Caradoc.

'Exactly. Now, let's go and have something to eat. And then we'd better get ready to go.'

'Are we leaving now?' asked Caradoc, happily following his father into the tent.

'Yes. We can't risk it if that Southerner gets back home, and we were going to set out soon anyway. If we march today, we should be able to reach the first city before they have time to prepare, even if their friend does warn them. It's just a shame that Morgan didn't manage to get any information out of him.'

Inside the tent, Caradoc helped himself to some bread and cheese. His ordeal had given him a good appetite. 'He said he'd never talk anyway.'

'The Southerner? Yes, he was impressively determined. Very loyal. I wish I had more men like him on my side. He might well have decided to die rather than tell us anything. But I suppose now we'll never know.'

*

After Kraego left him, Red kept on going without bothering about whether the griffin would be able to find him again. It didn't matter; Kraego wasn't going to help him, and getting back to Liranwee was far more important.

Red had meant to keep on at a run now he wasn't being actively chased, but in the end he realised that it wouldn't be possible. Now that he was out of immediate danger his exhaustion finally closed in on him, forcing him to slow to a kind of stumbling half-run that eventually became a walk. And even that would be too much to keep going.

His head had started to pound again, with both pain and tiredness. He fought it off for as long as he could, but in the end he saw sense. He couldn't force himself to keep going.

He checked the sky. No sign of griffins. It was probably safe to rest for a short while at least. But to be on the safe side, he kept going until he found a thick wattle bush. When he lay down under its branches he was invisible from the sky, and the bush was thick enough that he would have been difficult to spot from the ground as well.

It'd do.

Red curled up, making himself as small as possible, and dozed off.

He woke up in darkness, and his first feeling was relief. The headache had finally receded, and it would be much easier to make a proper escape of it at night. Most griffins wouldn't fly when it was dark, because very few of them could see in it. Humans were another matter, but Red felt pretty confident that he could deal with a few of those if he had to.

Feeling much better now, he crawled out from under the bush and slipped away into the shadows.

*

In the end, it took him more than a week to find his way back to Liranwee.

He took to travelling only at night, in case anyone else came after him. Once or twice he did see more griffins above, but both times he managed to hide and waited until they went away. If any humans came after him, he didn't see them, and he doubted that there were any. Griffins were the best hunters, after all.

There was almost nothing to eat along the way, and most of the time there was nothing to drink either. He had to get water from puddles and once a small stream, or even from dewy leaves early in the morning. He ate whatever berries or mushrooms he found, and eventually resorted to chewing on bits of bark just to help pretend he was eating something.

Over time, with poor nourishment, very little sleep, and fear hounding him day and night, he felt his mind starting to suffer. Toward the end of his journey, he would have been happy to just lie down somewhere and not get up again, and only the thought of the army he had seen stopped him.

When he slept, horrible visions filled his mind. He saw the Dark Lord's face glaring down at him with utter contempt, and behind him griffins and snarling Northerners ran through the streets of Liranwee, killing everyone they saw. He imagined Ranulf, and Talmon, and everyone else he knew, dying while he was out here in the middle of nowhere and unable to help them.

It was enough to wake him up even when he thought he was about to faint from exhaustion and hunger, and it drove him on even when his legs were agony and his head throbbed in time to his heartbeat.

Have to make it, he told himself, over and over. *Have to get there. Loyalty, duty, honour...*

He never saw Kraego again. Wherever the dark griffin was, he didn't care enough about his chick-hood friend to help him now.

Then, on the tenth day after his escape as he was shambling along through a stand of tall spice trees, he stepped on something hard and smooth. It shifted under his boot as he put his weight on it, and he stumbled and looked down dully.

Something shone under the leaf litter, and his heart leapt. Metal, it was metal!

He knelt and pulled the object out, and sure enough, it was his sword. Lying out in the open all this time had left it with a few spots of rust, but it was back in his hands at last, and he smiled for the first time in days.

But if his sword was here, then that meant...

Red straightened up, and looked southward. The trees gave way to an open plain, but on the other end of that was—

'Liranwee!'

Quickly, Red thrust the sword into his belt and scrabbled on over the side of the embankment at the edge of the trees. At first he thought he wouldn't be able to find it again, but as he shovelled the leaves aside his hand sank through a layer of rough cloth.

He pulled it aside, and climbed into the tunnel entrance – but had enough presence of mind to put the cloth back as well as he could once he was in.

Hidden in the cool, earth-smelling gloom, he sighed. At last, he was safe.

He didn't remember anything after that. Now that he was finally on familiar ground again his terror finally let him go, and he fell asleep on his feet, with his back resting against a soft heap of dirt.

Sleep was exactly what he needed. When he woke up he felt calmer and much more clear-headed despite the gaping void in his stomach. Food didn't matter now. He'd done it. He'd made it here before the enemy did, and that was everything.

Without further ado, he dropped onto all fours and began the slow crawl through the tunnel.

He remembered the last time he had used this tunnel, and how frightened he had been. But now, after days of being afraid of the sky, the small space felt comforting.

With the worst of his fear leaving, his mind felt clearer, and while he toiled along through the tunnel he started to think about what he would do once he reached the other side.

His first thought was to try and get into the Eyrie, but the more he thought about it the more he decided it wouldn't work. The Eyrie was always well guarded – commoners weren't allowed in without express permission. He could try disguising himself as one of the servants, but he was no Morgan, and he was too well-known. The moment any guard saw him he'd be recognised.

Come to that, there was a good chance he'd be recognised by just about anyone in the city by now. Whenever any known person was wanted for crimes as serious as his own, pictures of them would be put up in public places. And there would be rewards offered, too. By now the whole city would be on the lookout for him.

But he couldn't just let himself be arrested. If that happened he'd go straight to prison, with no chance of talking to anybody important. The only time he would get to see the Eyrie Mistress then would be when they executed him. And who in their right mind ever listened to a condemned criminal on the gallows?

Red shuddered.

No, the only chance would be if he could find a griffiner away from the Eyrie, and talk to them before the guards showed up. Maybe, just maybe, he'd be able to make them listen. He did know a few of them, after all – as a child, he'd lived among them. Since his mother had died when he was very small, some of the griffiner ladies with no families of their own had taken to mothering him and giving him little presents. No doubt one of them would be sympathetic if he introduced himself now. They might listen, if they remembered him.

The only question was where he would have the best chance of finding a griffiner outside the Eyrie. At one of the other public buildings, maybe? Or…

A grumbling pain from his stomach gave him the answer. Of course – the markets! They were supposed to be for commoners to buy their food and other items, but plenty of griffiners liked to go for a stroll through the stalls. They probably enjoyed the way the stallholders fussed over them, or just plain liked being away from the Eyrie and work for a while.

Red made his mind up. He'd go the the markets, and try to find a griffiner. At the very least he might be able to get something to eat, and the crowds would make it more difficult for anyone to spot him.

Just as well I ain't a griffiner, he thought. *They're always so damned easy to spot.*

As he wriggled through a narrow section of tunnel, his outstretched hand touched something cold. He stopped and ran his fingers over it, and his heart leapt – it was his medal!

He grinned in the darkness and wound the leather strip around his hand before he kept going. Once the tunnel widened again he stuffed the medal into his pocket, determined not to lose it again.

Getting through the tunnel was much more tiring than he remembered, and he stopped to rest several times. He dozed on a few of these rests as well; hunger had stripped away a lot of his energy.

Eventually, though, when he had begun to think it would take him the rest of the day and that he'd be forced to wait out the night, the tunnel came to an end.

He hauled himself out into the little cave, and inspected the medal while he took a breather. The feather was still attached to it, albeit broken and caked with dirt, and he could see now that the knot must have come untied when he went through the tunnel with No-Eyes. He re-tied it now, and put the medal back around his neck.

The journey had filled his pockets with soil. He scooped it out, and to his surprise he found a few coins underneath. They must have been there the whole time.

Feeling slightly uplifted by that, he climbed out of the cave and back into the little shack. It looked just the same as he remembered. He put the cover back on the tunnel entrance, just in case, and went to peer through a hole in the wall.

The sun still looked bright outside; he judged that it was about noon or just past it. Not too late, then.

Cautiously, keeping his hand close to his sword and praying that he wouldn't have to use it, he left the shack and set out into the city.

As he walked along those old familiar streets, he felt as if his heart were swelling. Could it really have stayed just as he remembered it, when he had changed so much? When *everything* was about to change? He felt as if he'd been away for months, but in all that time Liranwee had stood still, unaware of the danger.

The swelling feeling in Red's chest grew painful, and he smiled sadly. Before now he had never realised just how much he loved his home, but it reminded him of how determined he had been to save it at any cost.

Remembering that put new urgency into him, and he sped up, hurrying on out of the west side and toward the market district. Several people looked at him as he passed, but none of them seemed to recognise him. There were no threatening shouts. Maybe the hunt for him wasn't as widespread as he'd thought.

He reached the markets without incident, and the sight and sound of the bustling crowd made him feel better rather than nervous. Try as he might, he couldn't imagine these people wanting to hurt him. They were his friends and neighbours. He'd grown up among them. He was here to help them.

He ventured in among them, and his luck held. Caught up in the bustle of buying and selling, most of them were too busy to give him a second glance. Sensibly, he didn't try and hide, but strolled along as if he had a right to be there, checking the stalls he passed.

The moment he came across one selling food, he fished out some of the grubby oblong from his pocket and bought a bunch of carrots and a loaf of bread.

He gulped them down as he moved on, keeping his head up to scan the crowd for any sign of a griffin.

Please, he prayed silently. *Please, Gryphus, let me find one.*

But he had soon finished off his food without having seen anything. People were starting to give him odd looks because of his filthy clothes. It was only a matter of time before one of them recognised him.

Red put his head down, and ploughed on. His only hope now was of finding a griffiner before a guard found him. *And which,* he thought desperately, *which of those do you see more of in the markets? Gryphus help me, what was I thinking? I'm gonna get caught. I never should've come here.*

Panic started to prickle at him. Exhaustion and desperation had made him stupid. Any moment a couple of guards would come by on patrol – the markets were the best place to keep an eye out for trouble. And then he'd be caught, and it would be the end of him, and the end of Liranwee as well.

He had to get out of there. Get away and find a place to hide. He could rest a while and think of a better idea. Maybe he should've tried the Eyrie after all. Maybe—

Someone stepped on his foot.

'Watch it!' Red snapped without thinking.

The man glared at him. 'Hey, you wanna get in the way of that, go right ahead!'

'What—?' Red began, but the man had already gone on his way. Someone else pushed past him, and he suddenly noticed that they weren't the only ones coming his way. Up ahead, people were moving away from a single spot. Clearing a space for a griffin, and a human as well.

Red hissed in triumph, and ran forward. Up ahead he could already see the beast's huge beaked head rearing up out of the fleeing crowd. Nobody ever stood in a griffin's way, unless they were stupid or had no other choice.

Red was one of those in the second category, and possibly the first as well. He strode through the crowd toward the griffin, pushing people out of his way, his hopes rising higher.

Soon, he had made it out of the press and into an open space, with the griffin at the centre of it.

It was a large griffin – female and elderly, judging by the greying feathers around her face. But Red barely spared her a glance once he had laid eyes on the figure he had known would be there.

A woman in her sixties, finely clad like every griffiner, idly inspecting a pot.

Red's face split into a grin, and he made straight for her. 'Gallia!' he yelled. 'Lady Gallia!'

Immediately the griffin turned her head. Seeing the intruder, she raised her wings in a threatening gesture and hissed.

Red stopped where he was. 'Lady Gallia!'

The griffiner turned as well, and stared at him. 'Who are *you*?'

Red grinned at her. 'It's me, Red. Remember? Lord Danthirk's son? You used to call me the little Captain an' went on about how you liked my hair.'

Lady Gallia gaped. 'Kearney? You're Kearney Redguard?'

'That's me,' said Red, ignoring the gasps from the people nearby. 'Don't you remember me?'

'I do,' said Gallia. 'You're a wanted man, little Captain. What are you doing here?'

'I came lookin' for a griffiner,' said Red. 'There's somethin' I gotta tell you.'

Gallia glanced around at the crowd. 'Yes?'

'I…' Red took a step closer. 'Listen, I know this sounds loony, but I came all the way back 'cause I had t'warn you. You gotta tell Lady Isleen this. Promise me you'll tell her. I don't care what happens to me as long as you do.'

'Understood,' said Gallia. 'What is it?' She looked wary, but curious.

Red hesitated. Now that it came to it, he didn't know what to say. This was going to sound like pure insanity. But it had to be said. Throwing caution to the winds, he blurted, 'Gallia, he's come. The Dark Lord's come. I've seen him. He's come through the mountains with thousands of darkmen, an' griffins! He's comin' here to destroy Liranwee an' kill us all! You gotta warn Isleen, before it's too late!'

Gallia looked blank. 'What?'

'The Dark Lord!' Red repeated urgently. 'He's coming! Just like we always thought he would! He'll be here in a few days probably, with his army! *Tell Isleen*. I'm beggin' you.'

Gallia glanced at her partner. 'Kearney, the Dark Lord is dead. He's been dead for ten years.'

'I dunno about that or what's what, but he's comin',' said Red. 'I saw him, I talked to him. He had me prisoner, but I got away an' came back t'warn you.'

All of a sudden, he realised that the people around him were tittering.

He rounded on them. 'He's comin'!' he yelled. 'Are you all stupid? The Dark Lord's comin' to destroy Liranwee, an' the South! He'll kill you all if you don't do somethin'!'

Gallia had had enough. 'Guards!' she shouted. '*Guards!*'

Pushed to the edge of sanity by his desperation, Red didn't take his chance and run away. Instead he stood to attention, and saluted. 'Milady. I'm just a guard, an' I'm just doin' my duty. The city's in danger, an' I'm doin' what I got to to keep it safe.'

'He's mad,' said someone in the crowd. 'He's completely 'round the bend.'

'So'd you be if you'd seen what I saw!' Red shouted back. 'How'd you think this happened to my face? The Northerners had me in a cage. They beat me around the head t'try an' make me talk. They wanted to know about the defences. Don't you get it? They've come to take over!'

But nobody was listening. Gallia had already retreated to the safety of her partner's side, and the listeners in the crowd were either backing off or laughing at the madman.

Despair melted Red's insides. 'Fine, then,' he muttered. 'I've done my best. You wouldn't listen to Kraego an' you wouldn't listen to me. Maybe Kraego was right. Maybe you do deserve to get killed. But it'll be too late for me by then.'

It was already too late to escape. The commotion, and Gallia's shout, had brought guards. Two of them pushed their way past the onlookers.

Red's heart sank. 'Afternoon, lads,' he mumbled.

He couldn't bear to look either one of them in the face, but he didn't have to.

'Red,' said one of them. 'Holy gods. It's him.'

Very slowly, Red reached up and took off his medal. He threw it down at the feet of the fatter of the two guards.

'Keep it, Ranulf,' he said. 'I don't deserve it no more. I've failed everyone.'

Ranulf scooped it up, and silently put it into his pocket.

Red drew his sword, and the two guards immediately tensed, but he only threw that at Ranulf's feet as well, before slowly kneeling and putting his hands behind his head.

'I give up,' he said. 'I ain't lettin' any more guards get hurt, so just take me in.'

They both hesitated.

Red glanced up, and looked at the other of the two. 'Go on, Elthan,' he said gently. 'Your first arrest. I won't even fight back.'

Slowly, the young guard came forward. Ranulf came too, and took Red by the elbow. Elthan took the other, and clumsily manacled his wrists together.

Ranulf tugged on his arm. 'C'mon mate, get up,' he said. 'Let's go.'

Red stood up, and let them take up station on either side of him, holding him by the elbows just as a proper guard should. He could feel the stares of the crowd on him, but he couldn't bear to look.

He bowed his head as he was led away, and to his shame he felt tears wet his eyes. *Loyalty. Duty. Honour.*

They meant nothing now. He had failed, and it was all over.

Chapter Eleven

Innocent Blood

Ranulf and Elthan took Red to the prison complex without a word. Red didn't try to talk to them either, because what could he possibly say? That he was innocent? They'd never believe him. As far as they were concerned he'd killed another guard to escape, and that was all the proof they would need. He was a traitor not just to the city, but to the guards and all they stood for.

They reached the prison, and took him inside and into a room where he was searched by a couple of the wardens. They took his money and his swordbelt, and made him take off his boots so they could be checked for hidden weapons. Those were given back once he had been escorted to a cell and locked in.

Once he was alone, Red sat down and put his boots back on. That done, he looked dully around at what he knew would be the last room he ever slept in.

The cell had a bench bolted onto the wall which served as a bed, a large jar in one corner to serve as a toilet, and nothing else. The only light came from the corridor outside, and from a tiny window set way up high in one featureless wall, which let a little sunlight in. It was far too small to crawl through, too high even to look through, and they'd added some bars for good measure.

Red didn't really want to escape anyway, because what was the point? What would he have to look forward to other than a life as a fugitive in a land which would soon be overrun by Northerners anyway? Death would probably be better than a life like that.

I never had a son, he thought irrelevantly. *I never made another Redguard to carry on after me.*

Miserably, he lay down on the bench and stared up at the ceiling. Nothing to do now but wait.

Toward evening, when he heard a rattle at the door, he thought they had come to haul him off to the gallows already.

But when he went to investigate, he saw that someone had pushed a plate of food through the little slot at the bottom of the door. He picked it up, and heard a voice from outside.

'Eat up; the commander wants a word with you.'

Bewildered, Red sat down and bit into the bread and dried sausage. Surely they weren't going to listen to him now? What would Talmon want to talk about?

Then he realised what must be happening, and crumbled inside. They thought he was a spy. They must believe he had accomplices – after all, he'd been seen escaping along with someone else. That meant interrogation before he was executed.

Wonderful.

By the time they came to collect him, Red had decided he'd had enough. So when they took him into a small room where Talmon sat waiting at a table, he looked his former commander in the face and said; 'Just kill me. I'll tell you everything I know straight off, an' that's flat. So get it all down an' then just bloody well kill me, because I ain't stayin' around for you lot to go breakin' my fingers an' whatnot. Got it?'

Talmon looked slightly taken aback. But he pulled himself together quickly enough and said, 'Sit down.'

Red sat, and glared at him. 'I mean it. Just damn well kill me. I got nothin' to hide.'

'Understood.' Talmon glanced at the man sitting next to him with a pen at the ready.

'Go on, write it down,' Red told the man. '"Prisoner is pissed off but co-operative". Get it in ink.'

'That's enough,' said Talmon. 'Now.' He folded his hands on the table in front of him. 'I've been told that you've been saying things about Northerners you've seen.'

Red looked blankly at him for a moment. 'Yeah, I have,' he said slowly. 'But you all think I'm off my head.'

'Maybe,' said Talmon. 'But I want you to tell me everything about this army you've seen.'

Red was too angry at that moment to hold himself back. 'How'll you know I ain't making it up?'

'I won't, but there are a couple of reasons to think it might be true,' Talmon said calmly. 'Now tell me everything. Every detail.'

Red's heart leapt. 'Yes, sir.'

He took a deep breath, and told the whole story of everything that had happened to him since his escape from the barracks. Morgan, the Dark Lord, the army, the interrogation – everything down to the last detail. Talmon listened seriously, and beside him the record-keeper scribbled everything down.

'An' so,' Red finished, 'once I'd got clear away I knew I had to come back here an' tell the Eyrie.'

He sat back and breathed deeply. The only thing he had left out was Kraego; nobody would be pleased to hear he'd been chatting with a dark griffin. Thanks to the Mighty Skandar, a griffin like him would never be popular in the South.

'Is that everything, then?' asked Talmon.

'Yeah,' Red nodded. 'Far as I can remember it. I got beat up pretty badly, an' just about went crazy tryin' to get back here, but I did my best.'

Talmon drummed his fingers on the table. 'If it's all true, you should be getting another medal, not a death sentence. But that's not up to me. The Master of Law already decided.'

'It's true,' said Red. 'The Eyrie's got to be told. We can't have more than a few days t'get ready.'

'I understand, and I promise this'll get passed on,' said Talmon. 'The Master of Law will see it, and it'll be up to him to decide what to do with it.'

Red slumped in his chair. 'Better'n nothing, I s'pose. But what about me?'

'I'm sorry, Red, but it's out of my hands,' said Talmon. 'As I said, the Master of Law already decided what would happen to you. The order was given the day after you ran away.'

Red froze. 'What? What order?'

Talmon avoided his eye. 'The higher-ups want to make an example of you. It'll be carried out tomorrow morning.'

'But I…' Red trailed off, staring at the floor. When he looked up again, all the colour had drained out of his face. 'How?' he asked in a small, thin voice.

Talmon looked away. 'The traitor's death,' he said.

Red stood up so quickly that he knocked his chair over, and startled the two guards who had been standing over him. '*No!*' he roared. 'For the love of gods, no!'

He charged at the door, but it was locked. When the two guards grabbed him, he swung around and punched one in the face. He head-butted the other one, and ran at Talmon.

The commander of the guards had already drawn his sword. He thrust it up under Red's chin and kept it there, forcing him to stand still. The point broke his skin, and a little trickle of blood wet the rope scar left by the Hangman's noose.

Tears streamed down Red's face. 'Talmon!' he shouted. 'For pity's sake! You can't let them do this to me! I'm *innocent!*'

The two guards took him by the wrists, and twisted his arms behind his back. He lurched away from Talmon, wincing, but didn't try to fight back any more.

Talmon sheathed his sword. 'I'm sorry, Red,' he said. 'There's nothing I can do. Take him away.'

They took Red back to his cell, and shoved him through the door. He had meant to attack them again the moment they let go of his arms, but the door slammed before he could even turn around.

The moment he was alone, Red rushed over to the barred window and started to bash at it, trying desperately to break it open. But the solid iron wouldn't budge, and after a while a guard came by the door and shouted at him to stop.

Red went to the door, and slammed his fist into it. '*Let me out of here!*'

They ignored him now, but he continued to hurl himself at the door, cursing them at the top of his voice. It didn't matter that it hurt, or that he was going mad. They were feelings. His last feelings; before tomorrow when they would kill him and stop him from feeling anything, ever again.

In the end, tiredness stopped him. He let himself fall onto the floor and lay there, his back heaving. But he relished that, and the cold stone beneath him, and the pain in his ribs and arms.

It was amazing, he thought in a dim, distant kind of way, how much more everything mattered when you knew you were going to die. You never knew how precious life was until you could see its ending in front of you.

He stilled.

Slowly, he raised himself off the floor and turned to look at the window. The sun had gone now, and only faint starlight came through into the cell.

Red bowed his head, and folded his hands over his heart.

'Gryphus,' he murmured. 'I never prayed much before, but I never needed to. Please just listen to me now. You're all I got left. They say when there's no more hope, you're there at the end of it. They say you hear every true prayer. Well listen now, because this is the truest prayer I ever said.' He closed his eyes tightly, and whispered. 'Help me. I'm innocent. I never hurt nobody. Not even them Northerners. All I want is t'be a true Southerner an' protect my friends. Save me, Gryphus. Don't let it end like this. I'm beggin' you. Don't let the Dark Lord win.'

Only silence replied. No light came, no feeling of grace, no sudden courage. Only silence, in the place where there was no more hope and only death waited.

Alone, abandoned even by the gods, Red lay down on the cold floor of his cell and prepared to wait out the last night of his life.

*

Red didn't sleep at all that night. He couldn't. Whenever he started to drift off he would imagine that the door was opening, and snap awake again. If he slept, he would sleep away the last of his time in the living world. And when he died, he knew what would happen. After all, he had already died once before, just about.

He lay and stared at the wall or the ceiling or the door, and remembered the face and those icy hands that had dragged him into the darkness. *He got away, Master.*

Forced to stay awake, he finally got up and started to pace back and forth. He tried to think up something to say at the gallows, but how could he sum up all his grief and dead hopes in a few words?

I have to warn them one last time, he thought at last. *It's all I can do. If just a few of them listen, it'll be worth it.*

That made him feel slightly braver. He would go to his grave having used his last breath to serve his city, and that was as good as any man could hope for.

But he wished he could have said goodbye. To walk one last time through the streets of Liranwee, and share a last drink with his friends, and tell them how much they'd always meant to him. It would have been worth everything to him now. But nobody ever died without a few regrets.

When morning came and a pair of guards arrived to take him away, they found him standing in the corner by the window with his eyes on the shaft of pale sunlight that touched the floor. His last meal lay untouched by the door.

Red looked up at the two of them, and managed a smile. 'Morning, lads,' he said. 'I hope you got more sleep than I did.'

'Turn around and show us yer wrists,' one said by way of an answer.

Sighing, Red obeyed. Once the manacles were on, he turned around again. 'Don't worry, I'm done fightin',' he said. 'I might be out of a job but I'll always be a guard at heart, an' I won't hurt my mates.'

'…Thanks,' said the second guard.

Red had never worked in the prison before, and didn't recognise either of them. 'Listen,' he said. 'Could you do me a favour when this is over?'

'Yeah, what?' asked the second guard, suspiciously.

Red trudged along between them, following the narrow prison corridor. 'Pass on a message to Ranulf an' Elthan an' the others from the street patrol. Tell 'em… tell 'em I said I'm sorry for running off like a coward, an' I don't blame them for what happened. It was all out of our hands. None of us could've stopped it. And tell 'em I said… goodbye.'

'If I get the chance,' said the second guard.

'I'll do it,' said the first. 'I see their lot in the tavern some evenings.'

'Thanks,' said Red. 'It means a lot to me. What's your name, anyway?'

'I'm Tobin,' said the friendly guard. 'An' this here's Slone. Slow Slone, we call him.'

Red chuckled. 'I'm Kearney, but people just call me Red. I'm sorry I was a bother yesterday. Wasn't feelin' too good.'

Tobin's mouth tightened. 'I don't blame yer. I probably woulda tried the same thing.'

'Shut it, Tobe,' Slone snapped. 'No talkin' to prisoners.'

'Right, right.' Tobin looked away.

Red could have kicked Slone in that moment. 'I'm gonna come back an' haunt you for that, you miserable git,' he muttered.

Slone jabbed him in the ribs. 'You shut it too, traitor.'

Red nearly retorted that he wasn't a traitor, but he stopped himself. Why waste his time arguing with some brick-headed prison guard? His time was far too valuable now.

The little group left the prison and went out into the yard where the Hangman had died, and Red's heart quailed when he saw what waited for him there.

The gallows were still there, of course, but now other equipment had been brought up. A rack like a table, tilted to show its occupant to the crowd and fitted with iron shackles for wrists and ankles, stood near the noose. A burly, grim-looking man stood by it with a selection of huge knives and hooks hanging from his belt.

The hanging rope had been shortened, and a stool had been placed under it. The trapdoor wouldn't be used today; instead he would be let down slowly, to strangle rather than be killed immediately by a broken neck.

After that would come the rack, and the knives to open his body, and the hooks to drag out his intestines while he was still alive. If that didn't kill him, he would die when they finally tore out his heart and showed it to the crowd.

Behold the heart of the traitor!

The world spun around him. For a moment his vision blacked out, and he stumbled so badly that Slone and Tobin had to pull him upright.

He retched, and groaned. 'No. Oh gods, no.'

'C'mon,' Tobin said gently. 'Let's just get up these steps. Show how brave you are. You don't want to go yellow, do yer?'

Red pulled himself together. Going yellow to the gallows meant going like a coward, crying and pleading. But the last Redguard had to be braver than that.

He squared his shoulders. 'I ain't yellow, I'm Red.'

'That's it!' said Tobin. 'C'mon now.'

Breathing rapidly, but doing his best to hide his terror, Red climbed the steps onto the platform. *My last steps,* he thought in utter despair. *My last walk.*

Up on the platform, they made him stand by the stool where the noose dangled. He looked down at the crowd through wavering vision. There had to be at least three hundred people down there. Men, women, even children. The crowd looked even bigger than the one that had gathered to see the Hangman die. But how often did anyone get to watch a man die the traitor's death? Most of them wouldn't even care if he was guilty or not.

Red felt freezing sweat cover his back and shoulders. He had never imagined that anyone could ever be this afraid. The fear felt like a massive, living thing that had invaded his mind and body, drowning his very self under its numbing bulk. It could scarcely even be called an emotion any more. It had become so powerful in him now that it had moved away from that, and become a kind of physical force.

His senses had shut down to the point that he hadn't even noticed Lady Isleen and the Master of Law already there on the platform with him, or their partners standing by just as they had done when the Hangman had stood where he stood now.

Lord Eadion, Master of Law, came forward to speak. But Red scarcely heard him. His words came through in snatches.

'Kearney Redguard… high treason… conspiracy to assassinate… murder, resisting arrest… carried out.'

Silence fell, and Red realised that everyone was looking expectantly at him. He raised his head. 'Eh?'

'I said, do you have anything to say before the sentence is carried out?' Eadion repeated patiently.

Red looked at him, and then at the crowd. He felt close to fainting, but he knew he had to speak. It was his last chance. 'I'm innocent,' he said, and his own voice sounded so weak he could barely hear it himself. 'The Northerners are coming. The Dark Lord's coming. He's gonna destroy Liranwee. You gotta…' His former frantic urgency came back to him as he spoke, and he turned to look at Isleen. 'Eyrie Mistress!' he yelled. 'I came back to tell you that. To warn you, before it was too late! They're coming! He's coming! The city's got to prepare for war! *They're coming!*'

Isleen looked blandly at him, and turned away without a word.

'They're coming,' Red warned the crowd. 'I swear they are. You'll see. You'll see!'

A shadow passed over him as he raved on, warning them with his last breaths.

'That's enough,' Lord Eadion interrupted. 'Sentence will now be…'

He trailed off, as a shadow touched him too.

On either side of the platform, the two griffins began to hiss uneasily.

Lord Eadion looked upward, along with Isleen. Both of them

froze. Down on the ground, several people in the crowd screamed.

Red looked up too, and saw something that stabbed ice through his heart.

Griffins. Dozens and dozens of griffins dropping out of the sky, appearing through the clouds like phantoms. Every one of them had a glowing spot at its heart.

Moving as one, the flock swooped down on Liranwee. When it had come low enough, the first of them dropped the glowing spot it carried. The thing fell like a burning meteor, and landed somewhere among the buildings near the Eyrie.

Flames blasted into the air.

The crowd started to panic, but it was already too late. The burning missiles came down on Liranwee, and everywhere they hit, fire sprang up. The attacking griffins, free of their burdens, wheeled away into the sky. The city's own griffins were already flying up to attack them, and in a moment the air had become a battlefield.

Down on the platform with the smell of fire in his nostrils and the screeching of angry and frightened griffins in his ears, Red finally snapped. Looking down on the terrified crowd, he started to laugh.

'I told you so!' he shouted. '*I told you so!*' And he laughed like a lunatic.

Lord Eadion had already run to his partner's side. She let him onto her back, and took off in a flurry of wings, heading straight back toward the Eyrie. But Lady Isleen did not move. She stood stupidly on the platform, staring upward as if she couldn't believe what she was seeing. The destruction of her city had begun, and she had failed to protect it.

In all the panic, nobody paid much attention to Red any more. He sat down on the stool, ignored by the petrified Tobin and Slone, and tried to get a grip on his sanity. But just then, madness felt like the most sensible option. He'd been saved from his execution by the start of a war. Gryphus had answered his prayer after all.

A burning missile, dropped by one of the slower griffins, appeared out of the clouds and fell toward the platform. Glancing up, Red saw it, and jumped up off the stool. 'Run!' he yelled.

Tobin and Slone made a dash for it. But Lady Isleen hadn't moved.

Red ran toward her, hands still manacled behind his back. 'Get down!' he shouted, and slammed into her, hurling her off the platform.

He landed awkwardly on top of her and stayed there, shielding her with his body.

The platform exploded. Bits of burning timber flew everywhere, killing several people. Red felt the heat touch him, and some stray debris hit him, leaving spots of pain behind on his back and legs.

He rolled off Isleen and groaned when his injuries touched the ground. But he managed to lever himself upright, and knelt awkwardly by the Eyrie Mistress. 'You all right, milady?'

She sat up, wincing. 'Where's Arak?'

'Dunno, milady.'

The grey griffin darted over, visibly singed by the explosion but not badly hurt. 'Isleen!'

Red stood up again, and backed off. 'It's all right,' he said. 'You're both fine.'

Isleen leant on her partner, pale-faced with shock. 'Gryphus help us,' she said. 'I should have seen this coming. Why was I so blind?'

'You should've listened to me,' Red told her.

Isleen looked at him. 'Yes,' she said baldly. 'I should have.'

'Milady!' Two men came running. Tobin and Slone, both bleeding from cuts and grazes.

Lady Isleen's command came back to her. 'You two,' she said, pointing at Red. 'Set this man free. I hearby pardon him of all crimes.'

'Yes, milady.' Tobin removed Red's manacles. 'Looks like this is your lucky day.'

Red rubbed his wrists. 'Oh, sure. I feel like the luckiest man in the world right now.'

'That's enough.' Isleen climbed onto Arak's back. 'Go and help with the defence, all of you.'

'Right, but you make sure everyone else knows I'm free,' said Red. 'I saved your life, so it ain't much to ask, right?'

'Understood,' said Isleen. 'Now go!'

Arak flew off toward the Eyrie.

Red looked at Tobin and Slone, and shrugged. 'You heard the lady. Let's go. You'd better come with me. I don't want anyone thinkin' I'm still condemned.'

'You're not our commander,' Slone snapped.

Red straightened up. 'Actually,' he said, 'before all those lies got put about, I was made Captain. An' that outranks you, so shut up an' come with me. We've got a war on, an' there's no time for arguing about who's the boss of who.'

He sounded so completely certain that not even Slone complained any more. He fell in behind Red, along with Tobin, and the three guards ran off together into the city as if they had never been anything but a squad assigned to each other. Now, with chaos consuming the city like the fires that had broken out everywhere, the execution was miles away. Duty called.

Chapter Twelve

The End of the World

Red ran straight back to the barracks, and the dormitory. Inside he found a scene of total chaos. Guards were everywhere, pulling on armour and weapons, shouting questions and commands at each other. Not one of them looked as if they had any clear idea of what they were supposed to be doing.

Red groaned, but he knew he had to find his own gear before he dealt with them. With Tobin and Slone in tow, he went to his own bunk. It looked as if it hadn't been used, and sure enough, when he opened the chest, he found his belongings still inside.

He pulled off his lucky red tunic – now more of a lucky brown tunic – and struggled into his uniform. It fit a little more loosely than he remembered.

'Give us a moment,' he said, seeing Slone starting to look annoyed.

With his armour on he felt better. More certain. He smiled to himself as he straightened his breastplate. He was a guard again.

'Just the sword missing,' he muttered. 'Now, we'd better find Talmon an' see if he's got the first clue what's t'be done here.'

Tobin grabbed a passing guard. 'Here, you – what's goin' on?'

The guard shot him a look of mingled fear and exasperation. 'We're being attacked, stupid! What'd you think was goin' on?'

Red stepped in. 'Well done, clever britches, now tell us what we're meant to be doin' about it.'

The guard's eyes widened. 'What th— Red! You're supposed t'be dead!'

'I've just been pardoned,' said Red. 'Now what's the plan?'

'Er, well, we gotta get to the walls, double time. Talmon's probably already there.'

'Got it,' said Red. 'Let's go.'

He fell in with the guards leaving the barracks, looking around for any sign of Ranulf. His old partner was nowhere in sight, but he spotted another familiar face, and worked his way over to him.

'Elthan!'

The young guard glanced over at him, and stopped so suddenly that someone ran into him from behind. 'Red! What're you doing here?'

'My job,' said Red. 'Where's Ranulf?'

Elthan pointed accusingly at him. 'You ain't supposed to be here. You oughta be in prison!'

Red scowled. 'Actually I was meant to be cut up into little pieces by now, but when the Northerners attacked they decided I was tellin' the truth after all. Where's Ranulf?'

'Dunno,' said Elthan. His eyes narrowed. 'You shouldn't be here. We don't want you back after what you did.'

Red sighed. 'Elthan, I didn't do it. I'm not a spy, an' I didn't kill Bear.'

'Oh yeah, then who did?'

'No-Eyes did,' said Red. 'He was the real spy, an' he framed me t'get himself off the hook.'

'What, the old blind beggar?' Elthan sneered.

'He wasn't really blind, an' his real name's Morgan,' said Red. 'Look, we ain't got time for this. Let's argue later, when we don't have a gang of Northerners on the doorstep.'

He ran on, with the other guards, and managed to find Tobin again – reminding himself that it wouldn't be a good idea to go anywhere without him.

Fortunately, the other guards around him were far too distracted to be paying attention to him now. The city had turned into a nightmare.

Red ran along, smoke making his eyes and nose sting. Everywhere he saw fires devouring houses, people running in panic. Others lay by the wayside or in the street, dead or wounded. Ahead, a huge, hunched shape blocked the way, and the gang of guards parted around it like water around a rock.

Red passed close by it and saw the feathers all sticky with blood, the talons of one front paw stretched out toward him as if to ask for help. The eyes were half-open, and glazed by death.

Even as he left that sight behind him, another griffin fell out of the sky. It hit a building off to his right, and went crashing straight through the wall. He dodged away from it, and saw the wounded beast struggling to free itself from the shattered timber. But before it could recover, another griffin swooped after it and smashed it across the head with its beak. The wounded griffin went limp and died before its killer had even flown away, leaving its body hanging half-out of the broken building above a waterfall of blood.

Red's stomach lurched. Feeling close to vomiting for the second time that day, he broke into a sprint. It was only a matter of time before the enemy griffins finished off Liranwee's own griffins, and when that happened they would be free to start attacking the humans. The only place to fight back then would be the walls and the towers, with arrows and spear-launchers.

The ordinary guards had been given some basic training for a situation like this one. Red himself had been drilled in the procedure, and he remembered it now. When they reached the wall they spread out, going to different entrances that led to the parapet. Red chose the first one he saw, along with Tobin – he'd lost sight of Slone along the way.

The door in the wall led to a flight of stairs, which widened out into a room just below the parapet itself. Bows and bundles of spears waited on racks. Red grabbed a bow and a quiver of arrows, along with everyone else, and when he heard someone shout about the spears he took a bundle of those as well.

Up on the parapet the guards stationed themselves at intervals, and began to use their bows. The section where Red had emerged was already well-manned, so he kept on going. Further along, the crenelations rose higher and formed into a little roofed-in bit with tall, narrow openings in the walls. Inside it was a spear-launcher – a siege weapon that looked like a giant crossbow on a swivelling base. It could launch huge barbed spears in any direction, as long as it had a gang of men to operate it.

This one was already in use. As he reached it, Red saw the cable, as thick as his arm, slam back. The spear shot out through one of the openings in the wall, and he turned to watch it.

A griffin in flight was nearly impossible to hit, but there were enough of them in the sky that the spear hit one of them. It went clear through the beast's neck, and sent it tumbling down into the city.

I just hope it was one of theirs, Red thought.

He went on through the spear-launcher's shelter, and dumped his armload of spears with the rest that had been stacked in the corner.

Tobin did the same, and then pointed at the section of wall on the other side. 'There's a spot there for us – let's go!'

Red went on through the shelter, with a nod to the spear-launcher crew, and found a gap that needed a guard, next to where Tobin had set himself up. He took it, and unhooked the bow from his shoulder.

'Right,' he said. 'Let's just hope all that target practice was worth it, eh?'

Tobin selected an arrow. 'At least you practised,' he said gloomily. 'I don't reckon I could even hit the ground.'

Red had already notched an arrow onto his own bow. He raised it, pulled the string back, and loosed. 'You didn't practise?' he said as he pulled out another arrow.

'I'm a prison guard!' Tobin wailed. 'I didn't think I'd ever need to!'

'Then practise now!' said Red. 'It's as good a time as any!'

'Right!' said Tobin.

After that there wasn't much room for more talking. Red fought off his hunger and his desperate need to sleep, and sent arrow after arrow into the sky. If a griffin ever flew close enough he tried to aim at it, but most of the time he had to make do with just shooting at wherever they were thickest.

The griffins were quick to take advantage of the situation. As they fought on, they started trying to drive each other toward the wall and into the hail of arrows, and several of them died that way. The spear-launchers took out more, helped by their much greater range.

Before long Red's fingers were raw and blistered from the bowstring, and his hands and wrists felt like pieces of wood. He dearly wished that he had had time to put on some leather protectors to save his fingers and stop the bowstring from slapping him on the wrist every time he let go of it. But he hadn't seen any in the armoury, and now it was too late. *Just one more arrow*, he told himself, over and over. *Just one more.*

A shout finally brought him out of it. He lowered his bow and looked around to see what was happening.

'Look!' Tobin yelled.

Red followed his pointing finger, and saw his worst nightmare.

Outside the city, on the plain in front of the main gate, the Northerners were arriving. He saw them, rank after rank of armed and armoured men. Even more griffins came with them, and at the head was…

'It's him!' Red shouted. 'It's the Dark Lord!'

Even at this distance he thought he could make out the black robe flapping in the wind. The ruler of the North stood beside his partner, holding a banner with his own triple-spiral insignia on it.

Red snatched up another arrow, and aimed it at the hated figure. 'You're never gonna take this city, you son of a bitch.'

The arrow fell pathetically short. Not even the spear-launchers could shoot that far, and several did try. Nor did the army look as if it were coming any closer.

'What're they doing?' Tobin wondered.

Red pointed upward. 'Look at that – they're leavin'!'

Sure enough, the griffins that had been attacking the city were now flying out of it – rising high over the walls to avoid more arrows.

'They ain't giving up, are they?' asked the guard on Red's right.

'No,' said Red. 'No way. It's somethin' else.'

The griffins started to swoop onto the heads of the army. For a moment Red thought they were attacking it, but then he saw them rise up again with human figures in their talons.

When each griffin had picked up a human, it turned and flew back.

'They're ferrying them in!' Red exclaimed. 'They're – oh, shit. Tobin!'

'Yeah, what?' said Tobin.

Red put his bow down. 'We've gotta go. I just remembered – burn it all, if I hadn't been so wrecked I'd've thought of it yesterday!'

'Thought of what?' Tobin looked puzzled.

'How'd you think I got back into the city with everyone after me?' said Red. 'There's a tunnel! A tunnel under the city wall – an' the Northerners know about it! C'mon, we gotta get there before they do!'

'Shit!' Tobin threw his bow down as well, and ran after him.

Two other nearby guards, having heard what was going on, followed.

Red had no idea where he got his energy from, but he used it now, sprinting along the wall and down the stairs, unable to hear anyone telling him to stop. He kicked the door open and burst out into the city, where Northern soldiers were already being dropped onto the streets by their griffin allies. Red dodged them and ran helter-skelter through the city toward the west side. He didn't know or care much whether the others were keeping up. For all he knew the enemy could have started coming through the tunnel that morning. There could already be a hundred of them in the city, waiting for their signal to attack.

He cursed himself as he ran – why oh why hadn't he thought to block up the tunnel when he first came through it? The Northerners knew about it, so why in the gods' names wouldn't they use it?

A good part of the west side had caught fire. He skirted around it, and plunged on through what had been the most dangerous part of the city even before the war.

The shack up against the wall was still there. Red stopped and leant against it to rest a moment.

Tobin and the two other guards caught up, and stopped too.

'Is this it?' Tobin asked.

Red clutched at a stitch in his side. 'Yeah, it's just in here. Better get your weapons ready before we go in.'

Wishing he had a weapon too, he went in.

The tunnel entrance still had its cover on, just as he'd left it, and he sighed his relief. 'Thank Gryphus, looks like no-one's used it. But we'd better block it up just in case.'

He lifted the cover off. 'Anyone got any ideas about how to block it? We shouldn't wreck it; it might come in useful later, but we've gotta make sure nobody can get through from the other side.'

'Let's just stuff it full of rubbish,' said one of the two guards who'd followed Tobin. Red peered at him in the gloom. 'Oh, it's you, Slone. Yeah, that oughta work. But we should put something heavy on top. Somethin' like a block of stone or some bricks.'

'Rubbish should do for now,' said Tobin. 'Then we'll go tell Talmon or someone an' he'll get some lads in t'fix it up, or guard it at least.'

'Right,' said Red. He picked up an armload of garbage, and jumped down into the entrance cave with it. There he stuffed the garbage into the tunnel, packing it as tightly as he could. The others passed down more, and with their help he gradually filled the cave altogether. If anyone tried to get through from the other side they'd have a very difficult time clearing away the blockage, and might not even be able to get through at all. If they ever did make it, it would take a long time.

Red put the cover back on top. 'There!' he said. 'Thank gods we got that sorted out. Now we'd better go see what's happenin' out there. I reckon we'll have some ground troops t'fight now — it'd make a change from those bloody arrows, at least.'

'We should go to the main gates,' said Tobin. 'The bastards'll be tryin' to open them an' let their mates in, you bet your liver.'

'Good point,' said Red. 'It should be a good place t'start, anyway. I just wish I had my sword.'

He picked up a piece of wood that could stand in for now, and went back out into the city with his companions.

The Unpartnered had done their work well. By the time Red and his friends had reached the city gates, there were Northern soldiers everywhere. Half had gone to the gates, as expected, but the other half had gone to the Eyrie.

Liranwee's main gates were rarely closed, but when they were, it was by means of a huge set of wheels protected by the gatehouse.

A squad of guards was doing its best to protect the gatehouse doors, helped by others up on the ramparts with bows. The Northerners were outnumbered, but clearly well-trained — rather than trying a full-on charging assault they were hanging back, out of arrow-range, and harrying those on the ground with their own bows to try and draw them away. Unfortunately, it was working.

But the Northerners had made a mistake too: they weren't watching their backs. Red rushed up behind them, and smashed one over the head with his piece of wood. The man fell, and a moment later he and his three comrades were attacked.

'*Charge!*' Red bellowed, and slammed his wooden weapon into someone's face. It connected with an ugly crunch of breaking teeth, and he swung his arm around as he turned and knocked the sword out of another Northerner's hand.

The sword clattered onto the ground, and Red kneed the owner in the stomach hard before he could retrieve it. As the man reeled away, Red snatched up his sword.

The defenders at the gatehouse took advantage of the surprise attack, and charged.

'Drive them back!' Red yelled as he stabbed a Northerner through the shoulder. 'Push them into the archers!'

Without waiting to see if the others had heard him, he rushed toward the gatehouse. The Northerners in his way moved back to avoid his sword, and he took the opportunity to wound any who didn't move fast enough. Purely out of habit, trained into him years ago, he didn't go for the kill, but aimed to injure – slashing at arms and legs and knocking weapons away. Criminals should be taken alive whenever possible.

Around him, his fellow guards followed his command, as those who had charged from the gatehouse worked their way around to the front and began pushing the enemy into the range of the archers.

Some of the Northerners, unable to get back past their comrades, took arrows in the back and fell. Those nearer the front pushed back against the attacking Southerners, but, caught between two enemy forces, they had lost the advantage.

At the head of his fellow guards, Red swung his sword until his arm ached. He lost count of the number of enemy soldiers who fell down in front of him, but in the midst of the struggle, he soon realised that their numbers were thinning out.

'We've got them!' he shouted. 'Don't hold back!'

His friends heard him, but they didn't need encouragement. Flushed with victory, they advanced in a line and forced the Northerners away until they had backed up to the gates themselves. There, they died.

Panting, Red lowered his sword and looked for any sign of more Northerners. He didn't see any, apart from the wounded ones lying on the ground.

'We did it!' he said, not quite able to believe it. 'But we should—'

And then the world turned white.

Red felt his feet leave the ground, and an instant later something huge hit him side-on. A sound blasted into his ears, so loud it hurt, and he landed on the ground with a thud that rattled his bones.

The white turned red for an eyeblink, and then black.

He felt something cold and gritty on his cheek, and lay there in stunned silence for a while as he wondered vaguely what it might be.

Gradually, as his senses returned, he realised that he was lying on the ground. A dull pain pressed into his back, and he could hear a confusion of sounds above the ringing in his ears.

He snapped back to reality, and dragged himself up. His sword had flown out of his hand, and he groped around for it. He couldn't find it, but when he stood up and tried to work out where he was, he found another one lying abandoned not far from where he had fallen.

He picked it up, and finally took in what had happened.

The city gates had exploded. A huge hole, edged with broken wood and stone, gaped in the spot where they had been. Guards and dead Northerners had been thrown back by the force of it, and lay scattered everywhere among shattered timber and fragments of iron studs.

A single griffin stood on the other side of the hole. It wore armour that protected its head and back, but it didn't look about to attack. In fact, as Red watched, it sagged onto its chest in exhaustion. A faint glow of magic showed around its beak.

Behind it, the rest of the Dark Lord's army charged.

Red ran to help his fellow guards. Some of them had been killed by the explosion, but others were getting up. He found Tobin, cut and bleeding but alive, and hauled him to his feet.

Tobin clutched at his head. 'What…?'

'They've broken the gates!' said Red. 'They had a griffin with the right power – c'mon, we've got to try an' hold them back!'

Even then he felt like laughing at his own suggestion. Most of the few surviving guards were too hurt and confused to do anything, and when they saw the army pour in through the broken gates they either stood there stupidly and died, or tried to run and died.

Tobin pulled away from Red's hand, and ran. A moment later seeing sense, Red followed. He and Tobin were one of the few who made it away.

Behind them, the army of the North poured into the city. Hundreds upon hundreds of armed men and women, all black haired and black eyed, some wielding swords, some sickles, some spears. With them came griffins, on the ground and in the air. Some had humans beside them or on their backs, but many of them had none. They were the rest of the Unpartnered; the humanless griffins who chose to fight as one flock. They had never been defeated.

At their head was a lean and powerful red-feathered female, who wore gold and silver rings on her forelegs. Shar.

'To the Eyrie!' she screeched. 'To the masters of this territory! Come!'

On the ground, the King himself led the human fighters. 'To the Eyrie!' he echoed.

'To the Eyrie!' Red groaned as he ran. 'Tobin, c'mon! It's our only chance!'

Tobin did his best to keep pace, but he must have have guessed that it would be a futile attempt. The Northerners behind them were fresh and uninjured, and driven on by the victory they must believe would soon be theirs. Above, the Unpartnered easily pulled ahead of the two fleeing guards.

'It's no good!' Tobin yelled. 'We gotta get out of the way!' Not stopping to see if Red agreed, he dived into the first alley he passed, and disappeared.

But Red kept going. The Eyrie was the only place that would be safe now. If any of Liranwee's griffins had survived they would be in there, along with the rest of the guards under Talmon. And besides that, the Eyrie would be where Isleen and her council were, and even if the city was lost, he had to protect them.

Knowing that he couldn't very well run all the way there with the Northerners right behind him, he ducked into an alley much as Tobin had done, and followed it until it took him to a different street which also led to the Eyrie.

The only reason the Northerners didn't catch him along the way was that he knew the city better than they did, but as they spread out through its streets he had to be quick to avoid them.

In the end, he made it to the Eyrie before the bulk of the King's army, and nipped in through a door that had been battered open.

Inside, the building was curiously deserted. He saw a few other Southerners going ahead of him up the ramp, but no Northerners other than a few dead ones on the floor.

He risked taking a moment to rest while he looked around and wondered where everyone had gone. It had been a long time since he'd been inside the Eyrie, and he knew that, following griffiner custom, the more important rooms were higher up. The higher you went the more important they got, until you reached the Mistress' chambers on the top floor.

There was a good chance that Lady Isleen would be up there

now, or she might be in the Council Chamber about halfway up. Either way, he'd have to go up the ramp.

Damn.

Just as he was nerving himself to start the climb, movement caught his eye. He turned sharply, expecting to see the first of the Northerners coming, but he didn't. As he shook himself and made for the ramp, he realised that the movement had just been a tapestry on the wall. A breeze must have touched it.

Except that there wasn't any wind in the room.

Quickly, convinced he was about to get himself killed over nothing, Red nipped over to the tapestry and gave it a cautious poke. His arm pushed it straight back through the wall and into a hole on the other side.

'What the—?'

Shouts behind him made him turn, and he swore. The Northerners had caught up with him, and if he went up the ramp now they'd catch up in no time.

An instant before the first of them entered the tower, he pulled the tapestry aside and promptly fell down the stairs it had been hiding.

He landed on his face with a yelp of surprise. Shock made him stay there for a long moment, while pain slowly registered in his arm and ribs. Behind him, the tapestry fell innocently back into place.

Red heard the Northerners on the other side. Panic-stricken, he stayed sprawled on the stairs and listened. Their voices were full of horrible excitement. He could even hear the clanking of their weapons and armour. His breath froze in his throat, and he waited for one of them to find the tapestry and the stairs behind it.

But nothing happened, and he slowly pulled himself to his feet in the gloom. He was safe for now, and if he wanted to stay that way he'd better find out where this hidden passage went.

It was completely unlit, but he thought he could see light at the bottom of the stairs. He picked his way down with a hand on the wall to steady himself, until the stairs levelled out and he walked into a door. He ran his hands over it until he found a handle, and tried to use it.

The door moved a little, but then stopped as if something were blocking it. Red, aware of the sounds still coming from above, gave it a hard shove. He felt the obstruction tip over, and quickly squeezed himself through the gap he had made – immediately closing the door again once he was through.

A babble of voices filled his ears.

He turned, tensing for a fight, but relaxed again when he saw where he was.

The door had been hiding a big, stone-lined underground chamber. A few torches burned on the walls, and their light flickered over a dozen anxious faces. But they were Southern faces, and he saw immediately that they belonged to griffiners, and a few guards.

'Put the barricade back!' one of the older griffiners ordered.

Red picked up the small stone block that had been holding the door shut, and put it back in place. 'I don't think it's gonna help much,' he said. 'It didn't keep me out.'

'Maybe not, but it's all we've got,' the griffiner snapped.

'I'd put a few guards on it if I were you,' said Red. 'What're you all doing here, anyway?' He stopped, and stared. 'Lady Isleen!'

Isleen's sleeve was darkened by blood, and there was no sign of Arak. There were no griffins in the room at all. 'It's you again,' she said, by way of greeting.

Red saluted. 'That's me. Where're all the griffins?'

'Dead, mostly,' one griffiner muttered.

'Fighting,' said Isleen. 'We came down here to shelter. Griffins can't fit down the stairs.'

'Wonderful,' said Red. 'What is this place, anyway?'

Nobody looked about to reply, so he came further in and inspected one of the large stone boxes he had thought were tables. There were dozens of them, lined up neatly and filling most of the floorspace. Most of them were nothing; just simple stone rectangles with empty space inside. But others were closed, and elaborately carved. He looked briefly at one, and saw that the carving was of a life-sized person lying on the top of their box, as if they were asleep. This one was a woman with long hair. A small, stylised griffin lay under her head like a pillow.

'What *is* this?' Red wondered aloud.

'It's a tomb,' said one of his fellow guards. 'This is the griffiner crypt.'

Red immediately felt stupid. 'Oh, right. Is there another way out?'

'No.'

'Great, so we're cornered. What're you all plannin' to do next?'

'Whatever we're told,' the other guard said stoically.

Red muttered to himself, but he couldn't see much point in arguing – or in leaving, either. Going back into the Eyrie would mean walking into the enemy, and besides, he'd come to defend Isleen and her council, and they were here.

Also, he needed a rest. Actually he felt as if he could have slept for ten years, but as it was a rest would have to do.

He wandered around among the tombs, looking for a place to sit down. The empty ones looked just the right size to lie in, but he had a feeling that would be considered rude. *May as well take one anyway,* he thought despondently. *We're all gonna be dead before the day's out.*

To take his mind off things, he had a look at some of the occupied tombs. He had to admit that the carvings were beautifully done; if they hadn't been all in grey stone he'd have half expected them to get up. Every tomb had a name cut into the side – even the unoccupied ones. He even saw one with Isleen's name on it.

Now that's just horrible, he thought. *They can't be liking it much, sittin' here right next to the tombs with their names on 'em.*

At least there wasn't one with *his* name on it; frankly, he'd spent enough time recently thinking about his own death. As a commoner, though, when he died he'd be burned like everyone else who couldn't afford a fancy stone box to rot in. Not that it really mattered to him.

Moving along, he idly inspected another carving. This one was of a man, and if it was accurate he must have been burly in life. He didn't look much like a griffiner, with his square jaw and muscular shoulders. In fact he looked more like a...

As he stared at the cold stone face, Red suddenly felt as if he were falling. Dumbstruck, he moved closer and looked straight down at it, then crouched to see it in profile. Then, still not quite able to accept what he was seeing, he read the name.

DANTHIRK DANSON.

Red stood up, and took a step back. 'Dad...?' he said, in a voice that sounded small and quavering, like a little boy's.

He stumbled back into another tomb, and slid down it and onto the floor, where he sat and stared at his father's tomb.

In all this time he had rarely stopped to wonder what had happened to his body, but when he had, he'd never once imagined that it might be here, entombed as a griffiner's body should be with all the others.

This, on top of everything else that had happened that day, was too much. Red put his head into his hands, and thought of going mad again. 'Dad,' he said. 'Gryphus help me, I never…'

A shadow fell over him, and a voice came with it. 'Get up.'

Obediently, Red stood up. 'Lady Isleen.'

Isleen glared at him. She glanced at the tomb, and then took him by the chin and looked him straight in the face.

Her own face froze for an instant. 'It's you,' she said softly. 'I *knew* I recognised you! You're his, aren't you?' She let go of him, and pointed at the tomb. 'You're Danthirk's boy, aren't you?'

'Yeah.' Red nodded, wondering if he was in trouble.

Incredibly, Isleen smiled a thin little smile. 'It's been bothering me all this time,' she said. 'I kept on thinking… and in all this time I've never wondered what happened to little Kearney after his father died. I knew you inherited his money and belongings, but… well. Fancy that.'

'You're not gonna have me killed or somethin', are you?' Red asked nervously.

'What?' Isleen started. 'Of course not! It's against Cymrian law to punish a son for his father's crimes. But…' she glanced over her shoulder, and took a step closer to him. 'Listen.'

Red's nervousness grew. 'What is it, milady?'

Isleen looked troubled. 'We should have listened to you when you tried to warn us. But we didn't, and now we're paying the price. But I think there could be more to this than there seems.'

'What d'you mean?' asked Red.

'Twice now you've come to me,' said Isleen. 'The first time, you told me something I urgently needed to know. And then you saved my life. And now, even in the midst of all this chaos, you've found me again. And now I know that you and I are connected already, through your father. You travelled with the Winged Man, didn't you?'

The question caught him by surprise. 'Yeah, I did. Kullervo, his name was. We all thought he was holy.'

'He was,' Isleen said fiercely. 'Even if he didn't know it himself, he was sent by Gryphus. And he chose you to go with him. Why?'

'He didn't choose me,' said Red. 'I asked to go. What's this all about?'

'You travelled with the Winged Man,' said Isleen. 'You saw this disaster coming. You came back to us against all the odds.' She reached up, and gently ran her fingers through his hair. 'Red, like fire,' she said, in an odd, dreamy voice. 'Sacred fire. I believe that this is all a sign from Gryphus.'

Red pulled away from her, now thoroughly alarmed. 'What sign? What're you talking about?'

Isleen's expression darkened. 'Liranwee is doomed,' she said. 'No matter what we do from now on, the city will fall, and I will probably die when it does, along with my council. The Northerners won't let us live. I don't know what they'll do then, but they might well destroy the entire city and kill everyone in it. But they won't kill you.'

'Why not me?' asked Red. 'I'm a guard, an' this is my city. It's my duty to defend it, and you.'

'There's no point in that now,' said Isleen. 'And besides, there's something else I want you to do.'

Red saluted. 'I'm yours, milady.'

'Then get out of here,' said Isleen. 'Go to the other cities, and warn them. If Liranwee is conquered, ask them for help.'

'They won't believe me,' Red said flatly. 'You didn't.'

'No.' Isleen took a ring from her finger, and gave it to him. 'Take this with you. Only an Eyrie Master or Mistress can wear one. When they see it, they'll know I sent you.'

The ring was gold, with a sun embossed on it. Red put it on. 'All right, I'll try,' he said. 'But I dunno how I'll get out of here alive.'

Isleen smiled. 'From what I've seen, you have a gift when it comes to escaping. You got out of this city before without being followed, didn't you?'

Red nodded to himself as he saw what he had to do. 'Understood, milady. I'll do my best.'

'Thank you. Now you'd better go, before they find us down here.'

Red nodded formally to her, and made his way back toward the door. When he was partway there, he stopped and looked back. 'Good luck.'

'And to you too, Kearney Redguard.'

Chapter Thirteen

Red and Black

Night came to Liranwee, but it was a night without darkness. The fires that raged in the city gave it a ghastly light of its own — a light that showed anyone who saw it the fall of a city.

Griffins, given enough light to fly by, circled lazily among the columns of smoke. Most of them had come with the army, but others were natives of Liranwee. They had seen the greater power of their enemy, and had chosen to join them rather than fight them. No griffin had ever valued anything above his or her own life, and certainly not petty loyalties to mere humans.

Arak, though, was not among them. He lay at the top of the Eyrie with two of his legs shattered and his throat torn out. Shar stood over his body, and screeched her victory to the sky.

Down in the city, the Northerners ran wild, killing anyone who still tried to fight back, and helping themselves to whatever they wanted. Food, money, women — they were all spoils of war.

Inside the Eyrie, King Caedmon led others of his followers in a search for any griffiners or hostile griffins who had survived. But the hardest part was over. Liranwee was theirs.

*

Meanwhile, in a copse outside the city, Red hauled himself out of the tunnel and collapsed on the ground. Exhaustion and despair were hopelessly inadequate words to describe him now. He felt so completely and pathetically wrecked that he didn't think he even had the energy to sleep.

He fainted instead, and when he woke up some time later he could just manage to stand up. Wobbling like a baby taking its first steps, he staggered away through the trees. Liranwee was lost and he had to begin his mission, but first he needed somewhere to hide and rest.

A tired guard is a… The thought trailed off halfway through; he couldn't even remember how it was supposed to end.

The world span around him. He thought he might faint again. He stumbled into a tree, and then another one. Gods, this was hopeless.

'Are you ill?' a voice rasped.

Red gave a strangled yell, and managed to wrench his sword out of his belt. But when he turned around to look for whoever had spoken, he saw nothing. 'Great, now I've really gone mad,' he gasped.

'Perhaps, but that is not my problem,' said the voice.

Red had had enough. He sat down at the base of the tree, and dropped the sword beside him. 'Forget it,' he said. 'I've had enough. Just come kill me if you're real, and bug off if you ain't.'

'I will not kill you,' said the voice. 'I have already eaten.'

As it spoke, the shadows off to his left moved, and came to life. Red looked up, too far gone to be afraid any more, and saw a massive black shape emerge from nothingness.

'Kraego,' he croaked.

The giant griffin stood over him, and lowered his head to peer into his face. 'Red. I thought you must have died.'

Red shook his head. 'Nearly.'

Kraego looked back toward the burning city. 'Your territory is taken,' he said impassively. 'As I said it would be. Did they not listen to your warnings?'

'Not until it was too late,' said Red.

'As I warned you they would,' said Kraego. He sounded bitter, if a griffin could sound bitter. 'Shar is victorious again.'

'Yeah, an' you did nothing,' said Red.

'There was nothing I could have done, even if I had wanted to,' said Kraego. 'And nothing you could have done either, as you have seen now. But at least you escaped. What will you do now?'

Red closed his eyes. 'Go to the other cities. Warn them. Isleen sent me.'

'Alone?' said Kraego. 'And on foot?'

'If I gotta,' said Red.

'You will never make it,' said Kraego. 'I have flown to those cities; it would take you years to walk it.'

Tired anger gave Red back some energy. He gripped the tree bark and pulled himself upright. 'If it takes years, then I'll walk for years,' he growled. 'I ain't gonna give up just like that.'

Kraego eyed him. 'You are more determined than any human I have ever met. Shar has a powerful enemy here.'

'An' here, too,' said Red, pointing at Kraego. 'Why don't you help me?'

Kraego looked blank. 'What?'

'Let's go together,' said Red. 'Team up, like. Why not? We've got a common enemy. If you want t'fight Shar, but you can't with her army there, use me to bring 'em down.'

He spoke quickly, trying to get it all out before Kraego refused. 'Just think. We bring in all the armies of the South. Shar watches her followers get crushed. She loses everything. An' just then, when she's all helpless, you come in an' make your challenge. She'd die *after* seein' herself lose. Sounds like good revenge to me.'

Kraego rubbed his head with a forepaw. 'Interesting. Use your people to help destroy Shar.'

'Yeah,' said Red. 'You can take me along, 'cause you'd need a human to make other humans listen. I wouldn't be your partner; just a helper. A servant even. Remember how I brought you food an' carried you when I was a kid? It'd be like that again.'

Kraego put his head on one side. 'Yes,' he said slowly. 'This plan sounds good. I cannot sit here on my haunches and groom while Shar wins more power for herself. With your help, I could finally bring about her downfall.' He clicked his beak. 'Very well. I will carry you to the Eyries, and together, we will win.'

Red grinned. 'Perfect! But we'd better get out of here before we're found.'

Kraego crouched low, and offered him his back. 'Climb on, then, but do not pull my feathers or I will bite you.'

It had been a long time since Red had sat on a griffin's back, but he wasn't afraid. Wearily, he hauled himself up into the hollow between Kraego's neck and wings, and held on as well as he could.

Kraego straightened up, and took off with an easy flick of his wings. Red clung on as the giant griffin spiralled upward, and felt his stomach lurch at the motion. But even in that moment, he was aware of how lucky he was. For a wild griffin to carry anyone on his back like this was unheard of, and Red realised then that it went beyond even that. He had managed to win the allegiance of Kraego, the dark griffin, probably the biggest griffin in Cymria and certainly the most aloof and independent. And it didn't matter whether this counted as a real partnership or not. With Kraego he would travel faster, have the best possible protection if it came to a fight, and most importantly, anyone who saw them together would be instantly respectful. Any human who flew with a griffin so big was obviously important, and even other griffins would probably bow their heads to Kraego. He would scarcely need Isleen's ring now; any Eyrie Master would listen to him.

Finally, his luck had turned around.

Kraego turned south and passed directly over Liranwee. Red looked down from his back, and saw the disaster that had taken hold of his home. He could see the fires raging, and, faintly, he even heard the screaming of the people he had known and tried to protect.

His feeling of triumph, weak though it had been, disappeared, and a black hole in his heart replaced it. In that moment, all he could do was bow his head and remember that he had failed.

*

Kraego flew on for a good part of the night, and didn't stop until Liranwee was far behind him. He came down to land on a hillside, and Red fell off his back.

He sat up, and saw the dark griffin's blue eyes looking down at him. 'Why'd we stop?'

Kraego lay down on his belly. 'I have been using my magic, and I am tired.' He nudged Red gently with his beak. 'And you are half dead. I felt you nearly fall off me. Dead, you would be useless!'

'Yeah, true,' Red managed. 'We gonna rest here?'

'Yes.' Kraego laid his head down on his talons, and rustled his wings into a more comfortable position. 'Lie against me for warmth if you wish.'

Red obeyed, and fell asleep the moment he had laid his head against the giant griffin's flank.

But it was not good sleep. Sound, image and feeling followed him into the depths of his mind, and what made it all worse was that the sensations were not nightmares, but memories. Horrible and terrifying memories, winding around and around through his head as the trauma of all that had happened that day finally came crashing down on him.

Northeners chasing me, they're gonna catch me, no, it's griffins! Griffins after me. City's burning! But then that disappeared and he was back at the gallows, with the rope and the rack, hearing the Master of Law tell the crowd about everything he had done. And then his mind twisted the memory, so that the attack didn't come. The rope went around his neck instead, and he felt it strangling him, squeezing and wrenching while the crowd screamed, and he realised that the Master of Law was not the Master of Law, but had turned into the Hangman. The Hangman, swinging dead beside him but with his eyes still open, staring at him in hideous triumph.

Red jerked upright even as he woke up, and he heard himself give a distorted scream.

Kraego came awake in an instant, head rising. 'What is it? Are we in danger?'

Red's breathing had gone ragged, and his mouth tasted of blood. 'No. No… nothing…'

His breathing would not settle down, and as Kraego watched in bemusement, he did something that made him massively ashamed even then. He hunched down against the griffin's flank, and started to sob like a little boy.

His crying was an ugly thing. He took huge gulps of air that shook his back and shoulders as if each sob were a punch to the chest, and as they came out of him he shuddered violently. He clutched at his head and tried to make himself calm down, but he couldn't, and ridiculously, his inner voice ranted at him. *Stop it! You're not a child, you're a man! Men don't cry! Stop it, you idiot!*

But he couldn't make himself stop. Most likely he was too tired to even try.

Kraego sounded very alarmed. 'What is wrong? Are you sick?'

Red's sobs died down, and he managed to get out a few words between them. 'No – no – just – I… I'm crying. I'm sorry. Can't.' He broke down again.

Kraego curled himself around him. 'You must stop,' he said. 'We both need to sleep, and you will let enemies hear us.'

The griffin's deep voice and warm feathers were reassuring enough to calm Red down. Little by little his sobbing stopped, and he finally managed to take some deep, shaky breaths. 'Sorry,' he said. 'I'm sorry. I just couldn't… oh gods, I'm pathetic.'

Kraego put his head down again. 'I do not think you are weak, to have survived so much, but why did you do that? What does that sound mean?'

Red lay back against his friend, and made himself breathe slowly. 'It's a human thing,' he said. 'We do it when we're sad, or sometimes when we're real angry, or when we're just upset.'

'A distress call?' Kraego guessed.

'Yeah, somethin' like that.'

The giant griffin sounded curious, as he huffed softly to himself. 'Does it call to your parents to come and protect you?'

Red thought sadly of his own parents. 'Yeah, if you're a kid. Grown men ain't supposed to do it. I'm just glad nobody saw me do it except you.' He wiped the tears off his face with the edge of his tunic, and felt more embarrassed than ever.

'To show distress is a sign of weakness,' Kraego agreed. 'You must not do it again. I do not like it, and I will not carry a weak human with me.'

'Right,' Red muttered. 'I'm sorry. Let's just get some sleep.'

His tears might have been humiliating, but they had been a kind of catharsis. Afterwards when he went back to sleep, he didn't dream again.

*

On the night after the fall of Liranwee, once the fires had been subdued or put out altogether, the victorious Northerners celebrated. Every griffiner that had come with the army, and plenty of the more prominent non-griffiners, packed themselves into the Eyrie's various dining halls and enjoyed an impromptu feast.

In the largest and finest of those halls the King himself took up a table, along with his high command. He sat at the head of the table with Prince Caradoc beside him, while the griffins there spread themselves around the floor where fresh carcasses had been laid out for them.

The Master of War and his senior officers were there, along with some of the most prominent warrior griffiners from Malvern. But it was Morgan who sat at the King's right hand side. None other than Morgan, the man who had grown up in a shack in the poorest part of Malvern, and had never won the respect of anyone in the royal Eyrie.

He sat beside his adopted father, glowing with pride, and enjoyed the food brought to him by a group of humiliated Southerners. They weren't servants – or hadn't been up until that evening. But when some of the King's troops had found the Eyrie Mistress and her council hiding under the tower, they had taken them prisoner. Most of them had lost their griffins, and rather than killing them the King had decided to give them a taste of their new status.

Lady Isleen herself put a cup of expensive wine down by Morgan's elbow. He picked it up with an insolent grin at her, and drank it slowly to savour the rich flavour. He'd spent more than three months living in Liranwee as the poorest of the poor, and everything here tasted even better than it already was by comparison.

He glanced over at the King, who was busy tucking into a haunch of lamb roasted in cymran juice and honey. Caradoc sat on his left side, but he wasn't eating much. The boy looked slightly overwhelmed, and no wonder. Morgan had already privately questioned whether it was a good idea to have him here. But the King had been adamant. He wanted his son to be a warrior, and to do that he would have to learn about warfare. And learning by doing always worked best. Besides, despite the danger, Caradoc refused to be sent back.

'How is everything?' the King asked, interrupting his thoughts.

Morgan downed the rest of his drink, and waved the empty cup at Isleen until she came and refilled it for him. 'Wonderful!' he said. 'Tastes even better knowing how we got it! And how it's served, too.' He snickered.

Caedmon smiled. 'Yes – who would have thought that Southern griffiners could make such good servants? We should keep them.'

The revellers nearby laughed heartily at the suggestion, and Morgan joined in. Caedmon didn't, but he'd never laughed easily.

'What about you, then, little brother?' Morgan called over to Caradoc. 'You enjoying yourself?'

Caradoc nodded shyly. 'I wish Ceinwen was here too.'

Morgan grinned. 'Now then, you're a bit young to be worrying about that part of the celebrating!'

Caradoc, of course, didn't understand, and only said; 'She wanted to come too. She was very jealous that I got to go, but she doesn't have a griffin yet to protect her and her mother said no anyway.'

'Never fear, she'll be waiting when you get back,' said Morgan. 'And think of all the stories you'll be able to tell her! You should take her back some presents too; girls like that.'

'I will!' Caradoc nodded.

'My son did well today,' Caedmon said stoically. 'By the time this is over I think he'll be ready to join in the fighting himself.'

Caradoc pulled what he must have thought was a fierce expression. 'I want to fight! I'll kill lots of Southerners like a proper Northern warrior.'

'That's the spirit,' Morgan said with a laugh. He turned back to Caedmon. '*You* did well too, Sire. I lost count of how many Southerners I saw you kill. But I think half of them might have died anyway from fright. What with you being the Dark Lord and all.'

This time, Caedmon really did laugh. 'Yes, remember that poor idiot you brought to us? He gaped at me like a fish! Though, to be honest, I hoped it would happen. A little fear goes a long way.'

'True.' Morgan nodded seriously. 'Your cousin's legacy is important, and it'll keep helping us. Even knowing you're related to him would be enough to keep plenty of people scared.'

'But after today, what happened here will be more than enough to make it real,' said the King. 'To be honest, Morgan, all my life I've wanted something to distinguish *me*. Just being a Taranisäii isn't enough. I wanted to make my own mark on history.'

'And now you have,' said Morgan. 'And you'll keep on making that mark bigger.'

'Yes, with your help.' Caedmon hooked a dish of spiced river fish toward himself, and pushed it over to Morgan. 'Here, try some of this.'

Morgan forked some onto his plate, and took a bite. Delicious.

While he sampled the fish, Caedmon stood up. 'Quiet!' he shouted. And, when he didn't get everyone's attention right away, he shouted again, louder. 'Quiet! Everyone listen now!'

The hall went silent, and every head turned toward the King.

Caedmon inclined his own head slightly in thanks. 'Tonight we have plenty to celebrate,' he said. 'We've captured this city, and it was a great victory! We lost barely a handful of troops, and crushed all resistance in one day! They'll sing about this for centuries. Your names will go down in history.'

Cheers rose to the roof.

'But,' Caedmon went on, 'one name in particular must be honoured.' He turned, and gestured at Morgan to stand up. He did, and looked back proudly at the great lords and ladies, and the griffins too. Nearby, Echo, seeing what was going on, hurriedly left his food and came to his human's side.

'Morgan Taranisäii,' Caedmon intoned. 'My son in name if not in blood, but still my son. I took you into my family to repay everything that your brother Henwas did for me and for the North. But today you showed us that you, too, can do great things. This victory didn't come to us just because of the courage of our troops, and the good planning of our Master of War. It also came to us because of you. It's thanks to you and your incredible bravery, your cunning and your astonishing loyalty and resourcefulness, that we won so decisively today. And—,' he looked past Morgan, and bowed his head. 'And you as well, Echo.'

Shar, who had been sitting just behind her human, stood tall. 'Eck-hoo, you have done me a great service. As your human hid and used his great intelligence to help my human, so you have done the same for me. You are as cunning as a human, and as brave as a griffin should be, and so you too are honoured.'

Echo lowered his beak toward her. 'I do all that I do to dominate our enemies, and to bring more strength to you, Shar, conquerer of the Mighty Skandar.'

'Both Morgan and Echo are heroes of the North,' Caedmon resumed. 'And so, to reward them for this, I hereby give them the post of Master of Wisdom. But not merely to advise me!' he added. 'They and we know where their talents are, and they will be allowed to use them as they see fit and as I command! But now, cheer for them and show your own admiration and thanks!'

The griffiners there stamped their feet and gave shouted thanks and whoops of excitement. The griffins rasped and chirped, and snapped their beaks fiercely.

As Morgan and Echo stood there with their heads held high, Caedmon himself took a set of huge golden rings out of a bag, and snapped them closed around Echo's forelegs. Echo pecked them and hooted his pride.

As for Morgan, Caedmon honoured him with a hug.

'Now!' he said. 'Enough speeches! Let's drink!'

The revellers shouted in raucous agreement, and the drinking began in earnest.

'Thank you so much,' Morgan told the King.

Caedmon smiled at him. 'It's nothing less than what you deserve,

Morgan. I know you've never felt much at home among griffiners, even after you became one, but maybe this will help.'

'Can't hurt!' Morgan said cheerfully, and accepted another refill from a sour-faced Isleen.

Nearby, Echo and Shar fed off a pair of carcasses that had been put close together.

Echo ripped a large chunk of flesh away from the bone, and threw his head back to swallow it. 'I have won great pride today,' he said once it was safely in his stomach.

'You have earned it,' said Shar. 'But do not get above yourself.'

'I will not,' said Echo. But he felt bold enough just then to add, 'Some griffins were made to fight, and some to be powerful in other ways. I am not the largest of our kind, but I use my magic and my wits to win what I want.'

'Then they have served you well,' Shar said, clearly uninterested.

'There is one thing I have hoped for,' Echo went on. 'You know that I do not serve you out of pure loyalty. That is for humans and fools. I risked death because I hoped that you would give me something in reward.'

'So I have,' said Shar. 'Or are golden bands not enough for you, Eck-hoo?'

'They are fine and I am pleased to have them,' said Echo. 'But I had hoped for another thing.'

'Demand too much, and pay the price,' Shar warned.

'It may not be too much,' said Echo. He and Shar were speaking rapid griffish, rather than the slower, cruder form that humans could understand. Only another griffin would know what they were saying now. He risked coming closer to her, keeping his head low in submission, and raised his tail until it stood up stiffly over his hindquarters like a banner. 'You are a most beautiful female,' he purred. 'Most powerful. I have always admired you.'

Shar stood up sharply. 'So that is it!' she hissed. 'Another griffin would be happy with praise and status, but you wish to take me as well!'

'I have longed for it,' Echo admitted. His voice had gone low and rumbling — a griffin's way of sounding seductive.

For a moment, Shar looked about to attack him, but then she relaxed and chirped at him. 'You are a bold youngster.'

'Bold, and powerful!' said Echo. 'I am a fine male, worthy to mount any female!'

'You are also a fool,' said Shar. 'I have refused males twice as large as you; why do you think that you are worthy when they were not?'

Echo gave an affronted hiss. 'Size is not all that makes a male good for mating!' he said. 'I have powerful magic, and a cunning mind. My human is royal, and a high official. We have both served you well. I would give you many strong chicks.'

Shar flicked her tail-feathers across his face – a griffish signal of contempt. 'Come to me again with your tail held high when you have proven more than that,' she said. 'I demand a mighty warrior – mighty enough to defeat me. Do that, and I may accept you. Until then, retract your chick-maker or I will scar your face with my talons.'

Humiliated, Echo turned away. 'I will not forget this,' he vowed. 'One day, *you* will come to *me* with your head bowed and beg for my favour. On that day, hope that I am merciful.'

His threat was nothing more than a male's usual face-saving bragging, and Shar repaid him with a swat across the haunches. He squawked in surprise and pain, and skittered away to the other side of the hall.

Shar did not try and follow him. She returned to her food without another look in his direction, and for the rest of that night both griffins acted as if nothing had happened.

Meanwhile, at the table, Morgan celebrated. He ate until he was fit to burst, and drank until the room span lazily around him. Around him everyone else did the same. Even Caradoc had enjoyed several cups of watered-down wine.

As the night drew on, the revellers began to disperse and go in search of beds – many of them in pairs. Morgan, watching them go, remembered the old saying about how battle made men lustful. It probably did the same for women, too.

The King had retired as well, and Morgan, thinking he'd had enough to drink, decided to go onto the Eyrie roof and see the view. He wanted to remind himself of everything he had won for his adopted father that day.

His legs felt warm and a little wobbly around the knees, but he trotted up the ramps that ran around the inside of the tower, humming to himself. Echo came after him.

'How'd it go?' Morgan asked him in the happy, expansive tones of someone with half a jug of wine inside him.

'I ate well,' Echo said briefly.

Morgan grinned a little too widely. 'How'd it go with Shar? Did ye ask her for a little matin' flight?' As always when he was drunk, his old coarse accent started to come through.

'I did not ask her,' Echo snapped.

Even given how drunk he was Morgan picked up on his tone, and wisely dropped the subject. 'I'm just goin' up onto the tower-top to see the city again,' he said. 'It's ours now!'

'Yes, but you and I will not stay here long,' said Echo. 'Once the new Master is in place, we will move on.'

'Aye, the King's got t'have his advisors close by!' said Morgan. He had completely dropped his refined Eyrie voice by now. 'Imagine us!' he added. 'Master of Wisdom! Long way up from Malvern's gutters, that is.'

'You have risen high, with my help,' said Echo. 'And we will rise even higher.'

'So we will, so we will,' said Morgan. He hiccupped. A new thought occurred to him, and he immediately forgot what he had been talking about. 'I wonder what happened to that poor, stupid bastard Red? He did good, gettin' away from us. I'm bettin' he came back here, or tried to. Wonder if he made it? They would've just executed him, though, the brave sod. Too loyal by half, he was. I felt bad about turnin' on him like that, though, even if he was a Southerner.'

'He will be dead by now,' said Echo.

'Aye, probably. Hey, look, we're here!' Morgan stepped through the doorless opening to the Eyrie roof, and out into the fresh air.

Slightly fresh, anyway. The tang of smoke still hung over the city, and put a haze over the moon and stars. Morgan swaggered over to the edge of the tower, and stood recklessly close to the drop as he looked down over what he had helped to conquer.

'Fine sight,' he said. 'It'll take some rebuildin', though.'

'There will be plenty of slaves to do that work for us,' said Echo.

'Hah, yes.' Morgan cackled. 'Can ye believe the irony? Us Northerners, lordin' it over the South, an' usin' their people t'do our work for us! Just like the old days, only backward. If only more of the old guard were around t'see it. But if any of that lot complain, we'll just remind 'em where we learned about it!'

'Our territory has expanded today,' said Echo. 'Soon, it will expand even further.'

'Aye,' said Morgan. 'If the King's plan works out, which it will, in a few years the whole of Cymria will be ours. Maybe we'll even get our own Eyrie!'

'That is my hope as well,' said Echo. 'And perhaps then I will be powerful enough…' He trailed off and swished his tail over the stones in an irritable kind of way.

Luckily for him, Morgan was too tipsy to pick up on it. 'Ye an' me, Echo,' he said.

'Together,' Echo agreed.

They stood there together in silence for a while, until internal pressures gave Morgan an idea that made him smirk. Without bothering to move away for privacy's sake, he unbuttoned the front of his trousers and urinated over the edge of the Eyrie.

Echo watched him impassively. 'It is good to mark your territory,' he rumbled.

Morgan cackled as he tucked himself away again. 'That's how a real man does it, right enough. Damn I needed that, though.'

He watched the last of the fires for a while, and felt himself starting to sober up. Later on he would probably have a headache, but for now he felt sleepy and contented.

'Morgan?' A voice called from behind him.

He turned, and saw a woman emerging from the Eyrie with a griffin close behind her.

'Looking for me?' he called back.

The woman stopped for a moment when she heard him, and then came on toward him. 'There you are. Someone said you'd come this way.'

'So I did,' said Morgan. He squinted. 'Can't see you properly in this light – who are ye?'

The woman came closer, while her griffin idly sauntered off to look at the view.

'It's me,' she said, 'Lady Arwydd.'

'Oh, hello,' said Morgan. Remembering himself, he stood a little straighter and reminded himself to speak properly. 'Were you looking for me?'

'Yes.' Arwydd came to his side, and looked past him at the city.

'I'm glad the fires haven't spread,' she said.

'Of course they haven't,' said Morgan. 'Our troops knew what to do. Once the Southerners were subdued, we didn't need them any more. Can't afford to burn down *our* city, can we?'

'No.' Arwydd didn't look as if she were listening very closely. In fact, she looked rather tense.

'Why were you looking for me?' asked Morgan. 'Did the King send for me?'

'No, he's gone to bed,' said Arwydd. 'Oh, I suppose you heard that old Garnoc's going to be the Eyrie Master here?'

'Yeah, I helped decide that,' said Morgan. 'But that's not why you're here. What is it?'

'Er.' Arwydd looked away. 'I wanted to talk to you at the feast, but I was too far away.'

Morgan began to get impatient. 'Well you're talking to me now, so just say what you wanted to say.'

Arwydd looked out over the city again. 'Did you know I knew your brother?'

Morgan started a little at that. 'No – you did?'

'Yes, I knew him for just a few days.' Arwydd pointed at a stone seat that had been set up nearby. 'Let's go and sit down.'

'All right.' Morgan went to join her on the seat, intrigued now. 'When did you meet Henwas, then?'

Arwydd folded her hands in her lap. 'When Echo chose him and brought him to Malvern, I was there. The Qu – the half-breed, I mean – fell for it when he said he was just an ordinary commoner who'd just been chosen. She gave him an apprenticeship. To me. I was the Master of Gold back then, you see. At the party after his initiation ceremony, the Master of Law recognised him and he was arrested.' She looked sad. 'I was already secretly working with Lady Saeddryn – and Caedmon through her, of course. So when Echo disguised himself as Skandar and went to rescue Henwas, I helped. I never saw him again.'

'My brother was a clever man,' said Morgan. 'And a lucky one. No matter what happened he always managed to come out on top. But his luck didn't last forever.'

'No,' said Arwydd. 'But he was a great man, too. A hero. But I wish that I could have known him better. You're like him, you know. You look like him. And you're clever like him too.'

Morgan laughed. 'I'll never be half as smart as Henwas! He taught me everything I know. He hoped I'd join up with him one day, see. Be his partner in crime. But I was too young back then, and not so keen to go running off around the country.'

'But you've become great, just like he did,' said Arwydd. 'And you're a hero too. I didn't get to know him as well as I would have liked, but…' she looked down shyly. 'I want to get to know you, Morgan.'

Morgan's heart beat faster. Arwydd was one of the assistants to the Master of War, and came from a very wealthy family. She was also said to be one of the most attractive women in Malvern, and he believed it. 'You do?' he asked stupidly.

'I do,' she said. 'Very much. That is, what I wanted to say…' she blushed. 'Is that I like you.'

Morgan grinned. 'Oh yes?'

'Yes.' Arwydd shuffled her foot. 'I'd been watching you for months. I kept wishing I had the courage to talk to you, and it's only because I thought you might disappear again that I finally made myself do it.'

Morgan couldn't believe this. '*You* were nervous about talking to *me*? The jumped-up commoner? The boy the King pulled out of the gutter as a favour? *Me*?'

'It's not like that!' Arwydd exclaimed. 'You're a Taranisäii now, and… well, the truth is that you're a little bit scary.'

'Wh— *scary*?' Morgan gaped at her. 'What's so scary about me?'

'You're not like everyone else,' said Arwydd. 'You don't have an official position – or you didn't. You did your own thing and you never confided in anybody except the King, who's scary enough by himself. And the way you used to spend most of your time down in the city instead of in the Eyrie – we didn't know what you were doing, but we all knew how powerful you were. Don't think the nasty remarks in the Eyrie were made out of contempt; the truth is that most of us were nervous around you.'

Morgan couldn't contain himself any longer; he burst out laughing. 'And I thought you couldn't stand the sight of me! That's why I didn't stay around the Eyrie.' He frowned as his laughter died down.

'The truth is that I've never felt much at home around griffiners, even if I am one now. I grew up among commoners, and that's where I feel at home. Those are the kinds of people I understand. Why do you think I fitted in so well here among the Southerners? Their commoners are no different from ours.'

'Well, you don't have to waste your time with commoners any more,' Arwydd said firmly. 'You're Master of Wisdom now. Stay with us, and I'll help you make some friends. But I'm sure everyone will want to be friends with you now anyway.'

'I'm sure.' Morgan smiled at her. She really was very pretty, he thought.

Arwydd smiled back.

When the moment became awkward, she broke it by looking away. 'Where did Essh go?'

There was no sign of her partner, or Echo either.

'They flew off together.' Morgan laughed. 'Looks like Echo's going to get lucky tonight!'

Arwydd giggled. 'Essh said she thought Echo was a fine griffin. I suppose she must have really meant it.'

'We should probably wait here for them, then,' said Morgan. 'I will, anyway. I haven't found a room yet, and Echo won't be able to find me if I leave.'

'I'm not tired yet,' said Arwydd. 'It's nice here, anyway.'

They stayed on the bench together for a while, and chatted about this and that. Morgan felt himself relaxing in Arwydd's company, and enjoying her talk. She was smarter than she'd seemed.

He was trying to decide whether he should touch her, when a sudden downdraft made him look up. He saw a shadow pass between himself and the moon, and leapt to his feet. 'What the—?'

Arwydd stood too, and the pair of them watched as a massive griffin flew over their heads. It passed in front of a patch of open sky, and they saw its black shape against the stars. Then, with a flick of its wings, it flew up and away, moving beyond the city and off into the lands beyond.

'What was that?' Morgan exclaimed.

'Just a griffin,' said Arwydd. 'A very big one, mind you.'

'But it can't be one of ours!' said Morgan. 'None of our griffins are allowed to leave the city. No-one in the other territories can know about us yet.'

'None of them would bother about an Unpartnered,' Arwydd soothed.

Morgan's eyes narrowed. 'But they'd listen to the man I saw sitting on its back.'

'You could see that?'

'Yes, just for a moment, when it turned. There was definitely something on its back, and what else could it be if not a rider?'

Arwydd frowned. 'But who could it have been?'

'Maybe one of the enemy griffiners escaped, or maybe it was someone from another city. Or maybe one of our own decided to run off. Either way, the King has to be told.' Without waiting for her reply, Morgan strode away toward the entrance.

Arwydd followed. 'Surely it can wait until morning.'

'No, it can't.' Morgan turned to her. 'You stay here. Keep an eye out for anything else, and if Echo comes back tell him where I've gone.'

'All right,' said Arwydd, but Morgan caught a definite hint of disappointment in her voice.

As he went inside and darted off to find the King, he muttered his own disappointment. 'Damn them! Forget Echo; *I* could've had some company tonight!' Still, despite the lingering effects of the wine, he knew what was more important.

The King wasn't hard to find. He'd taken up residence in what had been the Eyrie Mistress' bedchamber, and the guards posted outside recognised Morgan and let him past.

Morgan knocked on the door.

'Come in!'

Caedmon was sitting up in Isleen's bed, with a lamp lit and an open book in his lap. 'Oh, hello, Morgan,' he said. 'Still celebrating, are you?'

Morgan bowed. 'No, Sire.'

'Caedmon, please.' The King gestured at a chair. 'Sit down.' He picked up the book and held it out. 'You'll love this – I found it hidden under the bed. You're in it!'

Morgan sat down. 'I am?'

'Yes.' Caedmon looked down at the pages. 'Listen to this.' He cleared his throat, and put on a nasally voice. '"*What can I do for ye now, Master Alaric?" Morgan asked with a bow. "If only I could help ye in this battle, if I weren't such a terrible coward!" Alaric smiled indulgently at him. "Don't worry, Morgan, I'll be fine. You do plenty to help me every day!"*'

Morgan choked on a laugh. 'Their Eyrie Mistress was reading

that?'

'Apparently.' Caedmon closed the book, whose cover bore the title *Alaric the Dashing and the Battle for Malvern's Freedom*. 'A bit of longing for the "good old days", by the look of it. Happy, faithful slaves and noble battles to, er, "rescue" Malvern from the dastardly Northerners. It's very badly written, of course, but what do you expect? Now, what's the matter?'

'I saw a griffiner,' said Morgan. 'Leaving the city.'

Caedmon started. 'You did? When? Do you know who they were?'

'No, I only saw a shape. I saw them fly over the Eyrie and watched them keep going on over the city and away westward. Whoever they are they're headed into Canran's lands, and if they're going to Canran then it's to betray us.'

'Damn!' Caedmon threw the book aside. 'Is that all you saw? Are you sure there was a human, if it was dark?'

Morgan nodded. 'I definitely saw a rider.'

Caedmon scratched his nose while he thought. 'This could be a problem.'

'One other thing, Sire,' said Morgan.

'Yes?'

'This griffin… whoever it was, that griffin was a giant. I've never seen one so big. Its wings were probably twice as long as my whole body.'

'I see.' Caedmon nodded once. 'This changes things. You're going to have to head out on your next mission early.'

'How early?'

'Immediately. Get yourself ready, find Echo, and fly toward Canran. Search for this griffin, whoever it is, but keep heading for Canran. If you don't find him, just go on to Canran and start work.'

'Yes, Sire. I mean, Caedmon. But—,' Morgan hesitated. 'Honestly, I'm not sure if Echo and I could handle that griffin. If it came to a fight, that is.'

Caedmon scratched his nose again. 'Fair enough. Take three other griffiners with you.'

'Who?' asked Morgan.

'Three of Cayne's men should be right. Young Eurig could do with some experience in the field. And Leolin's a good fighter. You can pick the third one yourself.'

Morgan smiled a secret little smile. He already knew who the third would be. 'I'll go and find them right away,' he said.

Caedmon, thinking the smile was for him, returned it. 'I trust you completely, Morgan. I'll see you in Canran soon enough, you can rely on that!'

'I can,' said Morgan. 'We both can. Good luck to you too, Sire.'

He left the bedchamber, but he didn't go to find Eurig or Leolin. Instead he went straight back the way he had come, back to the Eyrie roof. There he found Arwydd, waiting patiently in the cold night air.

She greeted him with a nervous smile. 'Hello. What's the news?'

Morgan grinned wickedly. 'Go and put on some warm clothes, and pack a sickle if you've got one. We're going hunting.'

Chapter Fourteen

The Chase

Red and Kraego travelled a long way during those first few days after their escape. At first determined just to put as much distance between themselves and Liranwee as possible, they headed in the general direction of Canran. Along the way they stopped at various farms and villages, where the locals were happy to provide food and shelter for what they assumed were a griffiner and his partner.

On the third night, when they had settled down in a barn, Red said, 'We're goin' to Canran, right?'

Kraego flicked his tail lazily. 'That is the nearest capital city. I know where it is; I have seen it many times before in my travels.'

'An' the others?' asked Red. 'D'you know where all the other cities are?'

'I know Canran, Withypool, Wylam, Sunton and Eagleholm,' said Kraego.

Red cocked his head. 'Eagleholm? You mean where Eagleholm used to be, right?'

'I have seen Dead Mountain,' said Kraego. 'That is what they call the place where the old Eagleholm was built. But I meant New Eagleholm, which is being built at a place near the mountains where two rivers meet. I have even been beyond it, to the island called Monag.'

Red rubbed his moustache. 'New Eagleholm,' he said. 'So they really did build it. Are Liantha and Seerae there?'

'I assume that they are,' said Kraego. 'I did not enter the city. It is not much; only a rough Eyrie and a few buildings.'

'Still, we should go there,' said Red. 'If they don't have proper walls yet, they'll need t'be warned more than anyone. I just wish I knew what the Dark Lord was plannin'.'

'I know what Shar's human means to do,' said Kraego. 'And he is not *Kraeae kran ae.*'

Red froze. 'What? How d'you know? What do you mean he's not – whatever that was you said?'

Kraego yawned. 'I was there,' he said. 'In Malvern. I was only a youngster, but I remember. It was the day I decided to leave the North. The human you called the Dark Lord is not King Arenadd, the partner to my father the Mighty Skandar.'

'Then who is he?' asked Red.

'He is Caedmon, son of *Kraeae kran ae*'s cousin Saeddryn.'

'What's this kray-kray thing, then?' asked Red.

'*Kraeae kran ae!*' Kraego snorted impatiently. 'That is our name for King Arenadd, who your people call the Dark Lord. But *Kraeae kran ae* is gone, and so is his pup, Laela. Caedmon has his throne now, and is master of the North's humans. But he does not have the dark power. He is only a mortal, and Shar is an ordinary griffin.'

'You sure?' said Red.

'I am sure!' Kraego snapped his beak. 'I told you: I was there. I was there the day Shar and her human took power. I saw the fall of Queen Laela the half-breed by the conquest of Caedmon and the treachery of Kullervo the man-griffin. Arenadd's children are dead or gone, and now the North is ruled by the son of Saeddryn.'

'Laela died, then?' said Red. Laela, the half-Southerner daughter of Arenadd, had been Queen of the North when Red was a boy.

'Yes, and left no offspring behind,' said Kraego.

'What about Kullervo?' Red's tone was urgent now – Kullervo had been a great friend to him once upon a time. 'Is he still alive?'

'I do not know,' said Kraego. 'I did not see him dead, but he disappeared when Caedmon and Shar took power. It is said he has left Cymria, if he is alive at all.'

Red sighed sadly. 'He said he'd come back one day,' he said, half to himself. 'He promised me he'd come back to Liranwee.'

'A promise he cannot keep now,' said Kraego.

'An' Caedmon?' said Red. 'You said you know what he's doin'.'

'I do,' said Kraego. 'On the day he and Shar were annointed in the Moon Temple in Malvern, Caedmon spoke to his people and told them what he would do when the time was right. He said that he would go South with his people, and make war. He said that he would capture your people's cities and make slaves of you, as your kind once did to his own. He and Shar promised that one day the dark men of the North would rule Cymria, and that the pale-haired ones like you would be their servants.'

'So it is a conquest, then,' Red mumbled. 'I knew it. They're not gonna destroy Liranwee; they're just gonna take it over.' Despite the enormity of what Kraego had told him, he felt slightly relieved. At least Liranwee wouldn't be razed. It would survive, more or less. It would still be there to save.

'They have already taken it over,' Kraego said impassively. 'As they will soon try to take over the other cities.'

'Then we'll warn them,' said Red. 'If they're ready when the Northerners come, they'll have a much harder time taking 'em over than they did with Liranwee. Places like Canran are much bigger than us, anyway. Bigger an' older, with more people an' more griffins.'

'Liranwee had never seen warfare,' Kraego agreed. 'But Canran and Wylam and Withypool survived the fighting between them, in the days before you and I were hatched. They will be much harder to capture. Shar will overreach herself if she thinks she can conquer them with only the forces of one territory. Do not despair, Red – remember that your people outnumber the dark humans, and that there are more griffins here than among the Unpartnered.'

'Yeah.' Red did indeed feel a lot better hearing that. 'When we tell Canran an' the rest, they'll help us. They might not be so friendly with us, but the Northerners are enemies to all of us. Every Southerner will want to help fight them off. But you an' I had better have a plan for how we're gonna go about this.'

'I have already thought of that,' said Kraego. 'I know the ways to fly around the South. We will fly to Canran, and after that we will go south to Wylam. From there we will go to Eagleholm, and then turn north and fly to Sunton and Withypool. From Withypool it will be a short journey to return to Liranwee. By then we will have gathered Shar's enemies, and it will be time to fight them ourselves. *Then* will be the time for me to fight Shar and defeat her, and you and I shall both have revenge.'

Red listened, and felt a savage excitement rise inside him. The armies of the South, put together, could crush Caedmon's followers easily. And Kraego could defeat Shar for certain; he was at least half as big again as she was, and much younger. He was the son of the Mighty Skandar, for gods' sakes, and everyone knew how invincible he had been.

'Sounds like a good plan to me,' he said. 'How soon 'till we get to Canran, do you reckon?'

'Not long,' said Kraego. 'I think we are in their lands already. A few more days should be enough.'

'Good,' said Red. 'Let's just hope the Eyrie Mistress takes us seriously, but I remember her being nice enough when I saw her before.'

'They will listen,' Kraego assurred him.

Red lay down on the heap of straw provided for him, and mulled things over for a while. Kraego had told him a lot that he hadn't known before, and some of it was a little difficult to take in.

So Laela was dead. He'd never met her, but he had met her brother, Kullervo. Kullervo had come South along with his partner Senneck – Kraego's mother – to negotiate a peace treaty with the Southern Eyries on behalf of his sister. Red had joined up with him when he had come to Liranwee, and had travelled to all the Eyries with him. He had only been fourteen at the time, but he'd asked to go and Kullervo had agreed out of simple kindness for the orphan boy.

Red remembered the mysterious, half-griffin shapeshifter very well. His huge size and ability to twist his shape into that of a griffin made him seem scary, and his ugliness hadn't helped. But any time spent in his company quickly showed how soft-hearted and gentle he was underneath the broken teeth and taloned hands. And now, it seemed, he was gone and probably dead.

'Wait,' said Red. 'What'd you mean about Kullervo's betrayal?'

Kraego looked up from his grooming. 'Kullervo betrayed his sister,' he said. 'He usurped her throne, and gave it to Caedmon. He ordered Malvern to surrender, and once Shar's followers had taken it, he fled and left Queen Laela to die. He also killed her partner, Oeka.'

Red gaped. 'He did what? But… Kullervo wouldn't do somethin' like that! I knew him back then, an' I never saw someone so loyal! He told me all about how Laela was his only family an' he'd never let her down. Why'd he turn on her?'

'Your Eyrie Mistress led him to it,' said Kraego. 'I saw it. Arak and his human, Isleen, persuaded Kullervo to betray his sister. They wanted to seize power in Malvern for themselves, and they tried to make Kullervo their leader. My mother agreed, and Kullervo would always do as she said. When Oeka tried to stop us, Kullervo killed her. But once Laela was betrayed, he in turn betrayed Isleen and her friends. He gave the throne to Caedmon, and drove the Southerners out of Malvern. Then he left, and my mother with him, and only I stayed behind. But I left soon afterward. I knew there would be no place for me in an Eyrie ruled by Shar.'

Red's head was spinning. 'You don't know where Kullervo went?'

'No, but if he had sense he would have left this land,' said Kraego. 'Do not think of him now. He is gone and is no use to us.'

'He just about raised you,' Red pointed out. 'Don't you care?'

'No,' said Kraego. 'Now be quiet and let me sleep. I have flown a long way today, and must do the same tomorrow.'

Red took the hint, and settled down on his own bed. He was very tired himself, but he had so much to think about now that he guessed it would keep him awake.

*

Kraego watched him for a while, but his own weariness soon made him lay his head down on his talons and close his eyes. Humans almost seemed to enjoy letting their problems keep them awake, but nobody slept easier than a griffin. Besides, Kraego was every bit as tired as he had suggested.

He drifted off in no time, sinking into the darkness that lay behind his eyes.

Outside that darkness, a shaft of moonlight fell across his beak and turned it silvery. It touched his eyes as well, and that was when the dream began.

He dreamt of an icy void, where he stood alone. Somewhere far away he thought he heard the whisperings of a thousand voices, too distant to be important. When he looked up he saw stars, glimmering faintly in the blackness.

Unafraid, he turned to look around and did not flinch when he saw utter nothingness.

And then, light came. It was white and pure, but it did nothing to dispel the darkness all around. The void simply swallowed it and gave nothing back.

Kraego turned again, and found himself face-to-face with another griffin. She was female, and unnaturally slender, but managed to look bigger and more powerful than even him. Her fur and feathers were white and silver, and one of her eyes was silver as well. The other, though, was missing. She didn't have a scar. Instead there was simply a hole in the side of her head, with blackness inside, like a portal into the void where they stood.

Kraego stared at her. 'What griffin are you?' he asked.

The white griffin's tail swished. *I am your master, Kraego.*

Her voice was not loud, but it was full of force.

'I have no master,' said Kraego.

You do, and I am that, the white griffin said sternly. *I am the one who gave you your great power, as I gave it to your father. You are my creature.*

Kraego snorted. 'My power was not given to me; I was born with it. It is mine.'

You were born with it because I willed it, said the white griffin.

'You lie,' said Kraego. 'Tell me what griffin you are.'

I am Scathach, said the white griffin. *I am the Night God. I am the god of the North, and the god of death.*

Kraego drew back. 'You! And you have appeared to me in a dream, but I know this is not a dream. Dreams are not like this. Then you are real, and not a fantasy created by humans.'

You are intelligent for a griffin, said the Night God. *Yes, I am real.*

'Then appear to me in your true shape,' said Kraego. 'I know that the Night God is human.'

Gods are not human, said the Night God. *We appear in whatever form is right. A human sees a human, and a griffin sees a griffin. Listen to me now, Kraego, son of Skandar.*

'Why?' said Kraego. 'Why should I listen?'

Because I have a command for you, said the Night God.

'I take commands from no-one, human or griffin,' Kraego said immediately.

But you will take orders from me! she hissed.

'Why should I?'

Because to follow me is to become powerful, said the Night God. *Why do you think your father became so great?*

'Because he was the mightiest of griffins,' said Kraego.

Because I made him mighty, and showed him the way to greatness, said the Night God. She came closer, and her voice took on a low, purring tone. *Do not think your hatching was for nothing, Kraego. I chose to touch another egg with my power because I knew you must come into the world. Another dark griffin, to carry my gifts. Now the time is right for me to tell you how to use these gifts.*

'I know it already,' said Kraego. 'I can use the shadows to hide and to move quickly, as my father did.'

Shadows? the Night God screeched. *Speed and invisibility? You think those are your true gifts? No!*

'I have not yet unleashed the dark power,' Kraego admitted. 'I shall when the time is right.'

The time is right, said the Night God, calming down. *You, Kraego, are the one griffin with the power to create the Shadow That Walks. To bring a single human back from death, and make an immortal of him. Create such a human and make him yours, and together you will have the power to conquer all of Cymria.*

'As my father did?' said Kraego.

As your father did. But he and his human did not go as far as I meant them to. The time to complete that quest has come. A new Shadow That Walks must rise.

Kraego thought it over. A legendary immortal, feared by all, to become his human? Tempting.

I have already chosen the one you must share your power with, said the Night God.

A vision appeared in front of him, of a tall, thin human with the barest stubble of black hair on his head.

Morgan Taranisäii, said the Night God. *Once the poorest and lowliest of humans, but a true Northerner all the same. And one of the great Taranisäii family.*

Kraego's eyes narrowed. 'You want me to find this one and give him the dark power?'

Yes. Finding him will not be hard; he is already coming after you.

'He will not catch me alone,' said Kraego.

He is not alone, but is flying with another griffin, said the Night God.

'Already partnered?' said Kraego. 'Two griffins cannot choose the same human.'

I know that, said the Night God. *When you find him, kill the lesser griffin that has claimed him. Then you must kill the human as well. He must be dead, for your power to work on him.*

'And then?' said Kraego.

Then, when Morgan Taranisäii has become the Shadow That Walks, you must return to King Caedmon and ally with him. Together, you will crush the filthy worshippers of Gryphus, and your name will be immortal.

'To have status, a griffin must choose a human,' Kraego admitted. 'And the greater the human, the greater the status. If my human were the Shadow That Walks…'

Then there would be none greater than you, said the Night God. *Even Shar, who defeated your father, would be nothing.*

Kraego slowly scratched his head with his front paw. 'I am already travelling with a human…'

Kill him, the Night God said coldly. *All Southerners must die or be vassals. You are the dark griffin; do not demean yourself by keeping company with sun-worshippers. You know that they hated your father, and will hate you as well for your black feathers.*

'They fear me,' said Kraego.

As they should, said the Night God. *Wake now, and begin your work, Kraego. Supremacy awaits you.*

As if on command, sleep slipped away from him and his eyes opened of their own accord. He raised his head and shook it dazedly, as light returned to his senses.

As his eyes adjusted, they focused on Red. The Southerner lay curled up on his side, with his face turned toward Kraego. He was asleep, with a restless frown hiding under his moustache.

Kraego's icy blue eyes were utterly impassive as he stared at Red. The human was completely helpless, so pathetically vulnerable that it felt as if a mere tap of the beak could kill him.

The void, and its master, lingered in his mind. *Make a Shadow That Walks,* his memory whispered. Or perhaps it was more than memory.

Kraego's tail began to twitch ever so slightly. Horrible ideas formed and grew in the privacy of his head. Barely audibly, he hissed to himself. 'Yeeeessss….'

*

Lady Arwydd was not enjoying herself.

She had been born and raised in Malvern, and after becoming a griffiner, she had stayed there to begin her apprenticeship. She had never travelled any great distance until joining up with the Master of War as one of his new underlings, and coming South with the army. Even then they had travelled at a fairly leisurely pace, since they had to stay with the more slow-moving ground troops.

Now, though, it was different. Now she and her companions

were alone, and they were chasing the giant griffin. And that meant speed.

It also meant sleeping on the ground every night, eating light travel rations, and spending most of each day in the air. Leolin and Eurig didn't seem to mind it too much – Leolin was an old campaigner and about as tough as an old boot, and young Eurig had joined up with him and was so eager to please his new mentor that he never once complained.

As for Morgan, he seemed to be actively enjoying the hardship, and Arwydd started to suspect he was doing it just to annoy her. He never seemed to get tired. He was the first up in the morning and the last to go to bed at night, and when he was awake and they were on the ground together he was *cheerful*. He even told jokes, damn him, and the other two laughed along with him and chattered away without paying any attention to her, or acting as if they even noticed how miserable she was.

As for Arwydd, when the first of the real unpleasantness of travelling began, she started to regret ever having flirted with Morgan. Obviously he hadn't taken her seriously at all; that was why he'd brought her along. She had thought it was because he wanted to spend more time with her, or even because he thought she might be a good fighter or resourceful or something. But now, she decided that he must have done it just to make a fool out of her. He didn't like her at all, and this was his way of teaching her a lesson.

Her hurt and resentment kept her from talking to him, and she kept to herself when they stopped to camp. They travelled fairly close to farmland, but of course they couldn't ask for shelter from Southerners. But keeping close meant that the griffins could steal livestock rather than waste time and energy hunting. As for the four griffiners, they had to make do with the dried food they had brought with them, and whatever else they could scrounge from the countryside.

Before long, Arwydd was stiff and sore in every joint and muscle, hungry, and constantly tired. The wind constantly blowing in her face while she was in the air made her eyes dry out, and tangled her hair so badly that it broke her comb when she tried to fix it. Her lips became chapped from sunburn, her face reddened and then peeled, and the harness left blisters on her palms.

Within a few days she was desperate to go back, but Essh

wouldn't let her.

'It is a matter of pride,' she said, by way of explanation. 'And I cannot miss this opportunity to catch the one that has escaped. If we succeed, it will bring us favour.'

'I don't care about favour,' Arwydd muttered, but she knew she was beaten.

Besides, Essh was far more interested in Echo. The two griffins went off together most nights, even once during the day when they had stopped to rest. Nobody remarked on it, not even the other two griffins there, but it was another source of unhappiness for Arwydd. Even her partner had lost interest in her.

After about a week of misery, she stayed up one night to watch the moonrise. The others were a little way off around the fire, either dozing or talking – she didn't care which.

Little by little the moon appeared over the treetops. It was bright tonight, and the white glow on her face made Arwydd feel better. It easily outshone the stars, and outlined the clouds around it with silver. The eye of the Night God, so people said, and tonight it was half open.

Arwydd smiled to herself. Checking that no-one was watching her, she got up and went to her bag, which she had hung from a tree. She rummaged around inside it and pulled out a small object wrapped in cloth. Holding it against her chest to keep it hidden, she crept off into the trees.

Once she was a good distance away from the camp, she found a small clearing. Bark, fallen from the pale spice-trees all about, littered the ground. She picked up a branch and, using it as a crude broom, swept it away. Soft grass showed underneath, and she sat down on it and unwrapped the thing she had brought.

Inside the cloth was a stone, about the size of her fist. It was flattened, and had a roughly triangular shape – like a shield, or a heart. It was wonderfully smooth in her hands, except where it had been carved on one side. A graceful, sinuous triple-spiral had been cut into the rock, with a circle carved around it.

Carefully, Arwydd put the stone down on the ground in front of her, where the moonlight would shine on it. Then she took the knife from her belt, and gingerly dragged it across her thumb.

She groaned at the pain, but quickly put the knife down and let the blood fall onto the stone. It hit the carving and flowed down inside it, and she began to recite the ritual words she had memorised.

'With this true Northern blood, I call to you!'

She waited until the bleeding stopped of its own accord, before she bowed her head and prayed.

'To you, who came to us from nothing, sent by the Night God's grace, I offer you my loyalty and my soul. Blessed one, heartless one, mighty Shadow That Walks, you are the master I choose. Watch over me, give me courage, help me to stand up when the whole world tries to push me down. Let me serve my people beyond life, beyond pain and beyond hope, as you did. Help me to survive this, with faith.'

She raised her head to look at the moon again, and chanted rapidly. 'Shadow That Walks, Master of Death, Dark Lord, Dark Lady, Man Without a Heart. Bless the North, bless our people, bless our King. And bless me. And...' she hesitated, and her manner became more personal. 'I know that what we're doing is dangerous. This invasion of the South won't be easy. If the King's plan fails, we could be wiped out – the whole of the North could be. So if that happens... if the danger is too much for us, then I beg you...' She hesitated again, afraid to say it. 'Return,' she blurted out. 'When we need you the most, come back to us. The ones who remember you will be there to serve you again. I swear it.'

She waited for a while in silence, and had the odd feeling that her prayer had been heard. The silence almost sounded... expectant. But what more could she say?

'We believe in you, King Arenadd,' she said impulsively. 'I believe in you. I believe that one day you'll return. I only hope that I'll be there when you do, so that I can follow you.'

She felt better after that. She imagined that the atmosphere around her felt satisfied in some way, and she felt it too.

The moon had gone behind a cloud now, so she picked up the stone and neatly wrapped it up again. She couldn't risk anyone finding it – if the existence of shadow worshippers like herself was ever discovered, accusations of heresy would quickly follow. And the priestesses of Malvern did not look kindly on heretics.

She walked back toward the camp, but just as the light from the fire had come into sight she saw someone coming toward her.

'Arwydd?' a voice called.

She stuffed the stone into her pocket. 'What?' Her voice sounded high-pitched and hopelessly guilty.

The dark shape came closer. 'There you are,' it said.

Arwydd made herself relax. 'Morgan,' she said. 'What do you want?'

'I was looking for you,' said Morgan. 'I noticed you'd wandered off somewhere. It isn't safe, Arwydd.'

'I'm fine,' she snapped. The thought that he might have caught her didn't help her to feel any more relaxed around him.

Morgan stopped. 'That's good.' Fortunately, he didn't ask her where she'd been.

Arwydd started to feel guilty. 'Well,' she said, 'I should probably go to bed.'

Neither of them moved.

'Actually, there was something else I wanted to mention,' Morgan said eventually.

Arwydd felt her heart beat faster. 'What is it?'

Morgan motioned at her to follow him. 'Not here. We don't want to wake the others up.'

Arwydd stumbled after him until he stopped a little way off. 'What did you want to tell me?'

They were standing so close now that she thought she could feel his breath on her cheek.

'We've been flying for ten days now,' Morgan said in a low voice, 'And we haven't caught so much as a glimpse of that griffin. According to the notes on our map, we'll be in Canran in a few more days. But if we haven't seen the griffin yet, I seriously doubt that we're ever going to. Maybe he's too far ahead or maybe he's gone in a different direction – either way he's given us the slip.'

'So what does that mean?' asked Arwydd.

'We'll have to revert to the original plan,' said Morgan. 'Echo and I will go on to Canran alone.'

'What about us, then?' said Arwydd.

'It's not safe for you three to stay out here,' said Morgan. 'Four are much easier to spot than one, and remember that Echo and I know how to disguise ourselves. But you'd be recognised in a heartbeat. You'll have to go back to Liranwee with the other two, and report to the King.'

Arwydd's heart sank. 'You mean we came out here for nothing?'

Morgan shrugged. 'At least I had some company. And I think

Echo was glad to have Essh along.' He grinned.

Arwydd's old desire to slap him came back. 'You mean all that travelling, nearly starving to death and getting burnt to a crisp by this horrible Southern sun was *pointless*?'

Morgan's grin disappeared. 'I thought you'd be pleased to know you're going back, since you've been sulking ever since we left.'

'I have not!' Arwydd snapped.

'Yes you have. You've been carrying on like a great, whiny baby for the last week. Gods help you if you ever have to really suffer.' Morgan's face was full of pity and disdain. 'That great clod of a guardsman I brought back to the King had three times your courage.'

Arwydd gaped at him. She wanted to throw something back at him, but she couldn't. Sheer outrage had taken her voice, along with every good retort she knew.

'Fine!' she screeched at last. 'I'm off, and good riddance! And I wish to gods I'd never tried to be nice to you in the first place!'

Morgan turned away in disgust. 'Go away, Arwydd, before you wake someone up. The dead, for instance.'

'I was right,' Arwydd flung at him. 'You really are like your brother. You're every bit the lying scumbag he was.'

With that, she stormed off. But by the time she reached the campfire her parting shot didn't feel half as clever as it had done at the time. By the time she reached her own sleeping place by Essh's flank, guilt had set in.

She curled up under the thin blanket that was her only bedding, and cried herself to sleep.

Chapter Fifteen

Canran

Nelia, Eyrie Mistress of Canran, sat alone in her garden and enjoyed the silence.

It had been a long day, full of work, and she had retreated here as she usually did when she needed to relax.

The garden had been planted at the top of the cliffside that held Canran's Eyrie, and must have taken a lot of work to create. Holes cut into the stone had been filled with good soil brought up from the valley below, and trees and other plants of all kinds grew there. Some were local plants – silver barked wattle and ghostly snow trees – but others were exotic, brought all the way from Amoran or Maijan as seeds. There was even a creeping rock vine with brilliant red flowers, said to have come all the way from Erebus. Nelia's favourite plant, however, was a squat and stunted oak tree. It had lived on the clifftop where she sat for hundreds of years, so people said – supposedly planted by the founders of Canran. Oaks weren't native to Cymria, and they were rare on the continent. They came all the way from Eire – far to the northwest, said to be the original homeland of all Southerners. Nelia sometimes wondered if any of her race were left living there, or if time had changed them so much that they didn't even look like relatives of Cymria's people at all.

Either way, the oak's bright green leaves were a pleasant contrast to the tough, waxy and greyish leaves of the spice trees that covered most of Cymria, and Nelia always felt happy when she sat on the stone bench under its branches.

So much to do, she thought. Ruling an Eyrie and a territory, even one as stunted as Canran's had become, was the hardest work she had ever known. It was just as well that there were so few griffiners left in the city; otherwise, she would probably have been assassinated and replaced by now. As it was, the others who lived in her Eyrie were generally either old, or even younger and less experienced than her. She knew she wasn't cut out to be an Eyrie Mistress, but the sad truth was that there was no-one better left. The real leaders, and the good fighters, were gone. Killed in the wars between the Eyries when she was a child, or simply gone – having defected to different rulers with better prospects.

Griffiners, Nelia thought, a little sourly. *They're as faithless and opportunistic as their partners.*

Her own partner, Lessk, wasn't with her just then. Most likely he was off flying with his new mate, or maybe he'd gone to find food. He had a huge appetite.

She didn't mind. He would have been quiet enough if he'd been there, but his absence made her enjoy her rest better. True solitude was a rare treat for an Eyrie Mistress.

She rested her head against the oak tree's rough trunk, and closed her eyes with a sigh.

'My Lady!'

Nelia's eyes opened, and she sat up at once. 'What?'

The servant who had appeared through the trees bowed hastily. 'There's someone to see you, my Lady.'

Nelia rubbed her eyes. 'Who is it? Can't Fenick see to them instead?'

'No, my Lady. They've come to see you personally. It's a messenger from Liranwee. Says he's come from Lady Isleen herself and it's urgent.'

Nelia stood up. 'Where is he?'

'Down below. Should I tell them to go to your audience chamber?'

'Yes–,' Nelia began, but she stopped herself. 'Wait. Bring them up here. I'll wait. Is Lessk around?'

'I'm not sure, my Lady. I haven't seen him.'

Nelia shook her head. 'I'll call him. Go and bring the messenger up.'

The servant bowed and left.

Once he was out of sight, Nelia went to the edge of the garden – also the edge of the cliff. Vines and other plants spilled down over the red rock face.

Nelia stood as close to the edge as she dared, and sent out a cry – screeching her own name in griffish as loudly as she could. It was an undignified thing to do, and bad for the throat – nowadays some griffiners preferred to use horns or whistles to signal to their partners. But calling like this worked perfectly well. Griffins were good at picking up the sound over long distances, and could recognise their partner's voices easily.

Nelia called five times, and went back to her seat to rest and massage her neck. If Lessk had heard her, he would come to find her soon enough. If not, she could manage without him, though it was considered rude for a partnered griffin to be absent when any outsider arrived to see him or his human. She would just have to see who got to her first.

As it happened, the messenger and his partner arrived before Lessk did. She stood up when she saw the human approaching, but nearly sat down again in shock when the griffin appeared, shouldering a pair of trees out of the way. He was so huge that the branches snapped like twigs when he pushed past them. He was also black.

Nelia's breath knotted itself in her throat. The name flew through her head like an arrow. *The Mighty Skandar!*

But she pulled herself together. This griffin clearly wasn't the notorious dark griffin. Apart from anything else, the sheen on his black feathers made it obvious that he was young, and something about the shape of his paws and legs indicated that – unbelievably – he wasn't even fully grown yet.

Dear gods, Nelia thought.

She hastily turned her attention to the human. He, at least, looked ordinary enough. He was a burly young man, broad-shouldered and powerfully muscled. His hair was a rich shade of flame orange, and he had the face of a soldier or a guard – square jawed and sensible, with a bushy moustache and a broken nose. It was a face that made Nelia feel safe, because it looked honest, even if its owner's clothes were torn and filthy and his eyes were hollow with fatigue.

The stranger bowed stiffly toward her. 'You're Lady Nelia?' His voice was deep and a little husky.

'I am,' said Nelia. 'Welcome to my garden. Please do sit down,' she added. 'You look exhausted.'

The man smiled – a weary, grateful smile that showed a couple of broken teeth. 'Thanks, milady.'

Nelia remained standing. 'Now, you'd better tell me what's going on. I've been told you came here from Liranwee?'

'Yeah, we did,' said the man. He coughed. 'Sorry, I'm a bit worn out. We ain't had much time for resting. My name's R— er, Searg— ahem.' He winced, and began again. 'Captain Kearney Redguard. Lady Isleen sent me. An' this is Kraego, my… well, my friend.'

Nelia nodded formally to Kraego, who stared back for a moment and then lay down to groom his wings.

'Lady Isleen, you say?' said Nelia, turning back to the black griffin's partner. She frowned. 'Why would she send you? You say you're a Captain?'

'More or less,' he admitted.

'Not a Lord?' said Nelia. 'And you're in this state… what's happened? Why would Isleen choose you to come here and not a diplomat?'

'I ain't no dipplowhatsit,' the Captain said brusquely. 'I'm a guard. An' if you don't believe I came from Isleen, here.' He took a ring from his finger, and held it out.

Nelia breathed in sharply when she saw it. 'Why would she give you that?'

'Proof,' said the Captain, putting it back on. 'I was the only one left. By the time Isleen gave me this, there wasn't anyone else left to send. They'd all lost their partners, one way or another. That or they were just dead.'

Nelia froze. 'What? What happened? Tell me everything.'

Lessk arrived at that moment, landing roughly close to his partner. 'What is this?' he rasped. He looked sharply at Kraego. 'What griffin are you?'

Kraego inclined his head toward him. 'I am Kraego. I have come as a messenger, with this human.'

Lessk hissed. 'Bow to me, black-feathers. I am master of this territory.'

For a moment it looked as if Kraego wouldn't lower himself to make a show of respect, but he finally bent his forelegs and bowed his head to the other male. 'I come in peace, without designs on your food, your females or your territory,' he recited in a bored voice.

'Better,' said Lessk. Mollified, he looked at Nelia. 'Messengers? What message have they brought?'

'Captain Redguard here was about to tell me,' said Nelia. 'Please continue, Captain.'

*

Red stood up politely. Then, briefly and brusquely, he told them everything that had happened. Nelia and Lessk listened closely, and as he talked he saw the look of horror appear on the Eyrie Mistress' face. Even Lessk began to hiss and huff in alarm.

'Enemies!' he finally said. 'What griffin leads these unpartnered scum?'

'Shar,' said Kraego, speaking for the first time since Red had begun.

Lessk looked at him. 'Female?'

'Female, and red feathered,' said Kraego. 'She fought the Mighty Skandar and killed him. Now she rules the North, with her human.'

'They've taken Liranwee,' Red concluded. 'And they'll be here soon enough t'do the same, you take my word for it. They want the whole South.'

'But surely they can't do that,' said Nelia. 'There aren't enough of them.'

'Not if the Eyries band together,' said Red. 'In the meantime, I came t'warn you. Get your people armed, prepare for a siege, do whatever you can, before it's too late!'

'I understand,' Nelia said gravely. 'And thank you. I'll summon my council immediately. Both of you are welcome to stay here for as long as you need to, and you'll be given food, fresh clothes… whatever you need.'

'We've got t'move on soon, to warn the other Eyries,' said Red. 'But we'll stay a while, and thank you.'

Nelia smiled. 'You've obviously come a long way, and had a hard time. This is the least I can do for both of you.'

'You can stay,' Lessk agreed.

'One other thing,' said Red. 'The Northerners gave themselves an advantage by plantin' a spy in our city. Chances are, they've planted one here too. I'd watch out for that if I were you.'

'I'll speak to the Master of Law about it,' said Nelia.

Red had said all he had to say, and he settled for a polite smile and a bow in her direction. Relief made him feel lighter inside. After so much suspicion and so many closed ears, Lady Nelia's willingness to listen – and more importantly, to take action – made him so grateful toward her that he just about wanted to give her a hug.

He didn't, of course. Instead, he went back down into the entrance that had been cut into the clifftop, and into the Eyrie below, where there were plenty of spare rooms. One had already been prepared for himself and Kraego, and some thoughtful servant had even filled a bath.

Red stripped off his dirt encrusted clothes and climbed into it without minding that Kraego could see him. What would a griffin care?

The hot water felt like paradise. He settled down into it and sighed beatifically.

Kraego lay down on his belly nearby. 'We have done good work today. But this is a small Eyrie now, and there are so few griffins. The Southern wars have hit them harder than I thought.'

Red didn't want to think about that just now. 'They'll be fine,' he said. 'They'll sort themselves out. Our job's done.'

'True,' said Kraego. He yawned widely. 'We will enjoy some food and rest before we go on, and be glad for it!'

'You can say that again,' said Red, and lapsed into a blissful silence.

*

When Morgan saw Canran for the first time, he was awestruck.

He knew what the city was like, of course – anyone who studied the cities of the South, as he had done, found out soon enough. But actually seeing what made Canran unique was something no amount of descriptions or even drawings could replicate.

Canran was sometimes called the Stone City or the Cliff City, and no wonder. It had been built in a spot where the Northgate Mountains curved around in line with the coast. Here, where mountains gave way to foothills and then plains, something had made the side of a mountain collapse. It had created an enormous cliff face of dark red stone, and a rounded valley below.

The fallen stone had been used to build the city itself, and there must have been a lot of it. Morgan couldn't see a single building of consequence that was made from wood. Burning this lot would never work, which was why Liranwee's strategy wouldn't be reused here.

Above the city was the Eyrie itself, and it was not made from fallen stone. At first glance it looked as if there *was* no Eyrie – only the massive cliff face rising up over the city, so sheer it could never be climbed. But Morgan knew better than that, even before he came close enough to see the openings cut into the rock. The Eyrie *was* the cliff. It had been carved into it, room by room. The books Morgan had read had warned him that not only could the Eyrie not be burned, but it couldn't be broken either. The openings all led to passages; none led directly into chambers or any kind of large space. Trying to attack the Eyrie with siege weapons would do nothing.

He explained all this to Echo, while they perched together in a tree and inspected the place from a safe distance.

'All of it built by us,' he added. 'All that carving out of the cliff, all the insanely dangerous perching on a rock face — all done by Northerners. Every last chisel mark. They say a hundred of us died making that Eyrie.'

Even Echo looked impressed. 'Every day I think I have seen all that humans can do, but every day I am surprised. Your magic is far more powerful than ours can ever be.'

Morgan cast a sideways glance at the spotted griffin. 'It's not magic; just hard work.'

Echo ignored him. 'Our powers are used to destroy. To burn, to break, to kill. Only humans have the power to create. That is why you are stronger than us.'

'Your power doesn't destroy,' said Morgan.

Echo snorted. 'My power allows me to wear a false skin, and use it to deceive my enemies so that I can kill them more easily. It cannot make something like this.'

Morgan was far too practised at self-control to let his astonishment show. He couldn't think of anything to say in reply to that, so he settled for, 'This city was made by Northern hands, and now it's time to take back what's ours. Are you ready?'

Echo shook his head in a quick rolling motion, like a dog drying itself off. 'I am.'

'Good. Have you decided where you're going to go?'

Echo pointed his beak toward the Eyrie. 'I will go into the mountains. When you give me your signal, I will go to meet the Unpartnered.'

'We'd better pick a place to meet afterward,' said Morgan. 'I'd rather not be in the city when the Unpartnered come.'

'You will not be able to leave it without my help,' said Echo.

'Maybe, maybe not,' said Morgan. 'It depends on whether I can move before the panic sets in. That shouldn't be too difficult; the effects shouldn't set in until a day or so later. Tell you what… if everything goes to plan and we get it done tonight or tomorrow, once I've signalled that to you I'll leave the city by whichever gate I can and come back here. This should be a good enough spot. If I can't get out, I'll go to ground somewhere and put up the panic signal for you. If you see that, it means I need you to come and get me out. I'll wait somewhere near the signal. Disguise yourself as one of their griffins and you should be able to get in and out cleanly.'

'I will do that,' Echo said immediately. A human might have paused to think it over, but like most griffins Echo assumed that his partner knew best.

'Right, then,' said Morgan. 'We may as well get some rest while we wait for nightfall. We'll need it!'

Without another word, man and griffin moved back from their vantage point on top of a small outcrop, and took shelter among some trees. They were far enough away from the city not to be spotted, but Morgan hid under a low-growing wattle bush anyway. Being seen now would be disastrous. Besides, the shade made it easier to rest.

By now he was more than used to sleeping in uncomfortable places, and he felt himself relax soon enough.

As he began to drift off, he wondered briefly whether the fleeing griffiner had made it into Canran. If so, it would be a setback, but only a minor one. The spies already in the city had reported back that Canran's griffins and griffiners were severely depleted, and even if they were alert to possible attack there was no way they would be ready for what Morgan was going to do. As long as he carried out his plan, victory would be a certainty. Canran wouldn't stand a chance.

*

Echo woke him up after sundown. 'It is time,' he rasped.

Morgan sat up at once. 'Have you changed your coat yet?'

'No. Prepare yourself while I use my magic.'

Morgan checked the contents of his bag; everything he needed was in there. He had shaved his head again, and now he fished out the strip of cloth that would cover his eyes. He tied it loosely around his neck for now, and stopped to watch Echo.

The griffin planted his legs well apart, as if to brace himself. A moment later his body went rigid. His beak opened, and a strange sighing sound escaped into the air.

The rigidity disappeared, and Echo shook himself vigorously. Fur and feathers fell away in one big puff, but underneath, instead of bald skin, was an entirely new coat.

This one was pure black in every hair and feather. In the darkness, Echo was almost completely invisible.

Morgan sometimes wondered what colour his partner had been at birth. He hadn't been born with the smart spotted fur he usually wore – as far as Morgan knew there was no such thing as a spotted griffin. Echo simply chose to wear that particular coat most of the time because he liked it. He could take on any colour or pattern he chose. Like Morgan, he could be whoever he wanted to be.

He stepped toward his human now, like a giant living shadow, and bent his forelegs so that his chest touched the ground. 'Come.'

Morgan climbed onto his shoulders, and took hold of the harness still strapped onto the griffin's head and neck. 'Remember, make sure it's somewhere dark.'

Echo didn't reply. He straightened up, and took off with a quick blow of his wings.

Fortunately it was a cloudy night, and the moon had been reduced to a dull glow behind the cover. It seemed the Night God was hiding her eye to help her two servants as they flew on to Canran.

Echo passed over the city walls in virtual silence. Below there were plenty of lights among the houses and official buildings, but there were plenty more places where darkness had swallowed everything. The black griffin touched down in one of them, and Morgan slid off his back the moment his talons had touched the street. He took the harness off Echo's neck, and ran away as fast as he could go.

Echo took off as soon as his human was away, and flew off out of Canran. He beat his wings hard for extra height, and once he was high enough to be invisible from the ground he wheeled away and went off into the mountains.

From now on Morgan had the hard job to do, and the most dangerous. Echo could live wild until then, and hope that his human succeeded.

He would, of course. There was no human better or more

cunning than Morgan of Malvern. Echo reminded himself of that as he flew. There was nothing to fear.

*

Back down in the city, Morgan didn't stop running until he was well away from the landing site. Fortunately he was wearing black, so he should have been about as invisible as Echo. But he didn't feel completely safe until he had hidden away in a handy corner and tied the cloth back around his eyes. It hid most of his face, but he could see through it well enough if there was some light.

In the dark, however, he was completely blind.

With a sigh, he unshipped the cane from his back. Just as well he'd spent so much time using it to feel his way before. He had come to have a lot of sympathy for actual blind people during his time in Liranwee. People with working eyes didn't have much sympathy for those without them – those drunks in the White Serpent hadn't been the first to try and steal his eye cloth. But they had come the closest to succeeding. Morgan hadn't been joking when he'd said that Red had saved his life.

Bag slung on his back and cane tapping on the cobbles, he shuffled away northward – an old, blind man once again.

It was going to be a long trip.

To keep himself occupied along the way, he went over the plan in his head. The other spies had described a statue that stood close to the centre of the city. That would be the rendezvous point. It would also be lit up at night, since it was in a big, open public space. Isolation was all very well, but crowds were just as easy to hide in and in some ways safer.

Once he found the statue, he would leave a sign there, and return at midday. If the other spies were still alive they would have found the sign by then, and would be waiting for him. Their reports had said they had a good shelter set up, and once Morgan had joined them there they would be ready to begin.

He ran their names through his mind now. Afan, Derfel and Gwynach. All good Northerners, who had already done a great service for their King and country. All of them had been promised high ranks in the new government once Canran was captured. They would certainly have earned it.

Of course, first Morgan would have to find them – and that

blasted statue. He wished he could wait until morning to look for it, but they would check it at dawn and he couldn't risk waiting out an entire day with nowhere good to hide.

With that in mind, he tapped his way to the nearest lit up spot, stopped to get his bearings, and set out in what he hoped was the right direction.

The night wore on, and while he found his way to what looked to be the centre of Canran, he hadn't found a trace of any statue. He had no idea how long he'd been looking, but he had a nasty feeling that dawn was getting closer.

Time to change tack, then.

There were still some people up and about in this part of the city where there were taverns and whorehouses open late. Morgan spotted a woman on her own, and shuffled over in her general direction. When she looked up and saw him coming, he stopped and hunched apologetically over the handle of his cane.

''Scuse me, miss,' he wheezed.

She frowned. 'Are you blind?'

No, I'm deaf, you sun-worshipping twit, Morgan thought.

'Blind as an ole worm, miss,' he said. 'Could you help an old man out, maybe?'

'I ain't got any money spare,' said the woman, sounding genuinely apologetic.

'That's all right,' said Morgan. 'Old No-Eyes only needs advice. Do you know the way to the statue of Nerther, miss?'

'Oh, is that all?' said the woman. 'Sure, it's west way, right near the Singing Goat. Y'know, the tavern with the broken sign?'

Morgan shook his head sadly. 'Old No-Eyes never saw a sign, or anything else. West, you say?'

'Yes, it's—,' the woman stopped and clicked her tongue. 'Burn it, I'm no good with directions. But I'm goin' over that way myself, so why don't you just follow me?'

'I will, an' thank you!' said Morgan.

The woman set out, too quickly for an actual old man to follow comfortably, let alone a blind one, but Morgan kept up with her easily enough – though he was careful not to make it *look* easy, as he kept deliberately wandering in the wrong direction and pausing to listen for her footsteps.

True to her word, the woman led him along several streets and took a shortcut through an alley before finally ushering him into a large, round open space. And, sure enough, at the centre was the statue.

'Here we are,' said the woman. 'Can you find your way from here?'

'I think so,' said Morgan. 'Thank you! Gryphus bless you, miss.'

'It's no trouble,' the woman said kindly. 'Here.' She pressed a coin into Morgan's hand.

He accepted it with a great show of gratitude, and once the woman had left with a pleased look on her face he hobbled over to the statue and rested.

He pocketed the coin, and looked up at the statue. It was carved from the same red stone as the Eyrie, and depicted a man sitting on griffinback. Nerther, founder of Canran, and his partner Resh. The two stood on a tall pedestal to keep them out of human reach – Morgan put his back to it now, and scowled under his bandage.

'Should've carved it in the shape of a bunch of kneeling slaves,' he muttered. 'Since that's whose backs they stood on in real life.'

He spat, and waited until no-one was looking in his direction. Once the coast was clear, he took a smooth black rock from his pocket and, standing as tall as he could, put it up on top of the pedestal, between Resh's stone talons.

With the signal in place, Morgan shuffled away to find a place to rest. He had been planning to go and find any old hole to put his head down for a while, but then he noticed the tavern signs around the edges of the statue's clearing, and an idea came to him. He had some money stolen from Liranwee's treasury – why not buy a room? He could even relax with a beer first.

It would be more risky than hiding out in a slum as he had done in Liranwee, but everything had gone off so smoothly so far that he was feeling bold. It would just be for one night, and he could keep an eye on the statue.

Accordingly, he chose a tavern at random – the Singing Goat, as it happened – and went inside. It was still fairly busy; apparently Canranians enjoyed their drink.

Sure enough, the owner said he had a room for hire on the second floor. Morgan paid for it, and bought himself a beer and a good meal while he was at it. He took it up to his new room rather than risk getting harrassed by drunks again, and was pleased to find that the room had a window overlooking the statue.

He ate, drank, and then went to bed – but only after he'd wedged a chair under the door handle, because he wasn't stupid.

He had anxious dreams of being captured, and dying a vile death at the hands of Southern executioners. But interspersed with those dreams were dreams of victory. Victory and slaughter. Another Liranwee, falling at his feet. Riches and glory.

Morgan drifted away from those pleasant visions, and into deeper sleep. Tomorrow, it would be time. Tomorrow, Canran's fall would begin.

*

Tired out from the journey, Morgan slept in late the next day. But when he woke up he did it quickly – getting out of bed before his eyes had even opened properly and darting over to the window in a kind of reflex action.

He yawned and rubbed his eyes, and then peered out of the window at the statue.

The black stone was gone. In its place was another stone about the same size, but this one was red.

Morgan grinned, and hurried off to put on his boots. He put the cloth back over his eyes, and picked up his bag and cane before he unblocked the door and went downstairs.

It wasn't midday yet, so he stopped in the bar room and had something to eat. Some of the other patrons there gave him funny looks, and no wonder – not many beggars could afford to hire a room for the night.

'My lucky day,' Morgan said loudly. 'Can you believe it – a woman I met gave me enough money to sleep in a real bed for once! Praise Gryphus!'

'Praise Gryphus,' one of the men there repeated. 'There's so many good and charitable people 'round here, aren't there?'

'Helping the less fortunate is Gryphus' holy work,' Morgan said sagely.

Having managed to throw them off, he finished his food and returned to the statue. There, as planned, he sat down directly beneath the red stone, put a small clay bowl on the ground in front of him, rested his cane across his lap, and waited.

The sun rose gradually higher and Morgan stayed where he was, sometimes muttering under his breath or humming a tune. Once or twice a passerby would drop a coin into his begging bowl, but he acted as if he didn't notice it.

Then, just past midday, someone wearing a hood strolled by and dropped something else into the bowl. Morgan glanced down, and saw a rusty nail lying innocently on top of the coins.

Without a glance in the hooded stranger's direction, he scooped up the bowl and walked away from the statue.

The stranger had already walked away. Shuffling along with his cane in his hand, Morgan wandered in the same direction – keeping well back and never raising his head to look directly at his target. But the hooded man moved slowly – slowly enough for Morgan to catch up with him as he left the square and went off into the city.

Once they were well away from anyone who might have been watching, the two spies fell into step beside each other. Neither one spoke, nor looked at the other.

Morgan let his new friend lead the way on a winding route through Canran's streets. He knew that by now the others would have worked out a nicely inconspicuous path to the hideout – or, better still, several inconspicuous paths. It always paid to be unpredictable.

Eventually, their journey ended in a small hatch hidden under a broken crate in an alleyway. The other spy opened it and gestured at Morgan to go through, before he followed.

The hatch led to a grubby cellar, lit by a single lantern. Morgan took the cloth off his eyes and blinked until he could see properly.

The ceiling was low, supported by two rows of wooden beams, and the walls were bare earth. The lantern hung from one of the beams, and illuminated three simple beds on the floor and a table with a few crates around it to serve as chairs. That, other than a few bottles and bags of food stored in a recess in the wall, was it.

Behind Morgan, the hooded man uncovered his head. He was bald, and had even shaved off his eyebrows, but the eyes gave it away.

Morgan squinted. 'Derfel, is that you?'

The man grinned. 'Aye, it's me. That's not you is it, Morgan?'

'Sadly,' said Morgan. 'Ye gods, you look like a freak. I don't reckon your own mother would know you now.'

'That's the idea,' said Derfel. He gestured at the table. 'Sit down.

The others should be here soon.'

Morgan leant his cane against a handy beam. 'Where are they?'

'Finding food,' Derfel said briefly. 'It's getting hard. Our money's run low.'

'But you've got plenty of water?' asked Morgan.

''Course. There's a whole barrel of it over there in the corner. But we shouldn't be here long enough to need all of it.'

'Best to be careful,' said Morgan. 'But I've brought plenty of money, so food should be easier to get a hold of.'

'Oh good.' Derfel sat down at the table. When Morgan had sat opposite him, he leant forward eagerly. 'So how'd it go? Liranwee – did it work? Tell me everything!'

'Wait for the others,' said Morgan. 'I don't want to have to tell it twice. But... it worked.'

Derfel grinned. 'Praise the Night God. I can't wait to hear how it all went down.'

Morgan grinned back. 'You'll hear it. In the meantime, you'd better tell me how things are going here.'

'They're good,' said Derfel. 'We've done everything we set out to do. Wait a moment...'

He got up and went over to the shelf that had been dug into the wall, where he unearthed a small roll of leather from inside a bag of flour.

He unrolled it on the table, and showed Morgan the map of Canran that had been drawn on it. Here and there on it, usually at crossroads, were little circular markers.

Morgan studied it closely. 'Is this all of them?'

'Yes,' Derfel said instantly. 'We've been at it for months, and this is all of them. We even know which one the Eyrie uses. See?' He jabbed the relevant circle with his fingernail.

'Do we have enough to do all of them?' asked Morgan.

'I think so.'

'I've brought some more, just in case. But we shouldn't need much.'

'Good.' Derfel brushed some flour off the map. 'Will we go ahead with it tonight?'

'Probably, yes. I'd say the sooner the better.'

'So would I. Honestly, the sooner we get out of here, the happier I'll be.' Derfel gave him a serious look. 'It's fraught, isn't it? Hiding among them like this. I mean, I knew it would be hard, but I never knew just how hard.'

'Neither did I, to be honest,' said Morgan. 'Pretending to be blind for months on end, not being able to talk openly with anyone… you live a lie for so long that after a while you start to forget. You know… toward the end there, just before I left Liranwee, I'd started to feel almost… I don't know, *lost*. As if I was losing touch with who I really was.'

'Same here,' said Derfel. 'You know, we've even started calling each other by our fake names here. You're the first one to call me Derfel in months.'

'You're welcome,' Morgan said absently.

The two of them talked on for a while after that, whiling away the time until Afan and Gwynach returned. They arrived separately, but not long apart from each other, and soon all four spies were sitting around the table and sharing a celebratory bottle of wine.

Afan had also shaved his head, but Gwynach, a lanky woman with a squint, had coated her hair with some kind of paste that had turned it a grungy shade of brown. The paste had also given her hair all the gloss and softness of a bundle of dried grass, but at least it wasn't black any more.

'I'll be a happy woman the day I wash this crap out,' Gwynach muttered in answer to Morgan's stare. 'Now, let's get on. Tell us everything!'

She and her two friends listened intently, as Morgan finally began his story. He told them about his spying work, described his escape from the city, and finally moved on to the capture of Liranwee.

Gwynach, Afan and Derfel all listened raptly, and gave a raucous cheer when they heard about the victory.

'Only one thing went wrong,' Morgan concluded. 'Someone escaped. Or two someones – a griffiner and his partner.'

Afan looked anxious. 'So what happened?'

'I chased after them, but never found them,' said Morgan. 'But I think they were coming here – they were heading the right way. Have you heard anything? Do you know if the Eyrie's had any kind of warning?'

The three spies shook their heads.

'I saw something funny yesterday, though,' Gwynach put in. 'Saw a damn great griffin flying over the Eyrie. Didn't recognise it. Only got a quick glimpse, but I'd swear…'

'Swear what?' said Morgan.

'I coulda sworn it was black,' said Gwynach.

Morgan swore. 'Are you sure?'

'Sure-ish. It was the biggest griffin I ever saw, let me tell you.'

Morgan rubbed his bald head. 'Then they did make it,' he said. 'The griffin I was chasing – I never saw it up close, but I did see that it was huge.'

'Damn it!' Afan gripped his cup tightly. 'What do we do now?'

'It's all right,' said Morgan. 'We're not finished. They might be expecting an attack now, but with so few griffins here there won't be much they can do against the Unpartnered anyway. And they won't know about *us*, either. There's no way. The only people who know our plan are us and the King. That's it.'

Afan relaxed. 'You sure?'

'Completely. But it means we'll definitely have to carry things out tonight. The messenger might know about me, and if he does he'll have warned the Eyrie Mistress to be on the lookout for spies. If he has, we can expect a crackdown by the guard very soon.'

'Tonight it is, then,' said Derfel. 'We're ready.' He glanced at his two friends for support.

'I've been ready for weeks,' Gwynach said immediately.

'I was ready the moment our map was done,' said Afan.

'Right, then,' said Morgan. 'Let's rest up a bit and go over things one last time while we wait for nightfall. We can't be too prepared.'

Derfel nodded. 'Let's check our supplies and make sure we've got enough to do them all.'

Working together, the three spies spread out through the cellar and came back with dozens of small stone bottles taken from different hiding places. They lined them up on the table and made several trips each before they had brought out all of them. Meanwhile, Morgan rummaged in his bag and produced his own supply.

Once the table was covered in bottles, all about the same size, Morgan did a quick count of them. There were plenty; more than they would need.

'Perfect,' he said. 'So we'll split these up between us, and each pick a portion of the city to do. Do you all have your own maps?'

'No,' said Derfel. 'We've memorised it. We all know the locations of every well in the city off by heart.' He picked up the map. 'This is for you.'

Morgan smiled. 'That's more like it! Now, let's start dividing.'

Together, the four spies divided the bottles into equal amounts, and packed them away into separate bags. After that they sat down again, and pored over the map, deciding who would go where.

In the back of his mind, Morgan decided that he had never felt so alive as he did at times like these. Planning… plotting. Feeling his intelligence working its hardest. It made him feel powerful, because that *was* his power, and he loved it.

Late that night, the four Northerners left their hideout. They went separately, each one headed for a different part of the city. Their mission tonight would be very dangerous, but none of them was reluctant to carry it out. Between them, they carried more than a hundred bottles of a solution called Viper's Tears, imported all the way from Erebus. More than enough to poison every well in the city, and sicken or kill everyone who drank from them. Canran would be brought to its knees.

Chapter Sixteen

Lingering

In the end, Red and Kraego stayed in Canran much longer than they had planned. Despite what he had said on the day of their arrival, Kraego soon changed his mind about leaving quickly as he started to enjoy the benefits of Eyrie life. He wouldn't admit it, of course – possibly not even to himself – but Red saw it quickly enough. Kraego was easily the biggest griffin in Canran, and even though he didn't have an official position, his sheer size was enough to do him plenty of favours. He had scarcely been in Canran for one day before females began to come to him. Other males were too intimidated to challenge him – even Lessk, who kept up a surly silence around him after their first meeting and soon afterwards avoided him altogether.

He very much enjoyed having food brought to him by servants, who also cleaned his nest out for him. A griffin healer even came by and gave him some medicine to kill any parasites living in his gut, and a powder that would cure him of fleas.

'See, living in an Eyrie's not so bad after all!' Red observed afterward.

Kraego sneezed. 'This dust smells foul.'

'Yeah, but it'll stop the itching.' Red noticed some powder still left in the bag, and surreptitiously pocketed it. 'Y'see why other griffins like living with us?'

'Yes, I see,' said Kraego. 'But we must leave here soon.'

'Sure thing,' Red said innocently. 'Now, I'd better go…' He snuck out of the nest and back into his own room, where he hid behind a screen, took his clothes off and doused himself with the flea powder. It did indeed smell nasty, but he sighed his relief anyway, and made a mental note to see if he could have some more to take with him. Living with a wild griffin had some unpleasant downsides.

He had a sneaking suspicion that Kraego would find a reason not to leave tomorrow either, so he put his clothes out to be washed and found a fresh set in a drawer. Better not wear the old set again until they'd been cleaned – there would probably be some fleas hiding in them.

Bare-chested, he wandered back into Kraego's nest.

The big griffin looked up. 'There you are.' He blinked. 'You have fur.'

Bewildered, Red looked down at himself. When he saw the thatch of red hair on his chest, he realised what Kraego was getting at. He grinned. 'Yeah, I might not have much on my head, but there's plenty just here.'

'I did not know that humans had fur,' said Kraego. 'You are bald-bodied and must cover yourselves in false skins to hide your shame.'

'We've all got some,' said Red. 'Men more than women. I remember Kullervo told me that in Amoran, they say us humans used to be apes. But then the gods decided to make us like them, so all our fur fell off. Somethin' like that. Load of ole nonsense if you ask me. Humans are humans an' apes are apes.'

'What is an ape?' asked Kraego.

'Dunno. Some kinda furry human-looking thing, I s'pose. Kraego, when are we leaving here?'

Kraego scratched his face with a forepaw. 'Soon. Tomorrow.'

'You said that yesterday. Look, I like it here too, but we really should get goin'.'

'You are right,' said Kraego. He stood up and shook himself, making a huge cloud of dust puff out of his feathers. 'We will leave tomorrow, at dawn,' he said, oblivious to Red's coughing. 'We have stayed here too long.'

'Right, then,' said Red, relieved. 'I'll go get ready. Gonna see if I can get a water bottle or somethin' to take along. I'm sure they won't mind.'

'And some dried meat for me,' said Kraego. 'It will save hunting time.'

'Got it.' Red turned to leave.

Kraego watched him, and when Red was in the doorway he suddenly asked, 'What is that mark on your shoulder?'

Red stopped. 'Hm? What mark?'

'That mark,' said Kraego. 'On your skin.'

'Oh!' Red turned back and patted his right shoulder. 'That's just my guard tattoo.'

Kraego looked blank. 'Your what?'

'Guard tattoo,' Red said patiently. He moved closer, and showed him. 'See the crossed spear an' sword? That's the sign of the guard. Every Southerner knows it. I got it needled into me when I joined up. Every guard's got one. It's part of the uniform.'

Kraego's blank expression had not changed. 'What does it mean?'

'It's just a sign,' said Red. 'Makes us feel more like we're together, you know? All one gang. See? I dunno, maybe you'd call it a flock? We all fly together?'

Kraego clicked his beak. 'Like plumage?'

'Yeah, like that.' Red sighed. 'No matter what happens, it'll always be there to remind me. As long as I've got it, I'll never forget what I am. Gods know there's few enough men in the world who can say that. Now, I'd better go see about that water bottle.'

'I will rest,' said Kraego. 'So that I will be ready for tomorrow.'

'Right.' Red smiled and nodded to him, and left the nest.

He had no money, or he would have gone out into the city marketplace and bought a water bottle. As it was, he had no idea where to start. But as he stood in the middle of his room and wondered what to do, a servant came in to pick up his clothes for laundering.

'Here, you,' said Red, moving toward the woman as an idea occurred to him.

She straightened up with his clothes folded over her arm, and made a brief bow to him. 'Yes, sir?'

'Er, I'm leaving tomorrow an' I was wonderin' where to get a water bottle to take along,' said Red. 'An' some other supplies.'

'I'll see to it right away,' the servant said promptly. 'What supplies do you need, sir?'

'The water bottle, an' some dried meat for my partner, an' some food for me. Light stuff. An' maybe a blanket to roll it all up in? Whatever a griffiner should take with him on a long journey.' That last part made him feel stupid the moment it was out of his mouth, but he ignored the feeling. He wasn't trying to impress anyone, and what mattered here was getting it right.

The servant, clearly well trained, didn't react beyond a polite, 'At once, sir,' and left, with a promise that his clothes would be clean and ready for him in the morning.

Red nodded to himself in satisfaction, and, since he couldn't think of anything else he should be doing just then, he decided to follow Kraego's example and get some rest.

Some books had been left in his room. He looked through them until he found one about combat techniques, and settled down to read it on the bed. He hadn't read a book since he was a boy learning how to read, and even now he was reluctant to be seen reading one that didn't have a suitably manly subject. Fortunately, this one was quite interesting.

He had just finished reading the chapter which talked about some effective uses for a spear when his supplies arrived. A different servant came in with a small leather bag that had a rolled-up blanket strapped onto it, which he placed on the table.

Red put the book down, and went to investigate. 'Is it all here?'

'Yes, sir, everything you asked for, but I'll wait while you check, in case there's anything else.'

Red opened the bag and inspected its contents. Sure enough he found plenty of dried meat, neatly wrapped up in some cloth, some rations for himself, the water bottle, and a map which he hadn't thought to ask for. There were also some bandages and a bag or two of a special healing paste.

'Is there anything else you need, sir?' the servant asked.

'No, that looks like everything,' said Red. 'Thanks a lot. Hey,' he added a moment later, 'Am I meant to pay for this, or-?'

The servant had already left. Red shrugged, and then cursed when he found the water bottle was empty. He'd have to go and fill it himself.

Ah well. It would be nice to have a look around at the Eyrie before he left.

He nipped into Kraego's nest to let the griffin know he was going out, but Kraego had already left himself. Off to find more females, probably.

Chuckling, Red took his water bottle and left.

He had seen some of the Eyrie's interior so far, but hadn't had the time or the inclination to explore the whole thing. But he did know that the well, which provided water for the whole building was down at the very bottom of the cliff, so he would see plenty on his way down there.

Navigating in an Eyrie, at least, was usually straightforward enough. Griffins found stairs either difficult or just about impossible, so like every building built to suit their needs, the Canran Eyrie had a series of ramps that went down in a zigzag shape through the different levels. It was tiring to walk on a downward slope for this long, but at least some metal railings had been set into the walls for human use.

Red trekked his way along the ramps, occasionally straying off into side passages to look at the different chambers and other spaces that made up the Eyrie's official areas. Everything was made of the same red stone as the cliff – almost everything of the structure was made of the original rock, and anything that had been installed later came from the Canran area and matched it in colour anyway. But here and there Red saw seams and patches of other colours, and once he came across a corridor that had a stripe of pure white quartz that went clear across the ceiling and down one wall.

Canran's Eyrie had been built with a kind of rough elegance, which made it look more workmanlike than luxurious, but that didn't mean it was plain or undecorated.

Like the other Eyries Red had seen, it had tapestries and shields hanging from the walls here and there, along with the occasional decoration made out of griffin feathers, which only griffiners were allowed to own. But unlike any other Eyrie, Canran's ornaments were also in the stone itself.

In some of the more opulent areas, where griffiners lived and worked, designs had been carved into the walls and ceiling. He saw patterns of vines, stylised trees, griffins of course, and other animals too. One corridor had a whole section of wall covered with a frieze of animals dancing on their hind legs – possums, ground bears, spotted tree cats and others Red didn't recognise.

He spent some time inspecting that particular carving, and could only react to it with a laugh and a disbelieving shake of the head. Maybe children lived hereabouts, or maybe there was a dancing hall nearby. He had no idea.

But he eventually remembered that, while he wasn't in a hurry, he didn't have all day, so he reluctantly found his way back to the main ramp system and resumed his journey to the well.

After what felt like forever – and after his legs had started to ache horribly from the angle he had to walk at – the ramps levelled out and he decided he must be on the ground floor.

To make sure, he went to the nearest window and peeked out. Sure enough, there was the ground. That was enough for him, and he carried on until he found a door and went out through it.

The space in front of the cliff's base was taken up by a kind of courtyard, with a wall around it to separate it from the rest of the city. There was a bit of garden there, and a pair of guards at the gate. And, more importantly, a well right in the centre.

Red went over to it with a sigh of relief.

'Oi,' called one of the guards at the gate. 'What're you doin' here?'

Red looked up in surprise. 'Getting some water, what's it look like?'

The guard tapped his spear-butt on the ground. 'I meant what are you doing in the Eyrie? You ain't on duty, not dressed like that.'

Red realised that he still hadn't put a tunic on. 'Oh, right,' he said. 'I don't work here.'

'Then why are you here?' the guard persisted. 'You're a guard, ain't you?'

Red started. 'How'd you know–?'

'Yer tattoo,' said the guard, pointing.

Red relaxed and grinned. 'Yeah, I'm a guard, but I'm not from here. I'm stayin' at the Eyrie. Got sent from Liranwee with a message for your Eyrie Mistress.'

The guard glanced at his partner, and came over to the well. 'Liranwee?'

'Yeah, that's right.' Red put his water bottle down, and started to lower the well's bucket down on its rope.

The guard, a burly middle aged man with a brown beard, frowned. Then, coming closer, he lowered his voice. 'Is it true?' he asked. 'The rumours about Liranwee?'

Red paused in his turning of the well's crank handle. 'What've you heard?'

'That Liranwee's fallen,' said the guard. 'Taken by Northerners.'

Red sighed and went back to turning the handle. 'Yeah, it's true. I was the only one to get away as far as I know.'

The second of the two guards came over. 'So they took over the whole city?'

'Yeah,' said Red. He heard a faint splash as the bucket hit the water, and waited a moment before turning the handle the other way to bring it up again.

The two guards looked openly frightened.

'Is it true that they're comin' here next?' the first one asked. 'If they've got Liranwee, will they want to take the other cities too?'

'Yes,' Red said baldly.

'You reckon so?'

'I know so. I dunno if they'll go after Withypool next, or here, but they're gonna attack every city in the South. Didn't anyone tell you?'

'Not really,' said the first guard. 'But they've stepped up patrols an' put more sentries up on the walls, an' warned us all to be on high alert. S'pose they didn't want t'get people too worked up.'

Red nodded. 'Best keep things calm. My name's Red, by the way.'

'I'm Ridley,' said the first guard. 'An' this here's my brother Tarn.'

'Pleased t'meet you,' Red said politely. 'It's good t'know Canran's got proper guards protectin' it.'

Ridley shrugged. 'It's griffins what really make the difference when it comes to a fight.'

'You reckon?' said Red. 'Maybe. But if y'ask me, a city's only as good as its guards. After all, you ain't just its protection; you're its people too. What'd griffins know about that? They don't know loyalty, or duty, or anything else that really matters. You know when they took Liranwee, with the Unpartnered an' all, plenty of our griffins joined 'em. The ones from our Hatchery, who hadn't chosen humans – they joined the Unpartnered an' they'll be here attacking alongside 'em when the Northerners come to Canran.'

Ridley and Tarn both shook their heads.

'Bloody griffins,' said Tarn. 'You wouldn't catch me havin' a thing to do with them. Sure they're strong an' the priests say they're holy an' suchlike, but far as I'm concerned they're nothin' but a damned nuisance.'

Red thought of Kraego. 'They're tricky all right, that's true.'

The bucket finally appeared, and he pulled it up out of the well. He didn't have a ladle or anything, so he balanced the water bottle on the low wall around the well and poured the bucket's contents into it. But the moment he tilted the bucket, something fell out of it and knocked the water bottle onto the ground.

'What the—?'

It was a small stone bottle. Some air had caught inside it, which must have been enough to make it float.

Tarn picked it up. 'Huh, how'd that get in there?'

Red stooped to pick up his fallen water bottle, and spotted something else on the ground beside it. He picked that up too, and tossed it over. 'Maybe this cork'll fit it.'

Tarn poked it into the bottle's open neck, and sure enough, it fitted. 'Fancy that. May as well keep it – bottles like this are ten oblong apiece down at the markets.' He stuffed it into his pocket.

Red finally finished filling up his own bottle, and put the lid back on. 'There, that oughta last me a while when I'm back on the road.'

'You goin' somewhere?' asked Ridley.

'Yeah. I'm not finished doin' my job yet,' said Red. 'My Eyrie Mistress said t'go warn all the other Eyries, so I gotta move on.'

Ridley glanced up at the sky. 'We'd better get back to our posts, in case anyone comes by. But it was nice meetin' you, Red.'

'Likewise,' said Red. 'I hope I'll come here again some day. If I do I'll be sure t'come by an' say hello.'

'An' if Liranwee's never got back,' said Tarn, 'you could always come join up with us. We can always do with another good man on our squad.'

'I'll remember that!' said Red. 'An' you.'

With friendly nods and smiles, the two guards went back to stand by the gate. Red felt better for having talked to them, as he waved his goodbye and went back inside. He hoped, for their sake in particular, that Canran would be able to survive whatever the Northerners did next.

*

Red returned to his room, and found Kraego waiting. The big griffin was standing in the entrance to his nest, with his tail twitching in agitation. The moment Red appeared, he came toward him. 'Where have you been?'

The question sounded more like an angry demand. Instinctively, Red took a step back. 'What's up with you? I went to get some water. I would've told you, but you weren't about.'

Kraego's tail twitched faster. 'I have been down into the city. There is danger.'

Red tensed. 'Danger? What kind? Not the Northerners?'

'Word is spreading among the griffins here,' said Kraego. 'There is a sickness in Canran. Everywhere humans are being struck down.'

'Oh no,' said Red.

'It is in the Eyrie as well,' said Kraego. 'Have you seen it yourself?'

'No, I've barely spoken to anyone all day,' said Red. 'What's goin' on, exactly?'

'I have heard that the sick ones suffer terrible pain, and are soon unable to walk. Many have already died.' Kraego's blue eyes narrowed. 'We must leave here immediately, before you become ill.'

'What, right now?' said Red.

'Yes.' Kraego was already standing up, wings rising as if he wanted to take off right where he was standing. 'Come, put my harness on.'

'Hold on here!' said Red, alarmed. 'We can't just bugger off right now – it'll be dark soon, an' we shouldn't travel before we've had a good night's sleep an' somethin' to eat. One night won't kill us.'

Kraego calmed down. 'You are right… I should not travel when I am tired. But you must stay away from other humans. I do not want you to be poisoned.'

'Can do,' said Red. 'I don't reckon the Eyrie Mistress'll mind if we just go; she's too busy t'worry about a couple of messengers an' she said we can leave whenever we're ready.'

'Then we will leave at dawn,' said Kraego. 'Be awake then, or I will wake you myself.'

'Got it,' said Red. 'I'll make sure we both get a good meal before bed. I always sleep better on a full stomach myself.'

'Bring food,' Kraego agreed. 'But do not become sick, Red. I will not allow it.'

Red grinned. 'Hearin' that, I almost think y'might just care a bit about me!'

*

That evening Kraego went for one last flight over the city, and then returned to his nest to eat. Sure enough, as promised, Red had ordered some food for him and he found it waiting. A whole side of venison – very good.

Kraego settled down to eat it. While his beak was busy his mind was free, and he took a moment to glance through the archway into the next room, where Red was busy eating his own meal. It looked unappetising, but that was human food all over. Humans insisted on spoiling their meat by burning it and covering it with horrible, inedible plants. And they had the effrontery to be disgusted by good, honest raw flesh with the blood still in it.

Kraego snorted to himself. Humans were such ridiculous creatures. They had no idea how to eat, or how to sleep. They didn't even have any proper ideas about mating. He'd seen how the males would simper and stammer around the females, begging for their favours when they should be fighting other males to show their strength and so win the right to fertilise the eggs.

Kraego had pointed this out to Red, but the silly creature had just laughed. No wonder he had not fathered any human pups. And he was at least ten years older than Kraego, who had mated with three females already!

Kraego crushed a bone and swallowed some of the shards, enjoying the rasp and scrape as they went down his throat. Red was just as foolish as every other human, but he was a good human to carry around. He was brave and knew how to fight, and he showed the proper respect to Kraego. His goal was one that the griffin could respect as well. Like a griffin who had lost his territory, he wanted to win back his home. And he wanted to kill Shar in order to do it.

Kraego wondered idly if Liranwee would become his territory after he killed Shar. After all, when one griffin defeated another he won that griffin's territory. Would he, Kraego, be master of the North as well?

But no – he could only rule a human territory if he had a human partner.

Perhaps I could choose this one, he thought, his eyes on Red. *With my partnership, he could become an Eyrie Master. With his, I could rule any territory I chose. But I am wild and he is a commoner, and we could only rule an Eyrie by right of conquest.*

It was an amusing thought. Give up the wild life and take an Eyrie for himself. He knew he could do it, but did he really want to?

Do I want to become my father? The Mighty Kraego? Do I want that?

Kraego didn't know.

The realisation disturbed him. He swallowed the last of his meal and automatically began to groom, while he thought of his father.

The Mighty Skandar. He had lived a good long life, and now his name was legend. He would be remembered by humans and griffins forever. But he himself hadn't lasted. Kraego remembered that part the most. In the end, despite all his power, Skandar had been defeated and had flown away into the wild somewhere to die. He had had everything, and Shar had taken it away. Everything he had been before that had only made his defeat worse and more humiliating.

No, Kraego thought. *I do not want to become like him.*

There had to be a better way for him to go, but what?

He wrestled with that thought long after he had finished grooming and curled up to sleep, while in the next room Red had some more of that vile red water humans drank, and looked as if he actually liked it.

Kraego snorted to himself in disgust, and went to sleep.

Chapter Seventeen

Poisoned Prize

Kraego slept deeply that night. And once again, the dream came.

The white griffin appeared, looking just the same as he remembered, with her coat glowing in the blackness.

Kraego!

Kraego looked up placidly at her, and said nothing.

Why are you here? the white griffin demanded. *Why have you not obeyed me?*

'I obey no-one,' said Kraego.

Fool! You have heard my promise. You know what can be yours. Do as I have said!

Kraego was not afraid of her. He yawned widely – a very rude gesture among griffins. 'No. I do as I please.'

Then die, she said, and lunged at him. Her talons hit him in the back of the neck.

Kraego felt his skin split, and blood ran down the side of his neck as he darted away from her. Shock hit him as pain did. She could not hurt him – she was only a dream!

But she did hurt him. She leapt again, this time at his face, and as he hit back he felt another set of talons slash him across the haunches.

Kraego rose up with a screech of fright and rage, and lunged at his attacker. Bewilderment rippled through his mind for a moment, until the real pain, the feel of real flesh under his beak, and the savage hissing of two griffins in his nest made him realise that he was not dreaming any more. He was awake, he was injured, and there were two griffins trying to kill him.

Even confused and half asleep, Kraego knew how to fight. He pushed forward, crushing the griffin in front of him under his greater bulk. The second one leapt on him from behind, but instead of trying to throw him off by turning around, Kraego reared up onto his hind legs. The other griffin fell off him, and he plunged back down again, talons first, ripping through the griffin that had fallen under him before she could get away. He felt his talons hit bone, and knew he had done enough damage to leave that enemy and attack the one behind him.

The griffin behind him was ready. He hit Kraego across the face as he turned, leaving a row of slashes over his forehead that bled into his eyes. Blinded, Kraego rushed in recklessly and slammed into the other griffin's chest. Caught off-guard, his opponent fell back, and if he had been able to see, Kraego could have killed him. But his beak missed the other's throat and hit the stone floor instead, making a horrible cracking sound.

The downed griffin struggled to rise before Kraego struck again. And then the second one, the injured female, hit the dark griffin from behind. Her beak tore through his back leg, which buckled and sent him thudding onto the floor with a scream of pain.

The other griffin, the male, got up. Before Kraego could recover, he slammed his talons down on the dark griffin's head, pinning it down, and struck the killing blow.

Or, at least, tried to. His beak came down aimed squarely at the fragile spot at the back of Kraego's skull, but at the last moment it suddenly twisted sideways and left nothing but a minor flesh wound. His talons slackened their grip, and immediately Kraego pulled himself free. He rose up furiously to kill the other griffin, but before he had even raised his talons his enemy fell down at his paws.

There, standing just behind him with a bloodied sword in his hand, was Red.

Kraego only hesitated for an instant. He struck the other griffin in the head, hard enough to break his neck, and whirled around to finish off the female who had injured his leg.

There were no other attackers in the nest. Once he was sure of that, Kraego subsided and began to lick his wounds.

Red wiped his sword clean on the dead griffin's feathers. 'Where in the gods' names did they come from?'

Kraego looked up sharply. 'You should not have done that!' he hissed.

Red stopped and stared. 'Done what?'

'It was my fight,' said Kraego. 'You should not have interfered.'

'I saved your life!' Red snapped.

'You humiliated me!' said Kraego. 'A griffin does not need a human's help!'

'What, you'd rather die than let me help you?' asked Red.

'Yes!' said Kraego.

Red's anger gave way slightly to surprise. 'Honestly? You'd rather *die?*'

'A griffin that cannot fight his own battles may as well be dead,' Kraego said, his voice softening slightly. 'Never talk about this to anyone. But now we must be quick. If I have been attacked, then you must know what this means. Come!'

He hurried over to the entrance that led to the open air, and Red came with him. Both of them froze.

Canran was under attack. Everywhere griffins were flying – griffins fighting, griffins killing. Normally, an attack in the middle of the night would be impossible. No griffin could or would fly easily in the dark.

But these griffins had brought fire. It lit up the night sky in patches, and Kraego saw everything that happened. The Unpartnered had come, and they were fighting Canran's griffins. Others must have already invaded the other nests in the Eyrie, just as they had invaded his. Partnered griffins must have been killed while they were asleep. Now Canran's own unpartnered ones were fighting back.

Kraego saw and realised all this in a moment, before he turned to Red. 'Quickly,' he said. 'Put on your second skin. And gather up the food you have for us. You and I must leave here at once, and we may have to fight to do it.'

'Got it.' Red ran back into his own room.

Kraego stayed where he was, and watched what he knew was the beginning of Canran's fall. With so many humans in the city weakened by disease, and the local griffins caught by surprise, the fight back would be a poor one.

He knew perfectly well that if he joined in, his presence could make a great difference. But he wouldn't. This was not his fight, and besides, he was injured and had his own purpose to worry about.

He waited impatiently for Red to get back, keeping a cautious eye out for any sign of more Unpartnered coming his way. Fortunately, while he could see plenty of them flying in and out of the Eyrie, none of them came close enough to see him. It was just as well – his wounded hind leg had already begun to stiffen, and the blood from his forehead had thickened all the feathers around his eyes and made it difficult to see.

Red came hurrying back to his side. He was wearing his armour, and had a bag on his back. He was also holding something that looked like a series of leather straps.

'What is that?' asked Kraego.

Red came closer. 'It's a griffin harness. I found it hanging on the wall in here. Bend down an' I'll put it on.'

Kraego jerked his head away from it. 'I will not wear a harness!'

'C'mon, don't be daft,' Red said impatiently. 'I need it so I can hold on properly. This is gonna be a rough flight out of here, an' if I've got nothin' to hold onto I might fall off.'

Kraego's eyes had narrowed. 'I do not care. I am not a partnered griffin, and I will not wear a harness like some oxen yoked to a cart!'

Red lost his temper. 'Oh right, I forgot,' he snarled, hurling the harness away with more force than he needed. 'You don't care about anybody but yourself. Me breakin' every bone in my body doesn't matter a damn, does it?'

The human's rage only irritated Kraego. 'Stop your squeaking and get on my back. We are wasting time.'

Red climbed on obediently, but he did it more roughly than usual, as if hoping to hurt the griffin.

Kraego only snorted grumpily. 'Hold on tightly, with your forelegs around my neck,' he advised. 'I will keep my flight level, but it will be up to you to protect yourself. Do not let go, no matter what happens.'

'I got it,' Red muttered.

Kraego launched himself into the sky with a quick blow of his wings. He didn't bother about trying to be stealthy, but he avoided the Unpartnered, and stayed out of the light. Not that he was overly concerned about being spotted. He would do his best to go unseen for as far as he could, and if any griffin came after him and couldn't be shaken off, he knew what to do.

If he fought in the air, it would probably be the death of Red. Even with a harness, few humans could stay on a griffin's back if it came to a serious fight. And that was a disappointment to Kraego, because, as he flew on over the city, dodging enemies left and right, he felt his blood start to heat up with the excitement of battle. The ache in his wounds only heightened it, and if he hadn't had Red on his back, he would have given in to it.

As it was, he pointed his beak forward and kept on steadily. He needed Red, and he needed to continue his journey. Killing a few Unpartnered here would be enjoyable, but it wouldn't bring him any closer to Shar.

By now, the fighting had spread out over the entire city. Some of the Unpartnered, having run out of other griffins to fight, had landed and were running through the streets, killing humans to amuse themselves. Seeing them, Kraego wondered idly what it would be like to give in to the most basic hunter's instinct like that, and slaughter dozens of weaker animals with reckless abandon. Not to defend a territory, not to eat, but just killing for the sake of killing. He hoped that one day he would be able to try it.

Watching the gruesome scene below had distracted him. A shout from Red made him look up sharply, and hiss when he saw another griffin descending on him. It was one of the Unpartnered, flying down to join in the sport, and when he saw the rider on Kraego's back he immediately came in for the attack.

With Red there, Kraego couldn't turn in the air to strike his attacker. He began to descend too, looking for an opportunity to get out from under the other griffin. But his unburdened enemy was faster. Before Kraego could move away, or try to attack, or take a moment to gather himself and use his gift to escape, something slammed into the back of his head so hard it made his vision turn red.

When his eyes cleared, he realised that he was falling. His wings flailed in the rushing wind, but they felt weak and his head was spinning, confusing him. The world lurched and reeled around him, refusing to stay in one place. He didn't know which way was up, or which down.

Even in the midst of his panic, he realised that – incredibly – Red was still clinging onto him. Kraego felt the human's arms wrapped around his neck like a collar, refusing to let go. But if he hit the ground, they would both die.

With a last, desperate effort, Kraego thrust his wings out. He lurched upward, made a short, rolling glide, and slammed into a rooftop. He felt Red fall away from him, and then he too was falling, rolling helplessly down the side of the roof before he managed to wrap his talons around a chimney. The bricks crumbled under his talons, but they were enough to stop him.

But Red was gone, and the enemy griffin was already coming down to strike the killing blow. Kraego heard him land on the rooftop somewhere higher than him.

Aching and confused, he managed to plant his paws.

When he saw the griffin that had brought him down, he actually snarled with rage. The Unpartnered was tiny – half Kraego's size, but obviously fully grown, with grey and rusty orange feathers that had a ruddy glow in the light of the fires burning below. Humiliated, Kraego began to make his scrabbling way up toward his enemy. 'What griffin are you?' he hissed. 'Tell me, so that I will know your name before I tear out your entrails.'

The small griffin looked smugly at him. 'I am Chot, the last son of Hyrenna. I have the power that she had, but stronger.'

Kraego was not impressed. 'And I am Kraego, the son of the Mighty Skandar, and *I* have *his* power, little chick.'

He used it.

*

The moment Red felt Kraego's neck wrench itself out of his grip, he knew that he was lost. The thought shot through his mind like an arrow in one frozen instant, and when he smashed onto the rooftop it shot away again, leaving his mind in a whirl of panic.

He bounced off the tiles, smacked back down again and rolled away helplessly over the eaves of the house that had broken his fall.

After that he fell again, one last time. He hit the street below with a bone-jarring thud, and for a little while after that the world fled away. He never knew for how long.

His senses came back with a slow, red dawning of pain.

He stayed very still, gasping with shock. He was lying in an awkward sprawl, with one arm trapped underneath him and the other one splayed out pathetically, as if reaching for help. His legs were stuck in a kind of sideways running position, and his spine had twisted. His heartbeat thudded pain through every bone and muscle.

Even after his senses had come back, he didn't dare move. He was afraid that if he tried he would find out that he couldn't – that his legs were broken, or worse, his back. Or, if not that, then moving would make everything hurt more.

His cheek felt cold and vaguely sticky, and he realised that this was because his nose was bleeding onto it.

It'll get all in my moustache again, he thought stupidly.

Back home in Liranwee, people had loved to make fun of Red's bushy moustache, but he'd always been proud of it. For some reason, just then the thought of it being mucked up was enough to give him an impetus to move.

Cautiously, wincing and gritting his teeth, he pushed himself up and managed to get to his feet. Thank gods, nothing seemed to be broken. His limbs were fine, anyway, and his back seemed to be doing its job. But his nose was bleeding vigorously, and he could feel other sticky patches here and there where cuts had opened.

He'd wake up in agony tomorrow morning – if he lived that long – but he was all right.

'I'm… all… right,' he groaned aloud, to try and reassure himself.

And now was not the time to be nursing a few cuts and bruises. As he leant on the wall and waited for the pain to die down, he finally noticed the screams and shouting coming from the streets around him. He looked up and saw griffins coming down to land, and realised what must be happening.

The horrors of Liranwee had come to Canran.

Grimacing at the effort, and the pain it caused, Red moved away from the wall and looked around more thoroughly. He couldn't see any sign of Kraego, and calling him would only make other griffins notice him. Besides, if Kraego was still alive then he would be fighting, and wouldn't have the time to bother about a human. Either way, Red was on his own.

His sword had fallen out of his belt, but he found it some way away and picked it up. He hoped to gods that he wouldn't have to do any fighting in this state. But he had a strong suspicion that he would.

Limping a little, he went to the end of the street where he had landed and peered out. He'd heard other people here only a moment ago, but they were gone now. Maybe some of them had run away, or maybe they were the corpses he saw lying where they had fallen. The Unpartnered who had killed them had already moved on.

Red knew what he had to do now: get out of the city as fast as possible. Kraego wouldn't try very hard to find him down here, but if he could get out into the open country around the city it would be easy enough for the griffin to pick him up again.

With this idea in mind, he set out cautiously – every sense alert for danger. Fortunately, he seemed to be in a clear patch for the moment – when he did see Unpartnered here and there it was only in passing. There were no other people about to attract them. No living people, anyway.

His bruised limbs had already started to seize up. He limped and swore, and hoped nothing was seriously damaged. His throat was hurting again as well.

But it wasn't long before he had other things to worry about. As he forged on toward the city wall, hoping to find a way out, he caught up with the Unpartnered. One of them landed not far ahead of him, and charged on without seeing him. Red quickly tried to turn back, but saw others coming in to land behind him, and hurried on.

He saw the one that had already landed reach the end of the street and burst out into an open space, and a chorus of pitiful screams rose up ahead of it.

Rage twisted in Red's aching body. Forgetting everything else, he drew his sword and broke into a run. He darted out into the open, and skidded to a halt when he saw what was happening.

A group of people had clustered together in a courtyard, and were trying to shelter around the base of a statue. One or two of them were holding makeshift weapons – knives and bits of wood – but none of them were trying to fight back.

A pair of griffins, including the one Red had followed, were circling around the statue. They weren't attacking yet, but they were keeping their victims penned in, hissing threateningly at them while they cowered pathetically.

Red saw the looks of terror and despair on the faces of the victims. They were about to die, and they knew it, and so did the two Unpartnered. They were toying with them. Taunting them.

Red knew that there was nothing he could do against a pair of fully grown griffins. If he attacked them now, or tried to interfere in any other way, he would die.

But the thought of doing nothing was more than he could stand.

He charged straight at them without a second thought.

His attack wasn't a mindless charge. Taking advantage of their distraction, he darted around behind the nearest griffin and struck at its hind legs. His sword went in deeply, and he backed off and ran.

The wounded griffin screamed. He didn't look back.

'Ruuun!' he yelled as he fled.

He hoped the others had heard him, and that they had taken the chance he'd given them. He couldn't risk stopping to find out.

He could hear the wounded griffin behind him – and judging by the noise it was possible that the other one was after him too. He sprinted for the nearest building.

A door loomed up in front of him. He wrestled with the handle for a few heart-stopping moments, wrenched it open, and dived inside.

Something hit him hard in the back. He tumbled sideways, landing with a cry of pain, and scrabbled away under a table.

The door broke into splinters.

Red was too frightened to look. He curled up in his shelter and tried not to move.

Just a few paces away from where he hid, the building's front wall juddered and shook as the griffins tried to get in through the front door. He could hear their talons ripping through wood and brick, and the snarls and rasps of rage. He could even hear their breathing, all harsh and angry with effort. This building, whatever it was, had not been designed for griffins.

But they were so close…

Please gods, make them go away, Red prayed silently. *Gryphus save me.*

Maybe Gryphus was listening this time too. After what felt like an eternity, the scrabbling in the doorway stopped. He heard the griffins hissing and snapping at each other as they left. There was too much easy prey in the city for it to be worth their time catching him.

Red stayed where he was for a while longer, listening to his own ragged breathing.

Finally, he dragged himself out from under the table and dusted himself down. That had been far too close.

'All right, that's enough,' he told himself. 'Just leave things be. There's nothin' you can do here, so just get away. Save yer own skin an' see if y'can't make things turn out better in Wylam.'

He left the building – cautiously checking that the coast was clear beforehand. The doorway had been half demolished by the griffins, but it had saved his life. He glanced gratefully at it, and went back into the courtyard.

The people he had tried to save were gone. He saw two of them lying dead by the statue, but the rest were nowhere to be seen. They had escaped.

Red smiled to himself, and went on his way.

After that, he saw plenty more Unpartnered, and more of their victims as well. Most of what he saw was far worse than what had gone before.

He hurried now, street to street, alley to alley, making for the wall as fast as he could. Along the way he saw Unpartnered everywhere. He saw them hunt their human prey, sometimes toying with them before finally going for the kill. But most of them simply charged through the fleeing people of Canran, cutting them down like wheat. Mindless slaughter.

Red didn't try and help again. He avoided the thick of it, and several times he hid until the coast was clear. But everything he saw stayed with him.

Griffins gone mad.

He saw a small child torn in half by a slashing beak. Saw women and the elderly trampled underfoot. Saw griffins with their coats splashed with blood, not seeming to notice the bodies tangled under their paws.

We let them in, Red thought dully, as he ran on. *We let those things into our cities. We let them breed. We fed them. We let them in.*

But even then, deep down, he knew who was really to blame.

His memory showed him an image of two men. They laughed and embraced each other like brothers as they stood over him, but when they looked at him their eyes were cold. Morgan and his King. They were the ones…

As he remembered those two, while he ran from Canran's massacre, hatred began to burn inside Red. It was a hate unlike anything he had ever felt before in his life. But as he went further on through the city, and saw death everywhere he looked, he focused on it, and nurtured it, and let it grow.

They did this, he thought, over and over. *They made this happen. It was them. I'll kill them. They're both dead. I swear by Gryphus I'll do it with my own hands.*

It was the only kind of comfort he could find, and he let himself obsess over it. He pictured himself killing the two Northerners. Caedmon had to die, definitely, but Morgan… Morgan would be the first. Red pictured him in particular. Yes, he would die first, and it would be slow and painful. It would be everything he deserved.

Red's mental picture of Morgan grew so vivid as he concentrated on it, that when he turned a corner and ran straight into him, he thought he must have gone mad.

The two of them stared blankly at each other for a moment.

Morgan was only half disguised – shaved bald, but with his eye cloth pulled up onto his forehead like a headband. He had a small pack on his back, and carried his cane in one hand.

Morgan pulled himself together first. 'You again!' he exclaimed. 'How in the Night God's name…?'

Red took two long strides forward, and punched Morgan in the stomach with all his might.

Morgan stumbled backward and nearly fell, but he recovered with surprising speed, and quickly tried to defend himself with his cane.

But Red was unstoppable that night. He swiped the cane away like a twig. Forgetting his sword, he simply wrapped one big hand around Morgan's throat and pulled him forward.

Morgan struggled and lashed out with his hands and feet. Red didn't even feel it. With his free hand, he punched the spy in the face as hard as he could, again and again until Morgan began to go limp.

'How d'you like me now?' Red roared at him. 'Son of a bitch! Godsdamned sodding coward! How d'you like it now you're facin' someone who can fight back? You ain't got me chained up this time! *Bastard!*' He shook Morgan violently, and hurled him to the ground.

Morgan, gasping audibly for breath, tried to slide away from him. Red caught up with him and kicked him spitefully in the ribs.

'You ain't gettin' away from me this time,' he spat. 'I told you I'd have yer blood for what you did to me, an' now I'm gettin' you for Liranwee an' Canran as well.' He kicked him again. 'C'mon, aren't you gonna fight back? Or is stabbin' a man in the back the only fightin' you know? *Well?*'

Morgan groaned. 'Please…'

'Please what?' Red could hear his own voice beginning to go ragged. 'Let you go? My arse! I'm gonna rip yer yellow guts out, you blackrobe scum. I'm gonna– *argh!*'

Morgan, looking up at him, saw the enraged Southerner's face suddenly slacken with surprise. A moment later he toppled over.

Lady Arwydd stood over him, holding a piece of wood in her hand. She looked slightly shocked as she glanced down at the groaning Red.

Morgan managed to get up. 'Arwydd!' he shouted.

'What?' She sounded panicky. 'I was just trying to help!'

Red got up, clutching at his head. 'Godsdamned Northern slag!' he growled.

Morgan darted past him, and grabbed Arwydd by the arm. 'Come on, move!'

The two Northerners ran for it, with Morgan dragging his rescuer behind him.

Red's head was spinning, but he wasn't about to let them get away. Forgetting any and all danger, he charged after them like an angry bull.

*

Ahead, Morgan felt panic pound through his head with the headache Red's punches had given him. He had never been hit so hard in his life. And he had never seen anyone look at him with so much hatred.

In all his life, Morgan had never known anyone who had so clearly wanted to kill him – or who had come so close to succeeding. It put more fear into him than he had ever felt before, and he ran as if all the demons of the void were on his tail.

Luckily for him, his speedy build and quick wit were still there to help him.

'We've got to head for the Unpartnered!' he yelled back at Arwydd. 'They'll protect us!'

'No they won't!' she shouted back. 'I've seen them; they've gone mad! *Let go of me!*'

Morgan obeyed. 'Then what do you suggest?' He could hear the desperation in his own voice.

'We go *this* way,' said Arwydd, darting past him and speeding off in a new direction.

Morgan followed her, glad that she was taking the initiative.

'Where are we going?' he asked as he caught up with her.

'To Essh!' Arwydd waved vaguely skyward. 'She's following us and we have to go somewhere she can land!'

It was easier said than done. The Unpartnered were everywhere, and, as Arwydd had said, they had gone mad. None of them would be likely to care much if they killed a Northerner by mistake. More than once they had to change direction, or duck into an alley to avoid them.

And all the while, Red chased them. He didn't seem to care about the Unpartnered, or any danger at all. He charged after the two Northerners like a man possessed, and it was surprising that he didn't catch them very quickly. But he seemed to be in some kind of pain – when Morgan risked a glance back he noticed the big guardsman was limping. There were some nasty looking grazes on his arms and legs. Clearly, he was in worse shape than he'd seemed.

*

Red was indeed in pain. His limbs had started to seize up as the fall from the roof finally caught up with him. He could feel the sting of broken skin everywhere. But he fought it down and kept going, determined that this time Morgan wouldn't get away.

'Hey!' a voice yelled, off to his left.

Red stumbled sideways away from it, raising his sword.

'Stop that!' said the voice.

Red lowered the sword and slowed down slightly. A uniformed guard had jogged over to run beside him. There were several others behind him, all armed.

After a moment's confusion, Red realised that the face of the first of them was familiar. 'Ridley!'

'That's me!' Ridley said, almost cheerfully. 'We're tryin' to get out of the city – come with us. Safety in numbers!'

Red stopped for an instant, and pointed ahead with his sword. 'Northern spies! Let's get 'em!'

He ran on without waiting for a reply, but Ridley soon appeared beside him. 'Let's get the bastards!' he shouted to his companions.

The gang of guards quickly formed itself into an organised column behind Ridley and Red, and went in pursuit of Morgan, all thought of escape swallowed up by the need for revenge.

*

Above, Essh saw what was happening. She came in for a hasty landing, dodging an Unpartnered, and touched down on the street just ahead of the two fleeing Northerners. They saw her and ran straight to the protection of her talons.

'Come!' Essh rasped. 'Climb onto my back!'

'But you can't carry both of us!' said Arwydd.

'And I will not!' Essh started to go into a defensive crouch as Red and his friends came closer. 'You are my human. Climb onto me, now!'

Arwydd grabbed Morgan's arm. 'I won't leave him!'

Morgan's face was full of undisguised panic. 'Don't be stupid; get out of here! You won't help anyone by dying.'

'Neither will you!' Arwydd drew her sickle. 'If we can't fly away, then we'll have to… we'll have to kill them!'

Morgan laughed at her high-pitched attempt to sound brave. 'Don't be stupid. I don't have a weapon, and you don't know how to use yours.'

Essh let out a snarl of frustration. 'Get out of my way. *I* will kill them.'

Red and the other guards had stopped and were hesitating, reluctant to get too close to the griffin.

'Anyone got a bow?' Red asked hopelessly.

'No!' said a woman behind him. 'Now let's bugger off outta here!'

The others started to retreat.

Only Red stayed where he was, his eyes fixed on Morgan. So close, but so far out of reach.

Red let out a roar of frustration. *'Bastard!'*

Ridley took him by the shoulder. 'C'mon, mate, it's no good. *Move!*

Essh pushed Morgan and Arwydd out of the way, and leapt.

Her wings opened as she sprang, and struck the air once. She shot up in an arc and came down again, straight at the two guards with her talons spread wide. She could not miss.

But she did.

In midair, Essh's pounce suddenly broke. She fell violently sideways and landed hard on her flank, one wing trapped beneath her.

As Red darted away from the screaming griffin, he saw blood darkening in her feathers. Three ragged slashes had appeared, travelling down from under her wing and onto her furred haunch.

'What the —?' Ridley muttered.

'Get down!' someone else bellowed from behind them.

The two guardsmen didn't stop to find out why. They shook off their confusion and ran away to shelter under a nearby window, and not a moment too soon.

The tussle down on the street had attracted Unpartnered, and as the group of guards tried to find hiding places wherever they could, three griffins rushed up on foot. Seeing the cornered humans, they immediately spread out to begin their hunt.

One of them came for Red.

Crouching in his pathetic shelter, he looked up at the approaching griffin and thought, almost coolly, that this time he was going to die. He was too stiff to fight properly, and there was nowhere to run. The Unpartnered would rip him to pieces, and Morgan would escape.

'Son of a bitch,' Red said wearily.

The griffin coming for him didn't bother to hurry. It was in command here; it knew exactly what to do. It must have done it a dozen times already.

Red pointed his sword at it. 'C'mon you bastard, just do it!'

Beside him, Ridley pointed his own sword, but he must have seen that it was hopeless too, because he didn't do anything else.

The griffin raised its talons to strike, and then fell over. It went down with a screech of surprise, and then began to flail around seemingly at random. Red and Ridley dodged a blow from one of its back legs, and backed away in bewilderment.

'What in the gods' names is wrong with it?' Ridley exclaimed.

Around them the other two griffins had also gone down – one dead and the other crippled by a blow that had almost torn its wing clean off. The third one struggled to get up, but even though there was nothing apparently stopping it, it fell back every time. Red, watching in complete confusion, saw injuries start to appear on its body – even though there was nothing inflicting them.

On an impulse, he raised his sword. 'Kill it!' he shouted, and rushed in.

The griffin could have killed him with one blow, but it didn't even seem to notice him. It stayed on the ground, fighting an invisible enemy and losing.

Red chose his moment. He waited until the creature's head was on the ground, and when the opportunity came he darted in and stabbed it through the eye.

The griffin's head jerked away so violently that it wrenched his sword out of his hand and nearly broke his arm in the process, but the damage was already done. As Ridley and the others took their chance and ran in to finish it off, the griffin went into a last juddering spasm and then lay still.

In the silence that followed, Red pulled his sword free and wiped it clean on the griffin's neck.

'We did it!' Ridley shouted suddenly.

The other guards gave a ragged cheer.

'How'd you do it?' one of them asked.

Red realised the man was talking to him. 'I didn't do nothin'!' he said. 'Why'd you think *I* did that? The thing was already down.'

'But you just kinda shouted an' they all went mad!' the guard insisted. 'They just fell down an' went on like they was bein' hurt!'

'They *were,*' said Red, looking at the injuries on the dead griffin. 'I dunno what happened…'

Something else occurred to him, and he looked quickly up the street. But Essh was gone, and so were Morgan and Arwydd. They had taken their opportunity and fled.

'Godsdammit,' Red muttered.

'Anyone know what happened?' asked Ridley. 'Anyone see anythin'?'

They glanced at each other, but nobody spoke up.

'It was *him,*' a guard said eventually, pointing at Red. 'He did it.'

'Don't be daft!' said Red.

'There's somethin' about you,' said the guard. 'I swear there is.'

'Lies!' a voice interrupted.

Red turned sharply, and terror turned his blood to ice.

Every one of the guards there took a step back, and one or two of them actually screamed.

A massive shadow had appeared. It was pure black, and it towered over Red. He could see the big, pale eyes fixed on him, the vicious curved talons, the…

'*Kraego?*' The name strangled itself out of him.

The huge griffin stepped out into the light. 'Lies!' he said again. 'To think this human could do that!' He snorted, and stared angrily at the cowering guards. 'Only the dark griffin has the power to vanish into the shadows, and kill his enemies from there. I saved you.'

Red could feel his heart pattering frantically, but he forced himself to calm down. 'It's all right!' he said loudly. 'He's a friend.'

'*Friend?*' Ridley repeated, sounding half hysterical.

'Yeah, his name's Kraego,' Red said quickly. 'I came here with him. He's the one who saved us.'

'I saved *you*, Red,' said Kraego. 'Now, come. We must leave the city at once.'

'Got it,' said Red. 'But…' he looked back at Ridley and his friends. 'We can't leave them here. Can they come with us?'

'I cannot carry so many,' said Kraego. 'I will take only you.'

'Please!' said Red. He was speaking Cymrian so the others would understand what was going on. 'If we leave 'em here they'll die. We gotta get them out of the city at least.'

'Yeah, let us come too!' a guard piped up. 'We'll take orders from you if you're a griffiner.'

'You are *not* a griffiner,' Kraego snapped. 'Leave them.'

Red folded his arms. 'Go if you want, but I'm stayin' with them.'

'No! You will come with me!'

'Then they're comin' too,' said Red.

'Do as I say, or I will kill you,' said Kraego.

'Stop that!' Red took a step back. He might call Kraego a friend, but he was more than ready to believe that the black griffin might actually kill him if he decided to.

'We have no use for them!' Kraego had begun to snap his beak threateningly, and his wings opened to make him look even bigger.

'We do!' Red quickly chose a new tack. 'They could be followers, right? Y'know, doin' what we say an' that?' He glanced apologetically at Ridley.

'Yeah, that's right!' Ridley joined in. 'We'll do what you say! We're guards; we know how t'take orders, right?'

The others there nodded hastily or called out their agreement.

Kraego began to look calmer. 'Servants for me?'

'Er, yeah,' said Red. 'You're such a big an' powerful griffin; you oughta have followers, right?'

Kraego glanced skyward for any sign of more Unpartnered, and slowly scratched his chest. 'I suppose that this could be a good thing,' he said at last. 'Yes. But they must do as I say, or be left behind.'

'Got it,' said Red. 'They'll be real helpful.'

'Sure we will!' said Ridley.

Kraego stood up. 'Come!' he called. 'Follow me and I will lead you out of the city. Fall behind, and you will be lost. I will not slow for you.'

'Let's go!' Red translated. 'Keep up an' Kraego will get us out of here.'

'Yes sir!' several guards chorused.

Kraego loped off, and the guards formed themselves into a column and followed. Red stayed at their head to begin with, but soon let himself fall behind, and kept an eye out for stragglers and any attacks that might come from the rear. Kraego might leave Ridley and his friends behind, but he wouldn't leave without Red, so Red should be able to save anyone who fell behind if he stayed with them.

While he kept pace with the column, he did a quick head count. Ten people, including Ridley. All of them were either guards in uniform, who must have been on duty, or at least had guard swords and tunics with them. The armourless ones had probably been off duty and hadn't had time to armour up. Either way they would be more than capable of taking care of themselves, and wouldn't have any trouble following Kraego's selfish whims.

All the same, Red privately decided that if anyone else tried to join up with them along the way, he would quietly give them permission. Kraego probably wouldn't notice; griffins weren't very good at counting. He had come too late to save Canran, but he had to do what he could to save its people.

With that thought, he squared his shoulders and marched on through the town, sword at the ready.

*

Elsewhere, Morgan, Arwydd and Essh also made their escape. Having used the Unpartnered attack as a distraction, they made a hasty retreat on foot. Essh took them to where Echo waited, and once Morgan and Arwydd had mounted up, the two griffins flew out of Canran.

They took shelter up in the mountains, well away from the city but at a vantage point close enough to keep watch over the devastation going on below. There Essh and Echo settled down to groom and rest, and Morgan and Arwydd sat down side by side to look down at Canran and catch their breath.

Arwydd watched the Unpartnered fly over the city, and shivered.

'Morgan, I'm so sorry I said that about you, and about your brother,' she said suddenly. 'I was stupid.'

'It's all right,' said Morgan. 'But what were you doing here? You were supposed to go back with the others.'

'I know, but we didn't.' Arwydd gave him a stubborn look, as if expecting him to tell her off. It quickly wilted, however. 'You're right,' she said, avoiding his eye. 'I'm useless. I decided to come after you because I wanted… I don't know. I thought I could help somehow, and Essh wanted to be in the fight, so we agreed. And then we met up with Echo and he told us you hadn't come to meet him, so we went in to find you, and…' She trailed off.

'I had it under control,' said Morgan.

'No you didn't! That guard was about to kill you!'

Morgan relaxed and grinned. 'All right, I admit it; you saved my skin back there. Thank you.'

Arwydd smiled back shyly. 'You're welcome.'

They sat together in silence for a while.

'What will we do next?' Echo asked, coming up behind them. 'Is it time to go to Shar?'

'Not sure,' said Morgan. He looked out over the skies beyond Canran, and his forehead furrowed. 'Echo,' he asked, 'you said you saw a giant griffin flying over Canran before. Did you get a good look at it?'

'I did,' said Echo. 'I saw him many times while you were in the city. Once he even came into the mountains where I was, but I hid from him. You have seen his colours?'

'No,' said Morgan. 'I only saw him from a distance. Why, what did you find out?'

Echo snorted uneasily. 'Morgan… this griffin we have been following is no ordinary male. He is a giant, and his feathers are black.'

Essh hissed. 'A black griffin?'

'Yes,' said Echo. 'Black feathers and blue eyes, and pale haunches. His scent is familiar to me.'

Morgan hissed his own shock, sounding uncannily like a griffin. 'Great gods, this is bad.'

'Why?' Arwydd asked nervously. 'It's just a griffin, isn't it?'

'No,' said Echo.

'He's right,' said Morgan. 'This isn't an ordinary griffin we're talking about. It's a dark griffin. The stories were true.'

'What are you talking about?' asked Arwydd.

Morgan glanced at his partner. 'You tell her, Echo.'

The spotted griffin clicked his beak.

'It is said that before he died, the Mighty Skandar fathered one last chick – a male. We know that he fertilised many eggs in his life, but this one was different. The others were mere griffins like myself. Large, but with nothing else special to them. But the stories told in Malvern at the time of Skandar's death say that his last chick was given his father's coat. Black and silver.'

'So?' said Arwydd. 'It's just a colour.'

'There is more,' said Echo. 'The black youngster's mother was Senneck herself, and she said—,'

'Senneck?' Arwydd repeated.

Echo rasped irritably at the interruption. 'Yes, Senneck. Her human was Erian the Bastard, who tried to kill Skandar's human and came the closest to succeeding. Senneck laid Skandar's egg, and she often boasted that it was a black egg.'

Arwydd began to lose patience. 'Why is this so important?'

Echo hissed at her. 'Do you know nothing? The Mighty Skandar was hatched from a black egg. Only he came from such an egg. If this young griffin was also from a black egg, and if he has his father's dark coat, then this means he may have his father's power.'

'Oh.' Arwydd looked at Morgan. 'What power did the Mighty Skandar have, anyway? I mean, specifically?'

Essh spoke up. 'The dark griffin has the power to make the Shadow That Walks. He may fly in the shadows, and his magic can strike down a hundred enemies in an instant. He is death in the sky, a master of the night. No griffin is mightier, or more deadly.'

'*No!*' Arwydd gaped. 'But… then that means… oh, gods. Is that what happened before? I mean, in the city, when you fell over like that? What did that to you?'

Essh's tail twitched.

'I do not know… it was as if a massive griffin struck me, but I saw nothing.'

Echo stood up sharply. 'You were attacked from the shadows?'

'Yes,' said Essh. 'I was attacked as I moved to kill the human with the red fur. Then when some Unpartnered came, they were also attacked.'

All four of them looked at each other in alarm.

'That makes it certain then,' said Echo. 'This black griffin is Skandar's son, and has his power.'

'And,' said Morgan. 'He's on the Southerners' side.'

'No,' Arwydd groaned.

Morgan stood up, and began to pace back and forth.

'This changes everything. If Skandar's son fights for the enemy, there's no telling how much damage this could do to us.'

'He's still just one griffin, though,' said Arwydd.

'One griffin?' Morgan shouted. 'Good gods, woman, haven't you heard *any* of the stories? The Mighty Skandar used his power to destroy entire armies! Now his son could do the same to us! And it's *worse* than that! If he's chosen this man – this Red, the guard – then they could destroy us! Every man in the South would run to follow a pair that powerful! If they managed to rally everyone against us, we'd be done for.'

Arwydd had turned pale. 'And what about the Shadow That Walks?'

Morgan hesitated.

'Well,' he said, 'supposedly, that can only happen with the Night God's blessing. Only a Northerner can become the Shadow That Walks. No, I don't think that'll be a problem. Which is just as well, because we already have a very big problem to worry about.'

Arwydd stood, and took him by the shoulders.

'All right,' she said firmly. 'So what are we going to do?'

'There's only one thing we can do,' said Morgan. 'If those two escape from Canran, then I have to go after them. They have to be dealt with before they cause us any more trouble.'

'Then I'm coming with you,' said Arwydd.

Morgan hesitated. 'Fine. We'll meet up with the others from Canran and send them back to the King with this information.'

'Agreed,' said Arwydd. 'But first we should rest.'

'Yes, you're right. I'm not due to meet up with them until the morning anyway.'

'This is a good plan,' said Echo.

'Yes,' said Essh. 'To kill the son of Skandar would win us much glory.'

'It's a pity,' Arwydd sighed. 'If only he was on our side.'

'If only,' said Morgan.

He looked down at the destruction of Canran, and murmured the words to himself like a mystical chant.

'Shadow That Walks…'

Chapter Eighteen

Tintilla

With Kraego's help, escaping from Canran was easy enough.

The giant griffin ran ahead of the band of guards, making no effort to help them keep up, but he was hard to lose. The Unpartnered saw them, but few of them did anything. Most of them, seeing Kraego, left in a hurry. If any came too close, a threatening lunge from Kraego was enough to see them off. None of them were willing to try and take him on, even in a group.

Along the way, other people did indeed join up with Red's group. Some were other guards, but most were just ordinary citizens. Red called to them to come with him and they, glad to find some kind of direction in all the chaos, obeyed.

Kraego must have already seen an escape route before he joined them, because he led them directly to a spot where the outer wall of Canran had collapsed, probably thanks to a magical attack of some sort.

The giant griffin charged straight over the rubble and out into the lands beyond Canran, where he found a sheltered spot in a rocky canyon.

There, he stopped and settled down to groom as if nothing had happened.

Red and the other humans clustered around him – albeit at a safe distance – and slumped down wherever they stood. Most of them were visibly gasping with shock and tiredness, some were injured; all looked relieved.

Kraego ignored them.

Red left him alone for the moment, and moved through the little group, checking to see if anyone needed help. Luckily, none of them was very seriously hurt, and most of the escapees who had joined up were strong adults – Red only saw two children, and they were unhurt and old enough to walk.

The guards had already moved toward him.

'Now what?' asked Ridley.

Everyone there looked expectantly at Red. He hesitated, but then he glanced at Kraego and realised what he had to do. To them, he was a griffiner. Therefore, he was in charge.

He coughed. 'We oughta be safe here for a bit, an' we should rest. In the meantime, I'd better do a headcount. Also, someone should go back an' see if there's anyone outside the city what needs help. But no goin' back in, understand? Anyone's still alive in there, they're on their own. We go back there, we die too.'

'Yes, sir,' said Ridley. 'I'll go.'

'Me too,' said Tarn, who had been one of those to join up along the way.

Two other guards offered to go with them, so Red gave them the go-ahead, and returned to count his new followers.

There were twenty-five of them, including the two children, who had come with their mother and were both crying with fright.

Red shook his head sadly. 'All right,' he said loudly. 'Before we do anythin' else, I should prob'ly introduce myself. My name's Captain Kearney Redguard, but you can call me Red. An' this is Kraego, my friend.'

'"Captain"?' one man repeated. 'You ain't a Lord?'

'Nope,' said Red. 'I'm with the guard. From Liranwee, though. Who are you?'

'Asple,' said the man, looking slightly embarrassed. 'I'm a brewer. Ain't you a griffiner? How can you be a guard if you're a griffiner?'

Red shrugged. 'Kraego an' me are just friends. Right, Kraego?'

'You are a fool who follows me about,' Kraego growled.

Red grinned. 'He's cranky, but he won't hurt you. Just stay out of his way.'

'You gonna lead us somewhere safe?' asked a nearby woman. She looked back despairingly toward Canran. 'Can't go home now, not no more. Where're we gonna go?'

Red scratched his moustache. 'I ain't from around here, so I'm gonna need some advice. Anyone here know a place we could walk to? Wylam's the nearest big city, but it's too far an' we got no supplies.'

Silence fell.

Then one of the guards stood up. 'Tintilla.'

Red opened his mouth to ask what that was, and stopped in surprise. The speaker wore a guard's armour and carried a sword, but she was a woman. She wore her hair short, and she was the most muscular woman he'd ever seen, but she was still clearly a woman.

'Uh,' said Red. 'Er. Tintilla? What's that?'

The woman's voice was as fierce as her grubby face. 'It's a town, sir. Where I grew up. We can go there.'

'Oh,' said Red, feeling stupid. 'Where is it?'

'Southways,' said the woman. 'I walked to Canran from there, so we can walk back.'

'You reckon it's big enough for all of us?' asked Red.

'S'got about three hundred people livin' in it,' said the woman. 'I reckon it's big enough. I still got a house there; we can rest up there.'

'Sounds good to me,' said Red. 'If you can show us the way, that's where we'll go.'

'I'll do it,' said the woman.

'Thanks a lot,' said Red. 'What're you called?'

'Name's Senna,' said the woman. 'Senna Wulfsen.'

"Sen" was the female version of "son" when it came to names, but a woman with a surname in honour of her parentage generally took her mother's name and "Wulf" belonged to a man. Several people there gave Senna odd looks.

She glared back defiantly.

Red pretended not to notice. 'Right then, that's the plan. I'll just go see how Ridley's doin'.'

He left the canyon and walked slowly back toward the open ground around the city. His joints had stiffened so badly that walking was agony by now, but he shook it off. Now wasn't the time to rest.

Ridley and the others weren't far away. Red found them at the edge of the loose rocks near the canyon, waving to some fleeing survivors to come to them.

Red joined them, and once the last of them had run over he led them back to the canyon where Kraego waited.

The giant griffin was already standing. 'Come,' he said. 'We cannot stay here; we must leave at once.'

'Right,' said Red. 'Everyone right for walkin'?'

'Where are we going?' asked one of the newcomers.

Red gestured toward Senna. 'Senna here can show us to a place called Tintilla. You lot reckon that'll work?'

'Should,' said Tarn. 'Tintilla ain't far away.'

'How far?' Red asked Senna.

'Two days, just about,' she answered. 'We'd better go now.'

Red looked back toward Canran. Dawn had begun to lighten the sky, but over the red stone city, smoke made the darkness linger.

'Yeah,' he muttered. 'No goin' back now. Kraego?'

'We will go to this place,' said Kraego. 'To rest and eat before we are ready to move on to Wylam. I will walk, so the Unpartnered will not see me.'

'Got it.' Red nodded to the others. 'Let's go.'

Slowly, wearily, the survivors stood up and began to walk away out of the canyon with Senna leading the way. Most of them had nothing but the clothes on their backs. Everything they owned had been lost in one night.

Nobody said anything, but Red could feel the despair that hung over all of them. It made his heart go heavy in his chest. Canran had been a home to him, just briefly, and now it was gone. Like Liranwee. And this time, he had no rage left to comfort himself.

The sun rose as the little group limped and straggled away south and into the open countryside. Its light shone weakly on their backs and faces, too feeble to do more than highlight lines and hollows. It touched Kraego's feathers, but it could bring no light there at all.

Red turned his head to watch the first pale rays point up into the sky from the horizon. Sunrise had always been a symbol of hope to every true Southerner, but this thin, watery light looked like nothing more than a mockery of it.

'Gryphus help us all,' he muttered, and turned away.

*

Senna had predicted that the walk to Tintilla would take two days, and maybe for her it had. But for the band of just over thirty of Canran's surviving citizens, it took closer to four. And no wonder. Only Red had any food or water with him, and the injuries of some of them slowed the group down even more.

And, before the first day had even passed, a strange weakness began to go through them. The oldest and the youngest among them were the first to show signs of it, but before long, everyone there felt unwell. Soon both of the two children were ill – feverish and confused. Soon they were unable to walk, and had to be carried.

By the third day, the illness had begun to affect the strong adults as well, including Red. He began to feel a strange lassitude in his body, even after his injuries had improved. Pain started to spike in his guts, and then his lungs as well. Sometimes, when he was particularly tired, it affected his mind as well. He started to have dizzy spells, and every so often his vision would go grey around the edges.

He shook it off as well as he could, and did his best to help the others along, but once the sicker of them had begun to weaken, they went on weakening.

They passed through farmland along the way to Tintilla, and the locals did what they could to help the "griffiner" and his friends – offering food and water. It helped, and the sickness seemed to improve. But it didn't go away, not completely.

As for Kraego, he of course did better than anyone. The farmers they met offered him the pick of their stock – believing that it would bring good luck – and he ate well and healed quickly. Once they were well away from Canran, he took to flying ahead, scouting out the land, and once he even came back with news of a stream he had found, where Red and the others could rest.

On the morning of the fourth day, as they set out again, Red moved to the front of the column to keep pace with Senna.

'Senna, when're we gonna get there?' he asked. 'It's been three days, an' I don't reckon those poor kids are gonna last much longer.'

Senna might have looked strong and fierce on their first meeting, but now she had grey smudges around her eyes and her face had turned pale. 'Can't be much longer,' she said. 'We're movin' so slow.'

'No surprise,' said Red. 'Ain't you got a better idea than that? Will we get there today?'

'Should do,' said Senna. 'I'm sorry; it's just been a while, an' I was on my own.'

'Yeah, I was wonderin' about that,' said Red. 'Why'd you come to Canran, anyway? Why're you wearin' guard armour? You ain't a guard.'

'Why not?' Senna snapped.

'Women can't be guards,' Red said bluntly. 'It's forbidden.'

She growled and straightened her helmet. 'I'm as good a guard as any of that lot. Anyway, Canran's gone. Ain't no law left now. Not there, anyway.'

'All right, but where'd you get the armour?' said Red. 'They didn't let you join up, did they?'

Senna spat. 'My dad was a guard. He wanted a son t'be just like him, but he got me instead, an' after that my mam couldn't have no more kids. So he trained me up instead. An' when he died, he left me his armour an' his sword. Said I should go to Canran an' join up. Fight for it, if I had to.'

'An' did you?' asked Red.

'Would have. Didn't get no chance. Them bloody griffins showed up first.'

Just as well, Red thought, looking at her with some sympathy. The guards were an old order, and set in their ways – they wouldn't let a woman join up, no matter how tough. It had never been allowed, so it never would be, and that was it.

'They let women be griffiners, don't they?' said Senna, glaring at him as if she had guessed what he was thinking. 'They let 'em be Eyrie Mistresses. Women can rule whole cities, but they can't join the guards?'

'Yeah, well, griffins change everything, don't they?' said Red.

Senna looked up at Kraego, as he circled overhead. 'Yeah, an' not for the better.'

'Not always,' Red muttered.

'That's a black griffin,' said Senna. 'Like Darkheart.'

'The Mighty Skandar,' Red corrected. 'Yeah.'

'Them's bad luck,' said Senna. 'You'd better watch that thing, mate.'

'I gotta admit,' said Red. 'I ain't had much good luck since I met him. But he's saved my life more than once. Saved all of you, too. I trust him.'

'Yeah, I see it.' Senna gave him a look. 'You're an odd one, Red. When we get where we're goin', you oughta tell us your story.'

'Sure I will.' Red winced as his muscles twinged.

They walked on in silence for a while.

'Look,' said Red. 'Tell yer what. I know what it's like to want somethin' so bad you'd just about die for it. An' I know what it's like t'lose a father too. I've been a guard since before I had more'n two hairs on my chest. I might have a griffin followin' me about nowadays, but a guard's all I am an' a guard's all I ever wanted t'be. Point is, I know how y'must be feelin'.'

'Yeah?' Senna looked cautiously at him.

'So I'll make a promise,' said Red. 'I'm in charge here, so that means what I say goes. Nobody here's argued with that, anyhow. So… you show me you know how t'be a guard, let me see you got what it takes, an' I'll swear you in.'

Senna stared. 'Y'what?'

'You heard,' said Red. 'I'll gather the lads here together an' we'll swear you in. Make a proper guard of you, if that's what you want.'

'You'd do that?' said Senna.

'Sure,' said Red. He rubbed his eyes – they were aching again. 'I reckon if we're gonna deal with the Northerners, we'll need good guards t'do it.'

Senna grinned, showing a broken front tooth, and clapped him on the shoulder. 'I'm with you, Red. An' thanks.'

Red shrugged. 'No problem.'

*

Thankfully, they did indeed reach Tintilla that day. It was a larger town that Red had expected, with several streets and plenty of good brick houses. It even had a small temple, right at the centre.

Senna led the exhausted group straight to a small house on the outskirts, and unlocked the door. It was musty inside, and there were only three rooms, but Senna soon had a good fire going in the fireplace, and brought out enough blankets to set up some makeshift beds on the floor.

Once they had settled in, Ridley and Tarn went out to buy some food and came back with enough for everyone to have a decent meal. Kraego, unable to fit through the front door, flew off by himself to find some food of his own.

That night, the survivors of Canran gathered in the main room. There wasn't anywhere near enough room for everyone to sit around the table, so Senna and a few others moved the chairs away and laid the food out on the table for everyone to help themselves. Red stayed nearby to make sure everyone got their fair share, and afterwards, when some of the weaker and sicker people had gone into the other two rooms to sleep, he sat down by the fire and shared some cider that Senna had had stored in a little underground cellar.

'So,' said Senna, once things had quieted down. 'Ain't it time you told us your story, Red?'

Red shrugged. 'Like what?'

The others there had already begun looking at him with interest.

'You're from Liranwee, right?' said Ridley.

'Yeah,' said Tarn. 'Tell us about that. Tell us how you got t'be flyin' around with a griffin. The whole story.'

Red took a drink. 'You interested?'

'Yeah,' said Senna. 'Go on. It's the right time for stories, ain't it?'

So Red told them. He started at the beginning, with a brief description of his father's life and death. Then he went on, and as he realised that more and more people were leaning closer to listen, he started to tell them everything. His travels with Kullervo, his time as a guard. The murders and the execution of the Hangman. His capture by the Northerners, and his escape, and everything that happened afterwards, up until the sack of Liranwee and Lady Isleen's final command.

Red wasn't a storyteller, or a poet; he told it all bluntly and matter-of-factly, like a guard reporting to his superiors. But before long the room had gone utterly silent. Everyone was listening intently, and others had appeared in the entrances to the other rooms to listen as well.

'An' so,' Red finished, 'here I am. Liranwee's gone, an' now Canran too. Guess I could say I feel like a failure, but puttin' a stop to all this is gonna take more than just me; it's gonna take everyone. Us Southerners have got to start workin' together if we want to save our land. As for me… well, I gotta finish followin' Isleen's orders. Gotta warn the other cities an' do what I can to make 'em band together. But after that, I got another thing I gotta do.'

'An' what's that?' asked Ridley, speaking for the first time since Red had begun.

Red scowled under his moustache. 'I got no Eyrie any more. No superiors. It's just me an' Kraego. He's taken a vow to kill the King's partner, Shar. An' me – I've made a vow too, an' I'll go to the ends of the earth t'see it come true if I have to.'

'What vow?' asked Senna.

'I'm gonna kill the King,' said Red. 'Gonna kill his lackey, too. Morgan the spy. These hands here,' – he held them up – 'are gonna be the hands that kill those two. I swear it by the proud old name of Redguard, an' by Gryphus himself.'

Senna, Ridley, Tarn and the other guards looked fierce.

'That's right,' said Tarn. 'It's a good oath, that. An' you know what? I'm gonna take one too.'

Everyone looked at him.

'Yeah,' he said again. 'That's right. I, Guardsman Tarn of Canran, swear that I'm gonna do everything I can t'stop the King an' his armies.'

'Me too,' said Ridley.

'And me,' said another guard.

'And me!' said a second.

'And me!' several others chorused.

'Yeah,' Senna growled. 'See, we're like you now, Red. We've lost our home. Our Eyrie. Lost 'em to *them*. So when the time comes t'fight together, we'll be there. I vow I'll take down a hundred Northerners before I'm finished.'

'She's right!' said Ridley. He stood up, and saluted. 'Captain Redguard, you've led us this far. Saved our lives. When it's time t'fight back, I'll follow you again – into battle!'

'We *all* will!' said Senna, standing and saluting too.

The others muttered their agreement.

Red stood up too. 'You're right,' he said. 'We gotta stand together on this. We're on the run now, but we won't run forever. We'll join up with the others out there, an' we'll show those bloody Northerners that you can't attack the South an' expect to have it your own way. We'll show the bastards what we're made of, won't we?'

'Piss an' vinegar!' Ridley shouted, making several people laugh.

'That's the one!' Red said savagely. 'An' if you want me to lead you, I will. But—,'

The others went quiet.

'Tomorrow I gotta leave,' said Red. 'Kraego an' me still have to go to the other Eyries, an' we gotta do it fast. But—,' he held up a hand to quiet their protests. 'I promise we'll be back. You can get started without us. In the meantime, I'm puttin' Senna here in charge.'

'*What?*' Ridley's outrage was echoed by plenty others.

'That's enough!' said Red. 'I've had time t'get the measure of all of you by now, an' Senna's the best commander here. So you'll do as she says. An' Senna – I'm trustin' you t'lead this lot properly. You reckon you can do that?'

'Yes, sir!' said Senna, her eyes shining with pride.

'Ridley an' Tarn are your seconds, an' they'll take over if anything happens to you,' said Red. 'After I've left it'll be up to you three to decide what to do next, but my advice is that you go to…' he hesitated. 'Eagleholm.'

'Eagleholm's gone!' said Tarn. 'Everyone knows that.'

'It's gone,' Red nodded. 'But it's comin' back. The survivors from Eagleholm have gone south to the Coppertops. To a place called Rivermeet. They're buildin' New Eagleholm there. The Northerners won't know about it yet, so you'll be safe there. I reckon it'd be a good place to regroup if the other cities fall. An'… I reckon they will.'

The others looked grim.

'Aye, we'll go there,' said Senna. 'If we have to. But first we'll go on to Wylam, maybe. If they're gonna send troops to Canran, we'll join up.'

'Right, then,' said Red. 'But Eagleholm'll be our meeting place. If I don't know where to find you, that's where I'll go. That's where you'll find me if you need me.'

'Yes, sir,' said Ridley. 'We'll remember.'

'There's only one question left,' said Senna. 'A squad needs a good name. What'll we call ourselves?'

Red rubbed his head. 'Let's call ourselves… the Last Guards.'

'Sounds good t'me,' said Ridley.

Chapter Nineteen

Dead Mountain

The next morning, at dawn, Red and Kraego set out for Wylam.

The journey to the famous "water city" passed uneventfully – much to Red's relief – and when they arrived, they found everything peaceful.

Wylam had a feature that made it unique among all of Cymria's griffiner capitals. Long ago, it had been built on low ground around the banks of a river. Once the buildings were complete, the river had been dammed. Now all of Wylam's buildings were surrounded by streets of water – protected from ground attacks, and even slightly safer from an assault by griffins, who did not like to fight over water.

As in Canran, Red and Kraego went straight to the Eyrie tower. There they were quickly granted an audience with the new Eyrie Master, the oddly-named Lord Ekra. Ekra and his partner Iraka listened seriously to Isleen's message.

'We already heard that Liranwee had been attacked,' said Ekra. 'But this news about Canran… we'll begin preparing for war immediately.'

'Thank you, sir,' said Red.

'In the meantime, you can stay a few days to rest and re-supply,' said Ekra.

Red and Kraego were both happy to accept.

This time, neither of them wanted to stay longer than one night. They had learned their lesson well enough at Canran.

But, even though he hadn't said anything to Kraego about it, Red had begun to worry. Not about the war, but about himself.

The sickness that had come over him on the walk from Canran still had not left him. Not that he felt *ill*, so much, but he did feel… weak. His insides ached dully, and he still had moments of lightheadedness. It was enough to bother him. If it got worse…

But it wouldn't, he reassured himself as he lay awake in his guest room. He was getting better. He'd be fine.

But he did not feel fine when he woke up the next morning. Even though he had slept deeply, he woke up exhausted. His head ached savagely, and his stomach as well. He was starving, but couldn't make himself eat anything.

Kraego appeared just as he was trying to force down some breakfast.

'We must leave.'

'Right.' Red put down his spoon. 'Just let me get my stuff.'

He stood up, and his head immediately started to spin. He stumbled over to the bed, and picked up his bag.

Kraego watched him. 'Are you hurt?'

'No.' Red leant on the wall and took a few deep breaths. 'I'll be right.'

'Come, then,' said Kraego.

Red slung his bag on his back, and managed to climb on. 'We're off to Eagleholm next, right? Gonna see Lady Liantha.'

'Yes,' said Kraego. 'The flight should not be long; I have flown it before.'

'Right.' Red tried to steady himself. Fortunately, the dizziness had died down.

Kraego loped out onto the balcony, and took off.

For a while, as he stayed still and let Kraego do the work, Red started to hope that he was getting better. Maybe he wasn't as bad as he'd thought.

But, before long, he began to realise that he was not well at all. He started to feel cold, but he could feel himself sweating even as he shivered. His hands felt weak, and before long he found his eyelids drooping and had to fight to stay awake. If he fell asleep now, he would probably fall to his death. He managed to keep going through that day, but he felt worse and worse as it dragged on, and

When Kraego finally stopped for the night, he managed to start a fire and lie down under the blanket he had brought – and even that felt like a heroic struggle. After that he fell asleep almost instantly, without having eaten anything all day.

*

Red didn't remember much of the journey toward Eagleholm. Within two days, the sickness had taken full hold of him, and as it drained his strength it brought fevers and confusion.

Even Kraego quickly realised that his friend was ailing, and he showed surprising sympathy – when Red became too weak to hold onto his back, the griffin took to carrying him instead – cradling him in his talons like a baby.

'You are very ill,' he said on the third day. 'I know of a leaf that may cure a fever, but it does not grow here and I do not think it will heal a human.'

'No,' Red mumbled. 'Got to get to… city. Other people. Need a doctor.'

'I understand this,' said Kraego. 'I will take you to Eagleholm and they will help you. But you must be strong until then.'

'Will be,' said Red.

Kraego lay down beside him, warming him with his flank. 'Do not despair. You are a strong human, Red. You have survived many things that would kill a weaker one. You fly with a griffin, and the strength of a griffin is yours. We do not lie down and die until our time has come. Your time is not now.'

Red grinned at him. 'Sounds like poetry.'

'I do not know that word,' Kraego said primly. 'Sleep now.'

And Red slept.

Some days after this, when the fever was at its worst, Kraego finally announced that they were getting close to New Eagleholm.

'Very soon we will be there,' he said. 'Tomorrow or the day after, perhaps. Tonight, we will rest at my true home.'

Red kept his eyes closed. 'Home…?'

'A place you know,' said Kraego. 'Once its name was Eagleholm. Now, no human lives there, and no griffin either. Now, it is called Dead Mountain.'

Red let himself drift away from the giant griffin's words, but they awoke memories in him all the same. Old Eagleholm, where his parents had been born. He had visited it as a child, with Kullervo.

Old Eagleholm had been a great city built on a mountaintop, but before Red had been born, that city had died. Destroyed from within, so they said, by a man called Arren Cardockson. Of course, nowadays very few people remembered that name. They knew him by the names he had taken up later. Lord Arenadd Taranisäii. The Dark Lord. The Shadow That Walked.

Some said that Old Eagleholm had been his birthplace. Not just the place where the dreaded Northerner had grown up, but the place where he had become twisted. Where he had met the dark griffin, Skandar, and been corrupted by him and by the Night God's will.

With the Dark Lord created inside it, the city never stood a chance.

When the mountain came in sight, Red watched it through dull eyes. He remembered it very well from last time he had seen it – but who could forget? The closer it came, the more he could see of the ruins.

The city had been built on top of a massive stone column – so huge it was more of a plateau than a mountain. Even then the occupants had expanded the space on top by building enormous wooden platforms to hold more houses. But the most important buildings had stood on the original stone. Red saw them now – or their remains. The skeletons of burned-out houses, heaps of rubble and garbage. Bones, too, somewhere among it all. And, right at the centre, was the remains of the Eyrie. Part of a wall, still standing among the tumbled bricks.

Kraego landed further out from there, among the remains of what had been the Hatchery, where most of Eagleholm's griffins had grown up. His mother Senneck had hatched there, and had returned more than forty years later to lay an egg of her own – Kraego's black egg.

Now the main building had mostly collapsed, but Kraego managed to shoulder his way inside. He laid Red down on the floor. 'We will rest here.'

Red curled up, shivering.

'You remember this place?' Kraego asked him. 'I have returned to it many times.'

Red rolled onto his back. 'Yer mother laid yer egg here,' he said. 'I was there. People... tried to kill us. Saw Kullervo. Thought he was his father. Arren.'

'Yes.' Kraego put Red's bag down beside him. 'Now, eat and sleep. In the morning we will go on to New Eagleholm. Do not be afraid,' he added. 'There are no humans here now. If danger does come, I will protect you.'

Red sat up, and hauled the blanket out of his bag. 'Thanks.' He wrapped himself up in it, and huddled down against Kraego's huge chest. 'I never thought you cared, but you do.'

'I need you,' said Kraego. 'You cannot die.'

Red closed his eyes. 'Brothers.' He started to shiver again. 'You're… only… the only one left. No family now. Friends… gone. Just you left. You an' me.'

'Rest,' Kraego commanded. 'We will talk later; you must sleep.'

'Yeah.' Red relaxed. 'Sleep.'

*

And he did sleep. But it was not peaceful sleep.

Even though it was cold on the mountain, the fever had made him hot – and he dreamt of heat. Heat that filled his body and scorched his face, as he ran through the streets of a burning city. Everywhere around him, flames rose into the sky. Houses glowed orange and then turned black, as the fire billowed out through windows and doors. He thought he could hear screams coming from inside them, but surely nobody could be alive in there. He couldn't help them, or even stop. He had to run.

But no matter how fast he ran, or how far, his enemies were always just behind him. He didn't look back at them, but somehow he knew what they looked like anyway. They were guards, that was it. Guards in their armour and their uniform tunics, whose faces were skulls. They made no sound. No warning shouts for him to stop, no cursing, no threats. Even their boots were silent on the ground. It was as if they knew that he couldn't escape, and didn't care about trying to arrest him.

They weren't going to arrest him, that was why. They were going to kill him.

There was no escape. His sword was gone, and he wouldn't be able to fight them off when they caught him. But he ran anyway. Gasping for breath, staggering as pain rose in his chest, he ran for all he was worth, doing everything he could to let himself live just a little longer.

His legs started to give out. He was slowing down. They were catching up, and soon they would have him.

Don't give up! a voice called from off to his left.

Red turned his head, and saw that he was not alone. There were others running alongside him – a man, and a griffin.

The man was a Northerner, and vaguely familiar. Morgan? Or his King? His curly hair flew out behind him as he ran, and he glanced encouragingly at Red.

Beside him, the griffin ran with its wings tightly folded. It was black. Not black as Kraego was black, but pure black, in every hair and feather. Its eyes were pale silver slits behind its massive beak.

Its head turned toward him, and the beak opened. *Run with us,* a voice whispered.

'But we can't get away!' Red yelled back.

The Northerner laughed wildly. *No-one can! But we run!*

So they ran, all three of them together, and with the others beside him Red found he could run faster. The skull-faced guards began to disappear behind him, and the flames on either side died down. But as they did the light they had made faded too, and darkness began to close in. Red saw the houses turn to charred skeletons that crumbled away, and the black griffin vanished – leaving nothing but its eyes, floating in the blackness.

'Everything's gone!' Red exclaimed. 'So where's the ground…?'

Then he realised that it was gone too – there was nothing under his feet, and he teetered in the air.

'Help!'

The Northerner was still there. *Come with us,* he said.

Red tried to back away from him. 'No… don't touch me.'

The man only laughed. He grabbed Red by the front of his tunic and hurled himself into the void, dragging him down and into absolute nothingness.

Chapter Twenty

Revenge

R ed felt himself trembling violently as the dream left him, but when he opened his eyes, he knew instantly that something had changed. He felt weak and shaky, but for the first time in days his head was clear. The fever had gone. So had the internal ache that had been troubling him for so long.

He was better.

Kraego stirred a little while later, and found Red busy munching on some stale bread.

'You are hungry at last?' said the griffin.

Red nodded, and swallowed. 'Feelin' much better – just starving is all.'

Kraego stretched and yawned, and got up to begin his morning groom. 'I can smell you easily. The odour of sickness is gone. You have recovered, and will soon be strong again.'

Red grinned and finished off the last of the bread. 'Here's hopin'. But I had the weirdest dream…' he trailed off and frowned.

Kraego wasn't listening anyway. 'Now you may ride on my back again, and we will reach New Eagleholm soon.'

'We're leavin' today, right?' said Red.

'Yes,' said Kraego.

'Good. This place gives me the chills.'

To his surprise, Kraego agreed. 'This is indeed a dead place. There is no food here, no warmth. A poor place for my egg to have been laid.'

'Yeah, we had a lousy time here,' said Red. 'Here's hopin' New Eagleholm'll be better.'

'You will see for yourself soon,' said Kraego. 'Now gather your belongings, and we will leave. It will not be far to fly now.'

*

They set out not long after this, but Red didn't enjoy flying much –

he was just as weak as he had thought, and holding on was difficult. The cold seemed to affect him more, too.

But the sun warmed his back, and he was happy enough just to know that he was better at last, and was leaving the depressing ruin of Dead Mountain behind. He didn't look back at it, but he imagined that he could feel it getting further away, and that made him happier too.

Not that the lands beyond Dead Mountain were very pleasant. On their way to the place – though Red didn't remember much of it – they had seen plenty of deserted villages, and former farmlands left to run wild. The fighting that had destroyed Eagleholm had destroyed its lands as well, and it seemed that nobody was left living in them for miles around.

But, as they moved further southward away from Dead Mountain, Red and Kraego started to see some signs of life. Maybe the war hadn't come this far, because the signs of destruction – the burned griffiner towers, the abandoned villages – started to disappear. They began to see signs of habitation instead – fields with farmers at work in them, and villages whose buildings were still occupied and in good repair.

When Kraego stopped for the night he stopped at one of those villages, whose occupants came out cautiously to greet them.

When Red asked them about their home, they answered that their village – and all the other villages in the area – were under the protection of New Eagleholm, its Eyrie Mistress Lady Liantha, and her partner Seerae.

'So they made it!' Red exclaimed. 'They built the city?'

'Yes, milord,' said the villager he'd been questioning. 'An' some of us commoners came out here t'make new lives in the old villages what got mostly abandoned in the wars.'

Red frowned and said nothing else. It was such a wonderful thing to see these ruined places being rebuilt and reoccupied, and the thought that they might be destroyed all over again was too awful for words.

The villagers gave him and Kraego shelter for the night, respectful as commoners generally were toward griffins and their partners, and the next morning the travellers moved on yet again.

'We will reach New Eagleholm soon,' Kraego said before he took off. 'One more night and one more day and it will be in sight.'

'You're sure?' asked Red.

'Yes. I have been this way before and have seen the city.'

'You've seen it?' said Red. 'What's it like?'

'When I last saw it, it was small and not yet fully built,' said Kraego. 'There are not many humans living in it, I think. But we will see how much it has changed.'

He took off, and once he had steadied out in the air, Red relaxed and smiled to himself at the thought of seeing Liantha again. He had only met her very briefly, but he remembered her kindness. He wondered if she would recognise him.

*

But Red and Kraego were not the only ones on their way to Eagleholm.

Morgan, Echo, Arwydd and Essh had tracked them until, two days away from the new city, their target came in sight.

Echo had flown ahead to scout out the land, and returned with the news.

'I have seen them,' the spotted griffin reported. 'They are not far ahead, roosting for the night among some trees.'

'Did you get a good look at them?' asked Morgan.

'Yes,' said Echo. 'You and I were right. The griffin is the same black griffin that I saw, and the human is the red-furred one that we took prisoner.'

Morgan swore. 'They didn't see you, did they?'

'No,' said Echo. 'I avoided their eyes. Now we must make plans, before they come too close to others who may help them.'

Arwydd had been listening. 'Why would they be close to help? The maps don't show anything around here for miles.'

'They must be going somewhere,' said Morgan. 'Maybe to hide out in the mountains, or more likely they're going to meet someone. Don't forget how old our maps are; those two might know something we don't.'

'My human is right,' said Echo. 'We must stop them, and soon.'

'Tonight,' Essh interrupted. 'We may not have a better chance.'

'That's probably true,' said Morgan. 'What d'you suggest, Echo?'

'The dark griffin is the danger,' Echo said immediately. 'He must die.'

'I'd say we should try and get him on our side instead, but it'd be a fool's hope,' said Morgan. 'As long as he's on their side he's a danger. If we can kill him, then the guard won't be a problem.'

'We will ambush him,' said Essh. 'Once he is asleep, Echo and I shall attack together. He will be dead before he wakes.'

'What about the guard?' asked Morgan.

'What of him?' said Echo. 'He is only a human.'

'Don't underestimate him,' Morgan warned. 'I did once, and I almost died for it. He's a lot stronger than you think.'

'Then you must come with us,' said Echo. 'We will kill the dark griffin, and you will kill his human.'

'Don't!' Arwydd took Morgan by the arm. 'Morgan, don't. He'll kill you! He nearly killed you once before; don't give him another chance.'

Morgan shook his head. 'Don't worry about me, Arwydd. He took me by surprise before, and I was unarmed.'

'I saw him,' said Arwydd. 'He's a brute. You're not strong enough.'

'Do not insult my human!' Echo snapped.

'Hey,' Morgan smiled to defuse the situation. 'You forgot that I'm a spy. My speciality is catching people unawares. I won't fight him face-to-face. I'll catch him sleeping and put him down the way I did to one of his friends back in Liranwee. A stab to the spine can take any man down.'

Arwydd let go of his arm. 'All right… but be careful.'

'Trust me, I will be,' Morgan said grimly. 'I've no intention of taking Captain Redguard lightly, ever again.'

'And if you cannot kill the human, I will do it,' said Echo. 'Once the dark griffin is dead. All we need is for you to keep him out of our way.'

'I can do that,' said Morgan.

'Good,' said Essh. 'We will wait until dark, and then go.'

'In the meantime, let's rest up and make some plans,' said Morgan. 'But we'll have to go without a fire. Can't risk them seeing the smoke.'

Instead, he and Arwydd sat down together at the base of a tree and shared some dried food, while the two griffins rested and groomed their feathers.

'I still think this is too dangerous,' Arwydd murmured.

'Maybe, but what choice do we have?' said Morgan. 'We can't

just keep chasing them like this forever. Sooner or later we'd lose them, or run into trouble. They're a threat, and we have to deal with them before they interfere again.'

'It's not very honourable, though, killing them in their sleep,' said Arwydd.

Morgan shrugged. 'The man who worries about honour when he's this badly outmatched, is the man who ends up dead. Besides, since when did I care about honour?'

'Nonsense. You've been braver and more loyal than anyone I've ever met,' said Arwydd. 'Even your brother.'

Morgan chuckled. 'I'm a spy, remember? It's never been an honourable profession. It's all about lies and deceit, and treachery as well. Still…' he lost his smile, and stared into the distance for a moment.

'What is it?' asked Arwydd.

Morgan shook himself. 'Oh… I don't know. I lived among the Southerners for so long… and you can't live among people without getting to know them. They're not really that different from us in the end. And that guard…'

'What about him?' Arwydd frowned.

'Captain Red Redguard,' Morgan said, half to himself. 'I got to know him too. All duty and ambition. All he cared about was his job, and to him, his job meant protecting people. Even me. He's a good man. Honest and loyal. He saved my life, and I betrayed him.'

'You had to,' said Arwydd.

'I know,' said Morgan. 'But that doesn't mean I'm proud of what I did.'

'And now you're going to kill him,' Arwydd pointed out. 'By stabbing him in the back.'

'Yes, and I have to do that too,' said Morgan. 'He's my enemy now, and he'd be more than happy to kill me too if I gave him the chance. Which is why I won't give him that chance.'

Arwydd looked troubled. 'Just be careful.'

'Don't worry,' Morgan smiled. 'I'm a survivor. Always was.'

Then again, he added in the privacy of his head, *so is Red.*

*

Some time later, when night had well and truly fallen, Morgan, Essh and Echo crept into the trees where Red and Kraego had camped.

They went on foot, since the canopy was too thick for a stealthy landing, and as the smallest and quietest, Morgan went first.

He stopped at the edge of the campsite, where the embers of a fire cast a faint light over the tree trunks, and peered out cautiously. Red lay on his side by the dying fire, with a blanket covering him. Kraego slept nearby with his head resting on his talons. Both of them looked soundly asleep.

Morgan nodded to the two griffins, and crept out into the open. They followed him, and got into position on either side of Kraego. Morgan crouched by Red's side, dagger in hand, and gave the signal.

Essh and Echo reared up to strike, and in that instant, Red's eyes snapped open and he let out a loud yell.

Fright jolted through Morgan, and just for a moment, he hesitated. He saw Kraego spring forward away from his attackers, toward Red – and himself as well. Panic-stricken, he reached down to grab Red by the hair and slit his throat.

But the element of surprise was already lost, and Red was faster than he looked. He threw himself backward away from Kraego, and smacked into Morgan's legs. Morgan fell awkwardly, and his dagger flew out of his hand.

Red got up as Kraego turned to attack the other two griffins, and grabbed Morgan by the arm, dragging him away from the campsite. Morgan tried to break free, but Red was an expert at holding people captive. He twisted the spy's arm painfully behind his back, and wrenched at it when Morgan tried to move.

Gasping in shock, Morgan heard the big guardsman growl into his ear.

'Gotcha, you bastard.'

Back at the campsite, Kraego had managed to beat Echo and Essh back through pure brute force, but it was clear that he wouldn't be able to defeat two of them at once. Or, at least, he didn't seem willing to try. He knocked Echo down with a brutal blow to the forelegs, and charged straight at Red.

Morgan saw the huge griffin bearing down on him, and tried to twist out of the way – but too late. Kraego's talons wrapped around his body and wrenched him sideways, into a freezing, black void.

Chapter Twenty-One

New Eagleholm

The journey through the void lasted for a horribly long time. Morgan felt Red's grip on him weaken, but there was no chance of escape. Kraego's talons were as strong as steel bands, but considerably sharper and colder.

There was nothing to see in the void, nothing at all. It was as if he had gone blind, and all his eyes could pick up in any direction was utter blackness. The cold was all around, too, and it was unlike any cold he had ever felt before. This wasn't just a cold that chilled the body, but a cold that felt as if it were sucking the warmth out of him.

He thought he could hear, or feel, Kraego's wings beating, and realised that they were flying – if it was even possible for a griffin to fly in this. But why not? Kraego was the dark griffin now, and everyone knew that the dark griffin owned the shadows in a way even the Shadow That Walked never could.

But the worst part of it wasn't just knowing that he was a prisoner, or that he had failed and lost Arwydd and Echo. The worst part was the feeling that being in the void gave him, and the longer the journey lasted, the worse that feeling became. At first he could dismiss it, but as it grew the dread of it grew until he began to panic.

He could feel the void slowly killing him. It wasn't a dramatic thing, or even painful – it was a simple fact. The coldness was draining him, taking the life out of him bit by bit.

But it didn't kill him.

Without warning, Kraego dragged himself and Red out of the void and back into the warmth of the real world. Morgan felt the thump as the giant griffin landed, and a moment later the talons had released him. He could have taken his chance and run for it then, but his limbs had gone stiff and cold and once he had fallen over he couldn't get up again.

Red had not let go of his arm, but his grip was just as cold as Morgan felt, and he sounded just as disoriented when he said,

'Where're we?'

'We have arrived,' said Kraego. He sounded completely unaffected.

'Eagleholm!' Red exclaimed as he stood up, dragging Morgan with him.

Morgan managed to stand up, and groaned as Red twisted his arm behind his back again. But he raised his head, and his heart leapt as he saw the last thing he had expected.

They were standing in a field. Ahead, mountains loomed. And, framed against them, was a city.

Not a very big one, or an imposing one. The walls around it looked brand new, and some of the buildings inside were only partly completed. But Morgan could see an Eyrie at the centre, and a few griffins circled overhead.

'New Eagleholm,' Red murmured. 'Damn me. We're here already?'

'Yes,' said Kraego. 'The shadows are a much faster way to travel.'

'Then why didn't we do that before?' asked Red.

'Because if I carry you through them too many times, you will die,' said Kraego, quite matter-of-factly.

'I can believe *that*,' Morgan mumbled.

'Shut up.' Red gave him a painful shove.

Morgan made the Northerner's traditional threatening gesture at him, making a throat-slitting motion with a finger and then thumping himself in the chest before pointing at the ground. 'Freeze in the void,' he spat. 'You got me, so just kill me and get it over with, you sun-worshipping dolt.'

Red smacked him across the face.

'I said shut up. I'd love t'kill you, but I reckon Lady Liantha'll be happier if we bring you in alive. You're a high official, ain't you? You know a lot that'd be useful, I'll bet.'

He prodded Morgan hard in the chest. 'Oh yeah, I learned a lesson from you. Now move it.' He drew his sword and rested the tip against Morgan's spine.

Morgan knew he was beaten. Even if he escaped, Kraego would hunt him down in a moment. He walked on ahead of Red, toward the city, and felt despair drain him dry like a new void inside him.

*

Red walked slowly toward New Eagleholm. The void had left him feeling chilled and with a weird sense of dread right at his heart, as if he had touched something that he shouldn't have, and come closer to death than any living man should.

But the sunlight shining on his back helped to make him feel better. Morning had come while they were travelling, and the rising sun always cheered him up at least a little.

Ahead, the city made him feel better too. He could hardly believe that it had sprung up here so quickly, but there it was, made of a kind of coppery-coloured stone he had never seen before, which almost shone in the early light. He could see the tiny figures of guards patrolling on the walls, but the main gates were open and looked welcoming to him.

He pushed Morgan on ahead of him, and walked briskly toward them.

At the gates, a pair of guards were waiting. They pointed their spears, and glared suspiciously at the pair of them.

'Who're you?' one demanded. He sounded more hostile than Red would have expected.

Red didn't have a hand free to salute, so he nodded politely instead. 'Captain Kearney Redguard, from Liranwee, an' this is Kraego.'

'An' that?' the guard pointed his spear at Morgan.

Red gave the Northerner a spiteful prod with his sword. 'My prisoner, Morgan Taranisäii. We're bringin' him to the Eyrie. Gonna hand him over to the prison guards.'

The other guard did not look mollified at all. 'Northerners ain't welcome in here, Captain,' he said.

'It's the law,' the other added. 'Any Northerner sets foot in New Eagleholm, we kill him on sight.'

'Why?' asked Red. 'Afraid Arren Cardockson's gonna come back an' destroy the new Eagleholm as well?'

'That ain't funny,' the first guard snapped. 'Yer friend can't come in here.'

'Look,' said Red. 'He ain't my friend. Trust me. I brought him here 'cause he's got valuable information. Information Lady Liantha's gonna need. I take it she's still in charge here?'

'Yeah,' said the second guard. 'What information, then?'

Red explained.

Both of them looked shocked.

'So if we're gonna find out what they're planning next, this sod here's the way to do it,' Red finished.

The two guards exchanged glances, and slowly lowered their spears.

'All right,' said the first. 'But you'd better fly in. If the people in the street see the bastard, they'll try an' kill him.'

'Right,' said Red.

Kraego had been listening. 'I can carry two humans,' he said.

He pinned Morgan down while Red climbed onto his back, and took off with the spy safely clutched in his talons – just as Echo had once carried Red. But Kraego was a much more powerful flier than the spotted griffin, and could lift two humans with ease. He flew up and over the city, and straight to the Eyrie.

The Eyrie only had a single tower, but it was a large, solid one, made of the same coppery stone as the walls. Like all Eyries it had a flat top, and Kraego landed there – quickly followed by the few other griffins that had been in the air nearby.

Red dismounted and quickly took control of Morgan again, while Kraego turned to confront the other griffins.

They landed and approached cautiously, heads held high and tails swishing.

'What griffin are you?' one hissed.

'I am Kraego,' said Kraego. 'And this human is Red. We come in peace, without designs on your mates, your food or your territory.'

'Wait here,' said the first griffin. 'And Seerae will come.'

They waited, and Seerae did indeed come. The sandy-coloured griffin was in fact Kraego's half-sister, but there wasn't much resemblance between them. Her human, Lady Liantha, walked beside her, and two guards took up the rear.

Seerae went straight to Kraego, and challenged him with a stare. He lowered his head politely, and after a quick exchange of rapid griffish the two of them relaxed.

'It is good to meet you, brother,' said Seerae. 'I see now that our mother was telling the truth when she said that your father was the Mighty Skandar. I saw him with my own eyes many times, and you cannot be the son of any other male.'

Kraego snorted back. 'And I see that you resemble our mother,

Seerae.'

'I do,' said Seerae. 'Now tell me why you and your human have come, and why you have brought this darkman with you.'

'He is not my human,' Kraego said at once. 'But let him tell you.'

'Thanks,' said Red. 'Lady Liantha, this here's Morgan Taranisäii an' he's my prisoner. Your guards can take him an' lock him up, but don't kill him. He's got information that could save your city.'

Lady Liantha nodded briefly. 'Understood.' She gestured to her guards. 'Take him underground and put him in a cell.'

Morgan spat at Red as he was dragged away. 'No Taranisäii's ever betrayed his people, sun-worshipper.'

'Yeah, but you ain't a Taranisäii,' Red shot back. 'You're just a jumped-up commoner, remember?'

He took a good amount of cruel satisfaction from the infuriated look on Morgan's face.

'Now,' Lady Liantha resumed once they were gone. 'Who are you?'

Red grinned at her. 'It's me, Liantha. It's Red! Remember me?'

She stopped to stare at him for a moment. Maybe she didn't recognise him right away, but he recognised her. Her hair was dark blonde, and her face was attractively freckled. When he had met her before, though, she had been little more than a girl and her clothes had been ragged. Now she wore the fine gown of an Eyrie Mistress, and a gold chain gleamed around her neck.

'Red…?' she faltered.

'Yeah,' said Red. 'From Old Eagleholm.'

Liantha's face suddenly lit up with a smile. 'Red! It *is* you!'

And then, to his utter astonishment, she rushed at him and took him in a warm hug.

Red laughed and hugged her back. 'It's good t'see you again, Liantha.'

'And you!' Liantha let go of him with a laugh. 'You've changed so much!'

'I ain't the only one!' said Red. 'Look at you; you're a real lady now!'

'And what about you?' said Liantha. 'A griffiner!'

Red shook his head with a smile. 'Not really. I'm a guard. Me an' Kraego here are just kinda helping each other out.'

Liantha glanced at Kraego with a slightly puzzled look. 'And this is Seerae's brother. From that black egg Senneck laid?'

'Yes,' said Kraego.

'Well then,' said Liantha. 'Come inside, both of you. I have a feeling you've plenty to tell me.'

*

Inside the Eyrie, in Liantha's private audience chamber, Red and Kraego told their story yet again. Liantha and Seerae both listened, and though Seerae gave away nothing much except by the twitching of her tail, the horrified look grew on Liantha's face.

'The only way we're gonna fight back is if all the Eyries band together,' Red offered. He knew it was cheeky of him to be giving advice to an Eyrie Mistress, but he didn't care.

Liantha didn't look offended anyway. 'That may be true, but the truth is that New Eagleholm doesn't *have* an army. We only have five griffiners here, and a handful of unpartnered griffins.'

Red shook his head hopelessly. 'All we can do is give the warning.'

'Understood, and thank you,' said Liantha. 'My council and I will discuss what to do. In the meantime, you've brought us a valuable prisoner. Hopefully this Morgan will be able to tell us more.'

Red had already told her everything she needed to know about Morgan. 'Yeah,' he said. 'The Northerners might not know yer even here. Ask him an' find out. Meantime, me an' Kraego should go. The others cities might need our help too.'

Liantha smiled at him. 'You're a brave man, Red. A man like you shouldn't be wasted working as a guard.'

'Nah,' Red shrugged. 'Guarding's all I know, an' it's where I'm happy.'

'Well, if it turns out that you can't go back to Liranwee when this is over, you're more than welcome to come back here,' said Liantha. 'We could use a man like you in Eagleholm.'

'I'll remember it, milady,' said Red.

*

That night, down in his cell, Morgan waited.

He wasn't afraid. Or, at least, not as afraid as he had been. He knew that there was no way he'd betray his King or his people. He had planned to die before his enemies got the chance to try and make him do it. Now, though, his confidence had risen. The prison under the Eyrie was brand new and roughly made, and though there were guards there weren't many. Most of them didn't have proper armour, and he had been watching them and noticed how undisciplined they were. To him they looked more or less like men off the street, crudely armed and trained. The crude training part had become obvious straight away. Any properly trained guard would have made certain to search Morgan properly before locking him up, and one of the first places they would have looked would have been his boots.

He slipped one off now, once the patrolling guard outside was out of sight, and carefully extracted the metal lockpick he kept hidden in the lining. He secreted it in his sleeve, put the boot back on, and went to inspect the lock. It was nothing special; definitely pickable, and once it was out of his way, these Southerners would find out what happened to anyone who was fool enough to lock up a Taranisäii.

So he waited. Patient and silent, he waited until the night was well advanced and the one patrolling guard had begun to look tired.

It was now or never.

Morgan had counted down the time it took for the guard to reach the far end of the corridor, and once the moment was right, he crept over to the door and set to work. After a few moments the lock clicked open, and Morgan quickly stepped back from the door.

He waited, one hand on the bars, for the guard to come back. After a moment or two the man appeared, trudging along past the cells with a bored look on his face. Morgan took a deep breath, and the moment the guard was outside his cell, he shoved the door open as hard as he could. It smacked into the guard, who fell over with a startled yell, and in an instant Morgan was on him. He snatched the dagger out of the man's belt, and slit his throat with it.

The dead guard's yell had alerted his friends back at the prison entrance. They came running, but by the time they arrived Morgan had already grabbed the first guard's fallen spear and ducked back into his cell. He kicked the door open again as two more guards arrived, and sent one stumbling into the other.

Morgan speared the first one and stabbed the second in the heart, and in moments the pair of them had fallen beside their friend. Morgan stopped long enough to steal their keys and weapons, and locked their bodies up in his cell before he left.

Of course, escaping from prison would always be the easiest part of his plan. He still had to escape from the Eyrie itself, and if anyone saw him out in the city they would kill him.

But none of that could stop him now. He would escape the city, or die trying. Either way, he wouldn't tell them anything. That certainty at least helped make him feel braver.

Trying to fight his way out would be suicide, but it wasn't the only option. He passed the guards up in the lowest level of the Eyrie by stealth, and let himself out through a side door. In the open courtyard around the building, he found the gate used for food delivery. Incredibly, it was unguarded.

Smirking openly at his good luck, Morgan strolled out through it and into the city.

*

Red and Kraego spent the night in a guest room, and left early the next morning — well before the news of Morgan's escape had reached Liantha. Kraego, typically for a griffin, was up first. He woke Red up with an unceremonious shove from his beak.

Red woke up sharply. 'What?'

'It is time to leave,' Kraego said brusquely. 'Do not keep me waiting.'

'Oh. Right.' Red climbed out of bed, and stumbled off to find his clothes. Travelling on the road had made him a light sleeper, and thank the gods for that.

Kraego groomed his feathers while Red got dressed, splashed his face and gulped down some food. Once they were both ready, Red slung the small bag of supplies Liantha had given him on his back, and the two of them headed out onto the balcony.

'Now,' said Kraego. 'We will go to Sunton, and then on to Withypool.'

'Gonna take a while,' said Red, stifling a yawn.

'It will not,' said Kraego. 'I have thought over what should be done, and I have decided that we will use the shadows.'

Red gaped at him. 'You what?'

'Yesterday was the first time that I carried another living creature through the shadows,' said Kraego. 'Now that I know it can be done, I shall do it again. We will reach Sunton quickly.'

Red shuddered at the memory of that freezing void. 'But didn't you say it might kill me?'

'Not quickly,' Kraego said blandly. 'I do not think it will kill you unless I carry you that way very often. A few times will not hurt.'

'You sure about that?' asked Red. 'You just said you never did it before.'

'The first time did not hurt you,' Kraego pointed out. 'We will try again. If you begin to weaken, I will stop. I do not want you to die.'

'Well…'

'You wish to reach Sunton quickly,' said Kraego. 'Are you too afraid to take a risk for it? If Echo and his friends are still following us, we will leave them far behind. If we are too late, the city may already be lost.'

'Right.' Red squared his shoulders. 'I'll try it. Let's go.'

'Then climb onto my back.'

Red obeyed, and an instant later Kraego rushed forward into darkness.

Chapter Twenty-Two

Sunton

Sunton, built not far South of Withypool, was another new city – founded not long before Liranwee. Red and Kraego reached it in a matter of days, and found it in a state of utter disarray.

Sunton was a fairly unremarkable place, built on a hilltop out of the yellow sandstone found in the East of Cymria. It had a wall around it and the Eyrie tower at the centre, and a large open space in the middle of the city itself where the market would normally be set up. Today, though, there were no stalls. The market square was full of people, and as Kraego flew over it Red looked down and tried to work out what they were doing. From that height, though, it was just about impossible.

The city's griffins were just as agitated; there were so many of them in the air that Kraego had to dodge several of them just to get to the Eyrie. And, when he landed on its top, about half a dozen other griffins immediately came down after him.

Threatened by their sheer numbers, Kraego threw Red off his back. The moment he had rid himself of his passenger, the giant griffin lowered his head and hissed. His wings lifted to make him look even bigger, and he opened his beak and showed his talons to warn the interlopers off.

The Sunton griffins, all of them unpartnered, hissed and snapped back – but had the sense to keep their distance.

Red stayed cautiously by Kraego's side. 'Kraego, stop it,' he said. 'We ain't here for a fight.'

Kraego rasped at him, but raised his head and addressed the other griffins. 'I am Kraego, and this human and I are here to speak with the master of this territory.'

'They will be here soon,' one of them snapped back. 'Do not move, or I will attack.'

Kraego huffed dismissively at him, and sat back on his haunches to wait. Very dignified.

Relieved, Red went to stand just under his friend's huge chest, and waited.

The wait was a long one, and made more uncomfortable by the watching griffins, who, wanting to make it completely clear that they had the upper hand here, occasionally hissed or made threatening comments at both of them.

After a while, movement at the back of the group announced the arrival of the Eyrie Master. Or, rather, the Eyrie Masters.

Red stared in complete bewilderment, as a griffin almost as large as Kraego shoved his way past his inferiors. Just in front of him walked not one but two people. Both of them wore the fine outfits of Eyrie Masters. And, even more confusingly, both the outfits and their wearers were identical. Both short and slight, both with pale brown hair and freckled noses. As far as Red could tell, there wasn't a hair different between them.

'Welcome to Sunton, my Lord,' said one of them. 'Who are you?'

Meanwhile, the griffin craned his head over the two humans, and sniffed suspiciously at Kraego. 'What griffin are you?'

Kraego introduced himself and Red, and looked disdainfully away without bothering to recite the ritual words about coming in peace and so forth.

'Uh, hello,' Red said awkwardly. 'Er…' He looked from one twin to the other, not knowing which one he should be paying his respects to.

The one who had spoken first laughed.

'There's no need to be embarrassed,' said the other. 'Nobody can tell us apart. We're the Eyrie Masters.'

'Both of yer?' said Red, unable to stop himself.

'That's right,' said the first twin. 'The Lords Brannon and Larkin.'

Well, at least they didn't do that thing where the names're just about the same, Red thought. 'You got chosen by the same griffin?' he said aloud.

'So we did,' said one of the twins.

'He couldn't tell us apart either,' said the other.

'And we've always worked best together anyhow,' said the first. 'Now, what brings you to Sunton?'

'Uh, well—,' Red pulled himself together. 'Kraego an' me have come to warn you…'

The twins and their partner listened.

'Thank you for the message,' one of the twins interrupted when Red was partway through. 'But we already know. In fact it seems we know more about the situation than you do by now.'

'Is that what all the fuss is about?' asked Red, gesturing down at the city.

'Correct,' said the second twin. 'Word is out. The Northerners have marched on Withypool, and we are going to fight them there.'

'Yes,' said the first. 'So if that's all you had to tell us, you may leave. Or if you and your partner choose, you may come with us and join the fight.'

Red glanced at Kraego. 'We were goin' to Withypool next anyway, so maybe…'

He trailed off and waited for Kraego to decide.

'We will go,' the dark griffin said. 'We have done what we set out to do. Now, it is time for us to fight.'

Red forced himself not to let his satisfaction show. 'We'll join up,' he said. 'An' we'll fight to the death if we have to.'

'Excellent,' said one of the twins. 'We plan to set out this afternoon – the foot troops will leave first. Until then, rest and eat. If you need weapons or armour, go to the armoury and take whatever suits you.'

Red bowed. 'It'd be my honour, milords.'

The twins nodded back politely, and left with their partner swaggering along behind. The unpartnered griffins dispersed, somewhat reluctantly, and Red and Kraego were free to enter the Eyrie.

*

That afternoon, the Sunton army left the city and marched on Withypool. As planned, the ground troops had already left. The last to leave, of course, were the griffins and the griffiners.

The Eyrie Masters flew at the front, both riding their partner. Behind him the other partnered griffins flew in formation: dozens of them, mostly young and newly partnered, but all eager for the fight. It had been a long time since a true Southern griffiner army had flown to battle, but every single man, woman and griffin there knew the stories. No ground-based force could withstand an attack by a real griffiner army for long, and few cities could survive a siege from one.

Behind the griffiner flock flew Sunton's Unpartnered – or some of them. Most unpartnered griffins refused to fight as a group – the great army of Unpartnered from the North was like nothing that had been seen in Cymria before.

Most of Sunton's own unpartnered griffins had stayed at home, where they would defend the city if it came under attack. Only a few had individually chosen to follow the army, for whatever reasons they might have.

And, of course, Red and Kraego were there too.

As an outsider Kraego should have been relegated to the back of the flock, but his pride had dictated otherwise, and he had instead taken up a place at the very front, just back from the side of the Eyrie ruler himself. If Kraego had been a smaller or a lesser griffin he might have been punished for this show of arrogance, but his sheer size and obvious power kept the other griffins at bay – even his superior, the Eyrie ruler, pretended not to notice.

Red didn't care. He leant forward on Kraego's back, wearing a leather breastplate and bracers, and a steel helmet he had taken from the Sunton armoury. He wished he still had his father's sword. It might be old and a bit rusted by now, but he would have felt stronger with it in his hand.

Still…

Red looked to his right and left, and back over his shoulder. He had never seen so many griffins flying together – not since the fall of Canran, anyway, and he had never seen this many griffins together that were on his side.

Ahead and below, he could see the human troops. Griffins refused to co-exist with horses, so the ordinary troops had to go on foot. Oxcarts laden with supplies trundled along at the rear.

Red thought of the Unpartnered, and the vicious Northern army they protected, and wondered if these men and griffins could finally stop them. With the Withypool army there as well, surely they would at least stand a chance. The Northerners had already fought in Canran and Liranwee – and they had won, but only through trickery and deceit. In open, honest warfare, it would be a different story. And whatever happened, Red would play his part. He would have his revenge, and win back his honour.

Before they had taken off, Red and Kraego had spoken – just briefly, on top of the Eyrie, while the Sunton griffiners adjusted harnesses and spoke to their own partners.

'When we get there,' Red had said, 'we're gonna find the King. Him an' Shar. That's who we're gonna fight.'

'Yes,' Kraego had answered. 'The others here may do as they please, but Shar is mine and the King is yours. We will kill them together, and victory will be ours, and you and I shall have the glory.'

The two of them had looked seriously at each other, and that was all that needed to be said. The agreement was made. They would work together one last time, and end this at last.

Now they flew together, each busy with his own thoughts. Red could feel the fear lodged in his chest like a great cold stone. He had come so close to death so many times, and now he was about to stare it in the face again. And there was a good chance that, this time, his luck would finally run out.

But if I die, he thought. *I'll take that bastard with me. The last Redguard'll die a hero or not at all.*

That made him feel braver.

To steel himself, he went back in his own mind, reminding himself of all the things that had brought him to this moment. Most of those things were horrors, and he let them fill his mind one last time, and bring him rage. So many lives lost. So much damage done. And so much more of it to come, if he and Kraego failed. This *had* to end, and it would, at Withypool. One way or another.

At least Morgan had finally been taken care of. That was a comfort. Hopefully, once he had given up his secrets, Lady Liantha would have him killed. He wouldn't cause any more trouble now, either way.

Now there was only one more of those hated faces left. King Caedmon Taranisäii. Red would find him, and when he did, the Northerner would die.

And then… Withypool.

Red had visited the city once before, with Kullervo. The half griffin shapeshifter had grown up there, and his mother had been born there as well. But its Eyrie Master had been unsympathetic. He had refused to listen to Kullervo's offer of a peace treaty with the North, and Red wondered if he would have listened to his own warnings about the invasion. Maybe, but no-one would ever know now.

Withypool stood near the ocean, and as the Sunton army

approached Red could see the water very clearly. He thought he could even see a few boats some way out from the shore. But he only spared them a glance, because, just outside Withypool itself, was something that made his heart quail.

The Northerners had already arrived. On the ground, westward from the city, the human troops had made camp well out of arrow range. The Unpartnered were everywhere, on the ground around the tents, or circling above them. If anything, Red thought they looked even more numerous than before. Had the unpartnered griffins from every other city in the South joined them? They must have. There were probably griffins among them from Liranwee. Traitors… but could a griffin even be a traitor? Loyalty was a human thing.

Red knew all that, but the sight of the Unpartnered still made his heart swell with rage. He hoped they all died.

Above Withypool, the city's own griffins circled uneasily. Red could see guards up on the walls, and spear launchers ready to loose. But so far, neither side seemed to be attacking. What were they waiting for?

But, with the arrival of the Sunton army, everything changed. The Unpartnered rose into the air in droves, sending out hoarse screams of challenge. Sunton's own griffins returned the call. And, on their backs, the griffiners opened their mouths and screeched, imitating their partners for all they were worth. On the ground, Red heard the human troops roar the name of their city.

He snarled, raised his own head, and roared his own challenge as hard as he could.

'*Redguaaard!*'

As if that was a signal, Kraego suddenly dived. He flew forward and downward in a rush of incredible speed, pulling his wings in tight so that he nearly plummeted out of the sky. Beside him, the other griffins with riders did the same.

Kraego's swoop carried him further and faster than the others, until he was hurtling along so close to the ground that his talons flicked through the grass. Ahead, Red could see the Northerners on the ground gathering themselves for the attack.

'Jump!' Kraego screeched over the roaring of the wind. '*Jump now!*'

Red jumped.

He fell off Kraego's back, but landed on his feet and stumbled forward a few steps. Kraego shot past him, and went straight back up into the sky again.

Red drew his sword. Around him, the griffiners were leaping from their partners' backs and drawing their own weapons. Not even a griffiner would fight in the sky.

Red didn't think. He joined up with the griffiners, with the ordinary foot army behind him, and charged.

Ahead the Northerners had pulled themselves together under their generals. All of them had their armour and weapons ready. They formed themselves into ranks, and rushed forward without hesitation. Red saw their pale faces painted with blue spirals, their hands clutching spears and swords and sickles. Many of them had decorated their hair with feathers and bone carvings. They screamed their own warcries in their own language – cries Red and his fellows couldn't understand, but which sounded wild and savage and completely without mercy.

For the first time in decades, North and South met on the battlefield.

The two armies hit with a crash of wood and metal, with screams and cries. Red heard them fill his ears, all ugly and discordant.

He didn't hesitate. He rushed in at the head of the Southern army, and fought. His sword slashed a Northerner's face open and threw the man screaming onto the ground. Red trampled over his enemy, and stabbed a second man through the chest.

'For Liranwee!' he bellowed.

After that, the fight carried him forward and away, into a mass of feeling that went beyond anger, beyond fear. He stopped thinking. He felt no pain, and didn't even know if he was being hurt. His sword and his arms seemed to have taken on a life of their own. He stabbed and slashed, knocked away weapons, punched and grabbed with his free hand and kicked at whatever came close enough.

Northerners fell before him, other Southerners fell around him, and once or twice a griffin fell from above. Red didn't stop to look or finish off anyone he wounded. He forged his way forward, killing whoever got in his way, and once the initial rush was over, he started to look for his goal. Where was the King?

No sign of him anywhere, but Kraego would find him. Kraego

would go straight to him, and that would show Red the way. For now… get to a clear spot.

Red fought on, searching now for a place where he could spare a moment to look for Kraego.

But there didn't seem to be anywhere he could go. Everywhere he turned another Northerner was there, coming in for the kill. He couldn't even see any other Southerners about. Had he left them behind?

Red thought he could still feel the faintest tremble of the fever in his body, as he killed several more Northerners and slowly forced his way back. He thought he could feel the touch of those icy hands of death again. He *had* to get out of this, and fast.

At last, he cut down a couple more men and found himself standing by a tent. He'd made it into the Northerners' camp.

Instinctively, he jogged on toward the centre of it. There were only a few Northerners about here, and most of them were running to join the battle. *Must have been caught napping or something*, Red thought.

He stopped by the remains of a campfire, and caught his breath. His head felt cold, and he finally realised that he'd lost his helmet. He wondered how that had happened – he had no memory of it at all. Now, for the first time, he felt the stickiness of blood and the sting of injuries. He hoped none of them were too serious.

Panting, Red looked skyward. It was a mass of griffins. Dozens and dozens of them, grappling in midair. Occasionally one would fall, and either recover itself and fly back to the fight, or tumble to its death. The chances of finding Kraego in all that were next to nothing. Nor could he see Shar anywhere.

'Damn it!' Red shook some of the blood off his sword, and rubbed his sweaty forehead, leaving a smear of more blood.

What should he do next? He couldn't get away from all this without Kraego. Maybe he should snatch a quick rest in one of these tents and rejoin the fight…?

Red smiled nastily to himself, as a much better idea occurred to him. He reached into the fire and grabbed a piece of wood whose end stuck out. The other end was still burning.

Red carried it to the nearest tent, and thrust it into the cloth. The tent quickly caught, and Red started to dart around through the camp, lighting every other tent he came across. He nipped into one or two of them while he was at it, and found a spare banner on a pole and some lamp oil. He set the banner alight, and used it and the lamp oil to make the fire spread even faster.

One tent was occupied, and when Red lit it, a panicked Northerner ran out. Red killed him without a moment's hesitation, and continued on his way.

Before long, most of the camp was ablaze and some of the Northerners, seeing it, actually ran back to their burning belongings. Their enemies took advantage of the distraction, and in moments the tide of the battle had turned.

Red, seeing a good part of the Northern army running straight toward him, threw away the remains of the burning banner and braced himself for another fight.

Then something hit him hard in the back. He staggered forward with a yell, but it was already too late. A massive grip closed around him, pinning his arms to his sides, and lifted him into the sky.

Red kicked hard, jerking his whole body and shouting in panic.

'Do not struggle!' a harsh voice rasped at him from above. 'We are going back to the city.'

Red stilled, and nearly choked on his own relief. 'Kraego!'

Kreago flew steadily, away from the battle and back toward Withypool. 'It was cunning to burn their nests.'

'Thanks.' Red looked down, and saw the Sunton army continue to drive the Northeners back into their ruined camp. His heart rose. 'We did it! *We bloody did it!*'

'Shar is not here,' Kraego interrupted harshly. 'And this is not all of their army. It is not over yet.'

Red's heart sank again. 'What…?'

Kraego said nothing more. He flew into Withypool, and touched down on the Eyrie roof. There, he put Red down and sank onto his belly. Red flopped down beside him, dropping his sword, and groaned at the pain that had started to throb in his limbs.

'We will rest here, and be ready to fight again when the time comes,' Kraego said brusquely. 'When Shar is here – that is when I will go. I should not have fought already, but I was too eager.'

Red inspected the cuts on his legs and shoulders. None of them looked very serious. 'Where are they, then? What's goin' on?'

'Clearly, they did not want to risk losing their entire force in one fight,' said Kraego.

Red looked out beyond the walls, to where the battle still raged. 'Well they ain't gonna take the city with that lot. Not now. Let's hope they didn't plan for this.'

'We will see,' said Kraego. 'For now… rest and be glad that you have survived.'

Red closed his eyes for a moment. 'Yeah.'

Chapter Twenty-Three

Waiting

Shar and the King hadn't shown their faces, but the fighting was over for the day. The remnants of the Northern army gave up and retreated westward, taking the depleted Unpartnered with them. Red hadn't even noticed it in all the chaos on the ground, but while the Sunton army attacked, the griffins from Withypool had flown out to join in the fight. Together, they had been enough to drive the Unpartnered back, defeating them for the first time since that day, nearly thirty years ago, when a griffin called Kaanee had led his fellows to betray the Mighty Kraal to his son Skandar, and created the first griffin army.

Red and Kraego had been given quarters in the Withypool Eyrie, and they stood out on the balcony together and watched the Northerners leave in disarray. The remains of the Sunton foot army chased after them, but let them go when they entered a forest and straggled their way back to the city. Even at this distance, Red could see the bodies of the dead and wounded left lying where they had fallen. He had never seen or imagined so many dead people in one place, not even in Canran. Compared with this, the conquests he had seen were nothing. This was real warfare, and in all his life he had never known how ugly it really was.

Kraego, of course, looked as cool and aloof as always. 'We have won the right to live for another night, but there is no telling what will happen tomorrow.'

Red felt the ache of his wounds mingle with a deeper ache. A deep, weary ache in his bones and in his heart as well. It felt like a tiredness, not so much of the body, but of the soul. 'Whatever happens,' he said slowly, 'We'll keep goin'. An' when it's over, if we're still alive…'

'I will live,' Kraego said shortly. 'And so will you.'

Red looked up at him. 'Why're you so sure?'

'Because you and I are both under my protection,' said Kraego.

'And I cannot be defeated.'

Red smiled to himself. 'What're we gonna do when it's over, then? When the war's finished? I mean, I know we had a plan before, but so much has happened an' we've been together for…' he trailed off, not sure what he was really trying to say.

But he couldn't let go of the feeling that he and Kraego were… were something. Maybe not so much meant for each other as just bound together by what had happened. All Red knew for certain was that he couldn't really remember what life had been like without Kraego there beside him, and couldn't quite imagine a future life without him either.

What'm I thinking? he asked himself. *I'm just a guard. I couldn't be a griffiner.*

But still the feeling wouldn't leave him alone.

Kraego slowly scratched his neck with his talons. 'I do not understand what you mean.'

Red shook himself. 'I mean, are we still gonna go off alone when this is finished?'

Kraego scratched himself more vigorously, and shook out his feathers. 'Once Shar and her human are dead, their followers will have no more reason to be here. They will leave and the war will be over. In return for your help, I will carry you back to Liranwee and you will be free to live as you did before. I will return to my own life, as it was before. That was always our plan.'

'Yeah,' Red said reluctantly. 'I s'pose it was. I just wondered if maybe you'd changed your mind.'

Kraego gave him a look. 'Why would I do that?'

Red looked back at him. 'So we really ain't partnered? After all this time?'

Kraego looked as if he were about to say something, but then he blinked and looked away toward the Sunton army as it entered the city, carrying its wounded with it.

Red decided not to press him. Instead, he followed Kraego's gaze and murmured mostly to himself, 'I wish the others were here. Ranulf an' Elthan an' everyone else. I dunno if any of 'em are still alive.'

'You will know one day,' said Kraego.

'Yeah,' Red said sadly. 'I hope so.'

*

With so many new griffiners in the Eyrie, nobody paid much attention to Red and Kraego. They were given food, some bandages and ointments so Red could treat both their injuries, but other than that they were left alone. Red was glad; he wasn't in the mood for much talking. All he wanted to do now was rest, and hope that the "tomorrow" Kraego had warned him about would be better than it sounded. Maybe the Northerners really were finished. Maybe they wouldn't come back. *Maybe* it was all over.

And, for most of the following day, it looked that way. The defeated Northern army did not reappear, and Withypool's own forces had plenty of time to gather supplies, treat the wounded and prepare for another assault. And if one came, it would find the city better prepared and with greater numbers on its side than before.

Finally, that afternoon, Red heard some news that made his hopes rise even higher.

He had decided to go out into the Eyrie and do what he could to help. There was plenty of fetching and carrying to do, and nobody asked questions when they saw a strong pair of arms, other than "could you just haul this up those stairs?"

Red agreed, and spent most of the day doing whatever the Withypoolians asked – mostly heavy lifting and delivering messages. It was good to keep busy. It stopped him from thinking too much, and worrying about what might happen.

When lunchtime came, he managed to join up with a group of off-duty guards and accepted some bread and cheese they were sharing out. Sitting on a crate of arrows, out of the way of everyone who was still busy working, he quickly introduced himself.

'From Liranwee?' one guard said in surprise. 'How'd you get all the way over here?'

'It's a long story,' said Red. 'What about you?'

'Well, I'm from Withypool, ain't I?' said the other guard. 'Name's Neth.'

The others introduced themselves too.

'Nice t'meet you,' said Red.

They ate in silence for a while, before Red spoke again.

'So,' he said. 'What's the news? No-one seems t'know exactly what's goin' on.'

'I do,' said Neth.

'Oh yeah?' said one of his fellows.

'Yeah,' said Neth. 'We took a few of their wounded prisoner. I was on duty down in the lockup an' I overheard what got said.'

'Which is?' asked a man to his right.

Neth took his time, on the pretext of eating a few more bites of bread, just to savour the moment. 'The blackrobe scum told us why their army's all split up,' he said. 'All of 'em said the same thing.'

'Yeah?' said Red. 'Where's the rest of 'em, then?'

Neth wiped the crumbs off his tunic. 'Seems they were comin' here, all of 'em together. But along the way they got attacked.'

'By who?' asked Red.

'By us!' Neth grinned. 'An army came from Wylam. Seems they was heading for Liranwee, saw the Northerners headin' out this way, an' chased 'em. So they got caught up in a fight, an' half of them came over this way t'make camp an' wait to regroup.'

'But the other half never showed up,' said Red. 'An' they didn't expect us to come up from Sunton.'

'That's the one,' said Neth. 'If the other half ain't shown up by now, then they're probably dead.'

Red whooped aloud. 'Then it's over. We've won!'

'Looks like it,' said Neth. 'If the King was with the other half, could be he's dead now.'

'Huh!' said Red. 'I hoped it was gonna be me who finished him off, but who cares? Long as he's dead, that's fine by me.'

'Damn right!' said another guard.

Red thought briefly of the little Prince. If he'd been with his father, was he dead too now? He shook his head sadly. Still, if both father and son were dead, then that would be the end of the Taranisäii family, once and for all. That was something for every Southerner to celebrate.

After lunch, he and the others parted ways and went off to get back to work. Toward evening, with everything starting to look much more organised, Red went back up to his room to get some rest.

He found Kraego there, and told him the news.

Kraego huffed uncertainly. 'Then perhaps it is over…'

'Let's hope,' said Red. 'But we'd better not celebrate 'till we're sure.'

To reassure himself, he went out onto the balcony and looked out at the view beyond the city. He couldn't see anything. And despite what he had heard, he still couldn't quite shake the feeling that something wasn't right.

It had all been just too easy.

Maybe he was just being paranoid, and trying to find a reason for there to still be a problem. Maybe he'd gotten too used to constant danger, and couldn't cope with the idea that there might not be any more danger.

It's all over, he thought, but putting it into words like that didn't make him feel any better.

Restless and irritable, he went to have a lie down.

*

A commotion woke him up from a doze. He sat up sharply, and fumbled for a lantern in the darkened room. He managed to get it lit, and looked around. Kraego was there, snoozing halfway through the archway that led into his nest, but elsewhere in the Eyrie he could hear shouting and the thudding of griffins moving around.

'Kraego!' Red hung the lantern from a hook on the wall, and hastily buckled on his sword. 'Kraego, wake up! I think somethin's happening!'

Kraego had lifted his head almost as soon as Red had said his name the first time. 'Red? What is it?'

'Dunno, some kind of ruckus,' said Red. 'C'mon!'

He hurried out of the room with Kraego close behind him. People ran past him along the corridor, most of them holding weapons. He could hear their panicked voices.

'Oh damn it!' he swore. 'What's happened?'

A griffiner hurrying by stopped long enough to answer. 'It's the Northerners! They're coming! Hurry up and get up to the roof!'

'Right!' Red glanced back at Kraego, and made a run for it.

Up on the Eyrie roof, dozens of griffiners had gathered with their partners. Lord Penrin, the ageing Eyrie Master, stood with Brannon and Larkin and waited for everyone to arrive.

The moment he reached the open air, Red ran to the edge and looked out. It was early evening, and by the slightly faded sunlight he saw something that shot fear down his spine.

Out on the coast, just beyond Withypool, an army had gathered. It was the missing half of the Northern army. But now that he saw it, Red knew that it had never been half. The part that had been defeated yesterday had only been a fraction of the King's followers. Now they had returned, on the plain west of the city, and here, on the East, their friends had gathered in their thousands. Red could see the triple spiral banners, the bristling spears, the Unpartnered in their full numbers flying overhead. And, down on the ground, in the midst of the army, he saw something that made his heart beat faster.

A red griffin, just visible among the troops, with her partner standing by her side.

'*Shar,*' Kraego hissed.

'It was a lie,' Red said numbly. 'Those prisoners… they must've been told what to say. There is no Wylam army. It was a trick, t'make us think we'd won, to get us off our guard.'

'Human cunning has won more wars than strength alone,' Kraego observed.

Red wasn't really listening. He went back to where the Eyrie Masters stood, and waited for them to speak.

By now, the last of the griffiners must have arrived. Red looked at them all, and felt sick to his stomach. There must have been about a hundred of them, but next to the Northerners… next to the Unpartnered…

Lord Penrin spoke up. 'Lords and Ladies,' he said. 'We don't have the time for long speeches, so I'll make this quick. Look out there.' He pointed toward the army that stood patiently on the beach.

'That is what you will have to face today,' he said. Around him, the men and women who ruled cities and dominated thousands murmured amongst themselves, and Red could see how pale they all looked. Most of them had probably never fought seriously before in their lives. Why would they? Griffiners were expected to know how to fight, but by now, after years of relative peace, most of them never spent any time on it. They were administrators, leaders, officials — not warriors. And why would they need to fight when they had their partners to protect them?

Penrin must have known that they would be thinking the same thing, because he went on, 'I can see the fear on your faces. Most of you have never fought in a battle in your lives. But you need to remember this: you are not ordinary men and women. You are griffiners! You were chosen by griffins, and so chosen by Gryphus himself. You were annointed to lead our people. For centuries, our purpose has been to lead and protect our race, in Gryphus' name. Think of the people down there in the city. All of them will be afraid too, but when they look up here and see us, they feel braver. And you know why? Because they know they have us to protect them. With us to lead them, they know they have a chance. This is our land! *Our* home. And no man or griffin has the right to take it from us. Think of everything you love, and ask yourself if it's worth dying for.'

'No!' Red interrupted suddenly. 'It ain't worth dyin' for, sir.' He drew his sword. 'It's worth killin' for!'

Penrin looked shocked, and then his look turned ferocious. 'Exactly!'

The griffiners had stood a little taller, and several of them even laughed.

'So let's go!' Penrin resumed. 'And deal with these Northern scum who think they have the right to take our home away from us!'

Red stamped his feet and roared his approval with the others. Then, in unison, griffins and griffiners lifted their heads and screeched a territorial call to the sky. It was a griffin's warcry, and in times of battle, a griffin's partner had to share his partner's ferocity.

Together, the griffins flew up into the sky and began to circle, screaming their challenge. Elsewhere in the city, Withypool's Unpartnered rose up to join them. Down on the beach and on the plain, the enemy griffins flew up as well. Red could see the burning missiles clutched in their talons.

Up on the Eyrie roof, only Kraego had stayed.

'Are you gonna go fight them, then?' Red asked him.

'No,' said Kraego. 'I will not waste my time with these lesser griffins. Only Shar will be enough for me.'

'But they need your help—,' Red began.

'And that is why you and I shall go now and find her,' Kraego interrupted. 'Come!'

The massive griffin offered his shoulders.

Red felt sick, but he knew there was no turning back now. He sheathed his sword, and climbed onto his friend's back. It was now or never.

Chapter Twenty-Four

The Battle For Withypool

The Northerners must have chosen their strategy long ago, and as Red flew with Kraego overhead, he watched them do just as they had done in Liranwee and Canran. The Unpartnered split into three groups. One flew to attack the Withypool griffins, and while they were busy, the second group dropped flaming pots of oil onto the city. The last of them carried Northern troops over the walls. But that wasn't all.

Kraego dodged the other griffins in the air, and flew on toward the army on the beach. As he left the walls of Withypool behind him, a deafening explosion sent out shockwaves that made the giant griffin buck suddenly in the air. Red jerked backward, and nearly fell off before he managed to lurch forward and grab Kraego around the neck.

He clung on, heart hammering, and risked a look back.

Below and behind them, the walls of Withypool had been broken. A whole section of stone had tumbled down, and the edges of the gap continued to crumble before Red's eyes. Smoke and rock dust wafted into the sky. The little griffin who had broken the gates of Liranwee had done his work again, and as he collapsed onto his chest with exhaustion, hundreds of Northerners charged past him and straight into the city. The seige was already over, and Red knew that unless he and Kraego succeeded, Withypool was done for.

Kraego hadn't even spared a look back at the destruction. He flew straight, his legs tucked neatly in under his belly, and when some Unpartnered came in to attack him, he effortlessly flicked a wing, rolled away from them, and dived into the shadows.

Red nearly threw up at the shock of entering the darkness again, but he didn't. He hung on for all he was worth, bracing himself for whatever came next.

Kraego knew exactly what he wanted to do. He had planned it long ago, and refined it, and now he carried it out.

He burst out of the shadows directly above the Northern army, directly above Shar, and screamed out his challenge in a voice so loud that the people on the ground shrank back in fear and shock.

'*SHAR!*' Kraego screeched. '*I am Kraego! I am the son of the Mighty Skandar! I am the mightiest griffin in the world! Shar, I challenge you! SHAR!*'

Red knew what Kraego would do next, or guessed it. He tensed in readiness, and tightened his grip.

Kraego dived. As Shar rose up and opened her wings, the great, dark griffin suddenly threw himself forward. The motion hurled Red straight off his back and over his head. In midair, Kraego caught him in his talons and threw him straight at the astonished King, who stood on the ground at the head of his troops. Then he was gone, back up into the sky, pursued by Shar.

Red slammed into Caedmon, throwing him onto the ground. For a moment the two of them lay there, stunned by the impact.

Red rolled off and managed to get up. Around him the King's personal guard was already rushing in to attack him. But all Red saw was Caedmon. All he saw was that dreaded, hated face. All he felt was rage.

He drew his sword, and hurled himself at his enemy.

Caedmon was fast. He had already regained his feet, and now he pulled out his sickle and deftly sidestepped Red's charge. The sickle lashed out and left a savage cut on the back of Red's neck. Blood trickled down under his breastplate as he turned and swung his sword with all his might.

Roaring, Red brought his sword down on the King's arm. Caedmon flicked it aside with his sickle, and cut Red again, this time on the shoulder.

Red's free hand shot out and grabbed Caedmon by the sleeve of his robe, and for a moment the two of them grappled with each other, before Caedmon twisted free. So far he'd been the only one to take blood, but he was at a disadvantage. The sickle was sharp, but it was a subtle weapon, meant to cut and twist. It couldn't parry a sword very well, and it couldn't stab. And Red's sword had Red's strength behind it, and his fury, even if he was the slower of the two.

Red didn't think of any of that. He threw himself at his enemy, oblivious to any need for defence or retreat, unable to feel any pain or fear. He rained merciless blows down on Caedmon's arm, trying to knock the sickle out of his hand. Caedmon dodged most of them and caught a few glancing cuts, but he had started to retreat.

And then, Red's sword hit the sickle directly in the middle of the blade. A sharp metallic crack split the air, and half of the sickle's blade flew off.

Caedmon looked up, wide eyed, and saw the huge Southerner bearing down on him, sword raised high, mouth open to bellow.

'REDGUARD!'

Red's sword hit Caedmon in the neck and shoulder, cutting straight through his robe and into the flesh and bone beneath. The King of the North fell with a strangled cry.

Red closed in to finish him off, but his advantage of surprise had worn off. Caedmon's bodyguards put themselves between their master and his attacker, and in a moment, Red found himself under assault from all sides.

He didn't care. Shouting his family name, he hacked his way through them like a berserker. It was only a matter of time before he was overwhelmed and killed, but what did that matter? He'd done it. Liranwee was avenged, and the last Redguard would be remembered forever as the man who saved the South.

Loyalty. Duty. Honour.

But the end didn't come then. Not even then.

Suddenly, as Red fought on, he realised that the Northerners around him were falling away. Retreating. He heard a chorus of screeching from above. The men who had been fighting him broke off their fight and started to run away.

Puzzled, Red looked skyward and saw something that made him stare in astonishment.

The Unpartnered were retreating. Flying back out of the city and returning to their master's army, all in disarray. But why? Was Shar dead? Had Kraego won?

Red couldn't see either of them anywhere.

What he saw instead was even more astonishing.

Griffins were coming – hundreds of them. He saw them flying over Withypool, through the smoke, to attack the Unpartnered. On the ground, pouring in around and through the city, were humans. Southerners, all armed and armoured.

Red stared at them while the Northerners fled around him, not knowing what he was seeing. Where had they all come from?

Then he saw the banners flying above the heads of the

newcomers, and his amazement turned to joy.

'Wylam!' he yelled. 'It's Wylam! They came!'

They had come, and as Red ran back to join his allies, he saw the faces starting to emerge, showing up at the head of the great army of Southerners. Lord Ekra, Eyrie Master of Wylam, leading his people. And Lady Nelia as well, with the survivors from Canran.

They had answered Red's call. They had come to save their people.

Red started to laugh, a wild, joyful laugh. He stopped running and let them come to him. The army parted to go around him, and once he was in their midst he joined them, and began a relentless march forward, toward the retreating Northern army.

Now it would end.

But, as Red advanced, he heard the voice. It came from up ahead, loud and confident.

'Surrender!'

It was not a Southern voice.

It was Shar.

The red griffin flew down to land not far in front of the oncoming Southerners. She was bleeding in several places, but alive, and her voice was full of command.

'Surrender!' she screeched again. 'And live!'

Red looked around frantically. There was no sign of Kraego anywhere. There was only Shar. And, around her, the Northern army starting to pull itself together again. From somewhere among them, a figure appeared and slowly limped over to join up with the red griffin.

Caedmon. Blood had soaked into his robe, and his arm hung limply by his side, but he was alive. He went to Shar's side, and called out with her.

'Surrender to us!' he yelled. 'Or die!'

'They're mad!' Red laughed derisively. 'C'mon, lads, let's finish the bastards off!'

Most of his fellows seemed to agree; he heard them laughing and jeering too. But others had begun to falter. Red glanced at them and saw the uncertainty on their faces – what was wrong? They couldn't possibly be scared by this sad attempt at bravado.

But something *was* wrong. The Northerners had regrouped behind their King, and even started to advance again. Red saw the ugly looks of triumph on their faces. Above them, the Unpartnered started to regather and return to the attack.

But why?

And then Red saw what the others had seen. He saw the force starting to mass behind the Northerners. And he saw more griffins coming. More of them!

'What in the gods' names is going on?' he said aloud.

'Look, there!' a woman yelled to his left. 'Look down on the beach!'

Red looked, and at last he saw what had happened. Downslope, on the beach behind the Northerners, ships had docked. Dozens of wide, flat ships with elegantly tapered sails. Griffins were flying up from the decks, and people leapt over the sides into the shallows and marched up the beach to join forces with the Northerners. Hundreds of people.

'Retreat!' a voice shouted from the Southern army. 'Back to the city! *Retreat!*'

The forces of Sunton, Wylam and Withpool had no choice. They retreated back into the half ruined city, led by the griffiners, and pursued by their enemies.

Red went with them, his mind reeling. How could this have happened? Where had these new forces come from?

He went back into the city through the hole in the wall, and wandered away through the buildings, too tired and despairing to think of fighting again.

Somewhere toward the centre of Withypool, by the Eyrie, he found Kraego.

The dark griffin lay sprawled on his side, one wing twisted underneath him. At first Red thought he was dead, but as he came closer he saw the griffin stir.

Red ran toward him, and stopped by Kraego's head. 'Kraego! What happened?'

Kraego groaned and slowly rolled onto his belly. His wing came free, and he raised it partway and screamed. The wing flopped back down.

'Kraego!' Red called to him.

Kraego snarled at him. 'Do not... come closer... I will attack.'

Red kept his distance, remembering that injured griffins often turned vicious. 'You all right?'

Kraego lay still, gasping for breath. 'I am… strong. I will live. We should… leave here.'

Red rubbed his face. 'Yeah… but where'd we go? This was our best chance.'

Kraego subsided, resting his head on the ground. 'We have failed,' he said. 'Shar has won.'

'Did you fight her?' asked Red.

'Yes.' Kraego glared at him, and refused to elaborate. 'And you?'

'I thought I had him,' Red mumbled. 'I got him. Cut him a good one down the chest. But he's still alive. Might die from his wound though.'

'It does not matter,' Kraego said bitterly. 'You saw what has happened.'

'I don't get it!' Red threw his sword down. 'We had the bastards! An' then that lot showed up – who are they? How'd this happen?'

Kraego winced in pain. 'It is… over. The Amoranis have come. Shar's human has allied with them. With the forces of the Empire against them, your people have no chance. Their fight is over and those here will be lucky to survive at all.'

'An' what about you?' asked Red. 'An' me? What'll we do?'

'There is no chance for us.' Kraego managed to stand up. He folded one wing, but the other trailed uselessly. 'I cannot fly, and do not have the strength to use the shadows again. You and I are trapped here.'

Red forced himself to breathe deeply. 'Then what'll we do?'

'The only thing we can do,' said Kraego. 'We will stay here, and make our last stand. When they take this city, we will kill as many of them as we can, and I will stay beside you until I am dead.'

Red picked up his sword. 'All right. There's nothing else we can do, so let's go for it. An' no matter what happens, it's been an honour flyin' with you, Kraego.'

Kraego huffed softly, and gave Red a gentle push with his beak. 'You have been a good human to fly with me, Kearney Redguard,' he said. 'You have the heart of a griffin.'

Red smiled and rubbed the top of Kraego's head. 'You're like a brother to me, Kraego. Always have been.'

'And you have been the same to me,' Kraego said solemnly. 'Now, come. We will find a place to rest and prepare for our last fight.'

'Together,' Red said grimly, and together the two of them walked away past the terrified citizens of Withypool, ready for the end to come at last.

Chapter Twenty-Five

The End of the South

Red and Kraego did not have long to find a place to wait. The enemy, Northerners and dark-skinned Amoranis together, relentlessly followed the fleeing Southerners straight into the city. There, among the burning buildings while the Unpartnered slaughtered any griffin still foolish enough to fight back, they mercilessly hunted down every Southerner in sight.

Red and Kraego followed the main street away from the Eyrie, until they found the nearest large building. The Sun Temple, its doors wide open. Inside, plenty of people had already come in to take refuge and pray for salvation.

'Right.' Red took up position just inside, in the entrance hall. 'Here's where I'm stoppin'. I'll protect the people in here as long as I can.'

Kraego sat on his haunches and gingerly pecked at his injured wing. 'It will be enough. There is room here and we cannot be attacked from above.'

Red looked back at the people inside the Temple. Many of them had gathered around the altar where the high priest had begun to chant a prayer. They kept their eyes on him, some murmuring the prayer along with him, and Red saw the looks on their faces. He saw despair there, but hope as well.

It was midday, and a shaft of gold sunlight shone in through the windows in the high dome of the Temple. Red looked up into it, and fixed his gaze on the golden sunwheel painted at the highest point of the dome. And he, too, prayed.

'Gryphus, save us. Don't let it end like this. Save us. Protect us. Please, Gryphus.'

Kraego heard him. 'Do not waste your breath, Red,' he said. 'The gods do not exist, and there is no true mercy in this world.'

'Gryphus exists,' Red said quietly. 'I know it. An' if I die today, I'll go to the golden fields an' see my Dad again, an' everyone else I knew, because I'm a loyal Southerner an' I know I'm a good man.'

To his surprise, Kraego lowered his head toward him and gave him the gentlest of nudges. The giant griffin rumbled deep in his throat. 'It is a sad thing to see you cling onto delusions to save yourself from the cruelty of this world.'

'Well where're you gonna go when *you* die?' asked Red.

'I shall go nowhere,' said Kraego. 'My body will rot and become part of the earth, as yours shall, and that will be the last remnant of me. And in time, all memory of us will fade. Life is fleeting, and death is oblivion, and all we have in this life is what we have the strength to take.'

Red gaped at him. 'You really think that?'

'That is what every griffin knows,' Kraego said calmly.

Red shook his head slowly. 'Sounds like you don't even care if you die.'

Kraego snorted. 'Do not be foolish. I am a griffin, and will live as long as I can. I will not die until I have fought my hardest.'

'That's the spirit,' said Red, but though he tried to sound brave, he couldn't shake the feeling of utter despair that Kraego's words had given him.

And what if he was right? So far, Red had seen nothing to suggest that Gryphus was trying to protect his people. If Kraego was right, then Red's father, and his mother, and so many others he had known, had become nothing. And when Red died, he too would go into oblivion, into the void. He too would be made into nothing. Maybe, then, it wasn't such a good thing to die, bravely or otherwise.

Red squared his shoulders. It didn't matter. He had to keep going, *had* to. He couldn't give up now.

It didn't take long for the battle to reach the Temple. Red heard it well before he saw it. He heard the screechings of griffins above, and the screams and cries of people on the ground. As the last battle for Withypool came closer, people started to come into the Temple. Red let them run past him and into the holy space to find shelter. Some, who could still fight, took up station in the entranceway as he had.

When the enemy arrived, they were humans. Northerners and Amoranis together. The Amoranis wore light leather armour and carried tall bronze shields. Red took a step back into the Temple, noting the weapons in their hands – spears, curved swords, clubs, and nets. He raised his own sword in readiness, and called out to his fellow Southerners.

'All right, let's make a fight of it! Make our ancestors proud!'

But most of the others were retreating rather than charging.

Kraego remained by Red's side, and now he lowered his head and extended his talons. 'Red, tell them to stand aside,' he rasped. 'I will go first.'

'Move away!' Red yelled. 'Let the griffin through!'

The others obeyed, pressing themselves back against the walls, and they had barely done so before Kraego charged. The black griffin bounded forward like a moving mass of feathers and claws, beak open wide to screech his own name.

'*Kraaaaeeeegoooo!*'

But the Amoranis were ready for him. They moved out of his path and threw their nets, some at his head and wings, and others down at his feet. Kraego's front talons caught in the webbing, and as he fell the Amoranis closed in, tangling his wings and his hind legs. The moment they had subdued him they swarmed over him, prodding him with long spears and bashing with clubs.

But not to kill. Rather than finish off the maddened griffin the Amoranis, with the Northerners' help, tied Kraego's legs and wings. They put ropes around his neck and attached them to his forelegs so he couldn't lash out with his beak. Around them others were already coming into the Temple to attack the humans.

'No!' Red yelled. 'Kraego!'

He ran forward to help his friend, sword raised to kill anyone who got in his way, and then to cut the ropes.

The Amoranis were ready for him. One of them lashed out with his shield, hitting Red hard in the face. Red grabbed the edge of the shield, trying to pull it away so he could get at the owner. But the Amorani held on, and as Red wrenched at it, someone hit him from behind. He staggered and fell, and in an instant a net had tangled him as well.

Red struggled, roaring in rage, and thrust his sword arm through the net to cut it away. But the Amorani who had thrown the net only tugged at it, tripping Red up. He fell, and the sword flew out of his hand. Immediately the Amoranis were on him too, wrenching off his armour and tying his arms behind his back. One of them tore Lady Isleen's ring off his finger, and another stole his belt.

Red rolled onto his side, and saw the same thing happening all around him. The other Southerners fell – some killed, but most netted and captured like himself. Red tried to break the ropes holding his wrists together, but they wouldn't give.

No, he thought. *Not like this. Not like this!*

But there was nothing more he could do. His last fight, and the South's fight, was over before it had even begun. The Northerners had won, and the Eyries, the cities, the great civilisation of the South, had finally fallen.

*

The Amoranis did not kill Red, or Kraego. After a while they were taken out of the Temple, along with the other prisoners – Red forced to walk, and Kraego dragged onto a cart. From there they were taken to the open city square in front of the Eyrie, where hundreds of people and even griffins had been shoved into what looked like holding pens for cattle. The Amorani leading Red took him to a pen holding about twenty other people, opened a gate and shoved him through. He staggered forward and stumbled into a couple of other people, whose hands had also been tied behind their backs. Unable to catch themselves, they staggered too and would have fallen, but the pen was so crowded that there was no room to fall.

Red managed to regain his balance. 'Sorry.'

None of the others answered. They only stared at him, all blank-eyed and mute, as if they had not only been penned up like cattle, but had become animals themselves.

After that… after that all Red could do was stand there and watch.

He turned around and looked out through the slats of the pen. It and its fellows had been set up in a rough ring, and in the open space at the centre of that, a group of Amoranis had gathered around one of their number, who looked as if he was in charge. He wore a strange outfit – some kind of skirt made from colourful cloth, sandals, and what looked like a spotted animal skin draped over his chest and shoulders. Unlike his fellows, who went bare-headed, this man wore an elaborate headdress with a golden griffin's head over the forehead.

Red watched as this man, with his offsiders or servants around him, stood and waited. One by one, people were taken out of the holding pens and brought over for him to inspect. The richly dressed man would speak to each one – though Red couldn't catch what he was saying – and his friends would touch the prisoner, feeling their limbs and prodding them here and there, and inspecting their faces with businesslike speed. Then the prisoner would be hauled away and placed in another pen with others who had already been examined.

At first, Red couldn't guess what was going on. But then a prisoner was brought out who walked with a limp. The limping prisoner endured a shorter and rougher examination than the others. The Amoranis inspected his crippled leg, flexing it experimentally while the owner winced in pain. Their leader spoke to him, and Red, straining to hear, saw the cripple shaking his head in answer to whatever he was being asked.

Whatever the man told his captors, they didn't like it. Silence came, and a moment's stillness. The Amorani in charge nodded to his underlings, and in an instant one of them grabbed the cripple by the hair and pulled his head back. A second Amorani came forward with a dagger, and slit his throat. The murder was over in seconds, and the Amoranis unceremoniously dragged the body away and dumped it off to the side while the next prisoner was brought forward.

That was what it was, Red realised dully. It was a test. Anyone they thought was too weak for whatever they had in mind was no use to them. Around him the others seemed to have guessed the same thing; he heard them groan and mumble to themselves. Red might have tried to say something comforting to them, but he couldn't find the words. His mind felt as empty and barren as Kraego's void.

And that was how it went, for the rest of that evening. Red stayed in his pen and watched as the prisoners were tested one by one. Some passed, others didn't.

A few tried to escape.

They died.

The sky grew darker, and gradually the numbers in the holding pens dropped. The pile of dead grew. They killed anyone who was badly wounded, the old, the frail, anyone with a disability, and some for reasons Red couldn't guess.

By the time his turn came, Red only felt numb. Everything seemed to have moved away from him. Sound seemed muted, nothing felt real or important. Even his vision seemed to have gone fuzzy.

As if in a dream, he let himself be taken forward by two Amoranis and went to stand in front of their leader. Even then, he was surprised to find himself noticing that the man looked tired.

Must've been a long day for him too, he thought. *Long day for all of us.*

His captors began to inspect Red, feeling the muscle on his arms and legs and prodding him unceremoniously to look for injuries. Red winced whenever they found one of the cuts the battle had left on him, but held firm.

The leader in front of him spoke. His Cymrian was cultured and refined, and spoken with a rounded accent that Red had never heard before.

'Name?'

'Captain Kearney Redguard,' said Red.

'Captain?' the Amorani repeated, with a glance at his underlings.

One of them took out a knife, and Red tensed expectantly, but they only grabbed him by the sleeve of his tunic and slit the fabric up to his shoulder, ripping it away to expose the guard tattoo.

The Amorani nodded. '*T'e, Re'pat*,' he said. Amorani, Red supposed.

'You are a guard,' the leader said.

Red nodded. 'Yeah, a guard captain.'

'Where are you from?'

'I'm from Liranwee,' said Red.

'"Captain",' the leader said. 'You know how to lead?'

'I do,' said Red.

'Skills,' said the Amorani.

Red looked blank.

'Tell me your skills,' the Amorani repeated patiently.

Red froze in surprise for a few moments, and one of the men holding him slapped him across the head to hurry him up.

'Uh,' he said. Then, sensing that this might save him, he quickly began. 'I can read an' write, I can use a bow an' a sword, I'm… uh… I know the laws of Cymria.'

'You read?' said the Amorani leader, sounding slightly surprised.

'Yeah,' said Red.

The leader nodded to his underlings, and said something in his own language. Red had passed, and he let himself be taken away, wondering if it would have been better if he had been killed instead.

But maybe not. Life was life, and if they let him live now then that meant they had given him a chance. And whatever that chance might lead to, he would take it.

*

That night, Red finally found out what his chance was. With the sorting finally over, he and the others who had been selected were led out of the city, and to a dock built in the bay where a very large Amorani ship had docked. There they were marched up a ramp and sent below decks, where most of the ship's interior had been given over to rows of steel barred cages. At the far end, at the back of the ship, another much larger cage had already been filled with captive griffins. They lay in rows, chained to the floor by steel collars fitted around their necks, and watched blankly while their human counterparts filed into their own cages next door.

Red found himself pushed into a cage directly next to the griffins, with only a row of bars between himself and them. Now, at last, his captors untied his wrists and he was allowed to sit down on a wooden bench at the back of his new prison. He slumped onto it and put his head in his hands, listening to the babble of voices from his fellow prisoners – some angry, some afraid. Now, at last, he understood what was happening. This was the Northerners' revenge for what Red's own people had once done. Now, at last, he and his fellow Southerners would understand what it had been like all those centuries ago, when their ancestors had invaded the North.

Red knew. Red understood. Like the Northerners so long ago, he had seen his home invaded, his people slaughtered, his pride taken. And now he had been sold, as the Northerners had once been sold. He was going to Amoran to live out the rest of his life as a slave, and all those who survived would suffer the same fate. The past had caught up with them at last, and this was their punishment.

Red looked up dully, and watched the griffins stirring in their cages. He wondered why they had been taken prisoner too. What possible use could the Amoranis have for them? Then his heart leapt, and he stood up.

'Kraego!'

The big griffin lay on his belly, like his fellows, but even then he towered over them. He raised his head. 'Red,' he said. 'So you are alive.'

Red pushed his way over to the bars, as close to his friend as he could get. 'Yeah. They got the both of us. But why'd they put you in here?'

'I do not know,' said Kraego. 'But the moment I am free, they will suffer. I will not endure this humiliation!' He wrenched at his chain, and snarled like a mad dog.

But Red shook his head. 'Forget it, Kraego. It's over. There's no gettin' out of this one.'

Kraego wasn't listening, but Red didn't expect him to. He sat down again and listened to the griffin's raging, and wondered if he too should be angry. Was there really any point in holding out hope now?

'What do I do now?' he asked aloud. 'It's hopeless.'

'It's never hopeless, Red,' a low voice replied.

Red froze. 'What? Who said that?'

'Down here,' said the voice. It was soft and rasping, and it spoke griffish – but it didn't sound completely griffinlike.

Red turned, searching for the speaker. 'Where are you?'

'Red, I'm here,' said the voice. 'I'd be so glad to see you again, if only it weren't here.'

Red looked down, and saw the owner of the voice peering up at him. It was a small grey griffin, chained up between two others. Its yellow eyes were fixed on his face, and though they looked like a griffin's eyes, there was no ferocity, no pride in them at all.

Red's own eyes widened. He knelt down, and reached out to touch the griffin's face. The griffin rubbed his head against Red's big callused hands. 'Red,' he said. 'How you've grown.'

'Kullervo,' said Red. 'It's you!'

'Yes,' said Kullervo. 'It's me. Listen, Red, don't despair. It's never too late, and it's never time to give in. There's always hope.'

'Is there?' Red asked in despair.

'Yes,' said Kullervo. 'There is. You've survived so much already, and so have I.'

Red listened to him and, seeing those eyes and hearing that gentle voice he remembered so well, he felt hope begin to rise in his chest once again.

'Yeah,' he said. 'We have. You're right. We're in trouble now, but it won't last forever. We'll find a way to go back, won't we? All of us. The South will rise again.'

Epilogue

The King and the Void

After the battle, when the Southerners had all been taken away, Caradoc was allowed to go into the city. He had stayed on a ship with the Amoranis while the fighting went on, with Ereska to protect him. The ship had stayed away from the shore, but he had stood up on the deck and had seen some of the battle inland. It was amazing, but scary. Once he had spotted Shar, but instead of making him feel better, it scared him.

He had kept his eyes on the faint red shape of the royal griffin, and prayed silently to the Night God, asking her not to take his father.

Ereska, though, had seemed angry. She shifted about restlessly and scratched the deck with her talons. Her beak opened, as if she wanted to eat something, or bite it.

Caradoc looked up at her. 'Do you think my father will be all right?' he asked. 'What if he gets hurt?'

'Do not be afraid for him,' said Ereska. 'Shar will keep him safe.'

'But what if she gets hurt too?' Caradoc persisted. 'What if she dies? What if Father dies?'

'Then it will be our time to rule,' Ereska said coolly.

That hadn't made Caradoc feel better at all, and he waited out the rest of the battle with an awful, fluttery feeling in his chest. It seemed to take forever before a griffin's call from the beach signalled to the ship, and the crew turned it around and sailed it back toward the shore.

Ereska huffed, and lowered herself onto her belly. 'Climb onto my back, and we will fly into the city.'

Caradoc obeyed, and held on tight as Ereska stood up and took off with a leap that made the ship lurch under her hind paws. Caradoc knew how to fly by now; he had learned how to hold onto the harness, and how to lean with his partner so he wouldn't unbalance her. A heavier rider would have had to worry more about that, but it was good practise for when he got older.

Ereska flew up and over Withypool, and Caradoc looked down and saw what the battle had done to it. Smoke wisped up here and there from the rooftops, and some of the buildings had been broken. He could see a few dead griffins here and there, draped over walls and roofs like broken toys. He saw live griffins, too. The Unpartnered flew over the city, or perched wherever they could find a clawhold. They had claimed another territory for themselves, and Caradoc could hear the triumph in their calls.

Ereska flew on toward the Eyrie, and Caradoc saw the prisoners in the open space outside its doors, being sorted so the Amoranis could take them away and sell them. He even managed to spot the Prince who led them; he was the Amorani Emperor's second son, and had come all the way to Cymria for the new slaves Father had promised. Caradoc was glad that Ereska didn't land there; he didn't want to see any more Southern prisoners, and the Amorani Prince was scary anyway.

Instead, the yellow griffin flew up to the Eyrie and landed on the roof of the main tower. Caradoc got off her back, and removed her harness.

By the time he had taken it off, a couple of other griffiners had already emerged to meet him.

'There you are,' one of them smiled. 'How was the flight? Did you see much of the battle?'

Caradoc smiled back shyly at her. 'I saw some. Is my father all right? Can I see him now?'

The other griffiner glanced at his friend, and nodded. 'The King is below with his partner.'

'Is he all right?' Caradoc asked again.

Their brief hesitation told him all he needed to know, and the fluttery feeling got even worse.

'Is he all right?' he persisted. 'Is he hurt?'

The woman griffiner touched him reassuringly on the shoulder. 'The King is wounded, but he'll live.'

Caradoc didn't wait to hear any more. He ran down through the entrance and into the tower. Ereska followed, and the two adults went ahead to show him the way. They led him to the Eyrie Master's quarters, and Caradoc wrenched the door open.

Inside, King Caedmon was sitting up in bed. His robe had been taken off, and he had a bandage around one shoulder and his arm in a sling. Shar was rising over by the fireplace, with a warning hiss at the intruders.

Caradoc ignored her, and ran straight to the bed. 'Father!'

Caedmon smiled and reached out with his good arm. 'Caradoc. There you are.'

Caradoc hugged him around the neck. 'Are you all right? Please don't die!'

Caedmon looked pale and tired, but his voice sounded as strong as always as he gave his son a one-armed hug. 'It's all right, Caradoc. It's all right. I'll be fine. It's just a cut.'

Caradoc nearly sobbed, but he forced himself not to. Taranisäiis didn't cry. 'I was so scared.'

'So was I,' the King admitted. 'But it's all right. It's over now.'

'Who hurt you?' Caradoc asked, letting go of him. 'Was it a Southerner? Did you kill him?'

Caedmon chuckled. 'Yes, it was a Southerner. He broke my sickle. I don't know what happened to him, but if he's not dead then he's going to Amoran now.'

'We won!' said Caradoc.

'Yes, we did. The South is ours now, or close to it. Withypool is certainly ours. And now that we've given the Amoranis so many new slaves, they'll be able to send our people back to us. All the Northerners still living in Amoran as slaves – they'll come home.'

'And great King Arenadd's quest to free all of us will be over at last,' Caradoc repeated from memory.

'Yes, just like that,' Caedmon smiled. 'And the whole of Cymria will be ours in the Night God's name.'

Caradoc didn't really care about that. All that mattered to him was that his father was alive.

'But the Southerners can't come back, can they?' he asked cautiously.

'Who knows?' the King gave a one-armed shrug. 'We've beaten them for now. As long as we're careful, we should be able to keep things under control. But as long as we have the Amoranis here to help us, we'll be more than fine.'

Caradoc nodded. 'We couldn't have done it without them, could we?'

'Maybe,' said Caedmon. 'Maybe not. But you don't need to worry about that. In the meantime, let's just rest and get ready to celebrate!'

'I will!' Caradoc promised.

Caedmon smiled and lay back on his pillows. 'That's the spirit. I'm very proud of you, Caradoc. You're a worthy Taranisäii, and a worthy Northerner as well.'

Caradoc smiled back, shyly. 'I had Ereska to help.'

'Yes, just as I have Shar,' said Caedmon.

Shar flicked her tail. 'What would you expect from the conquerer of the Mighty Skandar?' she asked playfully.

'Nothing less,' said Ereska.

'Yes.' Caedmon sighed and winced. 'King Arenadd would be proud of us all.'

*

Somewhere in the void, in that dark place where the dead went, someone watched. Someone heard. Someone knew.

The Night God smiled to herself. *At last. At last, my will has been done.*

Beside her, her servant watched too. His own face was almost as impassive as hers. 'Are you happy now?' he asked. 'Is that enough for you?'

The Night God glanced at him. *Are you bitter, Arenadd? Jealous that it was not you who finally crushed the South? Or do you pity them?*

'Me?' The shadow of what had once been Arenadd Taranisäii shrugged. 'What do I care? What's done is done. I don't want any more part of it.'

You were the greatest leader your people ever had, the Night God pointed out. *You gave everything of yourself for them. Now you say you do not care.*

'I don't,' said Arenadd. 'What's dead is dead.' His black eyes narrowed slyly. 'But don't forget that man. The Southerner.'

What of him?

'He was supposed to die back there,' said Arenadd. 'On the rope. I reached out to take him into the void just like everyone else.'

But he escaped, said the Night God. *I know.*

'Yes. And now he's alive, and swearing the South will rise again.'

It does not matter, the Night God said coldly. *He is only a mortal.*

'Of course.' Arenadd drifted away by himself into the void, where she could not see his smile. He looked out into the mortal world, alone, and laughed softly. 'Of course.' He watched over Red, peering out at him from the darkness, and laughed again. 'I let you go, Kearney Redguard. I let you go back. And I won't take you unless I have to. The South will rise again,' he added, half to himself. 'And one day, so will I. One day, both of us will be free.'

Other Books By K.J. Taylor

The Price of Magic

Broken Prophecy

The Land of Bad Fantasy

Tales of Cymria

The Fallen Moon
The Dark Griffin
The Griffin's Flight
The Griffin's War

The Risen Sun
The Shadow's Heir
The Shadowed Throne
The Shadow's Heart

The Southern Star
The Last Guard
The Silent Guard
The Cursed Guard

The Drachengott
Wind
Earth
Fire
Water

www.ingramcontent.com/pod-product-compliance
Lightning Source LLC
Chambersburg PA
CBHW040519170726
48295CB00012B/265